D1385639

Official
and
Doubtful

Ajay Close

Official
and
Doubtful

Secker & Warburg
London

The author gratefully acknowledges the
support of the Scottish Arts Council
during the writing of this book.

First published in Great Britain in 1996
by Martin Secker & Warburg Limited,
an imprint of Reed International Books Limited,
Michelin House, 81 Fulham Road, London SW3 6RB
and Auckland, Melbourne, Singapore and Toronto

A CIP catalogue record for this book
is available from the British Library

ISBN 0 436 20307 3

Phototypeset by Intype, London
Printed and bound in Great Britain
by Clays Ltd, St Ives plc

Yo bro!

'Postperson!'

She turns on her heel and lowers the angle of her head to make eye contact. Every day for three months and still he thinks it's funny.

'Yes, postmaster?'

He likes this, thinks she's flirting. And I am, she acknowledges in a sudden gust of self-loathing. His naked scalp is the colour of those unidentifiable cuts of offal you see in the butcher's down by the football ground. Someone should cook him, bile his heid, anything to change that pinkish-grey vulnerability. Even a nylon toupee would be preferable.

'How's the sleuthing going?'

'Nothing Sherlock Holmes couldn't handle.'

'Ha.'

Bullseye. Bullshit, light but not funny, nothing too smart: we aim to please. What's a girl like you doing in a job like this? Keeping her mouth shut and taking the money. She wants to move off, but there's an etiquette about these things, and he hasn't stirred. He is standing underneath a blinking fluorescent striplight, which aggravates but doesn't explain her sense of unease.

'Seen the papers today?'

She tries to recall the headlines from the eight o'clock news. Terrorist attack on the West Bank? Some bacteriologist warning pregnant women not to eat cling peaches? Unemployment up again?

'Chainmail organised a wee test for us. We didn't do very well.'

'The recorded delivery arrived after the postcard with the Green Shield stamp?'

She regrets it immediately, then hates herself for the reflex to regret.

'I'm sorry, I don't see the joke. I've just spent two and a half hours on the sixth floor and it's not an experience I care to repeat. In case you don't understand: if we don't get our delivery record up to one hundred and one per cent we're history. And if you don't get us some good PR in the miracle department, you'll be history a lot sooner than the rest of us. Message received?'

'You want me to sign for it?'

The miracle department or, to use the name that appears on memos, holiday forms, shift reports and other pieces of paper issued in triplicate, Returned Letters Section (Official and Doubtful), is in the lower basement. She shares the floor with Vehicle Spares and a colony of rats which she hears sometimes scuttling between the joists in the ceiling; she's not fond of the vermin but she finds them marginally less off-putting than the storesman in charge of Vehicle Spares.

The only natural light strains through a skylight made of little squares of opaque greenish-purple glass, crude as old milk bottles, set into the pavement above her. Long ago one of the squares was pierced by a steel-tipped stiletto heel and children like to push sweetie wrappers down the hole. Now and again one drops into her coffee. Her desk, an ancient iron fortress of battleship grey boobytrapped with guillotine edges, sits directly underneath. She endures the whistling draught for the sake of human contact, even if it is only rubber-soled feet, and because she needs the daylight. The shadowless industrial lighting gives her a headache and she keeps it switched off on all but the darkest days. The postmen joke about this dingy hovel, call it the Anderson shelter, and they're almost right. It is her bunker, her place of safety.

She walks over to the huge wire mesh basket of doubt-fuls. Cards posted to streets which don't exist; packets which ripen and split in the pillarbox, shedding their brown paper skins; envelopes dutifully addressed in the unreadable script of the Edwardian schoolroom.

Bending over, she rummages through the mountain of manilla and Basildon Bond and pulls out a white envel-ope. The postmark – local – is perfectly distinct; the name and address less so. Someone has spilt water over the envelope, and two curving rivulets have smudged the purple ink into Rorschach blots, leaving only fragments of the words intact. Standard procedure: 1) check back of envelope for return address, 2) if unavailing, open. This one is quality office stationery, self-sealing. Insinuate a finger under the flap and the stringy adhesive gives easily. She unfolds the sheet of notepaper. In the top right-hand corner is an eight-digit number, one too many for a telephone line. All at once her mouth is open very wide. She is conscious of the attenuated strands of saliva between her lips, the salty runnel of tears; one cry, almost a yelp, and then it's over. It happens sometimes. What's a girl like you doing in a job like this?

She reads the words again.

```
I SAW YOUR PICTURE IN THE PAPER
AGAIN TODAY. I DIDN'T WASTE TIME
READING THE LIES. YOUR FACE SAYS
IT ALL. YOU'RE PISSING ON US AND
PISSING YOURSELF LAUGHING
BECAUSE YOU THINK NOBODY NOTICES.
BUT THE JOKE'S ON YOU. SOMEBODY'S
NOTICED, SOMEBODY'S BEEN WATCHING
YOU A LONG TIME.

GUILT IS LIKE LOVE, IT EATS YOUR
```

LIFE. NOTHING ELSE MATTERS. TAKE
A LOOK AT THE FACES YOU PASS ON
THE STREET. IT COULD BE ANYONE,
ANYTIME. YOUR TURN NEXT. YOUR
DAY OF RECKONING. HOW YOU PAY
IS UP TO YOU.

A footstep on the stair outside the door. It's so dark by the baskets that she can barely make out the etiolated face and anaemic ginger hair, the navy-blue nylon anorak, standard issue on the rounds. She recognises him by more elusive detail: that stoop like the arc of an overextended couch-grass, the way he displaces the air, her own altered mood.

'I hear the poison dwarf had a go.'

He's barely six feet away when he notices the smirr of tears; he takes another, awkward, step towards her.

'What's up?'

She chooses to misunderstand the question.

'Who knows? One minute it's "come with me to the kasbah", next thing he's going to give me the push. Probably the male menopause, but I don't see why it should be my problem.' She stops herself. Any minute now she'll be into *who does he think he is?* the shopgirl chorus, to be heard in four-part harmony on every bus in Glasgow. She is possibly the last woman in Scotland to discover that they don't just pay you badly in the unskilled sector, they treat you like shit too.

'They tell me there's an offer on kneecappings in Blackhill: thirty-five quid for one, only fifty-five for the pair.'

It's a regular joke of theirs.

'Trouble is, the bastards pay me so little I'd have to save up for weeks to afford it.'

He looks at his watch. He's supposed to be emptying his bowels in the second-floor washroom at the moment.

'Gonnae take first break?'

'Lunch at eleven-thirty and hypoglycaemia by four o'clock? No thanks.'

He is her only real friend in the building, or, for that matter, out of it, the one she can talk to without having to filter her conversation for double-entendres, the one who doesn't refer to black people as coloureds or pakis, the one who wonders what a girl like her is doing in a job like this but has never asked. It occurs to her he may not know exactly what hypoglycaemia is. But then, she wouldn't like to sit an exam on it herself.

'Rab. Come and have a look at this.'

He turns back too quickly and she feels a little curdle of dread in her stomach. *He loves me, he loves me not.* He squints at the sheet of paper, holding the type six inches from his face. The dyslexic postman.

'Is it a wind-up?'

But he doesn't want it to be a wind-up. He is excited, something is happening. She envies the simplicity of his response, craving headlines and drama because they always happen to someone else. This is why she has always stopped herself from telling him, although sometimes she's come close. He'd be genuinely sympathetic, but thrilled. He couldn't appreciate how mundane it is when you have to live through it. The letter may be a joke, it has the cheap sensationalism of the bogus, but life's like that too.

Suddenly decisive, he holds out his hand for the envelope; if she watched more television she could probably identify the character he's playing.

'I think you should take it to the polis.'

'No.' She smiles. 'I'm not too keen on the polis.'

He is genuinely surprised.

'Why not?'

'I'd just rather deliver it.'

He examines the envelope, holding it so close that if she didn't know better she'd think he was inhaling the paper. His lips move soundlessly as he traces the surviving letters.

'Gonnae visit a medium to find out who it's for?'

Cross-referring between telephone directory, electoral roll and Greater Glasgow street index, she draws up a list. She has just fourteen letters: fragments of a name and address, archipelagos trapped between watery blurs. Working on the assumption that the target lives in Glasgow, by mid-afternoon she has whittled it down to three possibilities. If she's wrong, that leaves any number of Macleods in Lesmahagow, Linlithgow and God knows how many other rhyming burghs. She pulls on her regulation anorak. Technically, she should hand the letter over to a postman but, under the circumstances, she feels justified in breaking the rules.

Montpelier has long been on the list of fashionable Glasgow addresses, a pocket of solid five-storey Edwardian tenements served by broad continental door-ways crying out for a concierge. Staggering up the hill towards them from the bus-ploughed trough of Dumbarton Road, she keeps her eyes on her feet, only partly to minimise wind resistance. There's something wrong, fundamentally at odds with nature, about these massive, gravity-defying towers adding their steeper verticals to this vertiginous slope. Look up and perspective goes crazy. It's fine in the art gallery but you don't need it on the streets. She remembers the suburb twenty-odd years ago: grand, but precariously so, like a bride walking to church in wet weather, finery hemmed with mud. Since then the city seems to have lost some of its prissiness. Poverty, squalor, urban deprivation are now selling points to be noted on the estate agent's particulars. The Glasgow bourgeois claims kinship with the mean streets of Chicago and New York. Everyone's a hardman these days. In lowlife bars across the city, accountants and lecturers huddle up to stickmen and hoods. It used to frighten her until she realised that the eavesdroppers were too drunk to remember what they were hearing and the criminals too drunk to care.

On a sunny day with the red sandstone glowing like a saxophone solo, Montpelier could be a little bit of San Francisco by the Clyde. Today it's a colourless, windswept gully, but the view over the city is still breathtaking, or would be if she had any breath left to take. Rusting

7

gasometers, sloping shipyard cranes, a mirror shard of river, all the stock ingredients of post-industrial picturesque: a big draw for the postmodernist popstars, alternative comediennes and independent filmmakers who have colonised the neighbourhood. Below the snowline are a dozen sleazy drinking shops where they can rub shoulders with the people. And your average twenty-a-day housebreaker slogging it up from Dumbarton Road is wheezing so hard by the time he reaches the summit, who needs a burglar alarm?

She doesn't smoke, but still has to pause for a moment before tackling the half-dozen steps up to the front door. She presses the bell, waits for the muffled enquiry, then crouches to bring her lips level with the horizontal slats of the intercom box.

'Post Office: Mrs MacLeod in?'

A static hiss, in the negative. The door buzzes. That fleeting panic she always feels at autonomous inanimate objects.

'Top floor.'

Of course. She takes the five flights at one go, no stopping. It's the knees that really feel it. On the stairhead she rings the bell and waits for the looming shape on the other side of the etched glass panel. It's a young girl, twenty or so, in a shapeless acid-yellow sweatshirt. A toddler in candystriped dungarees clings to her legs. They're obviously not related. The girl could be a childminder, possibly a cleaner. Her skin has the greyish tinge of unfired clay; the child is fired and glazed too, shiny with health. Or money.

'They're not here.'

Whatever the girl's job description, it doesn't include initiative. Somewhere in the flat a phone rings. She disengages herself from the toddler's grip and retreats to answer it.

'Aye . . . uh-huh . . . no . . . there's a post . . . a wumman from the Post Office at the door . . .'

More monosyllables, then the girl is back, ushering her towards the phone.

'Imogen Reiss.'

That throws her. 'Oh. I'm looking for Mrs MacLeod.'

'That's my other hat.'

The routinely amused tone of the self-consciously civilised.

'How can I help?'

'I have a letter that could be for you. The address isn't very clear . . .'

'If it's money, Michelle's very trustworthy.'

'It's more complicated than that, I'm afraid. I have to see you in person.'

A sigh. Irritation starting to replace the amusement.

'Well I can't come home. Either leave it with Michelle or come to the paper. Ask for me at reception.'

She should have made the connection sooner. That hybrid accent, Mancunian iron fist stretching a North London velvet glove, the voice that talks women down from barbiturate highs on midnight phone-ins. *Now love, take your time* . . . The terracotta walls inside the flat, the absolute confidence that fashion will catch up.

In the days before women's lib became feminism Imogen Reiss was famous, glamorously angry, Cosmo woman with conscience, pin-up to a generation of adolescent girls who didn't want to be mother. One of the original campaigners. One way and another they'd got just about the whole shopping list. Perhaps that's why she's not so famous any more, less of a heroine, more of a hack. Wasn't there something about her selling out? Some remark about abortion being the easy option or there being too many one-parent families in the world?

9

These days her face graces the problem page of one of the nastier national newspapers.

She walks in past a pair of security guards. Chevrons, epaulettes, silver buttons, the paramilitary works. Nothing too soldierly about the slouch, though. Considering the London headquarters are regularly shown on the television news barricaded behind floodlights and razor wire, they could be more vigilant north of the border. She makes for the reception desk, an ostentatiously simple counter of blond wood. A matching receptionist smiling a professional smile. Next to her, a switchboard operator chanting her mantra, thank you for calling, with identical inflexion, time after time.

Directed upstairs, she chooses a chair fashioned by ripping the leather seat out of a 1960s saloon car and stringing it from a tubular steel frame. There's also a small pink satin sofa, mouth-shaped, after Salvador Dali. Even the black and white carpet is trying to be witty, parodying the marble-flagged entrance of a country mansion. Through an archway she can see a hangar-sized room full of people, some sitting in front of computer screens, most, inexplicably, just walking around.

After some time she manages to attract the attention of a woman with a Louise Brooks bob and very short skirt, who promises attention directly. Minutes pass. A couple of women in short skirts and siren lipstick head towards the stairs. Just about the entire staff seems to be female, and they're all wearing short black skirts and blood-red lipstick. The older ones vary the formula with the backcombed perm and shoulderpads look favoured by American soap queens of a certain age. They seem not exactly nervous but certainly highly strung, eyes and teeth flashing, hands signalling. Mayday.

A door opens. Three young women and a middle-aged man emerge. One of the women is crying; she's short-skirted, scarlet-lipped, with a precision haircut, but different from the others. Stringy instead of slender, deep circles under her eyes, and the ghost of another two concentric grooves level with her cheekbones. The man, gangster-chic in a black shirt and vanilla tie, checks the door is shut behind him and puts an arm round her shoulders. The other two walk with the whiplash gait of white fury, sharp heels striking sparks were it not for that chessboard carpet. All four disappear into the forest of green screens.

Two men in voluminous white shirts knock and wait outside another office.

'Last sniff I had was a Vicks Sinex.'

'Tell me about it.'

The door opens and they too disappear.

Louise Brooks is back, pouring herself a coffee from a filter jug on a low glass table.

Nan is half-way into an icy reminder when she realises it's not the same woman. At least this one bothers to search the newsroom. Five minutes later she returns with an apologetic smile. Imogen's busy, is she sure no one else can help?

'No.'

'Well, it's really not worth waiting.'

She is pulling on the anorak and getting up to leave when she recognises a face just the other side of the archway. The strong features blurring into middle age but still beautiful. Evidently she uses an old photograph at the top of her column. An odd sort of vanity: making yourself ridiculous to people who know you for the sake of readers you'll never meet.

'Excuse me.'

The woman turns her head with a neutral look and seems to be conducting some sort of grading process before committing herself to a smile.

'I'm from the Post Office.'

She is momentarily wrongfooted. 'Oh yes, I . . . it's my deadline day.'

'I won't take a minute.'

Reluctantly, the older woman crosses the carpet. Hooked over her shoulder is a leather satchel few schoolgirls could afford. She fishes out a pair of rimless glasses and scans the page of notepaper, clips the glasses away in their case again, and rummages in the bag. Eureka: a paper tissue. She crumples it, unused, and stows it up her sleeve.

'I can't see how it could be for me.'

'Sorry to have bothered you then.'

Something nameless stirs behind the executive poise.

'Hang on a minute. You say you're from the Post Office, do you have any identification?'

Regulation black lace-up shoes, grey stockings (a bit of a risk, this, Gorr likes to see her in American tan), navy-blue skirt, pale blue blouse under navy sweater, roundsman's anorak with its red go-faster stripe. She pulls out her identification card.

'Jeanette Magritte?'

Friendly again now.

'Megratta. Everyone calls me Nan.'

'Unusual. Is it Italian?'

'My grandfather came over in the Twenties. . .'

But Imogen Reiss finds this information surplus to requirements. Already she's turning back in the direction of the green screens.

'Sorry you've had a wasted journey. Can you find your own way out?'

'Gorr.'

He has the telephone manners of a pit bull.

'It's Nan.'

'Hello, Nan.'

'You've been trying to get hold of me.'

'Oh, aye. Where the hell have you been?'

He's on the phone but beckons her in. Nowhere to sit down; there's a pile of papers on the other chair. What a load of junk the modern communications manager accumulates: executive blotter, paperclip tidy, perspex penholder with Postman Pat trapped like a mammoth in a glacier, Newton's cradle gathering dust at the far end of the desk, occasionally snippy but ultimately compliant female subordinate still the fantasy side of thirty. The bureaucrat who has everything.

'... sure, sure, I see where you're coming from ... Well, any time you fancy a gubbing on the squash court you know where I am ...'

Is this performance for her benefit?

He replaces the receiver.

'So Nan, found Mrs Matheson's chutneys yet?'

'You what?'

He tosses her a sheet of paper. Basildon Bond. Her heart sinks. A fountain pen complainer.

'Green tomato, pickled walnuts and a prizewinning wild rowan jelly.'

Dear Sir, Nine days ago I sent my daughter . . .

'I don't *believe* she put them in the post. Anyway,' her

hands sketch out dimensions in the air, 'that's too big for us. It's Parcels' problem.'

He shakes his head.

'If you can be bothered to read it you'll see she packed the stuff in plastic bags.' There's a squeaky note of unacknowledged glee in his voice. 'Very well wrapped apparently.'

'I'll bet.'

She returns the complaint to the pile it came from, then, seeing his expression, retrieves it. Her problem now.

'So what's the story, Nan?'

She hands over the Macleod letter. He's impressed and mildly titillated but not about to show it; at least, not without prompting.

'It reads to me like a blackmail note.'

'Does it now? You may be right. On the other hand, it could just as easily be a practical joke, or a new recipe from the Joy of Cooking.'

She hates to gratify him by looking puzzled but on this occasion there's no alternative.

'Sex games between consenting adults: wouldn't be the first case of foreplay by post. You'd be amazed how some people get their kicks.' He gives her an arch look. 'Or maybe you wouldn't. Either way, I can't see the need for you to go hightailing it all over town.'

She sets about convincing him.

'I've drawn up a list of possibles and one of them is Danny MacLeod.'

Not a flicker.

'The MP.'

Now he's interested.

'He's been at the House of Commons all day, but he's due back tonight. Coming up to rally the troops in the byelection; there's a public meeting in Sanilands.'

He squares his shoulders, pulling himself up to his full

height, a fairly useless gesture given that he's sitting down and, even on his feet, she's a good two inches taller.

'I think it'd be better if I handled this.' He fingers his moustache, defender of the famous. 'Shit, not tonight. Have to be tomorrow sometime.'

'You'll be lucky, he's flying straight back for some big debate. Three-line whip.'

One of the perks of working for a seventeen-carat fake is that they rarely call your bluff.

'OK, see him tonight. I don't want it ending up as another gold star for the rubber heels squad. This one's chalked up to Official and Doubtful. But, Nan, try and employ a little finesse. We don't want him thinking we're accusing him of anything. And if you're going to Sanny I'd take your leather leggings.'

Now he's given her what she wants she doesn't mind returning the favour.

'Pardon?'

He smiles, anticipating his own joke.

'The dogs roam in packs up there. Now I think about it, so do the kids.'

Toiling past the 1930s semis on the passionless fringes of desirable suburbia, the bus shifts down a gear to take the hill. The approach is leafy mock-Tudor; at the brow everything changes. Sanilands is spread across the valley, contained by a cluster of hills, manageable, just as the architect's model promised. From here, it doesn't look as bad as they say. But it is; just bad in a different way.

For three years of her early childhood she lived on a housing scheme, not the most notorious, but one with enough of a reputation to teach her about stigma. Her mother coped by pretending it wasn't happening and punishing any reminder to the contrary. Eventually she married out of it, out of the city altogether, coincidentally

15

finding a devoted husband. Glasgow was never mentioned again. Later, when Nan talked about it, her teenage friends mocked her for downward mobility, bogus street-cred. They subscribed to a rigid apartheid; no one could have a foot in both camps. It wasn't anything as simple as snobbery, more like middle-class guilt. Easier to believe in the absolute quarantine of deprivation than in the powerful chimeras of class.

The old man at the bus stop directs her to a squat, pinkish brick community centre. Not decorative, not impressively austere in the modernist way, just mildly depressing, like all the buildings on the estate: street upon street of concrete maisonette blocks, each subtly different and yet utterly featureless.

The hall is lit by naked fluorescent tubes, a few fading posters on the walls. *Watch Out! There's a thief about!* So many old men with ruddy, pitted complexions: a lifetime of industrial toil touched up by a daily diet of Heavy; a few matrons, stomachs loosened by childbirth and padded with fry-ups, watery eyes magnified by National Health specs; a handful of kids wearing counterfeit labels and expressions of carefully nurtured contempt. More gaps than people in the rows of splintering stacking chairs. The audience can't number more than seventy, there are six thousand tenants on this estate. Democracy in action.

Seated at the front are the usual committee stalwarts, typical of the audience but for being touched by the mysterious zeal of activism. She feels awkward, conspicuous in the half-empty room, even though nobody's looking. Just as well she went back to Catriona's and changed, although perhaps the skirt was a miscalculation. What seemed demure enough amid the pot pourri and scatter cushions now strikes her as overemphatically feminine, even perversely provocative. Still, it could be worse: she could be Skinnyshanks in the corner there, avoiding eye contact with the three women swaying menacingly in their stretch jeans and burlesque heels. Who let him wear that sleeveless slipover? She chooses a seat, picks up an election handbill. *Malcolm Foy: Your Labour Candidate.*

There's no measurable increase in the noise but she registers his entry behind her, feels the electric prickle of excitement. Turning round, there he is, the man of the people. There's still a family resemblance, he has the same florid features, but his fingernails no longer end in a bottle-green crescent, the grey suit is a cut above, the green shirt saved from flashiness by a well-judged tie. He's gladhanding, working his way up the hall; a nod here, a special smile of recognition there, intimate laughter. Can he really know them all? Now he's at the table, easing in to his place, a confiding word to the committee men on either side. The one on his left stands up.

'Ladies and Gentlemen. Comrades . . .'

Danny MacLeod. The speech is predictable; a few jokes, the punchlines signalled minutes in advance and followed through with the latest instance of the callousness and injustice of the government. The crowd follows the cues: smirking, then expelling its breath in a collective hiss of disgust. He's good, as is only to be expected after twenty-five years on the stump. Wearing well, too; looking pretty much as he does on television. Even with the grey hair and suit, he's more vivid than the rest of the room. It must be the power, or fortune's smile.

And yet he still burns with the indignation of the dispossessed. How can you feel hard done by on thirty thousand a year? It doesn't seem faked. There is too much sadism in his rhetoric. Revenge is in the air. Someone, a long time ago, did him an injury, and they will never stop paying. This is hatred made abstract, class warfare. He may dress like the enemy, pick up their tastes and habits, but he'll never be on their side.

He's working the room, treating each target to their exclusive moment. Suddenly it's her turn. Involuntarily she colours; knowing it's a trick, it still feels like a tribute. His eyes are like marbles. Not grey or green. Eau de nil. Pale unflecked irises full of light.

The crowd claps enthusiastically enough, but there's silence when questions are invited from the floor. A couple of Labour plants raise their hands and bowl him some gentle balls. The chairman announces that the hall has to be cleared by nine. Chairs scrape on the scuffed lino as the audience get to their feet.

She makes her way to the front, snagging her tights on a splintering chair seat. He sees her but is pinned to the spot by a pensioner in a matted grey mohair coat. She edges nearer. He half-smiles over the oyster perm then stoops to address the old woman's good ear.

'Sorry, love, I promised I'd have a word with this young lady. I'll get the lassie in my office to ring up the Social for you. Don't worry, they're a bunch of chancers.'

He leans towards Nan conspiratorially. 'I owe you one. I've got enough to write the authorised biography and she was just warming up.'

'Could I have a word in private?'

He cocks an eyebrow, and guides her to a corner of the room, his hand glancing on her elbow. Now you feel it, now you don't.

Reading the letter he nods, apparently unsurprised, as if she's handed him an unreasonable gas bill.

'Are you in a hurry?'

She shrugs. Not now.

In the car he chats about Labour's chances in the byelection, namedrops *Tony* a couple of times, tells a story about some woman on the shuttle mistaking him for a newsreader. He has the knack of generating laughter at the not particularly funny.

'One of those half-famous faces. They know they know me from somewhere but they're not sure whether they were at school with me, or I once played the murderer in *Taggart*.'

He changes down to take a bend, the ring on his third finger glinting as his hand nudges the gearstick.

'Happens to everyone, I suppose. Threw me a bit when I saw you.'

'Why?'

'I had the feeling I'd seen you before.'

'I don't think so.'

'Never been on the box?' She smiles, signalling absurdity. 'In the paper?' If her expression flickers momentarily he misses it. 'Maybe I've just passed you on the street and filed your face away for future reference.'

'Your files must be pretty full.'

'Oh, I'm very discriminating about what gets into the system.'

Embarrassed, she cuts him off.

'I only moved here a couple of months ago.'

'Aye, it's a great city. Best people in the world, Glaswegians. Down at the House we have our differences, but if they try to pick us off we're tight as . . .'

Whatever the simile, it seems he's thought better of it.

'I'll have a pint of Special please.'

He stiffens slightly but brings her the beer, setting a whisky down for himself. She waits. He's taken the initiative so far; the silence is his problem.

'Not a bad wee bar, is it?'

She shrugs non-committally, wondering what she is punishing him for.

'Where do you stay, Jan?'

'Nan.' She relents. 'On the South Side, I share a house

with a woman who works in a beauty salon. Well, I pay her mortgage and get to sleep in the boxroom. I try to keep out of her way. She's got a hang-up about spending her day discussing combination skin and splitting finger-nails. Has Radio Three on at seven in the morning. Wears a pair of tortoiseshell glasses with plain glass in them. Thinks it makes her look intellectual.'

It's like sitting with two people, the man engaged in conversation, and the one with that level stare.

'You're not married then?'

'I was married then. I'm not now.'

'Aye, very wise.'

'A weekend husband must be the next best thing.'

'There are times even that's too much togetherness.' The eyes lose power for a second as if this wasn't the conversation he had in mind. 'Some of us are better housetrained than others. It does funny things to you. All-night sittings at the Commons. They call it working; it's no really, but you can't relax either. Pavlov's dogs, waiting for that bloody bell. If you're not front bench, and I chucked the chance of that years ago, you're a statistic in the division lobby and a social worker in the constituency. And that doesn't get you elected. You've got to get in the papers, on telly, become a professional personality, it's in the job description. You're always hyped up, on show. People get excited. It's a turn-on. Ach, I'm not saying anything new. But it doesn't make for a happy home life.' If this is a pitch it's a remarkably inept one. 'Amazing how many mistresses there are on the Terrace come May.'

'Is it? I would have thought it was obvious.'

He falls silent briefly, not sure if this is a snub.

'You don't strike me as your average postman, Nan.'

'I'm the wrong sex?'

'In my book you're the right one, but you're not exactly typical.'

'They did away with stupidity as a condition of entry a couple of years ago.'

No mistaking the rebuff this time. His eyes glitter, a flicker in the stare like a shutter coming up. Or down.

'I used to share an office with Bob Settle. He was sponsored by your lot. Said they were the biggest bunch of bastards he'd ever met — sexist as they come, too, if that bothers you. Made the printworkers look like a Sunday school. Maybe there's been a purge over the past couple of years, but I wouldn't put money on it.'

That's what you get for questioning the credentials of a professional socialist.

'Now you mention it, there are a few Neanderthals.'

'Are you on some sort of management training scheme?'

What's a girl like you . . .

'Just an ordinary postie?'

'Well, I'm not on the rounds, I work in Official and Doubtful.'

His laughter splutters a fine spray of Glenmorangie.

'And which are you?'

They are on their third drink before he broaches the letter. He asks to see it again, studies it, brushing an itch from his upper lip with his right thumb. Like the gesture boxers use in sparring.

'Are you sure it's for me?'

'No. You're on a list of three. I hoped you could tell me, save me some leg work. I thought . . .' *careful now* '. . . being an MP made you a likely target.'

He looks away, pursing his lips, then renews the connection.

'Can I trust you?'

No, but tell me anyway.

'I meet a lot of people in this job, and some of them are, frankly, raving. I can think of a couple of possibilities. One of them's a female, a mistake; I knew as soon as I'd started it. My wife knows anyway. I can handle her, if I have to, but it might not be anything to do with her and I'd rather not get in touch again to find out. The other lot call themselves Anarcho-Syndicalists, Libertarians, Animal Liberationists. Bunch of juvenile delinquents in bikers' leathers without the wheels. Most of them are kids, late teens, early twenties, Bostik for breakfast. Nutters.'

'What do they want with you?'

He smiles, almost convincingly. 'What they really want is to see me struck blind on the road to Damascus, or walking into the lobby in sackcloth shouting "Meat is Murder". They don't like my position on the Middle East, they don't like me sitting on the board of Sapro Pharmaceuticals – they do their research, I'll give them that. They turn up to meetings, barrack me, throw stink bombs, smoke bombs. I know: bloody ridiculous, but they're relentless. Fancy themselves as my own personal nemesis. I'm amazed they weren't in the Sanny tonight. The boys always get them out but there's usually some rough stuff first. My main regret is I've never been near enough to stick one on them myself.'

Beware the streetfighter in the Austin Reed lounge suit.

'So what are they after?'

'My balls.'

She wonders if the prize is worth it.

He sighs noisily. 'I've got problems in the constituency. Who hasn't these days? Militant don't help any. I've still got enough backing to survive reselection – as long as I don't get any *Sun* headlines about my night of love with juicy Julia. But I'm not sure the Black Flag brigade are as untouched by party politics as they make out. I don't know what they're trying; if they've been put up to anything by the paperback reds on the GMC I'll fucking tear them apart. But I need to know. And I need to know soon.'

He looks at her.

'Well, Nan Megratta, what do you say?'

'What do you want me to say?'

'They have a stall on Buchanan Street on Saturdays: Save the Seal petitions and a bit of patter on the Nazi revival. Some punk plays the penny whistle and the punters pay him to shut it. I can't go down there, it'd be street theatre, and if they've got nothing to do with it I don't want to start them thinking I'm looking over my shoulder. But you could do it for me.'

She looks down. His hand is resting on hers: silver cufflink, beautiful nails, little white scar on his index finger, a hand hardened in the shipyards.

'What am I supposed to say to them?'

He smiles. 'You'll think of something. Just don't for Christ's sake let them know I sent you.'

He switches off the engine outside her tenement. There's a moment of silence. The streetlight falls onto his lap, turning his trousers a shade lurid and sombre at the same time.

'You've got a ladder in your stocking, Nan Megratta.'

'Where?'

She realises her mistake as soon as the word is out.

Her legs are crossed, left over right; he turns, leaning towards her as he runs a finger lightly along her inner thigh, just below the hem of her skirt.

'There.'

She opens the car door. 'Full marks for observation.'

He straightens up and turns the key in the ignition.

23

'So you'll see those comedians at the weekend? Ring me afterwards and we'll meet up. I can debrief you then.'

'I'll make sure I'm wearing trousers.'

Too frequently for coincidence, she finds herself the victim of mistaken identity. Alighting on railway platforms in unknown cities, complete strangers rush towards her with outstretched arms, only faltering as they register the implications of a body braced for assault. Once, years ago, waiting in the departure lounge at Gatwick Airport, she was taken for a tuba player with the Manchester Youth Orchestra. The recognition isn't always so precise. The more surreal encounters, only minimally embellished, make handy icebreakers at awkward social occasions, but it's more common for her to be approached by people who need no introduction to claim the privileges of intimacy. Puberty taught her the necessity of the averted gaze on crowded pavements, that distinctively female unfocused glance, but still they sought her out: women guarding the driers at the laundrette who volunteered confessions of joyless promiscuity and slot-machine addiction, muttering scavengers reeking of electric soup who spurned the proffered coin and poured out their life stories, pedestrians falling into step on streets crazed by Christmas shopping, glue sniffers on the tops of buses, sandwich-board evangelists, and men. Men of all sorts and sizes, ages and degrees of sanity.

'You must look like their mothers.' She dismissed the comment at the time, wrote it off like the softly whistled opening bars of 'I'm just a gal who can't say no', another dig with a spadeful of unnecessary malice. It isn't as if she's beautiful. She's seen beauty and the effect it has on people: the extra emphasis in the performance, the laugh a little louder, the smile a little wider, the gaze insouci-antly off-target as if they hadn't noticed the radiance in their midst. Nan's looks pose no threat of enslavement so there's no need to demonstrate their independence. They don't care how they look, they're not interested in her approval. That's part of the magnetism that draws them to her side. In a world of judgement and censure she offers an involuntary haven. She has worked this much out, but there remains the other side of the equation: what's in it for her? Might the curse serve some subcon-scious purpose? Over the years she has learned to deflect the casual advances, schooled herself in the brisk sidestep, cultivated the shuttered look, although she's never lost the fear of provoking a reprisal. She's done as much as seems humanly possible and the cancer of random atten-tion is definitely in remission; but it never quite dis-appears.

She's almost safe at the bunker when Gorr hails her. The brilliant morning clouds a little.

'Howdy, Red.'

His other joke. Maureen O'Hara she isn't.

'You haven't forgotten the sections meeting?'

But she has. She dreads these fortnightly occasions where everything is discussed but nothing decided, full of pudgy men in ill-fitting sportsjackets who've spent a quarter of a century climbing to the top of their particular shrub and now they've got there, you'd better believe they're going to enjoy it. It was Gorr's idea to put her name on the list, making the fatuous case that, despite her three months' service, working in a department of one qualified her as a section manager. He wasn't doing her any favours; he finds these meetings as irksome as she does. She attends as his accessory, a personal plus in the chromosome algebra. She is, of course, the only woman there.

Someone has decorated the meeting room in the minimalist high-tech style which spread like measles in the mid-Eighties. Her employers latched on to it eighteen months ago. The walls have been skim-plastered with geometric precision and painted a faint clinical pink. The table is a monolithic slab of grey moulded plastic. There are cheap black uplighters, dated in that special way of objects which were futuristic five years ago, and matt black microblinds furred with dust.

The meeting begins with a round robin of reports. She knows these despatches are funny; the laborious

27

explanations, the policeman's notebook prose, these men have euphemisms for euphemisms, but the cumulative effect is too depressing for laughter. The most she can hope for is appreciating the joke when she rehashes it to Rab later. She knocks back the last of her Maxpax tea, grimacing at the mouthful of silt. The corporate Martian has the chair, his skin radiating an extra-greenish gleam today.

'. . . competing in international markets . . . merit culture . . . total quality management . . .'

She tunes out again. Graeme Bruce catches her glance and lowers his eyelids in a pantomime of coma. She smiles and looks away.

It took her a while to get used to these gatherings. She is the most menial member of staff present, still serving out her probationary period, but their awareness of her is such that she might as well be chairing the meeting. She feels like a cricketer in the nets, deflecting a barrage of looks, smiles, conspiratorial winks, comical faces and subversive comments she can never quite lip-read. A ninety-minute session leaves her exhausted with the responsibility of all those egos. Not that any of this was a revelation, it goes with the gender; harder to come to terms with was the recognition that despite – or because of – it, the price of making any contribution to the meeting was a sharp put-down. Easy to get above yourself when you belong in the basement.

Finally it's her turn to report. Her predecessor in the post was a sweet old codger coasting gently into retire-ment, a shoemaker elf with fluffy white hair, a baby's crumpled pink face, and the filthiest mouth in Glasgow. Not that this was held against him. But when he started clearing the backlog by stuffing anything from the Inland Revenue under the Queen's Park rhododendron bushes he was allowed to coast a little more quickly. Beside his record, she's a model of efficiency. She gives them the good news; let them draw their own conclusions about the rest. When she finishes Gorr leans across, close enough to smell his breakfast, and whispers, apparently for the benefit of the next street.

'Aren't you forgetting something, Sleuth?'

She opens her mouth to speak but he gets there first.

'Official and Doubtful have fetched up with a black-mail note; looks like someone's trying to put the pincers on a member of the government.'

There is a sudden spate of phlegm-clearing and buttock-shifting, which is as close as they ever come to expressing excitement. It's a shame to disappoint them.

'He's a Labour backbencher. And it's not definite. There are two other possibilities. I'm checking them out . . .'

Gorr cuts in.

'But if we help out a member,' he smirks, 'caught with his breeks down, there'll obviously be some gratitude in the right places, which can't do us any harm in the difficult months ahead.' Smiling now at the Martian. 'I think we'll all be following the progress of this one.'

Back in the bunker she's developed a tardy hangover and forces down a restorative can of Irn Bru. The phone rings. It's Imogen Reiss. Only she's not bothering with surnames any more.

'You caught me on the hop a bit yesterday. Maybe I should have another look at that letter. Could you come to the house? I'm toddlerbound at the moment so I'll be in all day. Michelle's got her Restart interview and you know how long anything to do with the DSS takes.'

Nan waits, remembering her afternoon in the newspaper lobby. Eventually Imogen breaks the silence, but when the words come, they sound less like a woman used to controlling the situation than a woman trying to control herself.

'Is there any way you could manage it, Nan? I really would be grateful.'

'It'll have to be after work.'

'Any time. Any time you can make it.'

There's no real reason why she can't call right away, but it's good for apostate feminists employing domestic labour cash-in-hand to know what it feels like to wait. She sets off for The Greasy Spoon.

She's never been to the Spoon before, but like everyone else in Glasgow, she knows all about it. A favourite haunt of what passes for the city's celebrities: television continuity announcers who consider themselves personalities, commercial radio DJs, a couple of novelists known for their sensitive portraits of working-class life, an assiduously notorious newspaper columnist, and the retinue who press their noses to their windows of these empty lives. The place functions as a high-priced media canteen, somewhere the clientele can be sure of finding the people they've been working with all day. The menu merits a couple of stars from Egon Ronay but a significant proportion of the plates go back to the kitchen still piled with food. It's much rarer to find the wine making a return journey.

When she phoned earlier, the call was intercepted by an answering machine. 'Hi, this is Callum Macleod. I'm out right now, or asleep, or maybe I just don't want to speak to you. Leave a message after the fart or ring me at the soup kitchen . . .' The second number connected with a waitressy voice which said yes, Cal was in all day, but no, he couldn't come to the phone. She looks at her watch: another forty minutes and it'll be lunchtime, the kitchens must be busy but if he's one of the table staff he might have time to see her.

A young, goodlooking doorman is employed to stand exchanging courtesies with the punters. He looks doubtfully at her uniform but directs her through the empty restaurant to a modern spiral staircase. She makes her journey through the tables as slowly as she reasonably can, taking in the wrought-iron furniture, more sculpture than seating, the abstract slab of opaque glass positioned pointlessly in front of the bar, the discreet ceiling spotlights like opticians' torches, the concrete floor sparkling with mica.

She knocks on a door of frosted glass etched with the word *bureau*, and enters a dazzlingly bright office which seems to be made of nothing but glass. Here and there, a white muslin blind has been drawn against the glare. A jet arcs its vapour trail across what should be the ceiling. A pale youth lounges against a desk, carrying his stylishness like an offensive weapon. The young, improbably small woman in an impossibly short pleated skirt is index-fingering a wordprocessor keyboard. Totting up her scores in the figureskating championships perhaps.

The door at the far end of the room opens and a blur of white, a tall man in a pale raincoat, bursts in. The tableau springs to life. The leather-clad youth detaches himself from the furniture while his companion rediscovers the lost art of two-handed typing. The newcomer is playing keepie-uppie with a child's football, dodging from side to side to follow its erratic trajectory, the schoolboy fringe and open trenchcoat flapping in parallel. The black and white plastic veers so close to the skylight that Nan is already backing away from the expected shower of glass but, miraculously, gravity takes over just in time.

The words come in clusters, punctuated by the thud of the ball.

'Tinkerbell, have you seen about that squash court?

Course not. You're waiting for Junior Gaultier here to kiss you out of that hundred-year kip . . . Passed any good mirrors recently, Chico?'

Unexpectedly, the youth darts forward, gives the taller man a measured shove in the chest, and captures the ball, boosting it skilfully with the side of his head and falling into an easy, assured rhythm. His opponent comes back, laughing, changing the game, repossessing the ball with a basketballer's swipe and bouncing it on the floor.

The girl squeals.

'Watch it, Cal, you nearly had it through the windae. And I didnae book the squash because Del rang up to cancel. His maw's taken a stroke so he's gone doon tae Kelso.'

He makes a feint towards her but doesn't let go of the ball, instead he buzzes it at Nan. For an infinite moment she hesitates, hands raised, not sure if he's thrown it or not. Then in a gesture of pure instinct, her palms close on the missile and she takes it to rest in her stomach.

His smile serves himself first.

'And what's Her Majesty's Mail doing here?'

'I've come to see Callum Macleod.'

'Larger than life and twice as lovable.'

A phone rings, to be answered by Tinkerbell with an elocutionary crispness.

'Cal, it's Mr Morrison.'

He jabs the second finger of his right hand upwards, American-style, in the direction of the receiver.

'I'm sorry, Mr Morri . . . No, that was someone else. He's in meetings all day.'

Giving the secretary the thumbs-up, he starts backing towards the door he just came through, picking his feet up with the exaggerated care of a cartoon burglar and beckoning Nan with the same pantomime of stealth. She follows him out and finds herself on a fire-escape. He's already skipping down the metal staircase; quick on his feet for such a big man. At the bottom is parked a silver-grey sports car.

She hands him the letter. As he reads, his expression loses its inverted commas.

Another candidate for blackmail.

'You play squash?'

'Never.'

He shrugs, opening the car door. 'What do you do to keep the cellulite at bay? Swim? Jog? Belly dance?'

'Not since I left the harem.'

He slides into the driver's seat and gestures for her to join him. The car is so low-slung, the seats so nearly horizontal, it's like slipping between the covers. She tugs the hem of her skirt downwards.

'Dig the groovy gear.'

It's not a big car and he takes up more than his share of space.

'Have you had lunch?'

'No, but . . .'

He guns the engine.

'We'll go to the club. They do a brammer of a water-cress salad. The bimbo on the desk will lend you your swimmies if you tell her you're with me.'

In the women's locker room there are neat piles of apple-green bath sheets, each the size of a small lawn, rows of matching towelling robes, and jumbo bottles of peach and coconut-scented lotions which set her salivating helplessly, their chemicals far juicier than nature's own. When she passed the sign to the squash courts it crossed her mind that this might be the club Gorr uses, then she realised he'd never raise the subscription fee. No question why she's risking a disciplinary being here in working hours: she'll never have another chance to see the inside of this place. As for Callum Macleod: she's

33

encountered the entrepreneurial public schoolboy type before but she suspects that compared to him they were apprentices. More often than not they're English, although in his case she can't be sure. The name could mean no more than sentimental parents in the home counties, an empty reminder of great-great-granny's heilan hame. Reading between the funny voices is almost impossible; his accent is a hybrid of London barrow boy and mid-Atlantic drawl, overlaid – or underlaid – with Scots; his vocabulary is the lingua franca of affectation, the same bracket of kitsch as Santa hats and leopardskin steering-wheel covers. But there's something genuine, an unforced playfulness, about his fakery. She'd like to call his bluff, only she's not absolutely sure he's bluffing.

There's no one in sight at the poolside. The rectangle of water is smooth as glass. She executes a rudimentary dive and recovers into a gliding breast-stroke, disturbing the calm surface as little as possible. The pool is Edwardian, miraculously preserved, the green and white tiling and the stained-glass windows with their sweet-wrapper colours all intact. Strange to swim in water which is water-coloured, not a gaudy municipal blue. The white vaulted roof is topped by a glass cupola, the winter sun rebuffed by the grimy glass like butter on greaseproof paper.

Gradually she becomes aware of movement to her left. He is swimming alongside her on his back, at the same steady pace. His body is unseasonably tanned, the blond hair darkened by wetness.

'Pretty cool, eh? Originally I was thinking of blitzing the building, keeping the pool but putting a new shell round it, going all out for Swedish health and efficiency. Glad I didn't now.'

'You own it?'

'Half share. Did you think I just had the caff? Couldn't

keep the Mazda in gas on that. Street Smarts is mine too, and we do the franchise for the Buccleuch Complex. And I'm opening a tapas bar down by the river to fleece the wide-os who've just discovered Bar-the-lona.'

'Anything else?'

'Only the bordello in Bearsden.'

He takes his time hauling himself out of the water, disdaining the aluminium ladder, sauntering over and lowering himself onto a wooden deck lounger. He's inclining to heaviness, with the slight balance problem common to very tall men, but it clearly doesn't bother him. His Bermuda trunks, a homage to Douanier Rousseau, are plastered to his flanks.

She is sitting on a canvas chair, swathed top-to-toe in her astroturf towel. He seems amused, but perhaps it's his natural expression.

'You're not a Moslem fundamentalist by any chance?'

'I'm not an exhibitionist either.'

'If you've got it, flaunt it.'

A teenage waitress in sweatshirt and leggings arrives with a tray and leaves it on a low table beside him. Nan moves across to the lounger on the other side of the food and takes a plate. He dabs himself dry without opening the towel, picking a pennant of bacon out of the serving bowl.

'How's the greens?'

'Brammer.' The inverted commas are catching. 'But the vinaigrette's pretty industrial. You should get the chef to try balsamic vinegar. And make sure he's using extra-virgin oil.'

'Nah, I'll just sack him.'

For a second she's not sure he's joking. Time to take the initiative.

'Are you Scots?'

'Inversneckie born and bred. Why?' Slipping into Fife Robertson. 'Are you questioning my bona fides?'

Odd how, all but naked, he still looks like money. Even the surplus weight suggests privilege: prime quality beef, glossy, grain fed.

'There's not too many sound like you in the Highlands.'

'Must be the old Alma Mater coming out.'

'I knew it.'

'What was the giveaway: stiff upper lip? Lovely manners? My easy charm?'

Beautiful feet, too, rosy-soled like a baby's.

'The public-school slang.'

'You're off-target there: that's all my own.'

'And the confidence.'

'I keep that in the bank.'

He pours two glasses of wine, half-emptying the bottle.

'How old are you?'

'Thirty-eight and I have two endorsements on my licence. Do you want to see my distinguishing marks?'

He's rattled beneath the smile; she savours a small victory.

'I've never met a man with three restaurants and half a health club before. Seems a lot for thirty-eight.'

Taking a fork, he leans over and lifts a piece of bacon from her plate.

'Nah. I've only just started. Before I became a leading light of café society I was in the building trade.'

'Hard hat and brickie's bum?'

'Soft sell and oops was that another grade A listed fell down in the night?'

He reassembles his mirth into mock penitence.

'Ooh dear, is there a conservationist in the house?'

She shrugs. No point getting trapped on the moral high ground.

'Anything you pulled down worth a threatening letter?'

That expression again. Or absence of expression.

'Anything's possible. Prince Charles could be waiting round the corner with a Kalashnikov, come to that.'

He tops up the wine, although she hasn't drunk any.

'So you work with the polis?'

'Christ no.' *Easy now.* 'I'm an old-fashioned public servant. Someone sends you a letter, I make sure you receive it. That's all.'

A man with a ponytail and small round spectacles enters from the changing rooms, registers the couple on the far side of the water, and hesitates. They lie like mirror images, hands behind their heads, the debris of a meal and a half-empty bottle between them. He leaves the way he came in.

'I've been straining the neurones and I do have a hunch who it might be from: friend of mine with a rather specialised sense of humour.'

'Not a blackmail note?'

'You won't find many people in this town dumb enough to try leaning on me.'

Showered and changed, she hovers uncertainly by the reception desk. The swing doors to the men's locker rooms ricochet and he appears, leather handgrip slung over one shoulder.

'I gotta go. Ask Sam to call you a cab. Nice meeting you.'

'You haven't.'

That three-hundred-watt grin.

'You're right.' He extends a hand. 'Callum Macleod.'

'Nan Megratta.'

They shake hands.

'So I can have the letter?'

37

'Not yet, there's a couple more people I still have to see.'

'I told you, it's for me.'

No funny voices now.

'And there are other people who think it's for them. I can't let it go until I'm sure. It's not a joke for them.'

'You trying to tell me that Glasgow is littered with members of clan Macleod convinced they're being blackmailed?'

He squints, the squall of temper displaced by a new thought.

'The Post Office is making a big deal of this, isn't it?'

She stares back neutrally, wondering if he's made a lucky guess.

'It should all be sorted out by early next week.'

'So I can pencil in a second rendezvous?'

Delving into the inside pocket of his trenchcoat he hands her a salmon-coloured card printed with black lettering.

'Tell you what: come along to the beano. *¿Qué Pasa?*, Paterson Quay. I'm getting in on the waterfront revival. In a couple of years you won't be able to spit for warehouse conversions and Martini umbrellas. You can't miss it: just off the Expressway, left at the doss house, right at the second-day bread shop. We open in a fortnight. Be there or be square.'

The woman standing on the threshold has undergone a transformation. In place of yesterday's discreetly expensive skirt and cashmere blazer she's wearing a pair of jeans and a man's check shirt. Her legs end in green fisherman's socks several sizes too large. On her shirt tail is a sticky-looking map of Australia, roughly the size of a toddler's palm. Even on the stair Nan could hear the strains of a counter-tenor lamenting some late-medieval woe; now the door is open, grief is unconfined.

'Welcome to Bedlam. Do you have any experience of voice-activated somersaulting dogs? Ours seems to be paralysed, which has left me with one very unhappy two-year-old. I know it's not the batteries, I tried the ones out of the clock, now I've no idea what the bloody time is. Non-gender-specific toys: cost a fortune and fall apart as soon as you take them out of the box. You don't get this sort of palaver with a water pistol.'

A child's querulous voice calls from another room.

'OK, Trouble, I'm coming. Have you had your tea? I was bracing myself for the egg soldiers Saul didn't fancy, but this is a great excuse to produce something more appetising ... *All right, I said I'm coming*. Kitchen's through there; put the kettle on.'

Nan walks through the door indicated. There's an inevitability about the room: it's clotted-cream walls, the heavy stripped-oak table, a matching dresser with its hanging bunches of herbs, the battered candystripe armchair and state-of-the-art white goods, a child's crayon sketch pinned up on the cork noticeboard alongside a leaflet from the local community association and a polaroid snap of a baby sucking on an outsize wooden spoon. It's like stepping into the set of a television drama, or a photograph in one of the Sunday supplements. The view from the window really ought to be Hampstead Heath and the householder a toiler in the metropolitan cultural industries, otherwise it's all there: the exotic domesticity of the upper-middlebrow, upper middle classes.

Imogen returns, puffing a sigh which ruffles her fringe.

'Now, Earl Grey or Lapsang, or a large gin? Think I'll go for the gin, myself.'

She opens the dishwasher, takes out two tumblers and mixes the drinks, keeping up a drily comic running commentary on her day: the man who came to mend the central heating, the cold-calling evangelist, opening the paper to find they'd put an ad for fishermen's waders next to a cry for help from the wife of a rubber fetishist. You'd think it had to be sabotage, but they haven't the wit to come up with a trick like that.

The words dip and soar. A handful of famous women in the Seventies had such voices: muscular, obstinately provincial, sexy without any trace of coyness. She's an accomplished performer, a mistress of the art of instant intimacy, gauging just how many leaps her audience can follow without footnotes, excluding any explanatory detail which might call to mind how distant their worlds really are. It's flattering that she takes the trouble, but somewhere around is the whiff of self-conscious sisterhood.

Nan feels her silence growing conspicuous and forces a pleasantry.

'This is a lovely flat.'

The envy clatters like a dropped fork, but Imogen is too polite to pick it up.

'Peter bought it in the Sixties when he was just qualified; wanted somewhere big enough for private consulting rooms, and thought he'd teach himself DIY. Luckily he's completely useless, otherwise we'd be wall-to-wall formica by now. I wasn't too keen about moving into the first Mrs MacLeod's bedroom when we married, but I'm glad I lost the battle now. God knows what it'd cost us at today's prices, even with the dodgy boiler and the penicillin on the bathroom ceiling.'

She pauses to take a sip of alcohol and make a quick assessment over the rim of her glass.

'Do you live round here, Nan? You look very familiar. I've been trying to place where I've seen you before.'

She shrugs. 'I shouldn't think you have. I stay over on the South Side.'

Imogen is silent, waiting for something more. Eventually she realises she isn't going to get it.

'How long have you been doing this job?'

'Three months.'

'How do you find it?'

'How would you expect me to find it?'

Imogen's eyebrows disappear under her fringe.

'All right, let's put it another way. What do you really do?'

'After I've put in an eight-hour day at the Post Office, you mean?'

'No, I mean before you started putting in eight-hour days at the Post Office. My guess is a small business, or shop, somewhere you were your own boss. Nothing too commercialised. Second-hand clothes? Pottery? Silversmithing?'

She remembers what it used to be like, before she was Nan Megratta.

'I ran a restaurant.'

'Maybe that's where I've seen you.'

'It was in England, a cosmopolitan bistro in provincial middle England.'

In the market by six, flirting with Terry over the fish slab, George giving her the rundown on global conflicts as indicated by the non-availability of fruit and veg. Planning the day's menu: French, Mediterranean, consulting Althea on the odd West African dish. Hoping he wouldn't be there when she got home.

'Was it a success?'

'The bank manager didn't think so, but I never had any complaints about the food.'

'You went bust?'

'I wound it up before it got that far.'

On the table is a newspaper, not the one Imogen writes for. Nan scans the headlines on the front page. *Five die in Gaza riots. Sapro drops Aids research.* Taking the hint, the hostess changes the subject.

'I had a letter from a woman who worked for the Post Office last summer. Sexual harassment. She had to leave. Nothing overt; if it'd just been 'drop your knickers' we could have had him at industrial tribunal, but he was the favourite uncle type: arm round her shoulder, ruffling her hair, a bit of tickling. She couldn't bring herself to say anything for months, not even really admit to herself there was a problem. The boss was being nice to her. Except that every man in the office got promoted and she'd been at the same level for five years. Amazing how long she put up with it. She wasn't the only one either. No one complained . . .'

Nan lifts her head from the newsprint.

'We're not all quislings in the gender wars.'

Imogen touches her hand.

'I'm not the enemy, Nan.'

The simplicity of the words coincides with a phrase of surpassing purity from the counter-tenor. She feels exposed, childish. *Why are you doing this? Because you admire her, and you're afraid there are reasons you shouldn't? Or because you want her to like you and can't think of a good reason why she should?*

'I just get the impression you could do with an equal opportunities policy over there. Change the culture. How many women in senior management?'

'I don't know any woman who wants to be. "The culture" is like Kafka on Ativan. No one in their right mind would want to be implicated. I'd rather be a conscript than a collaborator.'

'What about defeating the army of occupation?'

'You're joking? Cut one head off and another just grows in its place.' She's irritated with herself for trying to engage with that white-collar reasonableness. 'Anyway, they'd never let me within a million miles of management.'

Imogen looks sceptical.

'I mean it. And they're right: I screw up. All the time. It's a large organisation, and large organisations need procedures, systems, they employ thousands of people. If you get thousands of people all thinking for themselves, it's anarchy. So they put a little kink into the system to isolate the freaks who want to make it up as they go along. And the kink is to make everything just a little less straightforward than it needs to be, so that the simplest, most obvious solution is never the right one. It's not difficult to learn the system and stick to it. Any fool can do it. Except me. And I'm not high enough up the pecking order to get away with being a maverick. Perhaps you never are. So I screw up and get my knuckles rapped, and a few weeks later I screw up again. I suppose at some level I can't bear to tell myself: this is worth getting right . . .'

She stops, suddenly self-conscious.

43

'So, to answer your original question: I find it about as much fun as toothache.'

'Why do it, then?'

She laughs shamefacedly.

'Ridiculous as it sounds after all that, it has its advantages.'

'Such as?'

She considers lying but isn't enough of an actress to carry it off.

'No one knows who I am and no one cares, and I don't much care what they think of me. I might as well not exist. And that suits me fine.'

'How long have you felt like this?'

It occurs to her that this is how Imogen Reiss earns her living: listening to life and calling it mental illness. Another one for the casebook. She laughs again, a mirth-less exhalation.

'I'm not suffering from depression, if that's what you're driving at.'

'It's more common than you think.'

'I'm not depressed.'

It comes out louder than she intended. She drops the volume.

'I'm hiding.'

Imogen looks concerned, as agony aunts will.

'From what?'

Nan dismisses the question with a shake of her head.

'I thought you wanted another look at this.'

She lays the letter down on the kitchen table. 'If it makes any difference, there are a couple of other people it could have been sent to. One thinks it's a joke, and says he knows who wrote it, the other is certainly a potential candidate for blackmail.'

'Who isn't? One thing you learn editing a problem

page: everyone has secrets. Funny thing is how many want to be found out.'

'Not me.'

'You can't hide forever, Nan.'

She picks up her untouched gin and swallows a mouthful.

'No, but I should be able to manage for a few more weeks.'

'And then?'

The spotty neds with their turbo-charged Escorts parked outside. The women with teenage clothes and forty-five-year-old faces who could be almost any age in between. Telephoto lenses that can count the hairs up your nose from the other side of the street. The whole circus.

The front door slams and a man's voice calls in greeting.

Imogen starts visibly, and lowers her voice. Evidently she wasn't expecting him back so soon.

'What happens then?'

Nan checks over her shoulder: a tall, thick-set man in a shaggy Peruvian sweater is making his way towards the kitchen door. Just for a moment, she is tempted to tell; let's see how far sisterly solidarity really stretches. But the moment has already passed. As if paralysed, Imogen is staring at the letter on the kitchen table. Nan scoops it up and stows it in her pocket as he crosses the threshold.

Official again, she slides her arms into the standard-issue red and navy anorak and fiddles with the zip until the nylon teeth engage.

'Thanks for your help, Ms Reiss. We'll be in touch.'

At home there's a message asking her to ring Tarquin. She grimaces. The pleasure of hearing his voice is always tempered by the ordeal of getting through to him. He has a complicated private life and she never knows exactly who will answer the phone. Once she misattributed the barely-broken voice at the other end of the line. God knows what he had to say to get himself out of that one.

This time she's lucky. It's his master's voice: knowing, languid, a delivery which started as parody but ended up as the genuine article, or the only article he has.

'Well if it's not N–N–N–Nancy with the laughing face. How are you? I've been worried. I know how you mope, and it's not good for you.'

'I've adopted a new strategy: not thinking about it at all. Seems to be working fairly well, although it's hard to think about anything else, so I tend to spend more time than I'd like with my mind a complete blank. You never know, it might do me good. Isn't that what transcendental meditation is all about?'

'Well we don't want you taking off for some ashram. Not unless you're changing your plea to insanity.'

She smiles into the receiver. Behind the fancy upholstery he's sharp as a tack. He doesn't judge her and he doesn't pretend to understand. Being gay, it has nothing to do with him.

'Any sightings of our friends in the Fourth Estate?'

'Surely they'll be persecuting someone else by now.'

'Mmm.' He sounds doubtful. 'For the time being.'

Courtesies over, he gets down to business. She needs a character witness, someone of good standing who can testify that she's making a life for herself, establishing herself in the community.

'How about your boss?'

She imagines telling Gorr. He'd have apoplexy, take it personally. Or worse, perhaps it would excite him in some perverse way.

'Is it absolutely necessary?'

'Poppet, I don't want to put you in a tizz. I'm still very confident that we'll get you off scot-free, if you'll pardon the pun. Well, perhaps a suspended. But there's no point being negligent.'

The attenuated syllables tighten up. 'You'll need all the help you can get.'

She hasn't told anyone. It doesn't seem relevant. Another country, and besides . . . She did it to free herself, not to have it become the defining fact of her existence.

'I'm sure if you explained.'

'People are superstitious. They don't want contact with the sort of person this sort of thing happens to. It might be catching. I feel the same. Only I can't send myself to Coventry.'

'Even if you walk away at the end of it . . .' *If.* 'People are going to find out. It may not have penetrated the frozen north so far, but a trial is different. You'll have to give your address . . .'

'That'll mean instant eviction.'

'Like it or not you'll be headline news. Of course, if you did the sensible thing . . .'

'I've told you, Tarquin.'

'Yes you have, and it seems more than reasonable to me, but I can't see a judge taking the enlightened view.

I'm not nagging you for my benefit, you know. Quite the reverse.'

It's true. She's risking his neck as well as her own.

'I'll think about it.'

'That's a good girl. I've got to scoot now. Gino's doing spaghetti, and you know what Neapolitans are like about punctuality for meals. I hope you're still cooking, by the way, I'm looking forward to a cordon bleu feed once this is all over.'

I t is one of those temperate mornings, when clouds full of silver light protect the world like lint and the rumble of the city is kept at bay by birdsong. It was a morning like this the day it happened, freak conditions for November: that balmy start and then the apocalyptic storm. Even afterwards, after the squad car and the station and the reporters camped outside the hospital gates and all the rest of the game of consequences, the memory of that morning gave her hope: this is what life can be like.

Buchanan Street has the usual Saturday factions, the rockabilly buskers and their stiff-quiffed fans, the banjo player giving a bluegrass rendition of Scotland the Brave, an unsteady wino blowing nothing readily identifiable on his mouth organ. She realises she has seen Danny MacLeod's anarchists countless times before, swerving unthinkingly around them to avoid the trawl of petition-signers registering their protest against seal-clubbing, mink-farming, foxhunting, all the outrages that hijack attention from man's inhumanity to man.

About a dozen of them are grouped around a trestle table pinned with anti-vivisection posters and piled with photostatted news sheets. A couple of superannuated punks, scalps stubbled around the lacquered mohican crest, scabby knees and stripes of goosepimpled buttock visible through their torn jeans, a touch of inflammation about the nose ring, the ragged-trousered misanthropists. There's a white boy with dreadlocks, too, greenish-brown hanks of matted hair trailing on his shoulders. But most of them would pass without comment in a crowd: leather

49

jackets, single earrings, Doc Martens, cropped hair, every-day street style. She understands the MP's anxiety a little better. They're threatening, but not because of their appearance. The mercilessness of youth isn't frittered away on the distractions of fashion or rock, the children aren't playing. Nor, on closer inspection, are they all children. While the youngest seem to be in their mid-teens, one or two don't look much younger than herself.

One of them, in an army surplus sweater with a CND badge attached, sees her hovering and offers her a handbill urging her to *Stand up to the commissars at the City Chambers*. Now she confronts the question she was too drunk or disarmed to raise the night before last. Just how is she supposed to find out if they sent Danny MacLeod the letter?

'Are you gonnae come?'

She looks blankly at him, then it occurs to her to read the handbill. It announces a rally to protest about council house letting policies. She shrugs.

'How many do you think you'll get?'

'If you come that's another one.'

She reads on. *The Stalinist fat cats have been looking after their pals at the expense of working-class Glaswegians for too long.*

'Aren't Stalinists the last people to listen to demonstrations of public feeling?'

'They'll listen when there's a byelection coming up. It's "your pals the Labour Party" the now. "Gie's your vote and have a wee drink on us." Think we'll forget the six-month wait to get a windae fixed. They're in for a fright.'

'I was in Sanilands Thursday night, Danny MacLeod had them eating out of his hand.'

His face shows reflex contempt. 'That bastard.'

Over a khaki shoulder she sees a familiar figure, somehow less stooped without his uniform. As the anarchist turns to see what has distracted her, his face is transformed.

'How you doin', big man?'

Rab punches him on the upper arm.

'Brendan, how's the revolution? I shouldnae bother trying to recruit this yin, by the way, she's in the pay of the government.'

'Another wan changing the system from the inside?'

She's glad to be sidelined; it gives her a chance to consider, and reject, ways of raising the MP in conversation again. Rab evidently knows the army-clad pacifist well but they have some catching up to do. She's not sure if they're close enough in age to have been classmates. The lines about Brendan's eyes, the coarse five o'clock shadow, belong to a man nearer thirty than twenty, but his attitude is younger. Not carefree exactly, but careless, uncategorised, evidently on the broo.

Rab is starting to worry about her being left out, his concentration flickering as he attempts to listen to his friend and gauge her mood. Brendan is dropping names from their shared past, trying to tempt him along to some party. He gestures towards Nan.

'And yer lemon. As long as she brings some bevvy.'

Rab's smile dies before it reaches his eyes. They're friendly enough to be teased as a couple within the Post Office, but they don't socialise outside working hours. That's different territory and both know the ground rules. He doesn't want to be rebuffed, she doesn't want to rebuff him, but she would, if the need arose. Occasionally, late at night in her floral wallpapered cell, she wonders why there's never been any doubt about it. But Danny MacLeod changes things. Rab hides his surprise fairly well. They make arrangements, write down addresses. She wonders what the hell you wear to an anarchist party.

The flat is a three-apartment in Hillhead, a perennial student gaff with a pocket-handkerchief jungle between pavement and close mouth. They flatten themselves against the wall, running a gauntlet of bicycles at the bottom of the stairs. On the second flight they have to negotiate the overspill of the party: whey-faced Goths in a rainbow of black rags, dyed black hair lustreless as tarmac. They sit in pairs, hunched on the cold stone steps, nursing cans of lager and endlessly relighting anorectic roll-ups. Stepping across the threshold of the flat, she experiences a rush of social panic, a hangover from adolescence. The dozen or so figures in view barely glance up at the blast of air ushered in by the open door. A good sign: no one's waiting for the Cavalry.

Brendan is coming out of the kitchen with a baking tray of pizza, its wholemeal base the colour of soggy cardboard, the tomato puree topping enamelled to an adamantine finish and dotted with olives like shrunken heads. She bets herself there's a rice salad somewhere on the premises. Their host catches sight of them, shrugs elaborately to indicate that he will greet them as soon as he's dumped the hot pizza, then changes his mind and approaches, offering them the pick of his tray.

There's no time to warn Rab, who automatically takes a square. She pleads thirst and, brandishing the clinking carry-out, goes in search of the inevitable waxed paper cups. In the kitchen she fiddles with the corkscrew and takes stock. White rice dotted with peas and sweetcorn next to a soup plate of hummus and a half-eaten cheesecake. She cuts herself a wafer-thin sliver and runs her finger along the knife. Tofu: vegans.

But not all of them. It's a mixed crowd; there's the night of the living dead contingent, mostly teenagers, the slightly older street toughs in jeans and leather jackets and even a sprinkling of guests in their thirties. The women are stylish, if unconventional. Having reached an age where they can no longer risk the Oxfam rail and matted tresses, they have short, well-cut hair, immaculate jeans and chic boxy jackets. Their male contemporaries are close-cropped, defying the world and their bald patches, or else wear their hair long and tied back in a ponytail. Mostly they dress like sociology lecturers, street toughs who want you to know they've read Kerouac. The postmodernist black poloneck. Discuss.

Rab enters the room still carrying a rim of concrete-coloured crust. He dumps it on a dirty plate and holds out his hand for a paper cup.

'How was the pizza?'

He screws up his face.

'Boggin'.'

Something brushes against her leg and she looks down to find a piebald mongrel cleaning up someone else's indigestible leavings. In one corner a woman with a long plait is breastfeeding a baby. Talking to her is a man with John Lennon spectacles and a ponytail who looks vaguely familiar. Next to Rab, a couple of faces she recognises from Buchanan Street are discussing the finer points of recording contracts, not necessarily from first-hand experience. Unspecified artiness, leftist policies, and a sweetish layer of cigarette smoke hover above their heads.

'Who are all these people?'

He jerks his head towards a couple of chairs out of earshot of the rest of the room and they set up camp.

'Me and Brendan used to play fitba for St Pi's. My ma didn't like me knocking about with him: he was a wild boy. Clever but. Then he got political. Most of us were Grebos, or Skins or Suedes. I had the two-tone Sta-prest, button-down Ben Sherman, the Business. Not Brendan. He had to be the revolutionary reading Mao's Little Red Book under the desk. First he was a Commie, then he decided he was an anarchist. Used to go down to London on bash-the-fash awaydays; turn up at National Front marches and give them a toeing. I went with him once: it didnae seem worth it. They all looked like rejects from the retards class, you didnae have to batter 'em, Darwin had made sure they werenae gonnae make it.'

She marvels that he is able to talk about the past with such animation, as if it were still part of him. It can't be the drink making him garrulous unless he stopped off somewhere for a couple of shots of Dutch courage before meeting her. Usually they observe conversational parity: strictly third person, no glimpses of the inner life. I won't show you mine if you don't show me yours.

'At first it was just Brendan and a couple of clones. Then he started hanging about with the heavy team, older guys, a couple had done HMP, one of them was supposed to have a gun. As far as I could see it was just getting blootered in the back rooms of pubs and slagging the SWP and the RCP and the rest of the alphabet soup. The polis took it seriously, but. Kirsten's husband – you know, the Special at Clydebank – tried to warn me off. Bad company. I wasnae that keen anyway, I'd written them off as a bunch of bampots. And then there were all they letter bombs.' Her face fails to register the desired recognition and he rolls his eyes in disbelief. 'It was in all the papers up here. They had the polis changing their jooks twice a day. Democracy under siege. Half a dozen manilla surprises and bingo: pure panic.'

'Did anyone get hurt?'

He's wrongfooted by the note of censure in her voice: this is his party piece, she's supposed to be laughing.

'Naw, they looked up a few Scottish Office suits in *Who's Who*, hauf the addresses were out of date anyway and the bombs were a joke: mair explosive in a roman candle. But it put the wind up the papers. Every day it was "Police close in on the ringleaders". But there were-nae any ringleaders, they couldnae run a ménage – the only smart thing about them. Soon as anyone did anything they put out a communiqué claiming it: eejits setting fire to letterboxes, totie wee boys breaking windows. No one was a member, everyone was part of the movement. It was mental. The polis were chasing their tails looking for Mr Big, talking about IRA training camps and Libyan funding, and it was just Brendan and his pals and a load of heidcases they'd never even met.'

'And no one was ever caught?'

'Oh aye, a couple.' He scans the room. 'Max must have pissed off, but you see that baldy with the red jaikit? He did a stretch in the Bar-L, conspiracy to cause explosions. He was heid bummer at the Welfare Rights but they gave him the welly: sexual harassment of a lassie on the YTS. His personal politics are a bit on the iffy side. Max is OK. He got twelve but they let him out last year: good behaviour.' He laughs. 'Calls himself a free-lance journalist now.'

'The pen is mightier than the letter bomb?'

He laughs again, nervously; she's still missing the point.

'They were haunless. "Hitting strategic targets": they couldnae hit a cow on the arse with a banjo. Anyway, Scott and Max are reformed characters the now, have to be: if they crossed Argyle Street against the lights the polis'd be down on them.'

He lowers his voice as a trio of black-clad teenagers, plates laden with rice salad, drift within earshot.

'The vampire kids are running the revolution now, and you know what they're doing to bring capitalism to its knees? Superglueing the locks on the fur shops. Every night. Every morning the janny comes to drill them out again. Pathetic. They've some persistence, but.'

'What about Brendan?'

55

He shrugs. 'Him and his pals are getting on a bit for hunt-sabbing and liberating beagles with lung cancer. They do Saturdays on Buchanan. Run night classes in squatting; once a month go doon the City Chambers and gie it laldy in the public gallery . . .'

'Blackmail the odd public figure?'

His expression hovers on the brink of laughter, if only he could see the joke.

She gazes back, unsmiling.

'You know that letter I showed you? I narrowed it down to three people. One of them's Danny MacLeod. He thinks your pals might have it in for him.'

'Did I hear the name of our MP?'

She looks up to a thin-lipped smile, pennyframe spectacles and mousy blond hair pulled back into a ponytail. The yellowish tint of his skin is heightened by a peacock-blue shirt. She has always found unjustified vanity repellent.

'Max, the man himself.'

The smile broadens slightly, still not showing his teeth. She sees now how he could have arrived at their side unnoticed. He carries stillness about him like a shroud. His eyes don't blink, she notices; perhaps he's stoned.

'How's the man I made all those mailbags for?'

Not waiting for a reply, he turns to Nan. His gaze is like looking into a two-way mirror. If he's stoned, she'd hate to meet him sober.

'Not interrupting, am I?'

She looks to Rab, sending distress signals.

'This is Nan, she works at the post with me.'

'I know.' The eyes behind their glass shields are giving nothing away. 'So you're a friend of our Danny?'

'Not really. Are you?'

Rab registers the tension but misreads it as sexual, and sulkily crosses the room to the assortment of bottles and cans, full and empty, ranged underneath a steam-rippled poster of James Dean. Max slides into the vacated seat, his eyes never flickering from her face.

'I've some experience of the honourable member.'

She says nothing.

'Some friends of mine did a little job for him a while back: not entirely legit, but in my experience legislators are never too fussed about the law.' A tip of tongue snakes over his upper lip. 'You're a long way from home.'

He knows. As soon as the thought crosses her mind she recognises how irrational it is, but the paranoia, once conjured, doesn't go away.

'The South Side? It's not exactly outer Mongolia.'

'I thought you lived in the Sanny.'

She remembers the cheerless community hall, the pensioners and the poll-tax debtors still hoping for an amnesty. His face doesn't fit the picture.

'No, I just went along for the meeting – he's a good speaker.'

'He's a crook.'

'How do you mean?'

The smile tautens the skin over his nose, giving him a fastidious look, as if somewhere nearby is a very bad smell.

'You'll find it in the dictionary. Under C.'

His lips, now slightly parted, reveal tiny milk teeth; she is reminded of a Victorian wax doll: that smooth yellow skin, the perfect miniature dental work more sinister than the knowing stare.

'Is he shagging you?'

The blood sings in her cheeks. Old-fashioned phrases flash through her head: *I beg your pardon? How dare you! Or should she just fall back on an obscenity?* His lips purse, mock-impressed.

'Life in the old balls yet then.'

'I've met him once.'

'That's not necessarily a barrier for big Dan. They don't call him Desperate for nothing.'

She feels cheapened, and not just by the man in front of her; she is starting to harbour an obscure resentment towards Danny MacLeod. She speaks as calmly, as quietly as she can.

'Leaving aside that it's no business of yours who I shag, why do you think I'm shagging Danny MacLeod?'

Rab reappears, triumphantly bearing a bottle of Blue Nun.

'You owe me a medal: valour beyond the call of. It wouldnae be my first choice, in the Rothschild cellars, but it's this or Blue Stratos.'

She crumples the empty cup in her fist and tosses it on to the table.

'I'd rather drink the aftershave.'

There is the usual clutter of people in the hall, half-queuing for the bathroom. A delicate, almost androgynous youth with a completely shaven scalp and a Gilbert and Sullivan Chinaman's pigtail growing from the base of his skull is entertaining a handful of black-clad teenagers. A dozen earrings are racked along the curve of one ear like relics of reconstructive surgery.

'So I said, "The squat may not have a power shower but at least Sigmund isn't creeping round in his micro fucking bathrobe." Christ! I wouldn't let him near me, no matter how mental I was. You can't move for bogroll. Every time he goes to the shops he comes back with another pack of Andrex. And *he's* supposed to be the doctor. Something went badly wrong with his toilet training, that's for definite.'

Rab arrives at her side wearing his Chamberlain look: appeasement passing itself off as control.

'I thought you'd pissed off hame.'

'Where's Max?'

'Gone to a late-night show at the Grosvenor. Neglec-
ted Algerian masterpiece.'

He pauses, hoping the hiatus will make the question
casual.

'What were you two talking about?'

'We didn't manage a conversation.'

'He told me to tell you to ask your pal about his
oriental interests. What's he mean?'

She shrugs. 'How should I know? He's your friend.'

One of the Goths ahead of her in the queue, a girl in
a peasant skirt with tassels round the hem, starts rolling
a joint, forming a patchwork of cigarette papers, eviscerating a Silk Cut, arranging the ridge of tobacco down the
middle. She pulls out a ball of clingfilm and unwraps a
lump of resin about the size of a chocolate chip. Most
of it lodges under her fingernails as she attempts to crum-
ble it onto the tobacco. The others watch greedily, all
conversation suspended. So much anticipation for such a
pitiful high.

Rab taps her on the elbow. 'Let's go.'

They end up in George Square, the scent of hyacinths concentrated as air freshener, the grid-planted blooms of indeterminate colour under the architectural floodlights. In the mild Spring night the streets have an interior look, as if enclosed in a protective shell. Inspired by the memory of the pizza, they are free-associating on the theme of disgusting food: blackberry and apple puree the colour of slugs, bruised bananas, fishpaste, fili-gree-work fried eggs. Rab protests: he likes his eggs that way. They laugh, weaving and staggering a little, not drunk but unmoored, cut adrift from their usual context, suddenly self-conscious when the spurt of hilarity has run its course.

He sighs, drawing a line under their laughter. 'It was good crack the night.'

But she's superstitious about postmortems before the patient is dead. Opposite them is the Post Office, the relentless light picking out details they never notice on their way into work: a tiara of urns, the elaborately carved lion and unicorn on the royal crest. Aimlessly they circle the building. The night entrance is open but John the watchman isn't at his post. They cross the threshold, feeling the pleasurable flutter of rule-breaking without risk.

After the strip-lit staircase, the sorting office swallows them like a cave. It takes a while to adjust to the murk. She knows the topography off by heart: the grey cellulose mailbags and huge moulded plastic tubs, the wall of sort-ing frames bisecting the room. The den of an obsessional insect collector. But it's different at night. Without the constant backdrop of Radio 2 the acoustics are unfamiliar; creaks and echoes tease at the limits of her hearing, disorienting her. She walks into a row of drop-bag fittings and yelps, more in surprise than from the pain of her jarred knee.

'Nan?'

The panic in his voice is impossible to ignore. She explains, reassures him, but the echo of that frantic cry hovers in the air.

'See that letter?'

His tone is over-casual, a wobbly acrobat's recovering flourish.

'Mmm?'

'That blackmail note. You think it's for real?'

She shrugs invisibly. 'Who knows? All those respectable professionals getting jumpy about the skeletons in their cupboards seem to think so.'

'How serious is it, I mean as a crime?'

She wonders if he always turns philosophical after midnight.

'No idea. All I want to know is, if I deliver it, does that make me an accessory?'

But he's not disposed to humour. She always thinks of him as colourless, in that category of redheads who are drained of pigment, unlike herself, one of the ones who have too much. But in this strange filtered semi-darkness, he is finally truly monochrome, like the pages of a child's magic paintbook, the liverish images waiting for water to be brushed into life.

'When I lived with Mandy in that single end in Springburn and things were really shite between us, she just went on strike. Total non-cooperation. The house was a pure midden. I'd get in and the post was still on the mat. She wouldnae even pick the fucking bills up. After a few days I thought fuck it, I'm not gonnae pick them up either. Every day there was mair, maistly crap, supermarket coupons and fliers, but some proper letters. Then she left and I still didnae touch them. I'd be driving round Lanarkshire, delivering for the Co, and I'd think about them sitting on the mat waiting for me. I couldnae cope with it, it got so I didnae want to come hame. There could have been a postal order from Paul Getty, I wouldnae have picked it up. It was daein' my nut in. I used to open the door with my eyes shut. The neighbours must've thought I was radio rental.'

He pauses, lacking either words or will to make the fear explicit.

'When I flitted to Mount Florida the landlord must have binned them.'

She knows he has just told her something important to him, she even understands the terror stacking up in those unopened envelopes – better than he does, perhaps – but she doesn't want the information. She suspects a precursor to seduction, a clumsy attempt to advance intimacy, but it could be a simple attempt at human contact. Either way, she doesn't his pain. Somewhere, shut away, she has her own.

She turns her head aside, a minimal movement but eloquent in its way.

'I knew you'd understand.' His bitterness sounds accumulated. 'A credit to the Colditz Charm School. Name, rank and serial number. Anything else: you can forget it.'

She wonders uneasily if this is really how she comes across.

'You reckon Brendan's blackmailing that MP?'

'Not Brendan necessarily, but maybe one of his pals.'

'Does he fancy you?'

'Who? Brendan?'

'You know who I mean.' She remembers other inquisitions, the endlessly ingenious questions to catch her out in a foregone conclusion. 'Wife and weans in Bearsden, probably a researcher in black knickers keeping the water-bed warm in London. Danny MacLeod isnae gonnae crease his suit for you. I don't doubt he'll give you one, but if you're expecting anything mair out of it you want your heid looked.'

She's never noticed before how well-defined his Adam's apple is: improbable as a cartoon cat swallowing a tennis ball. Its exposure is almost painful. The mystery of masculinity: why men see themselves as the stronger sex. What could be more vulnerable than the phallus? If men are dangerous, it's got nothing to do with their bodies.

'Where's all this come from? Your head? Or Max's?'

He shifts slightly.

'Max knows the score. If he says Dannyboy's a bandit, you'd better believe it.'

'Why? What's he got against him?'

She feels his struggle, the temptation to deliver more than he knows, but she doesn't play that game and is unforgiving with those who do.

'Christ knows. None of them are saying and it's no because they're fussy about slagging an MP. I've known Brendan since he was blowing gub balls through an empty biro. He was always a hard ticket, you wouldnae kick him if he was six months deid, but his arse is nippin buttons the now.'

S he settles on eleven as the best time to ring Danny MacLeod: late enough to allow a long lie but too early to interrupt Sunday lunch. He doesn't strike her as the type to go to mass.

She's wrong. His wife says to try again later. She has a pleasant Ayrshire accent, soft and broad, less reconstructed than her husband's. Nan feels a brief, baseless pang of guilt. When she calls back Danny picks up the phone. He sounds polite but neutral. Impossible to know whether this is for his wife's benefit or for hers. They agree to meet at three-thirty.

She was the child of a broken home in the days before it became commonplace, and on access afternoons, the second and fourth Sundays of the month, her father would collect them from their douce dormitory village in the Trossachs and drive them into Glasgow, here, to the museum. Overcome by guilt and the need to earn a fortnight's love, he would buy them ice creams from the van on the tarmac outside. Ninety-nines: vanilla cones that tasted of cardboard and that lipid-rich, airpuffed peak impaled with a half stick of flaked chocolate. Their mother used to balk at a squirt of raspberry sauce. After they had brushed the wafer-dust from their duffelcoats they would take a turn round the Winter Garden, an Edwardian glasshouse whose waxy foliage fell so far short of the romance of its name. Then the museum itself. She loved it; not the worthy details of trade-union rallies and socialist Sunday schools, but the Brasso and tin baths and cakes of carbolic soap in the domestic displays. *How we used to live.* The notion was fascinating, she would stare, tantalised by the knowledge that this easy inclusivity didn't stretch to her. Premature mortality ran through both sides of the family. Her parents were orphans with a fetish for the new. No holidays with arthritic grandparents, no bouncing on uncut moquette, no ruckling the antimacassars. The home they made together was full of wipe-clean surfaces and drip-dry fabrics in garish primary colours. With a child's flawed logic, old things came to stand for permanence, security and love. The exhibits became surrogate relations, an extended family which would always be there for her. When she left home, or what passed for it, she took to scouring junk shops in an effort to make her rented bedsit more personal, looking for love among the backstreet bargains. One day, rooting through a wicker laundry hamper marked 'everything 50p' she glanced up and discovered Kilner, the unluckiest find of her life.

She gets to the Winter Garden five minutes late to make sure he is waiting for her; her need of this small psychological advantage is greater than his. She realises, as she scans the tea tables a second time, that she's expecting him to be wearing the same green shirt and grey suit as the first time they met. Since there is no one fitting this description, she is momentarily at a loss. She thinks of the morning's phone call, the adulterous guilt about a man she can't pick out of a crowd of twenty-five.

Turning to the counter, she is studying the plates of cakes in their perspex cells when she hears a voice behind her, close enough to bristle the hairs on her neck.

'I wouldn't touch the apricot fancy. Tastes like the cement mixer broke down.'

He's wearing a pigskin jacket the colour of Lorne

sausage. She wouldn't buy a second-hand car from him. Wires of dark brown chest hair work their way through the open neck of his shirt. She stares at them a fraction of a second too long. He insists on carrying her cup back to his table. She knows this is meant as gallantry but it makes her feel about ten years old. All around them children are getting their Sunday afternoon treats: fizzy orangeade and foil-wrapped chocolate biscuits. The air is moist and humid despite the greyness of the sky on the other side of the arched glass roof. She can smell things growing. He settles into his chair and, picking up a teaspoon, pokes at the skin puckering over the surface of his half-drunk coffee. The flesh-coloured membrane wraps itself around the metal. He dumps it, disgusted, in the saucer. Sparrows are dust-bathing under the arcing palms; their cheeping rings piercingly in the enclosed space.

'So, Nan Megratta, what have you got to tell me?'

The directness of the question, not even pretending an interest outwith himself, shocks her. Awareness of how easily she could have made a fool of herself brings on a momentary giddiness, like the adrenalin rush after a close shave with a speeding car. She wonders if the meeting will last long enough for a second cup of coffee.

'I was at a party with your friends last night.'

He raises an eyebrow. 'I asked you to find out about them, not become a card-carrying member.'

'They don't have membership, they're anarchists.'

'And they don't own anything because property is theft? Let's pass on the ideological one-upmanship, it's meant to be my day off.'

He takes a sip of coffee. 'Did you have fun?'

She avoids his gaze, wondering why it should be humiliating to respond to his flirtation, but not for him to flirt.

'The catering could have been better.' The flicker across his face may not be irritation, but the possibility is enough to release a flicker of her own. 'I don't know why you involved me in this. You're not top of their Christmas card list, but that doesn't mean they're going to risk blackmailing you. Trouble for you means trouble for them. You know as well as I do, with what they've got on you they're in no position to get heavy.'

In repose, his features look their age. Then he smiles to himself, as if disappointed in her, and swings his left fist round in a slow motion punch, gently jarring her jawline.

'Nice try, Nan.'

Oddly, the birdsong has stopped. She rises from her seat, feeling foolish, knowing the gesture was nothing more than a playful rebuke, a rough caress, certainly not meant to be taken seriously. But it isn't a joke for her.

He gets up too, reaching across the table to put his hands on her shoulders and motion her down again. She resists the pressure. Elaborately, like a man confronted by a sawn-off shotgun, he removes his hands and holds them up at shoulder height.

'All right, cards on the table time. Just sit down. Please.'

Aware of the glances from other tables, she complies. He sighs like someone about to explain the seasons to a member of the flat earth society.

'Yes, they've got something on me I'd rather not see passed around, for all sorts of reasons. And no, I'm not going to tell you what it is. If they have half a brain cell between them they'll know blackmailing me isn't a smart move. But at least one of them is such a mad bastard there's no knowing what he'll do.'

'Max?'

He reaches into his pocket and takes out a box of slim cigars, the reformed addict's crutch. He pulls the cellophane tag and unwraps one. At the next table, a woman in a black shell suit like a roughly-tailored refuse sack is smoking. He leans across, borrows a box of matches, lights the cigar and exhales. The tendrils of smoke bring back other men across other tables. Older flames.

'So he's back?'

She shrugs. 'He didn't say he'd been away.'

'Spain I heard. Swapping detonator technology with ETA. An International Brigades pilgrimage. Who knows what the Scottish urban guerrilla does off-duty? I was hoping that whatever it was, he'd be enjoying it too much to come back.'

'Do you know what he wants from you?'

'No.' He says it once more with feeling, an acknow-ledgement that his first instinct is to lie. 'No. I don't even know if he wants anything. If it's even him. If the bloody letter's even for me. I've had no other contact from them. I was hoping you might be able to shed some light on it.'

'How am I supposed to do that when you won't give me a clue what's going on?'

He looks directly at her.

'Tell you what: you first. I'd like to know what's going on with Nan Megratta. Behind the see-all-say-nothing routine.'

This again. Of course she's secretive, but she hoped it was within the limits of normal behaviour. She doesn't want to be seen as some kind of freak. Was there ever a time when she volunteered information, said the first thing that came into her head? Ah yes. When she fell in love with Kilner.

Danny is leaning back in his chair, waiting. What does he want her to say? What *is* going on with Nan Megratta? Sometimes she feels less secretive than simply blank, as if she's short-circuited some crucial wiring and the lights will never work again.

Fortunately he's not the type to sustain an indefinite period of silence. Like many hard men, he loses his nerve at the prospect of a conversational gap.

'Maybe you just don't like politicians?'

'Maybe I don't. I don't have much faith in political parties, that's for sure. The things really needing change aren't on the agenda for any of them.' She hesitates, then says it anyway. 'It depends on your definition of politics. I don't swallow the line about this socialist country that just happens to be socially conservative. I find the Red Flag-raising domestic-tyrant type hard to take.'

He seems to think he's got her measure. 'So we all join a consciousness-raising group and unemployment vanishes like snow off a dyke?'

'No, but if you give a man a job it doesn't stop him coming home and battering seven shades of shit out of the wife.' *Not this. Not now.* 'I just feel that anybody who wants power enough to be a politician ought to be barred by law from holding it. Strikes me as a pathological profession.'

She smiles, pulling the punch.

'And yes, since you're wondering, I do vote Labour.'

But he's not flirting any more. Carefully he puts out the half-smoked cigar in the tinfoil ashtray.

'At least in parliament there's some sort of control. It's the lunatics outwith the asylum you want to worry about. I'm not talking about bedsit Guevaras like your pal Max: thinks he'll go down in history because he set a civil servant's welcome mat on fire. There are honours graduates in widowmaking out there. Real killers. I marched with them at funerals, when I was still playing at history myself. I did my time as a fraternal delegate. Fact-finding missions in the occupied six counties. The warning light

69

was flashing even then, but I thought: maybe that's what heroes are like, maybe that's what it takes. All the normal people have too much to lose.'

He exhales contempt.

'Christ save us from the heroes with nothing to lose. You don't get mentioned in dispatches for serving on a select committee, but what's the alternative? Law and order by kneecapping. Psychos and juvenile delinquents with their fingers on the trigger. Those bampots you were drinking with last night, they'd've nuked Washington to get the subs out of Holy Loch.'

'Why did you get mixed up with them, then?'

He sighs. 'God knows. For badness, maybe.'

He stops himself.

'Nan, I told you, no fishing.'

The woman in the shell suit is looking over, an unlit cigarette between her lips. He treats her to a naughty boy's grin, the unrepentant thief, and tosses the matches into her outstretched palm. Another prospective voter happy.

Turning back, the smile has already gone. He runs a finger around the inside of his shirt collar.

'Let's get out of here. I'm not dressed for the tropics.'

When he takes the door into the museum, she assumes it's as a short cut to the carpark but he surprises her by climbing the steep, echoing steps leading to the first-floor galleries. At the top he pauses and she slips ahead of him. After all these years, there's no hesitation, she remembers exactly where it was. Rounding the corner, it's still there. A quick check for attendants, and she's swinging her leg over the wooden railing to enter the alcove, tracing the scalloped soap recesses in the white porcelain washbasin, running her fingers over the organ stop controls of the Victorian shower-bath, the rudimentary yet ambitious technology offering every variety of wetness from *cascade* to *deluge*. Even now she feels a quasi-religious awe. How we used to live.

His smile acknowledges her pleasure without being able to share it. Jerking his glance over the mocked-up room, his eyes come to rest on the elaborately decorated lavatory bowl with its monstrous, oxen-yoke wooden seat.

'Now I know what they mean by a pompous shit.'

As a remark it's both tasteless and insensitive, but it's she who feels embarrassed: ridiculous to expect him, or anyone, to share her feelings. From the other side of the barrier he reaches out to take her hand, a gesture which trumps anything he's done yet to surprise her.

'I want you to see something.'

He leads her to the trade union history section, old photographs blown up and card-mounted, dog-eared pamphlets under glass, the odd frayed banner and rusting lapel badge. At first she doesn't realise the display in front of them is dedicated to events that took place under thirty years ago. The black and white photographs and earnest offset-litho agitprop seem little different from the relics of Red Clydeside before the First World War. Her eye is caught by a photograph of men walking in imposs-ible, easy juxtaposition with the huge hull of a ship in dry dock, dwarfed yet oblivious, as if their concerns were the scale and measure of all things.

Danny is scrutinising the clusters of tiny, boilersuited figures. He points at an upright shadow, taller than the rest, wearing a safety helmet, facial features indecipherable in the grain of the enlargement.

'That's the boy.'

She nods, uncertain how to respond, feeling suddenly, achingly sad. That smudge of black must have been about the age she is now.

As if reading her thoughts he moves across to a photo-graph on the opposite wall.

'You were out of kindergarten by the Miners' Strike, I take it?'

This time there's no mistaking him. The hair is black, the moustache more luxuriant. These days, even the West of Scotland has woken up to the ambiguity of such hirsute display. But little has changed. The aggression of his posture, legs planted wide apart, chest barrelled, winds her. There's no obvious target, no riot police or blackleg labour he's trying to outface; it's an indiscriminate chal-lenge. With one proviso. She scans the crowd around him: strikers in their everyday clothes, picketline fellow travellers, all shapes and sizes; one sex. The paradox of machismo: a heterosexual ritual to which women are irrelevant.

'I did the soup kitchens in Rugeley.'

Her mood clouds, remembering. Handing out chip butties and seeing the kids didn't use too much ketchup.

'The wives used to try to sell me their wedding rings.'

'Ever tempted?'

'I had one of my own.'

She says it absent-mindedly, trying to unravel a memory. Something happened to Danny MacLeod about the time of the strike. Maybe afterwards. For a short while he became an easy laugh for chat-show hosts and Radio 4 panellists. Something to do with being found out – or was it set up? – by the tabloid press. A photo-graph. An anti-nuclear rally? TUC conference? Some occasion where his mind should have been on higher things, not to mention his hands. He was unlucky. The minor pop stars and bimbo royalty were lying low that week, the paparazzi had to find fresh game. The picture got a lot of exposure. There was a nickname. What was it?

'The hot-to-Trot.'

It comes out as a murmur, but it would have been better not coming out at all. The set of his mouth warns her she shouldn't refer to the incident a second time, but she wonders if there isn't a little secret satisfaction behind that grimly pursed slot. No such thing as bad publicity.

'They had me down as one of the ten most dangerous men in Britain: Livingstone, Scargill, Benn, myself. The Yorkshire Ripper didn't get a look-in. Then the guardians of public morals decided they didn't need any more bogeys so they turned me into a clown. I hung on though. Wasn't going to give the bastards the satisfaction of turfing me out.'

He starts to move towards the stairs.

'The wife was good about it, I'll say that for her. They were desperate for the dirt. Bundles of used fivers, holiday in the Caribbean, she only had to say the word.'

'And you think it was good of her not to?'

He shrugs, surprised by the edge in her voice. 'She'd never have done it for the money, but she might've for the revenge.'

They are passing a mock-up of a Fifties newsagent's, its shelves of Woodbine and Park Drive, penny dreadfuls and women's magazines pegged diagonally, like bunting. *Woman's Own. Secrets. People's Friend.*

'Do you still love her?'

She's still capable of surprising herself, even if he shows no sign of finding the question unusual.

'It's not a yes–no thing, Nan. If she died I'd be devastated; if she decided to walk out I'd help her pack. It ain't going to happen, anyway.'

Outside, in the open air, he stretches, pulling his shoulders back so the shirt tautens across his chest.

'That place gets to me. Sunday dads. Poor bastards.'

'How old are your kids?'

'Old enough to have grown out of hating me, thank God.'

'Boys or girls?'

'Do you really want to know or are you just pressing the bruise?'

She doesn't understand the question.

'I've been married a long time, Nan. Twenty-three years. Longer than most life sentences. Well, you don't get remission for good behaviour. Not that I'd be eligible. You being so hot on personal politics, you probably don't approve. It happens. I never set out to lie to anyone. Never thought I'd actually find myself saying "my wife doesn't understand me". I don't bring it up. As far as I'm concerned Jean and the kids have got nothing to do with anything. But it's part of the female kit: find the thing that's going to make you really miserable and then worry at it like a dog at a bone. Find your bruise, and press it.'

They are walking along an avenue of closely-planted beeches; under the dense canopy of leafless branches the path is gloomy as a Victorian parlour, the ribbon of sky above them a grey institutional blanket, the grass a vivid, nauseous green. Rain is imminent. She sidesteps to avoid a crevice in the potholed tarmac.

He is slightly ahead when he turns, blocking her path.

'I'm not going to lie to you, Nan. My wife and I understand each other perfectly. That's half the problem. I could find her in a sandstorm in the Sahara. I'd just know which way she'd go. I understand women pretty well: my specialist subject. Used to be, anyway. It's taking a little longer to work out your mental map.'

It's the tenderness that takes her by surprise, an affection that seems almost asexual. Her first kiss since Kilner. The emotion is frightening, as if her ribcage will cleave. When the first drops of rain fall, heavy as sap through the winter trees, she expects him to pull away. The rain falls faster, heavier, turning his suede shoulders to leopardskin. Rivulets gather in her parting and course down her neck. The newly-released smell of the earth mingles with the musk traces of his cigar. Some indefinable point has been passed now, she's waiting for him to stop, wondering why he doesn't; maybe he wants to capitalise on the moment but just can't work out the logistics of sexual intercourse in the middle of a municipal park in the pouring rain.

Finally, she takes the initiative, moving towards a tree at the side of the path. He kisses a drip of rainwater off the end of her nose.

'My car's back at the road, I think we'd better get you home.'

Desperate Dan. She pulls away.

'I can get the bus.'

Behind the smile he's sizing her up.

'Don't be daft. What is it? You live with someone?'

'I told you who I live with.'

'The intellectual beautician, I know. So what's the problem?'

It seems a small choice: whether to shrug it off or take the trouble to explain. Like flipping a coin. But she takes the trouble, which means it's not such a small choice after all.

'Even if I'm sexually interested in you. And I have no objection to bedding married men. And I haven't got some hang-up about sex being something you do in deep and meaningful lasting relationships, I'm not a constituency groupie. And that's how I feel: this week's parliamentary perk. How come it's all taken for granted? I thought they did away with *droit de seigneur* in the dark ages.'

He starts to protest but she talks over him.

'Let's rerun the tape from my point of view. You don't want to lie to me. Fine. But I can't be natural with you because if I am you'll read it as bruise-pressing or fishing for commitment and switch on to adulterer's automatic pilot. What it boils down to is only one of us can be honest at any one time. If I knew you well enough to be rude to you I might accuse you of trying to manipulate me.'

'Do I get to speak for the defence?'

He doesn't look angry, but she is too well schooled in the old dread not to register the possibility.

'I offered you a lift home in the rain. Where I come from that's not code for screwing the arse off you. Since you raise the subject, I wouldn't say no, but I wasn't planning to jump you on the doorstep.' He runs his thumb through the hollow in her collarbone, displacing a thimbleful of rain. 'And it wasn't me who mentioned commitment.'

There doesn't seem much point prolonging the discussion. She steps out from the shelter of the tree and starts walking towards the museum. Cursing under his breath at the unremitting downpour, he catches up and takes off the suede jacket, trying to drape it round her shoulders. She shrugs it off. He makes another attempt. She quickens her pace on the uneven tarmac, black splashes spitting at her ankles. The pink hide jacket slides down her back, he makes a grab for it but fumbles the catch. It falls to the ground behind her.

Both of them stoop to retrieve it and simultaneously register a presence behind them, the smoker in the shell suit, now sprouting a royal-blue umbrella; she must have been following them along the path, and now she's watching them. Or rather, she's watching Nan.

'I thought it was you but I didnae like to say anything in case I was wrong. You've done your hair different.

Looks nice. It said in the papers you'd left the country. Spain, they said. Mind, I wouldnae trust that lot to get the date right.'

Nan's mind is racing. Her pulse, too. What does the woman want? In a distant part of her brain she recognises that the overture is not malicious, not even sly, but the immediate emotion is a desire to hit out, to cause physical pain. Everyone feels this way sometimes. Don't they?

Danny, grimly holding his muddied jacket, is looking curious.

'They did the whole street. Knocking on doors. Asking if there were any men you were friendly with? I knew their game. Told them to fuck right off. Excuse the French.'

An anonymous face, flabby round the jawline yet with something sharp about the nose and the definition of upper lip, features fitting easily enough into memories of bus queues and women gossiping at the chemist's counter. *What the hell does she want?*

'I only ate at your place the once. My man's as happy with a Wimpy. Used to say we'd have to get a second mortgage to afford a sweet. Don't get me wrong. I'm not saying you were ripping anybody off; if they'll pay it, good luck to you. We had the salmon pâté to start with.'

Nan feels a strong but unfocused foreboding.

'Billy had steak and I had the rabbit with chocolate. You wouldnae have thought it would go but it was brand new. And then you were bringing us the sweet menu and he came out after you with that bucket . . .'

'It was a clean bucket.'

Nan reminds herself that she's not facing the Environmental Health.

'. . . and he chucked that green slime all over you.'

She can still feel the humiliation, so complete it was

77

almost liberating. The knowledge that nothing in the world could salvage the situation. He stood there in his long white apron, sleeves rolled up, waiting for her to respond. Like slapstick. Taking it in turns. Even in anarchy there are rules. She ought to have picked up the nearest sachertorte and ground it methodically into his features. Or borrowed Billy's steak knife. She looks into the woman's face and see eyes that are bright with the suspicion of tears. Nan too feels pity for that girl with the guacamole clotting in her hair – probably very good for split ends – the paralysed floor show in the middle of a packed restaurant. But who is that girl? It doesn't feel like her. Which would she rather be? The one with a home and a life and a career and a husband who threw pureed avocado at her, and that was just the hors d'oeuvres, or the one with no home and no prospects, and no husband? No contest. There are worse fates than having nothing.

The woman in the shell suit comes a step closer, drawing a crumpled white paper bag out of her pocket and offering it beyond the charmed circle of her umbrella.

'D'you fancy a sookie?'

Nan wants to laugh, but it's a sad joke. *What does she want?* She wants to offer you a boiled sweet. Dipping her hand into the bag, the crystallised sugar scratches her fingertips like unfinished metal.

'Take one for your friend.'

Obediently she picks out a second sweet, pebble-weight, brakelight red.

'We used to stay on Chamberlain Road. Billy moved down for his work. I could have stayed up here and just seen him at weekends but he'd've been up to all sorts Monday to Friday. When he got the offer to come back, I jumped at the chance. It's not that they're snobs, but they're no as friendly. Still not sold the house, but. Costing us a fortune.'

Was there a time when Nan, too, used to be like this? Was it the chill winds of the West Midlands that blew away the assumption that walking down the same street makes you part of somebody else's life? Who can say. If she can't claim the girl in the restaurant, what hope has she of remembering what went before?

Danny has had enough. He steps forward and takes her arm just above the elbow, more firmly than it might appear.

'We're going to have to get a move on if we want to be there on time, you know.'

But she lets the lifebelt slip through her fingers. It is the woman who retrieves it, looking understanding, even a little concerned at the prospect of this unspecified missed appointment. Nan wants to ask for her silence, but it's not worth the risk. To speak of trust is to raise the possibility of betrayal. And besides, Danny is steering her forward, keeping up the pressure. He doesn't let go until they reach the car.

'Well?'

She looks at him warily. 'Well what?'

He holds out his hand, palm up.

'Can I have my gobstopper now?'

Outside her flat he leans across to open the door then sits back, waiting for her to get out. She stalls for time, glancing over at his spattered jacket, tossed on the floor in the rear of the car.

'Will it be OK?'

'I daresay the pig survived worse in its time.'

'Thanks for the rescue back there.' Uneasily, she picks at a loose thread in her jumper. 'And thanks for not asking.'

He smiles, lips together, a hieroglyph she can't read, and gives her a brief chaste kiss on the cheek.

'You'll tell me. When you trust me.'

Nan opens her eyes: the luminous dial an afterburn on the blackness of the room. 4.07. The air is full of silence. That's why he didn't ask: he knows.

*D*ear sir, It is over a week since I wrote to you regarding the non-delivery of three pounds of home preserves posted to my daughter in Dalbeattie, and I have yet to receive the courtesy of a reply . . .

It's almost lunchtime when the calls start; the first a man who identifies himself as Andrew Burnett. He says he's a friend of Cal Macleod and sent him the letter as a joke.

'What sort of joke?'

There's a brief pause at the other end of the line.

'A joke. A practical joke.'

'I'm just wondering what was so funny about what you wrote.'

'Look, it's a private joke, all right? A long story.' He sounds English, which may only mean he's a friend of Callum Macleod's.

'It wasn't very practical to write the address in pencil.'

'Well I promise not to be such a silly boy next time.'

His tone says Post Office employees aren't supposed to get chippy with the public.

Her pen taps out a rhythm on the smudged purple ink.

'Thank you very much, Mr Burnett.'

The phone rings as soon as she replaces the receiver. It's Imogen. She's apologetic about the sudden end to their last meeting. What about coming round for supper? Under the polish there's a little scratch of anxiety. She doesn't ask Nan to bring the letter, but then she doesn't have to.

Next it's the slow, dogged bell of the internal line. She loves the heavy Bakelite receiver with its whiff of ancient halitosis. Dod, another relic of the past and, in person, similarly scented, informs her that there's a Dan Regatta to see her. It might not be funny, but it's not as deadpan as his delivery.

Emerging from the grey light of the bunker she climbs the final flight of stairs and finds herself squinting in the combined brilliance of a crisp, cloudless day and Cal Macleod's halogen-white trenchcoat. Teamed with the suntan, it smacks of old-fashioned, airbrushed Hollywood publicity stills, matinee idols and movie moguls. Dod's oven-ready pallor, overlaid with an ordnance survey map of broken capillaries, looks particularly unappetising today. Tucking in her standard-issue shirt, she sends up a short prayer that any resemblance between them ends with the uniform.

'I didn't recognise you with your clothes on.'

'Dan, isn't it?'

'Suits me, no? Think I'll use it for the new life in Rio.'

'You're planning on skipping the country?'

'Not immediately, but the excrement's bound to hit the Xpelair some day, what with the Vatman and all those wronged virgins on my case.'

Dod, who has been looking disapproving ever since the crack about her clothes, now shoots her the rank-pulling stare special to men who have no rank to pull.

'What can I do for you?'

'I've come to borrow your discriminating palate. I thought we could continue our quest for the perfect vinaigrette. I'm looking for a new salad chef. André came over a tad narky when I mentioned the olive oil, so I told him he could go stew in someone else's juice.'

'What do you really want?'

'Lunch.'

Dod's yellowing eyeballs are popping behind his mock-tortoiseshell spectacles.

'What, now?'

'I believe it's customary to lunch at lunchtime.'

The silver sports car is parked on a double yellow line just outside but they set off into the city on foot. She assumes they're heading for a Merchant City bistro with candles in Chianti bottles and bread rolls in warm napkins but he ducks into a pub favoured by the bank and travel agency crowd. In an effort to bestow instant character the saloon is filled with pre-war moquette settees and occasional tables. On the shelves of the stripped-oak dresser there's an artful assortment of second-hand books chosen for the cherry reds, slate blues and playing-field greens of their faded cloth covers. One of the occasional tables supports a black Bakelite telephone almost as old as the one in the bunker, the three-digit number still legible in the centre of the alphabet dial.

She hates it. She may go home each night to Catriona's confected environment, her last impressions before sleep the reek of sandalwood shavings, those knicker-pink blinds and the moonlit Pierrot weeping over her bed, but her aversion to these things remains as strong as ever. It's like her diet, which consists of cheese and coleslaw sandwiches, the occasional scotch egg, and cold quiche, always unnerving to the bite, that rubbery triangle set in waterlogged pastry. She hasn't lost her ability to taste, she knows the stuff she eats is uniformly disgusting, but the great advantage of cellophane-wrapped portions from the chill cabinet is she doesn't have to cook them. Her attitude to Catriona's flat observes a similar warped but defensible logic. Not making her mark on her lodger's cell, refusing to compromise its kitsch, is a disclaimer on the present and a statement of faith in a future she dare not contemplate. Sometimes it feels like all she has left: her taste, the way Nan Megratta doesn't live.

This pub is not so far from it. That's what offends: the reminder that what feels idiosyncratic and personal is common enough to be commercially exploited. She feels parodied, cheapened. Some design consultant on loan to brewery headquarters has taken her attachment to the old and turned it into niche marketing.

She gets to the bar first but he won't hear of her buying the drinks. He has the sort of manners she associates with men of near-pensionable age: the milky-eyed cheese merchant with the panama hat who drove a grey Morris Traveller riddled with woodworm, or the cap-doffing old codger she used to pass every morning, dragging his moth-eaten Jack Russell around the block. During the short walk from Post Office to bar Callum kept gliding round the back of her, from her left side to her right, vanishing and reappearing like some pantomime spook. It was a while before she worked out that the purpose of all this weaving was to keep on her kerb side in case some deranged motorist ploughed on to the pavement. Reaching their destination, he stood back to allow her down the narrow staircase, then sidled ahead to open the door, an absurdly complicated manoeuvre in such a confined space. At first she suspected satire, but it seems to be one of the few things he does quite unselfcon-sciously. She receives these courtesies with as much irony as she can muster, while not being quite rude enough to laugh. However neutral the ritual may once have been, time and novelty have turned it into a form of innuendo, conjuring sex as unignorably as if he'd enquired the colour of her underwear. She doesn't need to remind herself that there is a flip side to this Moss Bros gallantry, behaviour with as little justification and very different consequences. Enjoy now, pay later.

While he's at the bar she stakes her claim on a two-seater chesterfield and sits, dead centre, leaving him a green leatherette captain's chair. He returns with the drinks and eases himself into the inadequate gap on the sofa beside her.

'Modom doesn't like my choice of establishment?'

'It's not what I would have predicted.'

'I'm full of surprises.'

'I'll bet the menu isn't.'

His gaze takes in two laminated cards, face down on the next table, as yet unread. Glancing briefly towards the door, he leans across and snatches them, holding them to his chest like a poker player's hand.

'Come on then.'

It's not a difficult trick to pull.

'Prawn cocktail, melon with a maraschino cherry, pâté, garlic mushrooms, lasagne, minute steak, chilli con carne, chef's salad, a vegetarian option – probably baked potato and cheese but it may be spinach-and-something crêpe – Black Forest gâteau, strawberry cheesecake, sticky toffee pudding,' she pauses, face screwed up in thought, 'ice-cream and Rombouts coffee.'

He has a set of teeth of American perfection.

'You were wrong about the cheesecake: it's blueberry. And what happened to the minestrone soup?'

After all her scorn, the soup is homemade and served with fresh wholemeal bread. His eyes straying repeatedly toward the street entrance, Cal talks about his new tapas bar, the cabaret he's booked for the launch party, his half-formed plan to open a nightclub. Every subject provides a pretext for send-up, although the ridicule never strays too close to home. He talks though a permanent grin, almost a leer, but a leer in which any sexual charge is secondary to the thrill of display. She is reminded of adolescent boys experimenting with the idea of their own dangerousness. Theoretically, the corollary is vulnerability, but she can't get beyond the theory. Her normal reactions have been disconnected and she's fifteen again, toughing it out with the cocky boys on the bus; puffing at her menthol cigarette, gabardine skirt sausage-rolled at the waist to make it a mini. Never for a moment wanting to win the verbal jousting, just desperate not to lose. And at the same time, beyond the tightness in her ribcage, there's something liberating about his egotism: a dispensation to selfishness, absolution from the customary constraints of considering another's feelings. Part of her thinks: I can be dangerous too.

'How come you're such a gourmet?'

'I used to be in the same line of business as you.'

'Bankrobbing, extortion or pimping?'

'Restaurants.'

'Oh that. Hasn't made me an expert. All the same in the stomach, that's my motto.'

'As long as you can keep it down.'

Deliberately she turns to look in the direction of the door. He's there first, head moving so fast she can almost see the displaced air. Nothing. He laughs, caught out, but right on cue the door opens.

The figure that enters is lost in the no man's land sometimes crossed by goodlooking men between twenty and sixty. If pushed she'd plump for early forties, but she wouldn't argue with twenty-five. At some point in the future he'll turn eighty overnight, but in the meantime he seems not so much youthful as unmarked by time. He's dressed in a faded and rumpled denim shirt and a darker shade of jeans. Poly lecturer cred. No genuine member of the masses would wear anything so tatty. His hair is that shade of blond which is no colour at all and needs cutting, petering out into sparse curls over his forehead and ears. Unironed, unshaven, quite possibly unwashed. Not to her taste, but she can see it's a popular line.

The barman bends over the table to clear the empty glasses. An undergrown youth in a white polyester shirt so thin it is possible to trace the aureoles of his nipples and a few tentative chest hairs through the fabric. They watch him relay the message. There is a delay before the newcomer turns round, scans the lunchtime crowd, settles on them, and turns back to the gantry. Nan tries to catch Cal's eye but he's oblivious, intent on his quarry. The man takes a long swallow of beer, picks up his battered leather music case, and ambles over to their table. There's plenty of time to study him as he makes the journey. His expression is so neutral it's offensive. Up against this sort of sang froid, even Cal's public-school urbanity starts to look a little ragged.

'May I present Jack the Lad, mastermind of the Merchant City, nemesis of wee extensions, woks on the wall and the Black and Decker workmate classes. Councillor Ibster, this is Nan Megratta. Don't be fooled by the postie's togs, she's a secret agent for the Michelin Guide.'

Ibster acknowledges her with the faintest flicker of the eyes, unless it's an optical illusion caused by the excessive immobility of his features. Then he addresses Cal.

'Bit downmarket for you here, isn't it?'

Cal laughs. 'What is this? The lady doesn't like the scoff, you don't like the lowlife. I just fancied finding out how the other half live. Not that I'd put you in that category, *councillor*.'

The way he says the title is loaded with something. Whatever it is, Ibster doesn't react. The conversation continues, its meaning tucked just under the surface of the exchanges. Cal's smalltalk is banal but knowing, archly cryptic. Ibster is simply uncommunicative. Once she realises she isn't going to catch the subtext, her attention wanders. All she can glean is that Cal is trying to needle the other man without positively provoking him. She wonders if she plays any part in this project. Ibster isn't about to show whether he's needled or not, but it occurs to her that some inverse principle may be operating, and the more impassive his face becomes the more irritated he actually is. There's no way of knowing. He just stands there, providing a deadpan counterpoint to Cal's smirking monologue.

'I've got the best cook in Glasgow, and that's only the accountant.'

He turns to Nan. 'How's your paella? Fancy cooking in a hot *cantina* in up-and-coming Finnieston? We'd have to dye the rug of course. Not too many redhead señoritas around. Get you dressed up, ruffles a go-go. Couple of flamenco classes and *Olé!* Whole new career.'

The fantasy is beguiling. Bits of herself she'd forgotten rise to the surface again, gratified vanity, confident charms. She realises how desperate she is at the Post Office, tastes the relief waiting on the day she leaves. If she ever leaves. And right at the core of her, from somewhere she doesn't go these days, a voice says *life*. Life, unpredictable, dangerous, happens to her too.

Cal is grinning. Only playing. But it's a serious game. Within it she can be bought and sold, customised, Celt to Latin, for the price of a hair tint and a rope-handled carrier bag from Princes Square. Her smile fades, remembering the price of all that life. The reply that occurs to her comes out as B-movie flirting but has the partial justification of truth.

'You couldn't afford me.'

Ibster is watching the exchange with a complete lack of

interest which may denote utter fascination. His stillness reminds her of botanical documentaries, the patient camera recording for days on end, trained on a single stem, and the footage finally speeded up to reveal nature, predatory, carnivorous, the same old story. He drains his glass and Cal proposes a refill, rising from his seat despite the refusal. On his feet, he has a good three inches on Ibster, but the councillor won't concede the advantage. He raises his left arm and plants a hand on Cal's solar plexus, fingers splaying slightly against the cushion of flesh. It's the shock of being touched rather than the physical impact which stops Cal's progress. For a moment Nan thinks she's broken the code between them. But the link isn't sexual.

Cal looks down at the rapidly vanishing indentations in his crisp white shirt and shrugs. 'Your loss. I just thought you might be interested to meet Miz Megratta here. She's a Post Office detective. Keeping Her Majesty's mail safe for the likes of you and me.'

He has recovered that air of private mirth, his exclusive purchase on the punchline, and she realises, as she fails to correct his description of her, that she's relieved. Dislike of Ibster has created a tenuous bond of loyalty between them.

'I'm helping with her enquiries into a case of blackmail.'

For a split second something happens on the pale face. Perhaps he blinks.

'As victim or suspect?'

Cal doesn't smile. 'It's obviously a kid-on.'

Without avoiding his look, Ibster's gaze manages to stop just short of Cal's face.

'No need to worry then.'

To her surprise he vouchsafes her a fractional nod as

he turns towards the door. He doesn't bother bidding Cal goodbye.

The barman arrives with the rest of their food. Nan waits until he's laid down the limp salad – they're still garnishing with pineapple rings – and the lasagne, its ovenproof dish radiating heat like a blast furnace.

'So you think it's him?'

Cal turns overwide eyes on her. 'Did I say that?'

'I can't think of another good reason you'd drag me down here.' Her glance takes in the coffinwood reproduction grandmother clock ticking behind his head. 'Neither of us is dressed for drawing-room comedy.'

'I would have said country-house murder.'

'So we're here because you think the butler did it?'

He picks up his cutlery, fork in the left hand, knife in the right. She registers the implicit rebuke of her one-handed shovelling, but it's too late to change now. He cuts into the lasagne's bubbling crust, releasing a geyser of steam, then reaches for the condiments.

'You sure you don't want to come and cook dago muck for me? Give the neds a fix of España between Club 18–30 holidays?'

The sprinkled pepper, momentarily buoyed up by the dish's thermals, settles like volcanic ash. Taking up knife and fork again, he starts to eat. She sits, refusing to be the first to acknowledge the party trick, waiting for the sly upward glance, the puckered grin, but for once he's not looking for applause.

'What are you doing?'

'Eating lunch. Why, what am I supposed to be doing?'

So it's not a party trick.

'Are you right or left handed?'

He looks down, as if the question can only be answered

empirically. The knife is poised in his left hand, fork in his right.

'Oh that. It depends. I'm ambi.'

He switches the cutlery back in demonstration. 'Twice as handy.'

Embarrassed by the innuendo, she returns her attention to her plate. 'Well, I'm making some progress anyway. Whoever did send the letter, it's obviously not your pal Mr Burnett.'

Cal grins. 'He said you were a tad suspicious.'

'Why are you so anxious to get your hands on it?'

'Add to my stamp collection.'

She lifts an onion ring, exposing the plastic pillow of salad cream hidden underneath.

'I can do you a photocopy.'

He shakes his head. 'Only the real thing.'

'Why?'

'I'm allergic to reproductions.'

The conversation has lost its playfulness. His delivery is still laced with camp, but the joke is wearing thin and she isn't sure what lies underneath. Her father once told her that male and female of the same species never fought. Biology was stronger than the drive for food or territory. If she was aware of the anomaly to hand, in their own household, she doesn't remember now. Doubt set in one autumn, churning ankle-deep through the rust-crumbling leaves on her way home from school, when she came upon a snarling whirlpool of collie and black retriever-cross. In those quiet backstreets dogs roamed, collared but unleashed, throughout the day, turning up on the doorstep in time for the vile-smelling tin of treacle-dark jelly and the six o'clock news. She recognised both animals and knew the collie to be a dog, the mongrel a bitch recently pupped. The collie's matted candyfloss coat was streaked with vivid pink, a different colour from cut fingers and skinned knees, but in the frenzy she couldn't be sure which animal was actually wounded. Terrified, fascinated, she watched them, entered into the complex rhythm of their aggression, felt the energy ebb as if by agreement, only to surge up, renewed. Teeth bared, a marbled pigment was revealed inside the squashy curtain of flesh protecting the mongrel's gums. Sugar pink and black. Fear flared in the whites of its eyes. It was some years before she made the anthropomorphic connection, perhaps not really until she married Kilner.

'How's the lasagne?' She recognises the propitiary urge in herself, she might as well be cringing at his feet, belly up. Is this why dog and bitch don't fight? Because the female always gives in?

'Too hot to handle. We've got the basics of nuclear fission in here.'

'It wouldn't taste of much, cold.'

'Pasta comes from the wrong part of Italy?'

'Welwyn Garden City more like.' She reaches across the table and cuts into the glutinous layers, bringing the steaming forkful carefully up to her nose. 'Pasta is pasta, it doesn't much matter where it comes from. It's the other ingredients that count.'

'Not the olive oil again?'

'Tinned tomatoes. No garlic. Seasoned with a clapped-out bouquet garni.'

'How come you quit the restaurant business?'

She realises she has misjudged him. The only reason she's allowed herself to give so much away is that she never expected him to be interested.

'I liked the restaurant; wasn't so keen on the business bit.'

'You gotta have the killer instinct.'

At first it's just a smile, twitching at the corners of her mouth. She struggles with it for a while, which only

93

makes it bubble up with redoubled force. Briefly, a soft, high whinnying escapes her. Head bowed, she's almost weeping with the effort of control. Then she's crossed another threshold and she knows there are tears, real crying, waiting their cue.

She forces her head up. He's watching her levelly.

'Care to share the joke?'

'What was it we used to call him?'

Imogen pauses, one hand frozen over the cutlery drawer. Behind her, Nan is setting the kitchen table.

'That's it: Zapata. He had a classic, grown with a set square. It was supposed to be sexy: the 'tash and an Afghan coat. They didn't half pong when you went out in the rain. Not that he'd have been seen dead in the coat. Too much of a politician even then.'

The columnist is off her pedestal tonight, not playing to the feminist gallery. Nan still has the sensation that they're secretly being monitored for a fly-on-the-wall documentary, but she's beginning to suspect the self-consciousness is all her own.

'So you were contemporaries?'

'I was a year ahead but he was a good bit older. Took WEA classes while he was working in the shipyards and then came as a mature student. I couldn't stand him.'

She opens the drawer and hands Nan a couple of forks.

'MacHismo at its worst. A woman's place is on her back. Thought we were counter-revolutionary: middle-class ladies-in-waiting diverting the radical energies of the proletariat. Couldn't accept I was working class: I was English, you see. He hit me once.' She strokes her jaw as if the bruise is still tender. 'There was a sit-in. We wanted a women's representative on the GUU. They were trying to hold a ballot on Vietnam but we'd taken the fusebox out. We were into the heavy-handed symbolism: women's dark energies. I had a loudhailer and was doing my Pasionaria.' She pauses briefly but Nan cannot read the intricately-patterned sweater bent over the chopping board. 'He decided to shut me up; tried to get the megaphone off me, and when I wouldn't let go, socked me one. Tried to claim the moral high ground too. "You want equality, sister, this is equality Govan-style".'

Nan would have been three at the time.

'I can't imagine Danny MacLeod hitting any woman. It's hardly the image he puts over.'

'You don't think? If you ask me it's exactly what comes across. No swearing in front of the ladies, but do something he doesn't like and he'll put you in traction. He's cleaned up his act since, of course. Saw him on *Question Time* speaking up for a woman's right to choose last year. Suppose we ought to be grateful, but it just makes me wonder if I'm still on the right side.

'He was into revenge fucking as I remember. I don't mean the standard working-class hero Lady Chatterley's lover stuff. All those white-collar kids reinventing themselves and bedding the girlies too wet behind the ears to tell Stork from butter. Danny MacLeod was in another league. Chose smart, articulate women and humiliated them. Going out with the gang, ignoring the lucky girl until last orders, then dragging her back to his cave. That sort of carry on. They thought it was cultural, this was how the working classes behaved, so they couldn't really complain without being guilty of suburban imperialism. Drove me crazy.'

Nan doesn't want to hear this. She is managing not to connect the subject of these stories with the man she met in the museum the day before, but it's not easy. She does it by concentrating on peripherals, conjuring the pantomime fashions: women in PVC thighboots and see-through blouses, men in rainbow satin Sergeant Pepper suits. It disturbs her, the possibility of Danny MacLeod living in this joke age, but ultimately it's unimaginable.

'A good friend of mine, Katy, had a thing with him for a while. She was an embassy child: curtseying before she could walk, knew how to address minor branches of European royalty but never prised a hand off her bra strap until she got to the uni. She used to say he liked hurting her. Too coy to say what. As far as I could gather it was nothing fetishistic. I tried to persuade her to chuck him until I realised what a kick it gave her. She liked the idea of a taboo. We were all so busy being permissive, refusing to be shocked by anything, lying through our teeth about how we weren't hung up on jealousy. Experimenting. About as much fun as vivisection.'

She turns, running a quick check of Nan's features under cover of reaching for the garlic press.

'Looking at it now, I think it was just that she didn't want to play our game and that was how far she had to go to find something that broke the rules. Maybe she just wanted to reclaim sex as a subjective experience. And give him something the others didn't: her USP. That doesn't excuse what he was doing, incidentally. I used to have a go at her: letting herself down, reinforcing the myth of female masochism, you know the line. She enjoyed that too: made her feel closer to him. She was drugged with it. The rest of her life was just foreplay.'

Nan's internal blindfold has slipped. She picks up the sharp whiff of other people's sex, sees Danny on all fours, furred buttocks moving slowly, exactly, over a smoother, whiter pair. Despite herself, juices stir. He liked hurting: she tries to ignore the thought, but it's just persistent enough to snag her arousal without freeing her from desire.

She shrugs. 'Who knows what other people's relationships are really like?'

'Well, three hundred letters a month give me a few pointers.'

There's a hint of asperity in Imogen's voice. She unwraps a parcel of newspaper and takes the fish to the sink. It flexes in her hands, the supple, glistening body belied by a single lifeless eye.

'What I was too young to know then is that there's a time to stop understanding and just draw the line. I always did it with men; forgave women anything in the name of the underdog. It wears out as an excuse. These forty-five-year-old blondes still playing hunt the slipper when their men get home from work; the ones who pretend they don't know how much he pisses away in the pub; the punchbags; the split-crotch pantie wearers . . . I've had it with them.'

Nan is familiar with these arguments, they used to be part of her own personal torture kit, the penitent's scourge. In the end she realised you have to be careful. Overdo it, and the self-disgust becomes so pervasive that nothing much matters any more.

'What if they've no choice?'

Imogen is slicing the fish, working down from the head with clean, effortless strokes. It must be a very sharp knife.

'When you really get down to it, there aren't too many of those.'

'How would you know?'

Imogen puts down the knife.

'More to the point, how would you?'

Nan laughs. Not that it's funny.

'I think it's called the school of hard knocks.'

Imogen nods, unsurprised.

'How long were you married?'

'Eight years.'

'What . . . went wrong?'

She can tell Imogen is groping for the diagnostic phrase, a formula vague enough to cover any eventuality, yet sufficiently definite to suggest there's no point holding back: she knows everything. The art of the professional confidante.

What went wrong? She has a memory of walking along a backstreet in what had once been Birmingham's manufacturing quarter, a mammon-forsaken cityscape of Victorian workshops, chunks of sooty brick rich as Dundee cake, and prefabricated industrial units in synthetic mustards and dull turquoises, Teutonic pigments compromising between ornament and duty. That day the malign influences only brushed against her mood. She was teasing him, pirouetting around him. She can't remember the theme. He mimed offence, but his pleasure reeled her in towards him, laughing. There was a pub around the corner, a poky room which always had the same half-dozen old men guarding the same flat pints, chests rattling with emphysema, the sort of men who never lose their hair, however thin it becomes, however grey, forelocks yellowed from the upward wisp of smoke. And she remembers, some time later, sitting wordlessly across from him, two fresh pints of Mild on the beaten copper table, him reading the beermat and her thinking: will I still be sitting here when his hair is grey and thinning, the dead air between us full of all the things I'm not allowed to say? What separated these two memories? Even if she knew the dates, that wouldn't be an answer.

Imogen is watching her expectantly. All that understanding there for the asking. Sympathy just waiting to be poured. Nan backs towards the door.

As the last target on the home improver's list, she's always loved bathrooms. Imogen's is a beauty, with a claw-footed iron tub and chunky, art deco handbasin, although the lavatory has, disappointingly, lost its overhead cistern and skull-splitting porcelain-handled chain.

There's a pleasing disorder about the room, the huddled towels on the freestanding wooden rail, hairline cracks in the paintwork on the tongue-and-groove panelled walls, a jumble of blue and white tiles above the basin, Woolworth's Delft and, possibly, one or two of the real thing. None of this quite prepares her for the toilet rolls: a ziggurat of shades and textures, splintery recycled pinks, luxurious padded peach, marzipan yellow, baby blues and milky greens, ivory and cream and apricot, even a couple patterned with clover sprigs, which doesn't strike her as Imogen's style at all.

In the corridor outside, the wall is lined with bookshelves floor to ceiling; mostly well-thumbed paperbacks, but a single virgin spine catches her eye. Crammed between a feminist detective thriller and an old clothback edition of the collected Charlotte Brontë is a dayglo-pink volume. *Suburban Guerrillas* by Imogen Reiss. The blurb on the front cover makes the routine promise that this book will change your life. On the back the *Sunday Times* and *Guardian* testify to the author's blazing intelligence and forensic insight into contemporary society. She checks inside: 1971. Scanning the shelves above and below she pulls out another two volumes bearing Imogen's name: a dictionary of women's health and, she is surprised to discover, a slim paperback of verse. *The I of the Beholder*.

On the back of each book the familiar face stares out from a different disguise. She has an actress's knack of projecting her gaze outwith the photograph. The first is laughing, sexy, cut off at the collarbone without a trace of clothing, suggesting she might even be naked under the shiny dustjacket. It is one of those faces that never need a memory-jogging caption, emblematic of her time: free spirit of the Sixties, strident, extreme but, at least in retrospect, containably dangerous; a centrefold with a clenched fist salute.

She remodelled herself for the late Seventies in a dramatic black polo-neck, her hair cropped and bubble permed, unsmiling: the right-on revolutionary reborn as sexual Cassandra. On the cover of the most recent book, full of line drawings of women examining their breasts and doing pelvic floor exercises, the hair grows straight once again in an early version of her present club cut. It's the photograph she uses at the top of her column. The post-feminist pin-up, a face still youthful enough for the casual glance to take in eyes and lips without the distraction of veiled lids and sagging jawline. These days the image is smudged and grainy. It's been ten years since the last book; her current medium is recycled newsprint and local radio phone-ins. Chip wrappers and aural wallpaper.

Does she mind no longer belonging to that class of celebrity where idle jottings are immortalised as poetry? How can she cope with the knowledge that not one but three rival Imogen Reisses still exist, glossy, perfect bound: lurking on trestle tables at jumble sales, biding their time in archive footage to be hauled out whenever the BBC needs a Proustian tang of the summer of love?

Nan weighs the three books in one hand for a moment. Briefly she allows herself a thought bundled back into the darkness more than once over the past few days. It links a reconstituted memory of herself as a child, of how it was to see the world through a child's eyes, when Imogen's notoriety was at its peak, with the gleeful, chagrined knowledge that they now meet on level ground.

The simmering garlic hits her in the kitchen doorway bringing a rush of the old excitement, the six o'clock hit, anticipated overspill of the seductions and flirtations and simple good times to be played out at her tables. Kilner never understood her pander's pleasure, just as he was enraged by the ever-changing menu and her refusal to streamline the operation with a freezer and a battery of microwaves.

'*For Christ's sake, why not?*'

'*It wouldn't taste the same.*'

'*They wouldn't care if it was spaghetti hoops and pot noodle if the prices were high enough.*'

'*But I'd know, and I'd care.*'

Imogen is pouring red wine into two oversized glass goblets. 'Do you know Danny MacLeod well?'

'No. Met him a couple of times.'

On reflection, this is not as much of a deception as it felt when she said it.

'I wondered if I'd put my foot in it.' Imogen dabs a splash of wine off the table, sifting her words.

'I haven't run across him for years but you hear the stories. Newspaper offices tend to be better at gossip than they are at news.'

Nan's reply arrives a breath too late.

'I don't follow.'

'He's a bit of a chancer. Professional heartbreaker. Either that or he picks the sort who'll kid themselves on it's wedding bells. I even got a letter from one of them. Don't know if he still has the same bedside manners but she was one bitter lady. His wife's a real glamourpuss, bit too much of the stiletto heels and leather trousers for my taste but a very attractive woman. He's always got a younger model in tow. Classic male menopause. I see him on the box every once in a while and he's losing it, his looks are on the turn, you know the way with some men everything starts to shrink? They say his son's a goodlooking lad, just going up to university. Must be hard: being overtaken by the young pretender.

'A few years ago I was asked to go on a TV show. They name-dropped one of the good guys, Canadian psychologist, so I thought at least I'd be trivialised in respectable company. He'd just finished a survey of the sexual habits of MPs in Ottawa. Even making allowances for boasting, they had a bloody funny idea of the sort of behaviour you'd want to boast about. All men of course; not enough women to get a statistical sample. He came to the conclusion that national politicians have a higher libido than the rest of us. I think that's a pretty dodgy interpretation, myself, but they certainly seem to deviate from the mean.'

The telephone makes them both jump. When Imogen picks up the receiver, a woman's tones, high-pitched, agitated, filter across the silence to Nan. Another case for auntie. Imogen listens for some time, massaging the socket of her left eye absently.

'All right, Maggie, hold on, I'll be right over. Make yourself some strong coffee and send the kids next door . . .' The voice resumes but she cuts it off. 'I'll be there. Just sit tight.'

When she puts the phone down she looks older. Under her eyes are pouches of slack skin Nan didn't notice before. She turns off the gas under the skillet and leaves the room; when she returns she's pulling an anorak over the toddler's pyjamas.

Peter's car is a box-nosed Fiat, a film of Glasgow silt just taking the gleam off the black bodywork. Imogen directs her round the one-way system with an efficiency surprising in a non-driver, although not so surprising in Imogen. She seems preoccupied. Hands in her lap worry a recalcitrant cuticle. They drive along Dumbarton Road in silence, over Partick Bridge, between the red sandstone citadels of Kelvin Hall and Kelvingrove Museum, their posters promoting a bantamweight title fight and a Sickert exhibition, philistinism and art facing each other in the Glasgow stand-off. Hunger stirs in Nan's guts but the inconvenience of the expedition is more than compensated by the gratifying discovery that she can do something her passenger cannot.

As they approach Charing Cross, Imogen starts talking.

'She drinks too much, Maggie, but she always has. Who doesn't in this city? Amazing how few letters I get from lushes. Not really classed as a problem, of course. We've been friends for over thirty years now, I'll be seventy-two when Peter and I have that much on the clock. We met at school. Everyone called her Shrimp, as in Jean Shrimpton. There wasn't really any resemblance. Hair's the wrong colour. Just a nickname. Mine was Rice Pud. All that time standing in front of the bathroom mirror with the spot lotion and the eyelash curlers, wishing I could look like her. Now she could be ten years older. Don't know if I'm pleased about it, or just scared I might be. Not that it really matters how she looks. She has terrible mood swings though, forgets she's said things, or doesn't care if she says them again, and she can be a bitch to the kids. Only when she's drunk. Which is all the time.'

'Is she still married?'

Imogen's eyebrows rise and fall in a private gymnastics of derision.

'For what it's worth. Sometimes I look at her and see the sort of crazy you pass picking over the bins at Central Station. No, that's not fair. Next minute she'll be just like she always was; there's still no one can make me laugh like her.'

Her eyes crinkle, showing the years, not the crow's

feet but the Cleopatra eyeliner favoured by women of a certain age. Nan's now old enough to have her own generational giveaway, but it's like dust on your own windowsills: invisible.

'You know what it's like at fourteen: you know nothing but you're convinced the rest of the world is beyond redemption. Every Sunday afternoon, up in her bedroom with the record player on repeat, doing the personality quizzes in the women's magazines, sniggering at the problem page. Taking it all in, of course. All those exercises for trim ankles and longer legs. Hadn't a clue what cellulite was but keeping it at bay got us safely through adolescence. And then I built a career out of discrediting it all.'

Half-way up the tenement stair they hear whistling and quick, light footsteps descending towards them. Head down, watching his footing on the uneven stone, he makes way for them, drifting over to the inside of the stair without bothering to look up. Nan recognises him immediately. The blond tracing of stubble seems a little more established in this utilitarian light, the denims a little more crumpled, otherwise he looks exactly the same. Without changing pace, he draws level with Imogen and seems to murmur something, but as there's no reaction she assumes she's mistaken.

Maggie is not as drunk as Nan was expecting. Otherwise she lives up to the billing: a ravaged beauty with black hair straggling out of an Edwardian chignon and skin so translucently pale it shades into purple under the hyperthyroid eyes and between the blanched folds of her throat. She is paper thin, two dimensional as a playing card, the queen of clubs.

'You shouldn't have come, Imma. I was being silly.'

She laughs skittishly, the cusp of her jaw blueish under the stretched skin.

'Jack's back now. He was at Labour group. I wish he'd remember to tell me. I made fish pie, his favourite. Shame I threw it away.' That laugh again. 'Still he's back now. I shouldn't have dragged you up here.'

'I just passed him on the stair. Going out.'

It is not said brutally, but nor is it as tactful as might be expected from a mother confessor to the tabloid-reading classes.

Abruptly, Maggie slips past them and out through the open front door; Imogen grimaces, hands the child to Nan and follows. Clattering footsteps echo up the stairwell. Then, from a long way down, voices, one raised, the other calm and indistinct. The louder Maggie shouts, the lower Imogen's even murmur becomes, but her words are easy enough to guess from the other half of the conversation. Maggie doesn't want to calm down. What gives Imogen the right? Just because she can play god to a load of nyaffs too daft to go on the pill, she needn't think she can come it with her . . .

Nan waits in the hall, trying to keep Saul amused. Her sympathies are all with Imogen, not out of any particular loyalty but because she knows incontrovertibly that in any altercation involving Maggie she would always back the opposition. The decoration of the flat strikes a note of faded grandeur reminiscent of the householder's own. The chaise longue has a right-angle tear in its port wine upholstery and the Turkish carpet has fossilised in ridges. Several windowed envelopes lie unopened on the pine blanket chest under a furry coverlet of dust. She realises the shouting has stopped. All she can hear are Imogen's soothing professional tones. Slowly the volume climbs back towards the flat and the two women, arms linked, appear at the door. For the first time Maggie acknowledges Nan's presence.

'Did you find the gin?'

'Did you lose it?'

Maggie isn't sure how to react. Imogen moves towards Nan, keeping hold of her friend's hostage arm.

'Maggie, this is my pal Nan: a lifesaver. Drives like Damon Hill but what she doesn't know about cooking isn't worth knowing.'

A chariness about the eyes fleetingly acknowledges the inadequacies of this statement but Imogen toughs it out. Maggie smiles as if her tissue-paper face might tear.

'Maybe she can teach you to make something that doesn't involve pasta.'

She turns to Nan, allowing her gaze to linger on the regulation windproof jacket, currently amplifying her breathing with its nylon whispers. 'There's only so many Mozzarella Surprises a girl can take. Nice to meet you, Imogen's pal. Join the club. So many friends, so little time to see them all. She's a terror for taking work home with her. But I'm sure I don't have to tell *you*. I keep expecting her to run out of sob stories, but she always manages to pull a new one out of the hat. What would you do without our problems, Imma?'

Nan recognises the deal. Rough them up a little, then offer a truce. Temporary alliance at a price: in this case, rejection of Imogen. She's met the type before. They never win but then, they don't want to. Their percentage is the casualties.

Nan waits until the street door has closed behind them and they're out on the pavement before risking a glance at Imogen. Two perfectly circular spots of colour on her cheekbones bring out a passing resemblance to Mary Poppins.

'I'm really all she's got.'

It's not so much the sentiments that are surprising as the uncharacteristic diffidence of their expression, the same tone she used on the telephone when she was asking about the letter.

'Underneath it all she loves me, you know.'

'It's not enough.'

Imogen cocks her head, as if trying to restore some internal balance. 'She has more urgent reasons to change than to pass my personality medical and she hasn't done it yet. The one she's really hurting is herself.'

There is a brief pause before she continues. 'You didn't take to her?'

'I'm not sure who she reminds me of, but it's not a nice memory.'

Imogen is strapping the child into his moulded plastic seat in the back of the Fiat.

'It's low self-esteem, nothing else. In a warped way she carries on like that because she cares. We always used to feel like mirror images, it's not easy adjusting, for either of us, so she tries to cut me down to size.'

The child's harness finally clicks into place. 'She's got her problems, Nan.'

'And she seems to hold you responsible.'

Imogen backs out of the car, glancing up at the blank, curtained windows of Maggie's flat before getting into the front passenger seat. Only when Nan is in front of the wheel and the driver's door closed does her sigh indicate that the conversation is still live. She seems to have abandoned the case for the defence.

'I never realised there were so many things to be blamed for. Everything goes down on the balance sheet. She didn't used to be like this. Maybe it's just that my credit used to be better.'

Nan starts the engine but has difficulty putting the car

in gear, the cogs scream a protest. She has realised why she doesn't like Maggie.

'Isn't it enough?'

Nan doesn't answer. A calligraphic insect is dancing on the inside of the windscreen, now dotted with the first spots of rain. Closer inspection reveals an unseasonal mosquito.

'You said being loved wasn't enough.'

'Oh.' Nan pulls the car away from the kerb. 'People do all sorts of things in the name of love. Didn't the IRA love their country? The Intercity Firm love Rangers. The Wee Frees love God. Child-abusers love their children. Dog-fighters love their pit bulls. Rapists love their victims. Husbands love their wives.'

'What sort of trouble are you in?'

Nan opens her mouth, surprised, and then shuts it again. Imogen leans forward, her hair filling the rear-view mirror.

'Nan, how am I supposed to help if you won't open up?'

'I wasn't aware you'd taken me on as a case.'

'Don't *you* start that carry on. If I can do anything for you, I will. If you're not interested, I won't waste my time.'

Nan's stomach shrinks. The fear of displeasing her is too strong not to do so. They pass a school all lit up, women with portfolios and sketchpads filing through the door. So many friends.

'I notice the Freedom of Information act doesn't extend to telling me you've been having it off with Jack Ibster.'

What happens next happens very fast. Imogen sees the mosquito above Nan's head and as she slaps her hand against the headlining of the car Nan flinches, a movement so sharp that the Fiat swerves onto the opposite side of the road. An oncoming transit van, blaring its horn, brakes too suddenly and goes into a skid on the wet tarmac. Nan feels time attenuating, seconds stretching like chewing gum. It is this feeling, not the reality of road and rain and hurtling masses of metal, which frightens her. She knows it. It means death.

The transit recovers from its skid and veers past them with an outraged blast of the horn. Nan gets the Fiat onto the correct side of the white line. The toddler in his safety seat starts to wail. She looks for somewhere to pull over but the kerb is lined with cars, bumper-to-bumper. Imogen, seatbelt off, is leaning over into the back, comforting the child.

Back at the flat the two goblets of red wine are on the table as they left them, but neither can remember whose was whose. Imogen takes one and drinks deep before breaking the silence.

'So, he used to hit you?'

'Funny thing is, we never got on.'

Imogen pokes at the scarred tissue of wine and onion stock a couple of times then, losing heart, pours the cold congealing slops down the sink.

'I told her not to marry him. Never liked him much. Couldn't keep my hands off him, though. Makes you believe in pheromones. One good thing – it was so unlikely, nobody ever guessed.'

She is as near to embarrassment as Nan has seen her, which is still a long way from blushing, the shame balanced by pride in her ability to stare transgression in the eye. Nan finds the attitude a little queasy. The taboo that dared to speak its name was novel enough in the Sixties, but these days the taramasalata classes have caught up. Nothing shocks any more. In cynical times self-conscious candour is merely embarrassing, something to be left out for Oxfam with the ethnic shawl and the Chinese paper lampshades. Strip away the trimmings, you're still left with those old chestnuts right and wrong.

'What was the giveaway? When did you realise?'

Re-*alise*. Imogen has two voices: the clear, slightly flat English accent, streetwise, a London pavement pitted with Mancunian grit; and her more muffled delivery, to which odd scraps of Scots stick like burrs on a jumper.

'Just a guess. Lateral thinking.' Nan considers. 'Maybe what you said about book-keeping. People don't generally feel guilt unless they're guilty. Of something.'

Imogen reverts to streetwise; voice deepening so markedly that Nan can see the vibration at the base of her throat.

'I didn't say I felt guilty.'

Self-conscious candour obviously has its limits.

Imogen picks up a long, taper-bladed knife and cuts in to a dun-coloured loaf about the size and consistency of a half brick. The bread cleaves like butter, the first two slices curving away in slow motion with the grace of felled trees.

'No one knew apart from Jack and myself.'

'And the letter writer.'

The cassette is secreted at the back of a drawer full of wedding present linen: embroidered tablecloths and white damask napkins with a silvery sheen in the warp and weft. Imogen substitutes the tape for the one in the machine under the telephone. There is the tantalising twitter of the rewind function, then the microchip bird-song between messages, that split-second pause while the caller considers hanging up, and a voice.

'Hi Imogen, it's Cameron. Any chance of you writing a couple of pieces for us? Everything you need to know about cervical cancer and the plain woman's guide to yeast infections. We could do with a laugh. Give us a call.'

Nan smirks reflexively, not knowing what else to do and not yet easy enough in the other woman's company to do nothing. Imogen's face is blank. The electronic tone sounds again.

'You've been neglecting your mail, Miss Reiss. Mrs MacLeod. That's not polite. I know you're a busy lady, but don't get too busy, or we'll all be sorry.'

Nan listens, fear rendered almost pleasurable by the knowledge that these tones of intimate menace are not for her. The English north country accent sounds put on, but since her only exposure to the real thing is working-men's club comedians on television, stiff-necked in dickie bow and lilac ruffled shirt, the whole region is tainted with fakery for her. Maybe that's the way they really speak. Imogen is standing very still, her fingers clenched around the bread knife's stained wooden handle. The tape relays a final high-pitched bleep.

Nan considers and rejects half a dozen remarks. Eventually she opts for levity.

'Is that accent for real?'

The spell is broken. Imogen resumes her bread slicing.

'Your guess is as good as mine. He might be trying to disguise his voice.'

'Because you know him?'

'Could be. I know a lot of people.'

'What I don't understand . . .' Nan pauses, suddenly understanding. 'You've had another letter?'

She is reminded of Hollywood special effects; latex masks peeling off to reveal the infrastructure of gristle and bone.

'Not that I know of, but I'm not always first to the post.'

'Your husband?'

She shakes her head. 'He would have said something. But Sean has a pretty flexible attitude to other people's privacy. My eldest. Not Peter's. My love-child. Some euphemism. A mistake I'm still paying for seventeen years later.'

Nan's eyes flicker around the room looking for traces of adolescence.

'Left home about a month ago. Didn't say he was going. Haven't heard a word from him since. You'd think with his background he'd express his teenage rebellion by joining the Young Conservatives. But no. Ran away to linoland. Probably squatting in a bedsit under a *nom de guerre*. Impossible to track down. I tried a few pubs, wholefood cafés, found out who the dealers were. Not that they were ever going to give me the time of day. Even tried his father. First word for sixteen years.' She smiles as if something in her mouth tastes bitter.

'And he might have gone because of the letter?'

'He went because he couldn't stand Peter. A little Oedipal loathing dressed up as ideology.'

The exasperation passes and her attention seems to wander. She is looking at Nan, seeing something else.

'You know, women have a watershed. Never crossed my mind until I crossed it, but take it from me, on the other side you're untouchable. There's a gang of neds coming down the street, I still feel the old tension – watch yourself, what are they going to try? – but I'm winding myself up for nothing. I don't even exist. No point asking them about Sean, no point asking them anything. We're no longer inhabiting the same planet.'

Nan reviews what she hates about her own body – legs, stomach, that slight overbite – and experiences a sharp apprehension of a time when these imperfections will be irrelevant, perhaps even cherished, against the great deformity, Time. Imogen is bending over, rummaging in a drawer in the scrubbed table. Seen from this angle her face looks worn, skin starting to slacken like a favourite sweater.

'There was a photograph somewhere. Must have left it at work. Not much use anyway. Shaved off all his hair since then. Bald as a coot, except for the bum fluff on his chin.' Something teases at the edge of Nan's memory. 'Probably got gangrene by now. Ear like a colander with all those bloody earrings.'

She passes a hand over her face, the gesture of an undertaker closing the eyes of a corpse.

'As if life wasn't difficult enough.'

Nan is uncomfortable. She doesn't want to see Imogen

like this. She doesn't want there to be secret terrors behind that level gaze. She doesn't want her to be a failed mother. Or a blackmail victim.

'Are you sure the telephone call has anything to do with the letter?'

'You're suggesting he's a dissatisfied correspondent to the problem page?' Instantly she's grimacing an apology. 'I've been over every bloody letter of the last two months. The usual complement of sickos, but this feels different.'

'You'll just have to wait till they get in touch again, then. After all, what's the worst that can happen?'

Imogen holds the blade of the bread knife up to her mouth and taps it against her lower lip. Absent-mindedly she tests its point with her tongue. The blueish strawberry dimples at the touch of steel. The laser gaze locks on target.

'Maggie finds out. And I kill myself.'

If this is humour, it's the deadpan variety.

After the makeshift meal of toasted cheese, while Imogen knocks the crumbs off the hand-thrown pottery and stacks it in the dishwasher, Nan excuses herself. It's not a call of nature, but the need for ninety seconds of sanctuary, barricaded with the Dutch tiles and the Ali Baba stash of toilet rolls, is also a physical imperative. She's not used to uninterrupted company these days; the forty-minute lunchbreak with Rab is about her limit.

Just before the bathroom is a half-open door: a glorified cupboard turned into a dressing room. Half the space is taken up by a shopfitter's rail of women's clothes, the odd jacket or dress sheathed in dry cleaner's cellophane. Against the other wall is a marble-topped washstand and an old fretwork mirror, its delicate frame covered with coat upon coat of black paint, clogging the intricate pattern. Snagged on the spiky corona are a couple of chunky modern necklaces, an antique coppery chain, and a green tartan ribbon whose ends trail in a shallow basket of jumbled cosmetics, expensive goo, things it would never occur to Nan to buy. Lotions and gels and cremes she doesn't know the purpose of, fat lipsticks in the bold colours favoured by brunettes, shades she could never wear.

She unscrews a small glass jar and dips her finger into the yielding white emulsion. It feels oddly warm. She sniffs the peak of cream on her fingertip and hastily wipes it on the back of her hand. The smell lingers, faint but delicious, pulling at the sweet tooth of childhood, conjuring other people's mothers, grown women, initiates. She wears little make-up, some days none at all, never having learned to gauge just how artificial you were supposed to look. Red lipstick turns her teeth green: the complementary effect of raw meat and plastic parsley on the butcher's slab. Pink makes her feel frilly and fraudulent. Coral, probably most appropriate to her colouring, reminds her of those big-haunched women who used to sit in lilac chiffon headsquares under the dryers at the hairdressers, surrounded by plastic orchids, when she ran in to collect her mother on Saturday mornings. Nails buffed and shell-polished, hairless calves in sheer nylon, but something feral and coarse under the sneezy aura of talc.

Turning the pots and bottles in the basket, she squints at the labels in the borrowed light from the hall. Clear glass, white plastic, pseudo-scientific names she can't be bothered working out how to pronounce. Surprising to discover in this household. However irrelevant ladyshave politics are supposed to be these days, she finds the treasure trove faintly indecent. Also fascinating.

She never had much time for self-conscious femininity. With fifty-two per cent of the population, it's hardly an exclusive club, but Imogen possesses a quality she can only identify as womanliness, something more than gender or biology. Not dependent on these exotic preparations but, if she's honest, enhanced by them. Dimly, she wonders if her own basic alchemy, the fragrance-free moisturiser and grungy eye-pencil, might hold a parallel mystique. For Rab, perhaps. But what about Danny? What does she have for him apart from young flesh, sympathetic magic to defy time's gravitational pull? Her fingers root through the potions and palliatives, the deep treatments and special formulas. Fear dressed up as beauty, extortion distilled to smell like choice. So many needs masquerading as desire. Skin deep.

'They're samples.'

Imogen is behind her, wine glass in hand. 'The women's page gets them by the crateload.'

Too close to face her, Nan turns back again and speaks through the mirror.

'I always wondered if they worked.'

'Not for me. But I suppose if you're going to use the witch doctor you've got to have faith.'

The smile lasts a fraction too long, the glass holding their mutual awkwardness.

Nan tastes again that endless moment in the car when they crossed the white line onto the other side of the road; the memory flashing like neon before she has time to look away. *So he used to hit you.* She is waiting for Imogen to ask, as she knows she will.

'Nan?'

Their eyes meet in the mirror.

'Can I ask you something?'

She nods imperceptibly.

'Will you find Sean for me?'

The lank-haired cashier takes the money with her left hand, using the right to make sure she doesn't lose her page in the breezeblock-sized bodice-ripper balanced on her knee. Nan slides the ticket off the counter and swivels sideways so that her hipbone takes the impact of the turnstile. She's been thinking about this all day.

The water takes her like a lover; she's twisting in its coils, hardly aware of the exertions of her limbs. Hasn't swum for years. Except for that lunchtime with Cal. The thought disrupts her rhythm, breathing suddenly out of sync with stroke, and she swallows a little surprisingly sweet water. The municipal pool is full of children, bodies chunky yet lithe in their fluorescent lycra, a school of dayglo mackerel. She feels her face moulding to the contours of their excitement, smiling in that split-second swoop above the water, but there's an extra component to her pleasure, beyond the gulf stream around the inflow pipe and the layer of chlorine mist created by the squealing, splashing swimmers. All day she has been telling herself she won't bother going to the tapas bar but now, as she weighs the relative advantages of bus or train, she acknowledges the imminence of an event.

As she approaches the shallow end of the pool a tall, bearded man encouraging the edgy back-stroke of two small boys bumps into her. Oddly, amid so much unself-consciously naked flesh, antiseptically pallid in the merciless light of the tiled pool, she is stirred by the muscled curve of his upper back, the black, slicked-down hair on his forearms like calibrations on a ruler. He smiles apologetically, mustering his talismans of innocence out of her way. She sees herself, fleetingly, as a kindred spirit of those shifty spectators who used to hover by the school railings next to the hockey pitch waiting for a flash of wind-chapped thigh. But mostly she feels amazement and a tentative self-congratulation. She thought Kilner put out that fire long ago.

It's been one of the better days. Gorr was away somewhere. Work was as mindless as usual but just busy enough for it not to matter. Another letter from Mrs Matheson. *It is now a full month since I, acting in good faith, posted my daughter an assortment of home-bottled preserves . . .* And Danny rang. Just before lunch. At first she couldn't place the voice.

'Jesus, what sort of phone system have you got there? Ever considered upgrading to two tin cans and a length of string?'

'Danny? Where are you?'

'My office. Live from Westminster. Only your switchboard just patched me through via Dubrovnik.'

Between waves of gratification at hearing from him, she realised she had nothing to say.

'How's the exciting world of the GPO?'

'About as exciting as tidying your sock drawer.'

'I wouldn't dream of asking you to tidy my socks.'

A poor attempt at humour. Even bad jokes carry ideological baggage.

'Don't feel too sorry for yourself. I've got an afternoon in committee with the Road Drainage and Resurfacing amendment. Anything you want to know about loose chippings, I'm your man.'

'I'll bear it in mind.'

Pause. Her turn.

'How's the jacket. Will it clean up?'

'Probably not, but it'll be a wee souvenir of Sunday

afternoon.' The crackling silence suddenly tautened. 'Don't worry, I'll think of some way you can make it up to me.'

'I don't consider it my fault.'

That did it, broke through the awkwardness, overcoming the essential absurdity of intimacy with strangers. She felt him relax.

'So when am I going to see you?'

A nice touch, the suggestion that she might be the one having to find room in a heavy schedule.

They made a meal of the arrangements, enjoying themselves now, every suggested rendezvous a landmark on their virgin map. Eventually they agreed a time and place and exchanged goodbyes. The connection remained unbroken.

'Oh, I almost forgot.'

'What, love?'

'Last weekend, at the party, Max did say something. Not to me, to a friend of mine; it slipped my mind.'

No sound to interrupt the fizzing of the line.

'He said I should ask you about your oriental interests.'

She could hear the smile leave his face across three hundred miles.

In the changing cubicle, chafing herself dry with the crumbling hired towel, she suddenly remembers the letter. She grabbed it from the bamboo telephone table on her way out that morning. An unusual place to find her post; Catriona must have picked it up with her own mail and only realised her mistake later. This hiatus in delivery has removed any sense of urgency. It hardly seemed worth opening as she left the flat and it remains sealed, stuffed to the bottom of her bag.

She works a finger under the envelope's flap, unable to shake the habit of opening mail as carefully as possible.

Something about the paper, or the typescript, strikes her as familiar.

PEOPLE IN GLASS HOUSES SHOULDN'T
USE BINOCULARS.

That's it. Nothing else. A word processor. She turns the sheet of paper over, pointlessly, then picks up the envelope. Nothing. Just her name and address written in a costive hand, the gs with their tidily-closed loops, topped and tailed. Purple ink. Her mind spins like a fruit machine. She checks the postmark: Glasgow, but the date is blurred. Catriona could have been carrying it around for a while. The police files will know her as Kilner, although she never took his name. For a second she tells herself that whoever sent her the letter might not, doesn't *have to* know.

It's a fatuous hope.

She draws her legs up to the painted wooden bench to pull on her socks, forcing the stiff towelling between her toes. Out of nowhere, she sees his face when she said it, one of those irrational taunts that jump out of a quarrel; childish, regrettable.

'*Just what is it you want? You obviously can't stand the sight of me; you won't let me go. What am I supposed to do? Drop dead?*'

It would have been fine if he'd said yes, the dynamics of the argument almost demanded it: she was upping the ante, using heavier artillery. But he didn't. The fury in him suddenly died and a man she had never seen before looked back at her.

She sits in the changing cubicle, a white-tiled confessional booth. On the other side of the pink plastic curtain a child's whine is wearing down its mother's resistance to ice cream; to her right she hears the hiss of an aerosol deodorant; two middle-aged voices are batting gossip over the partition to her left. She starts to cry, her mouth full of fragmenting cotton fibre and the lingering taste of soap powder as she tries to muffle the sound. When she moved to Glasgow she thought that, whatever else she had lost, whatever the price, it had been worth it, at least she'd got rid of the fear.

Now she knows she was cheated.

It's no more than a blowy night, but the bunting strung between streetlights ticks sharply on its line, a continuous soundtrack, like cold-weather cicadas. The wine bar itself doesn't need decoration, ornament would only clutter the stark lines and unbroken curves of window. The design hedges its bets between ultra-modern and Bauhaus pastiche: a squat, cylindrical construction like a giant cotton reel discarded on the riverbank amid the detritus of motionless earthmovers, crusted cement-mixers and the builders' boards promising a mañana of luxury flats.

The youth in the suit with the mandarin collar doesn't bother with her invitation card, gesturing vaguely towards the noisy restaurant when she asks for Cal. At least he doesn't do a double-take on her skirt. Underneath the baggy jumper, she's resorted to school-uniform tactics: rolled twice at the waistband. The Tinkerbell look.

Inside, the tables have been pushed to the walls and the place is heaving with people she never sees on the street: slightly scaled-up, expensive-looking, dressed like characters in television dramas about boardroom power struggles. The women hold wine glasses scalloped with perfect red lip-prints, the men smile broadly, exposing very white teeth in very pink gums. It's a while before she notices the straggling weeds among these hothouse blooms: West End ponytails in scuffed leather jackets; a few undernourished women in chainstore lycra with ragged, shoulder-length perms; the odd 1950s cocktail frock gaping at the bony breast. No one she knows. But then, she doesn't know anyone.

At the far end of the room, their oiled hair just gleaming above the crowd, a five-piece band is playing salsa, which doesn't strike her as particularly Spanish. Now and again there's a flash of silver as the trumpet player flourishes his horn. When the music stops, the babble of voices inflates like a life-raft.

She already regrets coming, but what was the alternative? Sitting in Catriona's scented nest straining for the echo of a footstep on the tenement stair? Anticipating those tones of intimate menace every time the telephone rings? She scans the room again. There must be three hundred people on the blond parquet floor. Cal could be anywhere. But she's lucky: here he comes, weaving his way through the crowd in another peculiarly-cut suit over what looks like a white cotton turtleneck; she bets he didn't buy that in Marks & Spencer.

Seeing him in this company, she understands him a little better, or at least, identifies more accurately what foxes her. He wouldn't thank her for the comparison but he reminds her of all the computer programmers, civil engineers and food chemists met over the years at twenty-first parties and weddings, men standing on the periphery of conversations, emblems of the awkwardness and boredom which stalk organised enjoyment, coming to life only when talk accidentally brushes against their professions. All of them intimidating, refusing to acknowledge any priority above their own. Cal's expertise is not megabytes or molecular compounds, but money. Money and how you spend it. This, it strikes her, is the real meaning of materialism. Not a graffito insult but an intricate code whose mysteries will always elude her.

He walks right up without seeing her, snapping the fingers of one hand, but not in time to the music. She stretches out an arm to block his progress. Still his expression doesn't alter. This is worse than she could have foreseen.

At last he recognises her, grabbing the barrier hand in both of his and clutching it to his bosom as he addresses the ceiling.

'Thank you. Thank you, God. You might have a seriously sick sense of humour but you're not a complete bastard.'

He looks down, releasing her fingers just before she can pull them away. 'How'd you like to earn my undying gratitude, babe?'

'I can take it or leave it.'

'Name your price. How about the keys to the Mazda for the weekend? Your pick of the waiters washed and brought to your tent?'

Her sinuses tingle with the buzz of playing to an audience. Not that anyone's watching, but Cal carries his own sense of spectacle. He's already backing through the chrome-plated swing doors into the kitchens. A couple of teenage girls in party clothes are decanting a catering drum of olives into individual sundae dishes, otherwise nothing is happening. The stainless-steel worksurfaces are absolutely clear.

It's none of her business but she asks anyway.

'Where are the staff?'

The answer is returned to Cal.

'Mike Park and Cressida are playing footie out the back.'

'Kerist! Maybe if I'd hired Partick Thistle the beautiful people would have something on their plates by now.'

He's enjoying this, she realises, because he thinks she's going to save the day. No one has shown that sort of faith in a long time.

'Who's in charge?'

'You are. My thieving Dago chef did a runner ten minutes ago along with his bum-boys. Janice'll tell you what's on the menu, I've got to go mingle.'

She unhooks a starched white apron from its peg and throws it across to him.

'Forget it, I need you in here.'

By cutting one dish and trimming the more ambitious flourishes from the others she devises a workable menu. The footballers are recalled, the goodtime girls swathed in sensible pinnies, and Cal put to work.

To her surprise he follows instructions to the letter and does the job fast. He still treats it like an elaborate game, but she's starting to enjoy herself too.

'Must be twenty grand's worth of haircuts in this wine bar. Where'd you find them all?'

'Yellow Pages.'

'G for glamour?'

'F for freeloaders. You obviously don't mix in the right circles, Mrs Beeton. There's always something opening: restaurants, private views, first-night parties. All you need to sustain life in this city is a diet of canapés and a change of cocktail frock.'

'Give them enough money and they never have to pay for anything ever again?'

He shoots her an assessing look.

'You're joking. Half of them couldn't raise the cab fare home. It's a con-job. All done with mirrors.'

'I thought they were the Glasgow jet set.'

'If they are it's a charter flight to Benidorm. If you really want to add to your autograph collection there's that policewoman from *Taggart*. The Singing Patriot's too busy manning the barricades to cut records any more; but if you're feeling generous you could call him a local celebrity. You clocked that blonde with the Carmen Miranda fuck-me pumps? Big Robbie's significant other; he's filming in Canada at the moment or he'd have been here too. That's the total star count, I'm afraid. You saw Kirsty and Muriel, of course?'

She didn't but she's reluctantly impressed and, despite her best efforts, he can tell.

He spreads his hands.

'And you and me's stuck in the kitchen, Cinders. Ain't life a bitch?'

She can't think of an immediate reply but here in a working kitchen, a good knife in her hand, peeling the parchment from a bulb of garlic, it doesn't bother her. The remark hangs unclaimed and, in a spirit of mild sadism, she lets the silence grow. The skillet spits, ready to receive its first sacrifice. She shifts it off the heat and the blue flames, released, cast their mirage into the vacant air above. Her knife strips the garlic without scoring the creamy nut within, a dexterity of which she has always been proud. This is what she does.

His amused stare has the stiffening look of an expression held too long. She realises her lips have been moving but she hasn't a clue what she was thinking about. Thank God he can't lipread: he'd have more idea what was going on inside her head than she has. Embarrassed, she seeks refuge in kitchen protocol, checking on progress, giving instructions, setting new tasks. The onions need peeling.

'You won't make me cry.'

'It's an allergic reaction, not a test of machismo.'

'I know. Kid I was at school with nearly died of it. They were going through a phase of alternative punishment. Cleaning windows and cross-country runs instead of wee homoerotic perks for the bachelors in the staff-room. Thursday was always Lancashire hotpot. Ever tried peeling onions for five hundred? Matron wanted to write him up for the *Lancet*. Plan B was to send the polaroids to Hollywood and option him to Stephen King.'

'Did no one know he was allergic?'

'Why do you think they made him do it?'

Unwillingly she feels her face firming into censure. Why is he telling her this? His smile is sardonic, yet forbids her sharing the joke. He wants her to react this way. It occurs to her that he's getting her to do his feeling for him and then mocking her for it.

'They went back to belting us after that.'

'What had he done?'

This time the laughter is genuine. 'He mowed the cricket pitch.'

'What?'

'We're talking about an English public school. You're better off sacrificing a goat in the chapel. The turfworm loved that pitch. Took him twenty years to get it like that. Spent more time on it than on Mrs Turfworm, that's for sure.'

He starts cutting up squid, leaving the onions untouched.

'They punished him for mowing a pitch?'

'Well, it was more *what* he mowed. Horticultural graffiti.' His eyes shine with infectious delight. 'You could see it miles away. Two months later it still hadn't grown out. "God Save the Queens" – there was a serious TB outbreak in the lower school.'

Seeing her confusion, he translates. 'Turdburglars. Fudgepackers. Shirtlifters. *Heterosexually challenged.*'

The knife slips and suddenly there's an indigo semi-colon on the white sweater, an unlucky splash within a couple of millimetres of the edge of his pinafore. He curses colourfully and lumbers over to the sink. Dabbing at the stain with a dishtowel, he doesn't notice the youth, the one he called Chico that first day though God knows

128

if that's his name, hovering by the door. A lock of brilliantined hair curves down over his forehead, artless but not, she suspects, accidental.

'Boss.'

He looks up. The aggression is instantaneous, so concentrated that the boy flinches, and disappears. The air vibrates with his absence yet Cal seems oblivious, his expression wiped clean. He picks up the knife to continue eviscerating the squid.

'That's what happens if you burst the eye. I should sling it and start again.'

To her own ear she sounds nervous, but he doesn't seem to notice, scooping the curling tentacles into the bin obediently enough.

'So the poor little sucker died in vain.'

At ten o'clock she puts down the knife and blissfully straightens her spine. She's out of practice, or maybe the worksurfaces are the wrong height.

'I need a breath of fresh air.'

'Well you won't find it outside. But be my guest. Must have something going for it: a couple of hundred alkies can't be wrong.'

The city sky is cloudless, its apocalyptic orange glow darker than usual but providing more than enough light to make out the fragments of brick and flinty stones embedded in the impacted earth, the row of industrial refuse bins, the cardboard packing cases – *Glass With Care* – a dozen upended paving slabs stacked like dominoes ready to topple and, a little further off, the abandoned football.

Out of the corner of her eye something stirs, scuttles, on the ground. She forces her head down to look. Just the wrapper from a cigarette packet pushed by the wind, a cellophane ghost still moulded to the shape of its former contents, the four corners intact, gold ripcord fluttering. Relief makes her civic-minded. She stoops to retrieve it and walks over to the nearest of the giant dustbins.

She knows exactly who it is upside down among the eggshell and old newspapers, whose feet in those antique sneakers, the ridged rubber peeling away from the canvas. Legs in jeans worn to floppiness. The denim jacket threadbare at the elbows, the pocket peeling; the grey vest riding up over a pale slash of stomach. At the bottom of the bin his head is jarred forward on to his chest, forcing a narrow fold of double chin, shadowed with pale stubble. The eyes are open. That unblinking stare, as if his whole life had been a rehearsal for this.

She knows it's a bad thing to happen to her, but it's just knowledge. No feelings. If she were watching it in a film there'd be a frisson of horror, an urgent sawing of cello strings. Pity, awe at a life destroyed, cross her mind only as she registers their absence. No point in pretending. He forfeited her sympathy along with his last breath, the power to cloud the mirror. Her eye fixes on an ankle. Funny, she wouldn't have put him down as a towelling sock man. Her second dead body. If that makes any difference. Time is passing. Maybe seconds, maybe longer. She should move, take action, but she's in the grip of something like peace. Everything is balanced, motionless, poised like a stopped pendulum. She's reluctant to restart the mechanism, the play of action and reaction. Here we go again.

Cal's still in the kitchen, slicing tomatoes and flirting with the party-girls. Something about her face holds the wisecrack in check. She beckons him into the corridor leading to the yard.

'Jack Ibster's body's in a bin out there.'

She moves towards the back door, assuming he'll follow but he catches her upper arm and pulls her through a doorway to the side, into a cramped washroom. He locks the door behind them and they're face to face, the seatless toilet bowl still bandaged in brown paper, the shadeless bulb overhead, a miniature sink speckled with tile-grouting pressing into the small of her back.

'How do you know?'

'I looked inside.'

'How do you know it's Ibster?'

Odd hearing him use the surname. Evidently it doesn't do to claim too much intimacy with the dead.

'I met him with you, remember?'

She would like some sympathy, nothing too elaborate: *Is she all right? Must have been a nasty shock.* His mind is working on other channels. He's surprised, but not quite in the way she was.

'Much blood?'

'Not that I saw.'

He checks his watch. 'We'll have to ring the polis.'

She looks at him in simple panic.

'We can't move it. All it takes is for whoever left this little surprise to tip them off and the forensic boys'll be crawling all over this place.'

She seems to be included in that first person plural. He's no longer screening his words with inverted commas, she notices.

'Let me go home first.'

'What's the point? You might as well talk to them here.'

They're locked in a half-finished toilet with a dead body in the garbage outside. It's no time for coyness.

'I can't afford another brush with the police.'

'Another?'

She looks at him steadily. 'With a councillor dead in

131

a dustbin on opening night, you're already front page news. If the press get hold of my name they'll think all their birthdays have come at once.'

'What the hell did you do?'

She savours his surprise, aware that she's just become more interesting. Self-disgust follows hard on her satisfaction.

'Nothing you need to know.'

He doesn't have time to pursue this. 'OK, I'll arrange for somebody else to find it but you'd better stick around. Mhairi and her pneumatic pal may not be Mensa material, but even they might get suspicious if Cinders left the party before midnight. Must be wondering where we are now. Probably think we've taken five for rumpy-pumpy in the cold store.'

The cubicle suddenly seems smaller. For a moment it's as if his body is closing on hers, but he's merely reaching over to release the lock. He draws the bolt and opens the door.

Back in the kitchen the goodtime girls exchange significant glances but nothing is said. Cal rounds up the waiters and organises distribution of the next relay of food, taking a tray out himself. She mixes up batter for churros.

She's bending over the fryer when the door from the restaurant opens and a tall but slightly-built figure appears. Beside him, in the doorway, Cal gestures in the direction of the passage leading to the back yard, then withdraws. The boy's skimpy teeshirt and voluminous combat trousers lend him the surreal proportions of a circus stilt-walker. His delicate skull is shaven, his left ear clustered with tarnished rings, some commercially faceted, some describing homemade parabolas. Two minutes later Cal is back. He stands very close, blocking out the rest of the room.

'Any sign of him?'

She gives a minimal shake of the head. He disappears down the passage and returns gripping Sean by one pallid arm, fingers tight around the childish bicep.

She glances anxiously at the party girls but their attention is fixed on the spitting oil in the fryer.

Cal draws nearer, which means his hostage comes too, though by a curious tact neither of them acknowledge the situation.

'I'm going to be tied up for a while.' His lips don't even quiver. 'You're holding the fort.'

She remembers the children's party game Murder in the Dark. Hysteria. Fear and laughter you couldn't tell apart. Bodies crammed in the hideyhole, giggling, tickling, shushing; it's fun to be dead. But the sounds never came from the places she heard them. In the end, she was the only one left. Fleetingly, he rests his free hand on her hipbone, a touch proprietorial and, just possibly, pleading.

'Attagirl.'

She takes the last batch of churros through to the restaurant herself. Her hair is hanging limp against her forehead, heavy with sweat and vapourised oil; she needs a drink. The flashing blue light surprises her with a familiarity born of countless television dramas; much more alarming somehow to see it without the whooping siren. Cal is by the entrance with a uniformed constable and a man in an outfit so catalogue-casual that he can only be a plainclothes policeman. Outside in the squad car Sean sits, head bowed, with another detective and a WPC. He looks guilty in the way of innocent people suddenly faced with authority. She wants to call Imogen but she's scared to be seen using the phone, nervous of drawing attention to herself. Cal never so much as glances her way.

Seeing him from this distance she marvels that they could have felt like allies a mere thirty minutes ago. It's a question of focus, she supposes. Up close, vision is blurred; this perspective offers a sharper definition. That overlong fringe, the slightly effeminate way he has of tossing it out of his eyes, the confident bulk of the body in that exhibitionist tailoring, the little jokes he's making for the benefit of the police. He stands out of reach but leans in towards them for the wisecrack, eyelids drooping, mouth parted expectantly as if to receive, not deliver, the punchline. Intimate flattery. The officers smirk, the shaven margin behind their ears pink with pleasure. She wonders, fleetingly, if they're on the take, but can't think of any compelling reason he would have for bribing them. Maybe just insurance. One of the guests comes over with a question. Cal turns away from the policemen, his deadpan expression an eloquent betrayal.

The police set up two tables at opposite ends of the room and proceed to note down every name and address. For such a simple process, it takes a very long time. As her turn approaches she has to fight the impulse to run for the Ladies', but the sluicings and churnings remain just within control. The detective behind his table with his neat pile of paperwork never even looks up. Three minutes later she turns to hold the door open for the footsteps behind her and finds a thin-lipped smile, tow-coloured hair drawn back into a ponytail and hooded eyes behind their twin discs. He's holding a motorbike helmet.

'Well, if it isn't Desperate Dan's favourite dish. Or was that cow pie?'

'Hello, Max.'

'A corpse on opening night. Just like Agatha Christie. Let's hope the poor bastard didn't die of food poisoning.'

His bike, an old-fashioned machine heavy with metal and chrome, is parked on the pavement. He straddles it and kicks the engine into a traumatising volley of noise.

'I'd offer you a lift but . . .' he taps the helmet, 'only got the one, and we wouldn't want to break the law.'

She walks for a long time before finding a public telephone. Then she gives Imogen the news that her son is in police custody. The rest she can find out for herself.

Next day it makes the front of the *Herald*; almost a third of a page including the picture, a red-eyed snapshot from some topping-out ceremony. Even clearly drunk, the pristine trowel dangling unheeded in one hand, he still looks self-possessed. There are a number of less-than-heartfelt tributes from political colleagues and a summary of his 'occasionally controversial' eleven-year stint as chairman of planning in the city. The funeral is to be a family affair up north, no flowers, no displays of civic mourning. The report is so lengthy and ingeniously worded that it's not until she reaches the end that she realises it's told her almost nothing. They don't even mention the dustbin. The only new fact is the cause of death: a gunshot wound. Police are appealing to the public for information.

The roughnecks in the seats across the aisle pause between slugs of lager, cans in hand, and snigger. Nan's lips twitch. Opposite her, Maggie is slumped, hat askew, mouth open, a runnel of glistening saliva between cracked lipstick and crooked teeth. Every now and again, randomly, she emits a low but distinct snore. No one should be exposed like this, but if Imogen doesn't think it's worth waking her up, who is Nan to argue? With three gin and tonics inside her, Mrs Ibster is probably less of a spectacle unconscious than she would be awake.

When Nan spotted them on the station platform she nearly turned and ran. The widow is dressed top-to-toe in black. Sheer stockings, chainstore Chanel suit, wide-brimmed frisbee hat as worn by royals paying their last respects to foreign dignitaries. She's even found a pair of those black gloves which wrinkle becomingly at the wrist. Until confronted by this costume, Nan had been vaguely anxious about the informality of her own outfit. Her skirt is ironed to shininess and still hangs like a tea-towel but the shoddy fabric seems morally superior, a principled asceticism, set against this display of funeral chic. Imogen has come closest to getting it right: neither Jackie Onassis nor Little Match Girl. The navy-blue skirt and jacket are borrowed from her working wardrobe, sober, but not melodramatic.

The widow wasn't pleased to see her. But then, Nan wasn't pleased to be there. It's strictly a favour to Imogen, a witness to private grief. Or so she supposes. She was too flattered by the trust to call it into question. The line is that she met the deceased through the Labour Party. Understandably, Maggie's suspicious. Perhaps she knows her husband was having an affair and has *her* fingered as the guilty woman.

Imogen refolds the newspaper and suggests a trip to the buffet car; she still hasn't acknowledged the snoring. Safely out of the carriage, they pause. Eyes closed, the older woman swivels her head in a circle. Yoga for travellers.

'Wish I could fall asleep just like that. Well, perhaps not exactly like that. Feel like I haven't been to bed for a week . . .' She reaches out and touches Nan on the forearm.

'Thanks, by the way.'

'For what?'

'Phoning. Coming along today.'

On this stretch of the journey the railway hugs the coastline, the nibbled ledge of turf suddenly dropping away into the rocky sea.

'How's Sean?'

'Good question. Stayed just long enough to get his washing done and put a ring round the bath and then he was back to the integrity of his bedsit. At least I've got an address now. No phone of course. Seems to have coped with the experience fairly well,' her lips compress to whiteness, 'considering it was his Uncle Jack. Just wish I knew what the hell he was doing going through Callum Macleod's dustbins. What he was doing at Callum Macleod's at all, come to that. Says a friend took him along. The idea that his friends are friends of Callum Macleod is bad enough. What were *you* doing on the guestlist?'

'I've met a lot of people called Macleod just recently.'

Imogen raises her eyebrows.

'Now he is worth blackmailing. Mister Big. At first I

137

thought Sean had gone there for drugs, but I suppose if he'd had anything on him the police would have found it.'

There's not much scope for misunderstanding but she asks anyway.

'Cal Macleod's a dealer?'

'More of a wholesaler. Or that's what they say. Never pinned anything definite on him but he's obviously into something a lot fishier than lemon sole, however pricey his restaurants may be. The paper had a team working on it for a while. Gave up in the end. Reckoned he was too well-connected in the CID.'

She thinks of the spotless white trenchcoat, the sunbed tan, those slightly soft hands with their perfect cuticles. She can't picture him picking his way through the discarded syringes on the housing schemes or even grubbying himself to deal with the middlemen. As it is he hardly seems to inhabit the same city. The sports club and the sporty car and the flashy wardrobe aren't compatible with the Glasgow of rain and litter and skippers trying to tap you for spare change, let alone the junkies and their notifiable diseases. It's a fantasy, Callum Macleod's parallel universe, a collage of advertising clichés come to life. But whose fantasy: his, or hers?

'The police told Maggie it looks like a professional job. Maybe somebody brought up from London. Who'd've thought anyone had a better motive for killing him than me?' She doesn't smile. 'Wonder what *he* was doing at Callum Macleod's party.'

'He wasn't.'

Imogen frowns.

'He wasn't a guest. Or if he was, I didn't see him, and Cal wasn't expecting him. He was as surprised as anyone.'

It's not quite the truth, but it has the advantage of economy.

'I'll bet he was. Nasty, finding a total stranger in your dustbin.'

Now Nan's confused. 'Hardly a stranger. They knew each other quite well. Least, they seemed to when I saw them together.'

'When was this?'

It comes out quickly, almost an accusation. Posthumous jealousy, perhaps.

'A few days ago. Cal took me for lunch and we bumped into Jack. That was the only time I met him, apart from passing him on the stair that night at Maggie's.'

Outside the window the sea is grey as slate, the speeding turf impossibly green. But then, the glass is tinted.

'Maybe they got to know each other after you two split up.'

Imogen looks incredulous, as if unable to decide whether Nan is guilty of extreme stupidity or deliberate provocation. It's always been her Achilles' heel, believing people; failing to calculate the importance of the little lies.

The door beside them opens and an old man in a herringbone sports jacket emerges, tottering slightly, adjusting his flies. His eyes water with the effort of focusing behind his off-the-peg spectacles. They move aside to let him pass. The automatic doors twitch and click in a frenzy of hydraulic indecision. They're standing too near the sensor.

'I'm sorry. I didn't realise. It must be terrible.'

Imogen pouts judiciously. 'No-o. I spent so long telling myself his life was none of my business, there's no real reason why his death should be any different. Just another thing he did when he wasn't with me. Maggie's pretty much a nightmare just now, but then I'm used to that. And she *was* his wife, which affords certain privileges.'

Nan waits, knowing there's more.

'Obviously it's going to hit me at some point. I've done my share of bereavement counselling. I'm familiar with the stages. Numbness. Anger. Grief.'

She closes her eyes.

'Funny, I really have no desire to know who did it. Maggie, now: she has to find out; it's eating her up. Mind you, she must be the number one suspect at the moment. Isn't that what they say: it's almost always the spouse?' She stretches discreetly, arms by her sides, flexing her back. 'Odd about him knowing Callum Macleod, though.'

Nan remembers the tang of his aftershave in that wash-room. Why did she tell him? She knew she was offering a hostage to fortune, but she didn't care. Now she has something on him, too, but it's a knowledge which makes him more dangerous, not less.

The mother of the deceased seems to be sublimating her sorrow in attention to detail. Either that or she's always been a pernickety old trout. She insists on a strict order of precedence in the funeral cortège but only seems able to arrive at it by working through every possible permutation of mourners, shuttling cousins and aunts in and out of the charcoal-grey limousines and borrowed family saloons while the idling engines choke the afternoon with fumes. Nan wonders if there is some secret calculation at work, if the ordering principle is not blood but feeling, which the old lady can only gauge by manipulating the mourners like abacus beads. Supposing that were the case, where should Imogen sit? In the back seat of this Sirocco, or alongside Maggie in the Daimler? Before long Imogen provides a sort of answer. Renouncing their places in the Ford, she hails a cab.

It's a roadside church, one of those eighteenth-century boxes she can remember modelling out of cornflakes packets when she was at primary school. Inside, the obsessively unfussy walls have a curiously insubstantial feel, as if they really were cardboard. She remembers her amazement when she moved south and discovered Anglican churches, their delicious fusty clutter, the elaborate haberdashery, the camp antiquity of it all. Here there are no candles, no crosses, no embroidered altar panels, no altar either, nothing but the back-breaking wooden pews.

The taxi driver must have brought them the long way

round; the relatives are already threading along the seats, replaying the pantomime Nan and Imogen abandoned in the station carpark. A huge turn-out. They can't all have known him, let alone liked him. She guesses it's the entire congregation; a duty of the godly to pay their last respects to a fellow worm of the dust. It's as if she's been sucked back to the 1950s. All these nuclear families on display, squeaky clean, godfearing; the men upright and unchallengeable in their heavy black suits, their wives less certain, torn between God and the children. Wee boys in their sombre Sunday best, hair brushed from unnatural partings; girls in berets and felt boaters. All at once, out of nowhere, she's envying them, these children of a stern but dependable father. They don't look happy, but there's a comforting consistency to their misery.

She didn't want to come to the funeral. Not because she has anything against funerals; it's the departure from routine, the double novelty of location and activity that upsets her. The usual programmed responses won't work. She has to react spontaneously and notice details and, at their worst, these things make her want to cry. It may be a reaction to the intensity, or the recognition that things are so rarely intense. She knows it isn't feasible to go through life like a perpetual adolescent, hypersensitive to every falling leaf, but is this deadness, this conveyor-belt existence, her only prospect? It seems to her that there was a time when she was happy, but it was a pleasure lost in her busyness, jostling for attention amid all the other circumstances of her life. These days she can't cope with too many distractions. She tries to keep the components down to manageable levels, one thing at a time. Even when it works, it's a cheerless victory.

By tacit agreement they sit near the back, separate from the family, their view of the yellow wooden coffin on its surgical steel trolley conveniently obscured. To their left, a couple of rows ahead, a woman sneezes. She seems to have a few cubic inches more space around her than the other mourners. Even from the back, with only a brown velvet hat and marmalade tweed coat to go by, Nan recognises her. She's the one standing alone in the bus shelter when you decide to walk to the next stop; the one children chant rhymes about, transposing their nameless fear into farting jokes and naughty words, comfortable taboos. Nan too walks down the street skirting those who are too fat, too loud, too ugly, too unlovable. Not even pitying them, just giving them those extra inches and wondering idly how they can bear to go on living. Only nowadays, weaving through the obese and the drunken and the obviously forsaken, she has the feeling she's sidestepping herself too. No one's noticed yet but it can only be a matter of time. Scanning the pews, she's held by the mystery of other people, their rhythms, their expectations of being alive, things she never thought about, until she lost them. Four minutes. The time it took Liam McVay to read the midnight news. Odd to find a Scot working on a Midlands radio station, a Sean Connery stumbled into the Archers, at least if you believed his voice; she always hoped he'd come into the restaurant one day.

Beside her, Imogen is turning the pages of the Bible, apparently searching for a specific passage, using a finger to steady the teeming print. A shred of lower lip is caught by the tip of her left canine. Nan's noticed it before, this glinting, feral detail. She's not sure just when she started to watch Imogen, collecting her mannerisms, wrapping them like apples to be stored until winter. Talking to Rab one lunchtime, she caught herself out in a hand gesture, a twisting of splayed, curving fingers she remembers from second-year physics lessons. A memory jogger to the Corkscrew Rule, whatever that was. Reproducing it in the formica-panelled canteen, surrounded by crusted sauce bottles and the debris of a sausage and egg sandwich, she knew it was Imogen's. She's started to think in her voice, too. Not all the time; just snatches of talk. Certain words – it has more to do with the sound than the sense – are so pleasurable she finds them running through her head again and again, like the hook of a song or the rote-learned fragments of her Sunday school childhood, *the bodies of men return to dust and corruption but their souls neither die nor sleep*, they say crucifixion is still an occasional ordeal on the wilder side of Glasgow, only nowadays they nail you to the floorboards. Wonder if that guarantees you a place upstairs.

The first hymn is announced, a tune almost avant-garde in its flouting of harmonic scale. She goldfishes it, occasionally guessing the next note out loud, not always correctly. Imogen looks around her, mouth and prayer-book firmly closed. The grandmotherly figure to her right proffers her own handsomely-tooled hymnal, assuming she's having trouble finding the page. Imogen shakes her head, smiling. Displeased, the good neighbour turns away.

They're mid-way through the fifth verse when the door opens. Nan's eyes are on her Bible but Imogen is watching.

'Look who's here.'

He's restricted himself to a grey suit, white shirt and sombre claret-coloured tie but he can't tone down the complexion. The rest of the congregation seem to have put on pallor with their mourning weeds, but even in the dingy, near-sepia light filtering through the lozenges of stained glass his colour is high, unseemly; rude health. Preoccupied with finding a pew, he doesn't notice her. Nan turns to Imogen and mimes a query.

'They were on the council together, before he stood for parliament.'

Mrs Ibster treats them to a dominie's stare.

Despite her expectations of hours of fire and brimstone, the service is over remarkably quickly. A psalm, a few prayers, a lengthy tribute from the minister based on the highly selective promptings of mother-love, and that's it. No one cries. Imogen's face remains neutral throughout, coming to life just once, during the minister's address, when she listens with one eyebrow raised in involuntary satire. Danny sits through the service head bowed, as if doing penance for his latecoming. It occurs to her that he might even be praying but, given that he's Catholic, she puts it down to discretion in the lion's den.

They're nearing the end of the second hymn, the organ chords spreading like ink on blotting paper, when the verse is pricked by a shrill electronic piping. Danny looks up to locate the source of the noise and their eyes meet. His surprise is so complete that for a moment he just stares. The intensity of his stillness, conspicuous as a shout, attracts curious glances from the nearest mourners. The moment hangs, somewhere between telepathy and paranoia. Too late, he smiles. Behind her, there is the sound of shuffling and muttered apologies. Turning, she sees a young man in crossword-puzzle checks standing in the aisle, murmuring into a mobile phone. Something tells her he is not a regular in the congregation.

When the bearers move forward she assumes they'll hoist the coffin up onto their shoulders, or at least carry it out at thigh level, but a foot slides under the trolley, releasing the brake, and the deceased is wheeled to his final resting place like a selection of steakhouse desserts. Maggie is first to follow. As she waits for them to negotiate the narrow aisle her shoulders start to heave like a diva warming up. Clearly they can expect a performance before long.

Outside, the leaden sky is insulated by a dingy layer of kapok cloud diffusing a strange chalky light. Danny is waiting for her by the door; he slips an arm round her waist and draws her to him in a sidelong hug, jarring her shoulder against his ribcage. Somewhere to the left, on the periphery of her vision, the light intensifies. She registers the anxiety before she understands why. Then she spots the cameras. They've come over the churchyard wall: three of them in the uniform of their trade, waxed jackets with corduroy collars and bulging poachers' pockets, modish green walking boots that never yet saw scree, leather-trimmed canvas shoulder bags capacious enough for all the tools of precision prying. They stand together at a distance that would be discreet, were it not for that unmistakable insolence.

She feels Danny's body tense and then rein itself back, his arm disengaging from her body. The trolley continues its unsteady progress towards the neat rectangle excised from the turf. Ahead of them Maggie is crying, her bloodless face creased and puckered like perished rubber. Imogen has extended a protective arm but is looking back at Nan and Danny. Her expression is unreadable but Nan can supply her own gloss.

There are more of them now, young men in cheap and baggy suits cut after the fashion of five years ago, chewed string ties bunching collars never meant to fasten, concessions to respectability only serving to enhance the impression of disrespect. As one they move, reporters and photographers, jogging over the mounds of earth, trampling the occasional clump of daffodils, overtaking the slow file of relatives on the gravel path until they're alongside the widow, cameras raised.

Casually Imogen glides around the back of her friend,

blocking their view. One of them treats her to a snarl of professional indignation. This is getting ugly. Some of the mourners tut, scored lips tightening; others watch, avid for spectacle. What could be duller, more routine, than death and its retinue, whereas these rakishly-clad cowboys, these shoot-out merchants with their narrowed eyes and frontier morals are something new, mesmerising, heedless in the face of mortality.

The congregation seeps towards the grave in a slow spiral, the living draining into the vortex. Trapped in black, Nan has no choice but to go with the flow. Danny is half a pace ahead, eyes lowered, when the procession bunches and stalls.

'Maggie! Over here!'

It's a schoolboy trick but she falls for it. They all do, turning towards the lens. That startled, unfocused expression, family resemblance of victims and criminals everywhere, is captured on film. He lowers the camera for a moment, revealing that half-witted, triumphant leer. Now she knows him. The one face she took as a keepsake from the dozen loitering outside the hospital gates. Even if the recollection isn't mutual, her face is in that picture. By tomorrow she could be on the front page of half a million newspapers. Tiny, out of focus, but still potentially recognisable.

Something coldly jagged presses against her palm and her fingers close on a set of car keys. Sensing rather than seeing a weak spot in the wall of people behind her, she turns and shoulders her way through. His car is parked a hundred yards from the kirk. She barely has to adjust the driver's seat. Odd how short tall men's legs can be. The engine starts first time. She slows down outside the church as Danny reaches the pavement, not quite braking as she opens the passenger door. Perturbation shadows his face as he realises she intends to drive.

147

By the second vodka she knows they'll have to stay for something to eat. God knows why she started on it, she's not used to spirits. Getting accustomed to them, though. This one slips down much more easily than its predecessor.

Suspicion rides the bubbles to the surface.

'Was that a double you bought me last time?'

'I thought you could do with something to relax.'

'You mean you don't want me driving any more.'

They have the beer garden to themselves. It feels reckless to be sitting out this early in the year but the late afternoon sky is warmer than it looks, reneging on its promise of rain. The premature buds on the horse chestnut above them are motionless. In the distance, cows are lumbering home to the milking.

'Most women would assume there were other reasons for getting them drunk.'

She doesn't smile. 'I thought we were past the Me-Tarzan, You-Jane stage.'

'OK, I give up. What's the courtship etiquette where you come from? Would you rather fill in a form: Name? Sex? Preferred position?'

He takes a mouthful of gin. 'Get up.'

She remains seated.

He asks again, more gently.

'Come on, a wee experiment.'

Guardedly she rises to her feet.

'You don't like playing the game by the traditional rules? Fine. Let's swap. Turn the tables, You be me and I'll be you.'

He catches her by the elbows before she can sit down again.

'Come on. Show me just what it is I do. Think of it

as a service to the sisters. Consciousness-raising for the remedial class. Give it a go.'

The moment feels forced. Neither of them is quite drunk enough for this but her curiosity is stronger than the suspicion that it's a stunt he's pulled before. Besides, her failure to explain that panic among the tombstones has been hanging like a dustsheet over the conversation. They could both do with a distraction.

'No use waiting for me.' He smiles unpleasantly. 'I'm you, remember, and you never start anything.'

Embarrassment pins her by the shoulders, the complicity they shared in the churchyard quite gone. She recalls Imogen's face just before she left the funeral. The service over, technically she had fulfilled her supportive brief, but she still feels uneasy about disappearing.

Right now, however, there are more pressing problems.

He is watching her, his posture uncharacteristically closed, eyes flickering between her face and the space just over her shoulder, engaging, disengaging, not a mannerism of his she's noticed before yet one that strikes her as vaguely familiar. Finally she makes the connection, and knows she ought to laugh, take it in good part, but the subtlety of the performance is close to malice. She has to fight the impulse to walk away. What she really wants is five minutes with a mirror and the privacy to assess the accuracy of his impersonation.

'Anyone ever told you, Nan, that talking to you is like conversation under exam conditions? Let me give you a tip: ice maidens are out this season. I'm getting tired of being the one hand that's clapping. Maybe we should cut our losses: I'll find someone prepared to meet me half-way, you pop down to the supermarket and see if you can't pick up a frozen cod that takes your fancy.'

'I thought this was supposed to be role-play, not character assassination.'

For a moment she mistakes his silence for compunction, then she realises there's someone else in the yard. She turns to find a couple of bikers, whiskery slobs in scuffed leather jackets, frayed denims greened with years of grease. They make for the furthest table. The bigger one spins his garden chair through a hundred and eighty degrees and straddles it like a cowboy. A skull and cross-bones is flaking from his leather back. Danny, too, sits down. Game over. She remains standing. Her turn now.

'So which Danny MacLeod shall I be? The honourable member for Testosterone West, or the Mr Softy underneath? We can flip a coin if you like. I'm sorry my acting isn't up to both, but I wouldn't say yours was either.'

His nostrils dilate as if he's short of oxygen. The bikers are staring, although she's pretty sure they're not close enough to hear.

'About time you got rid of one of them anyway, preferably the fake one, if you still know which is which.'

A step closer.

'How about the Westminster hard man.'

She notices for the first time that he's thinning on top.

'Or are there too many advantages?'

Another step and her nipple will be up his nose. She insinuates a knee between his legs. Involuntarily he strains backwards, but does nothing to stop her.

'There must be a lot of people like being pushed around.'

She fingers his lapel, feels the stippled stitchwork underneath, the fabric's surprising softness. 'Or manipulated, anyway.'

She's standing straddling his thigh, lips brushing his ear. The Hell's Angels look away. 'Nice work, being a hard man.'

Her tongue traces the curl of cartilage, like licking an envelope. 'As long as you live up to the billing.'

At last she gets a reaction. The moment has lost its irony and she realises with a shock the proximity of sex. So she's still in the game after all. Past embarrassment now, Danny draws her down. The chapter pick up their pints and walk back into the bar. She feels his hands slide under the bunched skirt.

It's not an elegant coupling; awkward prisoners of their underwear, moving to different patterns of urgency, rhythms hampered by the effort of will needed to banish the fear of discovery. Once, twice, they're almost together, but losing herself in the moment she loses the moment in surprise. *Still in the game.* The moulded plastic chair creaks loudly, erratically, the afternoon light insistent on her eyelids. He climaxes suddenly, almost imperceptibly, his expression suggesting the development is unexpected, even to himself. She's still registering the disappointment as he extricates himself, deftly buttoning his flies, scanning the horizon, surreptitiously tidying his hair. She straightens her skirt, closing her legs to trap the lukewarm gloop slipping down her inner thigh. On his way to the car he flicks her clitoris through the concertina'd fabric as, once upon a time, favourite uncles chucked toddlers under the chin.

The hotel lobby is a collage of styles: buttock-numbing gothic thrones, padded window-seats, the disingenuous simplicity of the arts and crafts movement, delicate French gilt, two leather chesterfields, a chiaroscuro of chintz-shaded forty-watt bulbs and the flickering of a spitting log fire. Gracious living. Olde England according to Hollywood, recreated in Scotland. She turns uncertainly to Danny, man of the people, poacher turned laird. He cocks an eyebrow.

'What's the matter? Think they might throw me out?'
She takes in the precision cut of the cloth over his

shoulders, the perfectly-chosen tie. Funeral etiquette has toned down the gangster's edge in his dress sense and he looks patrician, to the manor born.

'No, but they might me.'

He laughs, pleased with the idea. 'Not if you're with me, doll.'

'They know you here?'

It takes a while to occur to him that she might be feeling something other than impressed.

'Does it bother you?'

'Doesn't it you?'

At last the blanket good humour frays a little.

'We can book you into a separate room as my researcher. It's not cheap here but I'll do it. But I can tell you now,' he looks her up and down, 'no one's going to be fooled.'

'What's that supposed to mean?'

He leans over and kisses the bridge of her nose, a light, dry suction leaving no traces.

'It means you're a cracker, Nan.'

Glasgow City Chambers is one of those buildings which exist in the mind only as an exterior, an Italianate stone frontage whose grandeur is crowded by neighbouring architecture and usually veiled by rain. Inside, however, there's nothing to cramp its style, the clashing masonry, its liverwurst granite columns and licorice-allsort mosaics, all the high-calorie ostentation of municipal Victoriana.

The mailroom isn't far from the lobby but the door through which she's directed might as well be a checkpoint between conflicting ideologies. On the other side is a narrow, functional corridor whose plain plastered walls, once a cold-morning grey, are now shading into nicotine twilight.

She can't work out how it took her so long. Forty hours a week playing letter detectives and she's stumped by something that drops on to her own mat. It finally struck her at work, as she thumbed through the not-knowns, half-listening to Gorr's plans for a team-building Outward Bound course in the highlands. For one horrible moment she assumed her name was on the list and shudderingly imagined five days up a mountain with Gorr on the other end of the rope, but she needn't have worried: junior status has its advantages. He's been getting friskier of late, but somehow she doesn't mind as much. He's constantly commenting on how well she's looking, but if he's waiting for her to return the compliment, it'll be a long time coming.

'A lot of the stuff is taken from SAS basic-training, so

I'm warning you: if you get a midnight caller dropping in through your bedroom window it's not necessarily the Milk Tray Man . . .'

Suddenly it came to her. As soon as Gorr left she scrabbled for the envelope, crumpled at the bottom of her bag since that night at the swimming pool. As she thought, not a stamp, as with the original letter, but a licence number. *Postage Paid Glasgow 526.* She checked the register. 526: Glasgow City Council.

The mailroom is staffed by the usual combination of war heroes and dead-end kids, two of whom are fighting for control of a small transistor radio, scraping the dial between a heavy metal band's efforts at long-distance trepanation and bursts of heedorum-hodorum accordion-playing. A bulky, white-haired man with a startling tangerine tan lifts his head enquiringly; she wouldn't have thought a mailroom paid well enough for winter sunshine. She opens her mouth and is overwhelmed by the hopelessness of the quest. How many thousands of staff must they have? But the clerk takes her envelope between his fat yellow fingers, forestalling further explanation.

'Purple ink: that'll be the Devil's choirboy.'

It's such a simple piece of luck but the surprise of it brings her close to tears. It's been years now since she counted good fortune as her birthright, took it for granted that the lost earring would always turn up, the train she was running for be delayed at the platform. Everyday omens, tiny signs that she was blessed. She asks where she can find him. The smile fades.

'Naw, hen, that's Councillor Ibster's hand. The guy that was shot at yon fancy restaurant. Last writing he saw was on the wall.'

He's not very clear about why she wants to see the office, which isn't surprising given her extemporised mumblings about official procedure and closing the file, but he's an obliging old codger and not averse to wasting ten minutes on a stroll around the building.

The planning chairman's office is even more spartan than the mailroom. The dado is panelled in what looks suspiciously like hardboard, Bisto-stained and comb-dragged to give a cursory impression of timber; the upper walls are primrose pegboard, each circular indentation harbouring its crescent of dust. The vinyl typist's chair has the beginnings of a nasty tear in the backrest, the edge of the chipboard desk is scarred with dowt-burns. On top sits a cheap wordprocessor, a split-ended spider plant, and a large cardboard carton packed with files and papers.

Her guide opens a drawer. Empty. He nods, satisfied.

The door opens and a tightly-permed head pokes through the gap.

'Oh, sorry, Jimmy. I thought it was Mrs Ibster. I'm waiting for her to collect the last of his papers.'

There's a brief silence while all three register the absence of sorrow in her tone.

'Are you wanting any help?'

To her relief, Jimmy explains. It sounds more plausible in his mouth.

The secretary shrugs in the direction of the cardboard box.

'You're welcome to have a look through that lot. Everything else is away.'

Rapidly and, she hopes, officiously, Nan starts riffling through the committee minutes, past the clumsily-typed appeals for clemency over illegal porches and illuminated signs, the photocopied memoranda and meaningless jottings on sandwich-shop serviettes. An old-fashioned script with its double-looped gs. Purple ink. Half-way through, the search loses impetus, about the time she dredges up a torn-off corner of brown manilla envelope, scribbled on which is her own name and address.

Catriona can't wait to hand over the post, breaking out of her pink bubble of perfectibility to present herself, peach spandex leotard clashing with a deep aerobic flush, at the kitchen door. It is the trampoline hour. Bounce to fitness in the comfort of your own home.

'This came for you.'

A printed card, the dotted line filled in by an uncoordinated hand, the uncertain strokes of a black ballpoint. In the white space she reads the luminous polyester blankness of the regulation shirt, blank as she knows the face will be, that absence of expression which makes policemen's skin so noticeable, workhouse pallor, tawny freckles on a smooth cheek, a neutral screen for the projection of guilt. *Please contact PC Redpath, ext 4328.* So this is how it happens. All the drama of a dental appointment card. Not even a sergeant. It's about Jack of course. Routine enquiries. When her time comes they won't bother posting advance warning through the letterbox. But she was fooled for long enough to know that she can expect the same sense of unreality, panicked yet removed, the same detachment as she listens to the distant thudding of her own pulse. Unless she moves first, which of course she will. But not yet.

Catriona hovers in the doorway, avid for explanation. Wordlessly Nan reaches for her coat. She'll use the phone box on the corner.

Technically, she is on the run. A romantic notion to rebellious adolescents but, at her age, a bad idea from every perspective. Tarquin has run out of new ways of telling her just how bad. Bound to tip the balance over the charges and influence the judge when it comes to the sentence. But they have to catch up with her first. Not that she says this. He only remains in contact on the basis that she intends to go back, an undertaking which inhabits the unfenced plains between possibility and deception. Tomorrow is another day. In fact, through repetition at regular intervals the prospect has acquired a certain substance, as real to her as full employment or freedom of speech or Scottish self-determination, or any other principle without deadline in which she high-mindedly believes.

It's an unforgiving late winter morning, dusk just around the corner, the brittle blue sky criss-crossed with vapour like the skidding traces of pencil rubbings. The police station has the temporary look of all buildings that date from her lifetime; a single-storey block whose concrete and glass and homogeneous terrazzo amount to architectural nihilism, polar opposite of the moral certainties of the magisterial Victorian lock-up. Whoever designed it believed not in justice but in sociology. Passing the pub opposite, she's almost tempted by the morning-after staleness seeping through the open door. She could do with a drink, even a cigarette, any prop used by people in her position. It's the affinity not the stimulant she needs.

Inside, the building has the buzzing emptiness she associates with hospital corridors and railway waiting rooms late at night. The Post Office too. That unnerving combination of order and forsakenness, a place where functionaries take comfort in inflexible rules, the bureaucracy of life and death. In the reception area is a wall-sized bulletin board crammed with fugitives and malefactors, wanted and missing. Photo-booth likenesses, school photographs, and snaps of such primitive menace that the subjects would surely have had them destroyed. And if she finds herself among them, what then? Tarquin reckoned they wouldn't bother circulating a photograph north of the border in a case like hers, certainly not to a city she'd left as an eight-year-old, but he did spot her in *Police Gazette*.

'*Quite a good picture – curls suit you. Looks a few years out of date, though.*'

'*Graduation portrait.*'

'*You're not wearing a gown.*'

'*It wasn't obligatory at Walsall College of Food Technology.*'

She studies the wall. *Beware of Bombs*. Artists' impressions of a series of Adam fireplaces hacked out of empty country houses. A couple of seamed photofits. A rapist and a squint-eyed conman preying on pensioners in sheltered housing. And where does she rank in this league table of villainy? Somewhere between terrorist and mantelpiece thief.

PC Redpath turns out to be a woman, a Border collie with a checkered hatband despatched to round up the party animals and present them at a staggered series of ten-minute appointments. The morning batch is running about fifteen minutes behind schedule, but since she's late anyway Mr Rodger is just about ready to see her. The policewoman knocks softly on the chipboard door, a one-knuckle tap. It opens and a puppyish figure with a beat-nik-revival goatee emerges. Behind him is an older man who reminds her of the amputee pigeons found in diesel-clogged corners of the city, beady-eyed, scraggy-necked, picking at the shreds of tobacco stuck by viscous saliva to his lower lip. He has the Glaswegian's chisel cheek-bones, not genetic, but sculpted by decades of hungry smoking.

She stands aside to let the younger man pass, but this

is not, after all, a fellow witness. He angles his left hand, inviting her in.

'I'm Detective Inspector Rodger, and this is Sergeant Colin.'

No wedding ring. Once upon a time she would have counted this a bonus: fifteen minutes of low-level flirtation given extra piquancy by the presence of his tubercular colleague. These days she has other things on her mind. Still, to remember that much is a tribute of sorts, it must mean she's attracted; but to what? The bleached blue eyes in their circles of thinned blood, that young man's complexion, the pink and white of Gainsborough ladies, his body sausage-waisted under the softly-draped shirt. The shirt is good, a rich bottle green, buttoned to the neck but worn without a tie; and she likes the beard, a subtly dissident detail. But mostly it boils down to the shirt, a secret signal to all her sex: soft, tactile, discreetly luxurious, a shirt that promises *I'm on your side*. She never met such men before. Or if she did, she knew they weren't for her.

He sits down at the table, inviting her to take the seat opposite. His older but junior colleague (how does that go down in canteen culture?) sits to his left, in front of a brown cardboard folder and a pile of forms. Her eyes rake the inverted lettering, the block print swirling in front of her eyes, some interference at the periphery of her vision like the slanted shooting stars when she stands up too quickly in the public library.

'We'll just take down a few particulars.'

There's a music-hall joke in there somewhere, but she doesn't feel like laughing. She has no particulars. Her distinguishing feature is anonymity. She feels a muscle tremor in the pouch under her left eye. He can't know, but if he does there's nothing she can do about it. She's at the mercy of coincidence, chance and memory. She could have the mouth of an old girlfriend, the surname of a classmate at school, his mother's birthday, any meaningless detail might render her conspicuous. In which case it's only a matter of time before the pieces fit.

Sergeant Colin is having trouble with the name. It was the same for the constable at the tapas bar, his dyslexic difficulties with gs and js; in the end it seemed easier to let him get it wrong. The appointment card glossed over the problem with an illiterate scrawl, so the version on his list comes as a surprise. A liberal translation, almost as creative as the original pseudonym. After three and a half months of use she's just about worn it in.

'There was nothing out of the ordinary that night?'

She tilts her head. 'Not that I can remember. I was in the kitchen. There is a window but it was pitch black out there and it doesn't look out on the dustbins anyway.'

The policemen exchange glances.

'The dustbins?'

'That's where the body was found. Isn't it?'

Another significant look. The pigeon puts down his pen.

'What gives you that idea?'

'Cal Macleod said something.' *Bad choice.* 'Or maybe it was Imogen Reiss. She's a friend of mine.'

DCI Rodgers raises his eyebrows briefly.

'I have to ask you not to mention the dustbin to anybody else. We're bending over backwards to keep it out of the press . . .' He turns and murmurs to the sergeant. '. . . Have to have another word with *Mister* Macleod. And the kid's mother . . .'

Turning back, he maintains the confidential tone.

'It may not sound much but we need all the help we can get with this baby.'

'Is that with or without a comma?'

He has no idea what she means.

'In a carpark!'

Nan lowers her voice, unsure of the soundproofing.

'Look, it was a beer garden. Back of nowhere.'

Imogen raises an eyebrow.

'However primitive they may be north of Inverness, not even the Teuchters screw al fresco in March.'

The vacuum lasts perhaps half a second, then implodes under the pressure of their mirth, the pagan laughter of siblings under the bedclothes: Imogen's a throaty barmaid's cackle, Nan's an ambiguous mewling that could almost be taken for tears.

Effortfully, she regains control.

'There wasn't a soul for miles around. Anyway, if they'd blinked they'd have missed it.'

That sets them off again.

The door opens and a towel turban briefly appears in the strip of daylight. Guiltily, Nan draws her knees up to free a section of the slatted bench, but it's too late, the woman has gone. Imogen has no such qualms, she remains full-stretch, propped on one elbow like an art-school Venus.

At first Nan was self-conscious, elbow-clamping the apple-green towel to cover breasts and pubic fuzz. Imogen has tucked hers into a casual toga around the midriff, revealing dark nipples the colour of old brick-work, coarse grained and fissured, the teat robust, steep sided, with a greyish bloom which reminds Nan of the dull fur of freshly picked raspberries. She finds them curiously repellent but is aware that it's a minority view; in the world's eyes those warty nipples are a token of sensuality more prized than her own pale aureoles, now smoothed to invisibility by the melting heat.

Women aren't meant to compare and contrast in this way but most of them do. Divide and rule. She wonders if in some secret corner of Imogen's sisterly subconscious she's doing the same. There's certainly something artificial about her abandonment, that blissful sphinx expression. It's not *that* relaxing barbecuing yourself in this sweatbox, the caramelised air singeing the nostrils, heat filling the throat with a luxury just tinged with panic.

It's Nan's first time in a sauna but already she's sorted it into the category of overrated pleasures along with alternative comedians, facepacks and homemade pastry. Nevertheless she's sticking it out, still hoping to be convinced by the older woman's pleasure, maybe even to understand a little of how it feels to be Imogen Reiss. Not for the first time she thinks how easily her attachment could be misunderstood: solicitous, admiring, affectionate, physical, who knows, at some level probably sexual too. Only the absence of hostility distinguishes it from love.

'Did you climax?'

It's exactly the question she would expect of Imogen, and entirely to the point, but that doesn't help her find an answer. Imogen's mouth puckers with delicate amusement.

'Suppose not, what with the wind chill factor.'

The grin broadens. 'What about since?'

Is this really what Sixties children discuss in saunas, trading bedroom details like bubblegum cards, holding impromptu workshops in technique? Or is it another example of Imogen's idiosyncratic wiring, a professional's shock tactics?

'I don't think I'm relaxed enough. I have to be. Very. It's not that he's not attentive or affectionate. *Cosmopolitan* would score him very highly. It's me. It's enjoyable. But. I'm just not. Relaxed.'

Imogen purses her lips, evidence of a heroic effort to defer judgement until she's heard the full facts. A wasted effort. Nan knows her well enough to read the expression as the sentiment it's there to forestall.

'Of course it takes two, but in this case it really *is* my problem.'

She expects some contradiction, or at least an attempt to probe further, but Imogen doesn't reply. She is staring, eyes narrowed, at Nan's breasts. Looking down, Nan realises the towel has slipped and in the aquarium light of the sauna the scar is darker, more defined than usual. Perhaps it's a heat reaction.

'Did he do that?'

She's shrugging in confirmation before she realises the misapprehension.

'No, no, not him, Kilner.' She hates the expression but in the interests of clarity she hasn't much choice. 'My husband.'

Imogen's face is neutral, forensic. Seen it all before.

'What was it, cigarette?'

'Kebab skewer. Vegetable satay. Straight off the grill.'

Imogen nods as if ticking it off her checklist of domestic weaponry.

'He used to start it in the kitchens. Usually between eight and nine. Rush hour. I couldn't even raise my voice in case the customers heard. I had this green top on. Don't know what it was made of, something stretchy and synthetic. It shrivelled up and started sticking to the wound.'

The smell of melted fibre and seared flesh, the latter disconcertingly close to the mouthwatering tang of sealing meat. Worse than the pain, the thought of that nylon skingraft. She fingers the scar absently.

'It was Pam's night off so I was on the tables as well as cooking. She had this big butcher's apron which covered you from the neck downwards, I put it on and no one was any the wiser. I thought about going up to Casualty, but the satay was getting cold.'

Evidently the joke is not to Imogen's taste.

'He made a habit of attacking you when you couldn't retaliate?'

She cocks her head, considering.

'Not always. I think actually he wanted me to hit back. Anything for a reaction. Does it sound mad to say he was jealous of the restaurant? Of the customers. Anything that wasn't him. I could've screamed at him or gone off to hospital, or closed up for the night, but,' she pauses, knowing she'll be misunderstood but saying it anyway, 'if I'd done that, he would have won.'

This is the first time she has made a story of it and it converts well. Amazing that she can find the vocabulary to render her experiences intelligible. Fraudulently so of course: not even a blow-by-blow account could begin to convey what was really happening. Linear narrative, cause and effect, get lost in the switchbacks of love and survival. The screaming fits, the suicide threats, the silent treatment, the talking cures. The marital fruit machine: so many flavours, so many ways to lose. But not infinite. It is possible to exhaust the permutations of appeasement; one day, there's nothing left to try.

It was the night of the storm, a Monday. The restaurant was closed. She went to Althea's to see the new baby, an unusual expedition: she didn't go out without Kilner and she'd long since learned not to pay social calls with him. He'd wanted to come, though, wanted to see her hold the child; wouldn't she like a little baby of her own? She

165

always said she had no maternal instinct, but she could feel the stirring even as he wheedled her, miming the sucking reflex at her breast, babytalking, nudging against her stomach, changing the game from product to process, Mummies and Daddies. Yes, she had the instinct: she would protect her child at any cost, even that of not being born.

After the initial nervousness, the terror that she might inadvertently snap the sunflower neck or crush that soft-boiled skull, she was caught in the baby's magnetic field, tugged into the rhythm of its underwater mouthings, slow-motion sneezes and the mysterious language of its puckers and creasings. She felt the undertow of life, knew that for those minutes, to the thing in her arms she was everything; and knew even as she savoured the experience that she was excluded from it, a tourist in the land of the living.

Althea teased her out of her trance.

'You only think he's cute because he's a piccaninny. I can see he's an ugly bug and I'm his mother.'

And then the child cried and Althea caught her lip in joke-remorse and took her son to her, the grasshopper limbs folding neatly against her shoulder, the mother beating a slow, hollow tattoo on the wishbone ribcage until the angry eyelids uncrumpled and fluttered in sleep.

Nan said she'd pick up a cab on the main road but in truth she wanted to walk, to prolong the connection with everyday lives before returning to her desert island, the Crusoe and Friday world she shared with Kilner. They were known locally as a close couple. As they walked along the street hand-in-hand, road gangs would snicker, construction workers catcalled that 'they must be in love' and the invisible handcuffs would tighten, binding them still closer. They were everything to each other, misery and consolation, ally and foe, life and death. She would have left him, but her imagination failed her.

Stepping out of Althea's overheated hallway she was surprised by the turbulence. The wind grabbed her hair in its vertical hold and tugged her upwards. The front door bucked in her grasp. A pair of no-entry signs guarding the junction rattled. Entering the commercial sector, burglar alarms ricocheted into life. A reproduction carriage lamp blew out like a candle, its glass crashing to the pavement. She clung to walls and doorways, street silt stinging her legs like birdshot, while her fellow pedestrians, learning to walk in the teeth of the wind, pushed off from the knees like figureskaters. Now and again she'd pass through unaccountable pockets of calm, her limbs suddenly light, the night air almost caressing. The next moment, just as inexplicably, she'd be forced off her path by the whim of the storm, like crumbs swept from a table.

Clutching at lampposts to save herself from oncoming traffic, watching the chaos, hearing the distant screams, she knew it was dangerous but felt only exhilaration. He might own her life; he didn't own her death.

'Did you go to the police?'

The question takes her by surprise.

'Why?'

'Nan, that isn't a love bite. If it looks like that now, it must have been serious. How long ago was it?'

'Four months.'

For the first time Imogen looks shocked.

'My God, he's not still around?'

She smiles softly.

'No, he's not still around.'

The day after the storm the city had an oddly clean look, as if the whole world had been wrung out and hung up to dry. The pavements were strewn with unseasonal debris, winter twigs mysteriously in leaf, clumps of fresh earth, fragments of stone and pottery. The pale, surprised blue of the sky, purged by the night's travails, suggested life reborn, a minor miracle, like a drinker spared his hangover the morning after a twelve-hour binge. She walked the deserted streets treasuring details: sunlight caught high on a seagull's wing, the measured progress of a cat doorstep to kerb, a van turning out of the bakery trailing its thin sweetness of spun sugar and white flour, the enveloping sense of peace.

'So where is he?'

She's known for some time that if she is to open up to anyone then Imogen is the one, but the words don't come. *Do you really want to know?* It's hardly worth asking; however urgent Imogen's curiosity, it couldn't register on the same scale as her own feelings. The question is rather, does she really want to tell?

She shrugs, 'Who knows? Probably back where he came from.'

'Which is?'

Nan meets her eye, as one must when being less than candid.

'He was Liverpool Irish.'

'And do you miss him?'

She acknowledges the flash of inspiration even as she is incensed by it.

'Now you come to mention it I do miss waking up wondering which ordinary household object might be used as a weapon today; feeling relieved to notice he's left his rings by the bathroom sink – that cladagh ring was a bastard to heal. Yes, I miss not having to run the minesweeper over every chance remark. Not mapping out entire conversations in my head, checking for ambushes and boobytraps, before I even get round to opening my mouth. I miss having to bite my tongue to stop myself saying I don't feel like fucking today, because at least if he's randy he's not going to start playing football with my head. Having him on top of me, asking if I love it, *baby*, and afterwards, saying he loves me, and do I love him, and how much, and is it forever, and thinking yes, it's forever, this is for fucking ever.

'I was lucky, really: he didn't hit me that often, sometimes not for weeks on end, I just thought he was going to all the time. That really pissed him off, the way I used to flinch for no reason. He was always sorry afterwards, he didn't know why he did it, I just wound him up so much; he loved me, if he didn't I wouldn't be able to wind him up. Obvious. I should have been able to work it out for myself, I was the most loved wife outside Rillington Place. Is that the sort of help you offer your readers? Don't quit the house of horrors, you'll miss him when you've gone?'

She had forgotten misdirected anger could be so satisfying.

Imogen gets up from the bench and crosses the narrow floor to stand beside her. Wordlessly, she opens her arms and presses Nan's head downwards to fit the cummerbund of skin between loosening towel and falling breasts.

She doesn't doubt the comforting purpose of the gesture, but that chaste zone of flesh is so crowded with complications, it's a relief when the time comes to pull away.

'I wasn't trying to deny what you've been through, Nan. But consistency isn't necessarily part of the kit. If you talk to abused women,' Nan's lips tighten, 'which is a label no one welcomes, one of the worst things, sometimes worse than the actual violence, is the ambivalence. You don't stop loving or missing, you just feel implicated.'

Now she sees the source of that sudden insight. Not

such an uncanny access to others' souls after all. No X-ray specs. It's Imogen's own entrails which are twitching.

Nan walks over to the pail of water and releases a few seconds of steam from the volcanic rock. That slight delay before the heat bounces off the ceiling.

'But Jack didn't hit you.'

Imogen smiles, acknowledging that the tables have been turned, perhaps also that this is what she intended.

'No, not that at least. He had his share of undesirable habits, but he wasn't physically violent.'

'What was he, then?'

Imogen returns to her side of the sauna and stretches out on her back.

'Oh, an egotist, like all politicians, and a bit of a shit, that goes with the territory too. A black cynic, but without the usual pastel undercoat. No animal-loving, flower-sniffing tendencies in our Jack. Probably a depressive, clinically, and as convincing as depressives usually are.' She smiles. 'Sounds a bundle of laughs, doesn't he? I wasn't always this clear-headed. Hindsight's a wonderful thing.

'We met in Paris. I know: such a cliché. If I never see another documentary about '68 I'll die happy. I was levering up cobblestones with an umbrella spike, I looked up and there he was. Tear gas, CRS snatch squads, and Jack strolling through the middle. Came up to me and suggested if I wanted a souvenir I'd be better chipping a corner off Notre Dame.'

Nan knows she should be wearing an answering smile.

'I don't expect you to understand. I was *there* and it's hard to remember how different it was. The contrast control was turned way too high, on everything. You were either a revolutionary or a capitalist running-dog. One side of the barricades or the other. And then there was Jack: no one knew what to make of him. I always liked that. You've never seen a sharper operator. Born in a smoke-filled room. Taught me a lot. Well, taught me that it was going to take more than a sex-discrimination statute and lessons in clitoral stimulation to set the world to rights.

'Maggie spotted him first and I never trod on her toes. It wasn't supposed to matter, but nobody was fooled. He was ringed all right, free to fly as long as he came home to mamma. God knows what I'd've done if he'd chosen me up front. Not that it was ever on the cards. Couldn't take the competition. Behind all that cool he was red-hot to make a name for himself. Didn't want it to be Mr Imogen Reiss.'

Something about the confessional makes Nan uneasy; it's too fluent, almost a party piece. Not that there's no feeling there, rather that it makes its appearance bang on cue. Given the touchiness of the subject matter, this polished performance is a surprise; unless of course she's rehearsed it on the analyst's couch, a diverting alternative to aromatherapy or an hour in the flotation tank. Maybe that's why she's addressing the ceiling.

'It was years before we went to bed, but from the day we met it was a foregone conclusion. I remember going on a course in Pitlochry of all places: group dynamics, some visiting American. First day, they got us together, all strangers, and asked us to pick out one person we were attracted to. Just walk in, look around, make your choice. It was like Noah's ark. Everyone found their matching pair: only children, kids who'd grown up without fathers, mother's little helpers from big families. I picked a bossy elder sister who hated her mother. Frightening. Maybe Jack and I had more in common than I care to think.

'We were never cosy together, no pet names or sharing the same fork, the only way to survive was to be as emotionally insulated as he was. I was amazed I could do it; not just do it, enjoy it too. Obviously there was something a little pathological about it, but it had its advantages: no post-coital childhood memories for a start. Can't tell you how sick I was of listening to them talking about their mothers. I've heard every variation of filial trauma, and believe you me, there are depressingly few. Jack just wasn't interested in boiling himself down to the Oedipal soup. And he could be very funny. We had a good time, as far as you could tell with a man who never smiled. And then it just got too late. The whole thing was so fitted into our lives, we couldn't have stopped it without everyone noticing something was up. Would have been like a divorce. Probably two divorces. So we carried on. And after that it really was like a marriage. Sometimes there was sex, sometimes there wasn't, some-times we didn't talk properly for weeks on end. Obviously when I married Peter we packed it in; I first took up with Peter to *help* me pack it in, but he was setting up the practice night and day . . .'

Nan is fascinated. She never knew adultery could be so grey. Nor had she guessed at Imogen's own dishwater streak. Is this what the feminist rhetoric comes down to? Compounding betrayal in the name of routine? She feels a nudge of cruelty, or perhaps a desire to administer aversion therapy, in which case you could call it kindness; an impulse to punish her fallen heroine, this woman so careless of her own best interests, and of other women's needs. She wants to tell her: you know this man, your lover? well, it turns out you didn't know him at all.

Imogen closes her eyes, speaking slowly as the thoughts assemble.

'Of course I knew it was his ink. I thought they'd used it to pile on the pressure.'

She shakes her head. 'No, it's just circumstantial, it doesn't make sense. I wouldn't put anything past Jack, but I just don't see what he stood to gain.'

'That depends who he was blackmailing.'

Imogen opens her eyes. 'At least now we know it wasn't me.'

Something Nan has been trying not to think about glimmers in the shadows.

'I think we probably know more than that.'

The sauna door is pulled open and a man's bulk blocks the shaft of light. Nan doesn't bother looking up, assuming that the intruder will withdraw in embarrassment.

'Well, this is an unexpected one.'

Later her memory will return to the moment the door opened, running and rerunning the sequence in her head, trying to spot the troubling detail, to focus her blurred sense of excitement, but at this moment she registers nothing out of the ordinary. He's grinning down at her as she hitches the towel a little more securely around her breasts, his eyes following her fingers as she tucks the fabric tighter. It's her discomfort he's enjoying, not the peep show.

Imogen, just beyond his sightline, disdains any adjustment. Her voice, when she speaks, is deeper than usual.

'Wednesday is Ladies Day, which means you're off-limits, pal.'

He's about to reply, but Nan gets there first.

'I'm afraid he owns the joint.'

Cal pantomimes a leer.

'Which buys me the odd perk.'

It's the first time they've met since the opening of the tapas bar. He seems heavier, unless it's just the effect of exchanging his tailor's *trompe-l'œil* for the merciless candour of those squash whites.

'La Megratta a member of my club: I'm honoured. Hope you dropped my name and got a discount on our extortionate fees.'

'Imogen's the member. Post Office wages don't run to health clubs, however hefty the discount.'

The fringe is held out of his eyes by a towelling sweatband so ridiculous it's almost endearing. She reminds herself that buffoonery and menace aren't necessarily mutually exclusive.

'Well, you know the answer to that one. I've told you: there's always a place for you in my kitchens. What say we meet up later in the week and I make you an offer you can't refuse? Give Theresa a ring; fix up a time.'

When he's gone, Imogen tilts her head in a parody of demure enquiry. Nan starts to bluster, at first purely for comic effect, but the more emphatic her denials, the less chimerical the possibility becomes.

'Anyway I couldn't work for a killer.'

She doesn't know why she said it. It certainly puts paid to the hilarity.

'You think he killed Jack?'

She twitches her shoulders.

'I don't know, but it looks like it was him or Danny MacLeod and I really don't believe Danny is capable of it.'

She pauses to consider the truth of this statement.

'Or I don't want to. I suppose it might not be either of them. Could have been something else altogether. But a blackmailer who winds up dead: it's an interesting coincidence.'

Imogen's face is grave.

'If you're right about Jack and he knows you've made the connection, whichever one of them it is, he's going to be pretty anxious to get his hands on that letter.

Something to bear in mind next time you get offered a job in catering, or the member for Clyde West starts whispering sweet nothings in your ear. In your place I'd give them both a wide berth.'

Like much incontrovertible advice, she doesn't seriously consider it.

'I was thinking there might be something in Jack's papers to narrow the field. Do you think Maggie . . .'

Imogen shakes her head.

'Too late. She burned the lot.'

'What? Why?'

Imogen stands up, readjusting her towel, tightening the toga into a sheath.

'Didn't have room for it, I suppose. This is Maggie we're talking about. She doesn't need a why. Motivation's pretty superfluous if you're not going to remember what you were doing in five minutes' time.'

She presses her face to the porthole in the door, peering at the clock on the outside wall.

'I promised Michelle she'd be away by seven: I'd better get going. You too, unless you want another encounter with Fatboy Macleod.'

In bed that night, leaning against Catriona's padded head-board, thinking about the moment the sauna door opened, remembering the elasticated sweatband, those soft, slightly cushioned thighs beneath the whiter-than-white shorts, all the embarrassing details that failed to disturb his equilibrium, the thing that's been bothering her finally sharpens into focus. Not once, not when he opened the door, not when Nan referred to her by name, not even when she spoke to him, did Cal so much as attempt to look at Imogen. Now, why should that be?

U nusually, she meets the postman on her way out in the morning: a tiny man yet perfectly proportioned, as if he's simply shrunk in the wash. Seeing her uniform, he's thunderstruck; evidently it has never occurred to him that Post Office employees get their letters delivered too. He seems to regard it as a coincidence on a par with doppelgangers and being born under the same planetary configuration. On discovering that she's based in George Square, he works his way through the payroll in the hope of finding acquaintances in common. Eventually she lies: yes, she knows Wullie. Now he wants to know if Mrs Wullie has dropped the wean yet. Improvising something about being just back from holiday, she is past him and safely on the stair when he asks her name. She makes a mental note to be sure to leave the flat ten minutes earlier in future. He shuffles his sheaf of mail and hands her a long white envelope. Office stationery. Side opening. Self-sealing.

'One for you.'

She'd know those looped gs anywhere. Purple ink. Her fingers close on the stiff paper but she forces herself to wait until she gets to the bus stop. A random discipline, a compromise between the compulsion to tear it open there and then and the possibility of carrying it around with her, untouched, in perpetuity.

Standing at the roadside, she holds the envelope between finger and thumb probing the inside with the first two fingers of her other hand, next she turns it upside down, taps the open end against her palm. The bus whistles past leaving a lungful of thick, sweet diesel exhaust. In the gutter, a quintet of pigeons are pecking at a pool of sick. Not quite believing it, she puts the envelope to her lips and blows. No mistake. It's empty.

The policeman at the door has lacquered apple cheeks distending a smooth polyurethane mask of skin, an effect inanimate yet daunting, like the laughing sailor before a coin tickles him into mirth. Smiling her most diluted smile, eyes reflecting his depthless stare, she has the distinct and quite irrational impression that he recognises her. His response to the name is too neutral; the tone in which he repeats it to the man with the clipboard needlessly amplified. Yet even after all this, when Danny appears, briskly preoccupied, red rose pinned to his lapel as if he's some lonelyheart on a blind date, it's with the plastic polis she spins the invisible skein of affinity. Without challenging the MP, he manages to exude scepticism; ever a risk, she's observed, when the man of the people meets his public. As usual, Danny doesn't notice, or chooses not to.

Having beckoned her over the threshold into the warmth of the hall, he's on the point of clipping the laminated pass to her shirt when, with a lopsided smile, he presses it into her palm instead. Half-way down the corridor a middle-aged woman is staring at him, mute but peremptory, her ragged fall of grey hair brittle as winter laburnum. Fleetingly, without a ripple in the rest of his face, his left eyelid closes in a wink.

It is the time between times that is fruitful in adultery. She now recognises that their hours together will unfold largely independently of human will. Things happen, sometimes dictated by circumstances he hasn't confided, less often as a consequence of her own agenda, but mostly it feels as if neither is exercising control. They meet, and it's vaguely disappointing or, occasionally, vivid with a pleasure which, through unpreparedness, she's unable to appreciate until afterwards. There's no time for self-consciousness; reflection is a luxury which doesn't fit their schedule of meals in Italian restaurants where they know the service is quick, drinks in bars which are not quite his sort of place but not different enough to make him conspicuous, a new rendezvous every time, just in case he's recognised, and always within a ten-minute drive of Catriona's flat.

Alone again, Nan retells these meetings, interprets the missed glances and unexpected tenderness, does her grueing at remembered embarrassments, and returns with her expectations subtly adjusted, wariness tempered, intimacy reinforced. A week of absence offers more developments than a daily tryst. In all, they've met half a dozen times.

Aware of the rival claims on his attention, she rations her thoughts of him, aiming for emotional parity, but even when he's not in her mind there are moments when the newsprint loses focus and her attention is caught by changes of pressure in her internal plumbing, a sudden plunging of the gut. Objects detach themselves from their surroundings with preternatural clarity, impressing on her consciousness with obscure significance. Routine is plagued by minor disruptions. A forkful of salad seems almost chemically enhanced, the unfamiliar dressing under her nose disturbingly evocative, of what she couldn't say. She wakes at twelve minutes past five every morning, nerve ends straining, system racing. Being so far from love, she finds it interesting, this parodic infatuation, the riot of the senses, excitement's *coup d'état*.

How it works for him, she doesn't know. At first she suspected his affection was the generous overspill from a marital loving cup, making no distinction between bed and board. Then she put it down to manners, all form and no content: he was simply housetrained. The final possibility she does not allow herself to consider.

The Clyde East byelection count is being held in the Stour Hall, a hideous marriage of cod classicism and mercantile flash, mismatched to excite the jaded palates of the late nineteenth century. Following the left-hand stem of the dividing staircase up to the gallery, she is amazed at the profusion of marble: marble of toothsome treacly browns and cinder toffee yellows; marble from the abattoir, purple and fat-veined as beef on the butcher's slab; marble like cracked leather and cabinetmaker's veneer; white marble with lithograph scorings; marble like capillaries under the microscope, like cappuccino froth, like biblical boiling seas, like vast skies over eighteenth-century landscapes. Trestle tables have been set up along the length of the hall below, where volunteers are opening the black boxes and smoothing out clusters of voting slips. Ham-fisted students and arthritic do-gooders develop the deftness of bank-tellers before her eyes. Danny, now wearing a red rosette, is leaning against one of the trestles talking to the woman with the tumbleweed hair. A portly gent in mustard tweeds waves him away too brusquely to be ignorant of the MP's identity. Danny shrugs pointedly and moves a couple of inches further from the votes.

The woman is talking earnestly, head tilted, brow scored. Even at this distance, it's obvious she's sexually interested. Odd to have knowledge of a man you cannot publicly own. The brain makes sense of it by separating the clothed from the unclothed figure. The one walking around the hall is a stranger, someone whose eyes she can't quite meet. The one she encounters in bed, with his cuddling and his candour, is a revelation to her, but not, if she's honest, as exciting as the prize bull down there with his red rosette. The irony is that he can afford to trust; by some tacit agreement she doesn't remember striking she is the one who takes responsibility for his marriage, she makes sure their loveplay doesn't become the real thing. Secure in this knowledge, he's unstinting in his attentions; she is the one who is giving short change.

From beneath her in the lobby comes the sound of a fracas, muffled cursing and the grunts of unaccustomed exertion. She leans over the balustrade in time to see the tweedy official put on a surprising turn of speed to join the policeman in roughhousing a donkey-jacketed intruder out of the main entrance. Through the commotion she glimpses Brendan's desperado stubble. There seems to be a secondary disturbance in the doorway itself, a chorus of jeering is severed as the door slams shut. Democracy: one. Anarchism: nil.

Danny comes to find her, muttering an apology for his absence; she knows how it is. And of course she does. His next words are hijacked by a shout from the floor below where the Labour candidate is grinning up at them. He's swapped his slipover for a new suit so stiff she wonders if he's removed the hanger.

'That's the last of the votes in. They're talking about half-one for a result.'

Danny acknowledges the news with a thumbs-up then, for her benefit, rolls his eyes.

'And it's been half-one at Stour Hall since sonny down there was toiling to tell his big hand from his little hand. Day before yesterday, by the looks of him.'

Her eye follows the suit and its wearer as they pace up and down the tables, almost in step.

'What are his chances?'

He shrugs. 'I reckon his chances of needing his shoes resoled by half-past one are pretty high. And yes, he'll be making his maiden speech before the recess. It's not tellers you want in this constituency, it's a weighbridge. He'll maybe lose us a few hundred votes, but who's counting? They'd elect an inflatable banana if we sprayed it red . . .' He blows out a sigh. 'I earned my seat with fifteen years in the union, arguing the toss over every toilet break, every case of whitefinger. The only time in his life Little Lord Foy's got his hands dirty is when he dressed up like the thing from outer space and dumped a radioactive growbag outside the Scottish Office. Know what he does for a living? Runs a site of Special Scientific Interest. Designated wetland. Otherwise known as a stank behind the Upwell Flats that's got the maws up to high doh in case their weans end up drowning in it. A pro- fessional leech-preserver, that's what the electorate have put their crosses by. A tree hugger. Christ knows what they'd have made of him in the yards.'

He doesn't often talk about that life so she's surprised to find it brandished as a benchmark of authenticity.

'What would they make of you these days?'

It's one of those jokes that teeters on the edge of seriousness, threatening to roll back on its sponsor.

'No bad for a burner. Six bars in his place of work. Gets paid to bore the arse off folk about politics, which he always did anyway. Gets himself on telly. Hangs about with fast women.'

At times like this she finds earnestness the most effec- tive sabotage.

'Do you ever miss it?'

For a moment, seduced by his own legend, he almost acquiesces; but his honesty is one of the things she likes about him.

'Naw. No really. I wouldn't say it to many but they were ripe for the picking. They talk about overmanning now; there's no comparison. Men coming on the back-shift for a kip, going home again, up all day, back into work for their shut-eye. There was a guy, Wiggy, he was a caulker to trade but fancied himself as a barber, he'd picked it up hanging about his da's shop when he was a kid. The Vidal Sassoon of the shipwrights' toilets. Everyone knew Wiggy's cubicle; he had his mirror, scissors, clippers, something for the bloody weekend if you needed it. Fifty pence a time. He was run off his feet. Still drawing his pay. Never touched a caulking hammer from one month to the next. The gaffer would have had to be deaf, daft and blind not to notice. And it wasn't just Wiggy; there was Cremola Tam the sweetie man, and Senga in the office who sold cigarettes, wee Matty with his library of dirty books . . .'

She sees the shadow out of the corner of her eye but the only explanation is so improbable her brain just doesn't take it in. Danny seems to know by instinct, wheeling round, reaching for his portable phone as if it's a six-gun. His assailant is quicker. Legs find purchase on the MP's suited back, leaving hands free to wrest the mobile from his grasp. Struggling under the boy's tarantula grip, Danny staggers, half spins one way, then back again, twisting like a hanged man, his face old and effortful and angry. Then, with surprising energy, he's moving backwards. There's a jarring as his passenger's vertebrae make contact with the oxblood pillar. Suddenly Danny doesn't look old any more. Turning, he's headed towards the balustrade, his body already tensing for some final push. Sean seems paralysed, willpower gone, eyes fixed on the vacant air just the other side of the marble rail, clinging to Danny's shoulders like a toddler riding piggyback.

Without conscious thought, Nan reaches out, grabs the short black pigtail at the base of the shaven skull, and yanks. He squeals like a puppy, a yelp of pure pain, reflexively loosing his grip. Lightened of the burden, Danny turns and grabs him by the shoulders, the slender joints slipping his hold, leaving him clutching twisted handfuls of canvas jacket. The seams cut into Sean's armpits so that his arms dangle like a marionette's. The boy is pinioned, immobilised. In the set of Danny's body, the taut sinews of his neck, she recognises the stark efficiency of violence, but for a second she can't work out what he's about to do. The head pulls back, gathering strength, and then she knows.

Sean is limp as a rag in his grip, almost acquiescent, the injury a foregone conclusion. In that single expanded moment she takes everything in, searching the options: balls, shins, solar plexus, back of the knee, the tender crook of the elbow. Sean's body blocks all access. She anticipates the crunching cartilage, the blossoming capillaries as the delicate bones in that porcelain skull cave in. Her fingers close on the empty air, and before she knows it she's screaming, a banshee note of protest startling to her own ears. But also familiar.

Surprise drains the moment of its danger but Sean seems too dazed to take advantage, as if his mind's momentum has taken him through the impact and beyond, into concussion. Belatedly he registers the reprieve and stumbles across to where Brendan, Max and the others are watching. At the other end of the balcony three security guards are lumbering towards them, torn between dignity, urgency and the effects of a heavy tobacco habit, the vibrations of their approach tickling her shoes. The anarchists disappear down the staircase.

'Everything OK, Mr MacLeod?'

Danny jerks his head towards the stair. 'Make sure they're out of here.'

His diaphragm is heaving under the light wool jacket. To her surprise the shoulder seams are intact. *Beware the streetfighter in the Austin Reed lounge suit.* He flexes his shoulders, stretches his neck, lips grimacing in a smile, or an apology, or some combination of the two.

'Build-up of lactic acid. It'll go in a minute.'

She wants to smile back but her features have forgotten the social niceties. Her sternum is taut, a steadily increasing pressure on her ribcage. She spans her fingers across the ridges of bone.

'I could do with a drink.'

He nods and makes for the staircase, then unexpectedly turns, backing her, too, into one of the marble pillars, but slowly enough to avoid the suspicion of aggression. His weight crushes her; beneath the discomfort it's oddly satisfying, a purging embrace, bone to bone, destructive, self-destructive, who knows? His breathing calms and then starts to gather pace, she feels his erection just as he pulls away.

'Let's get that drink.'

In the deserted hospitality room a series of red paper cloths have been drawing-pinned to the long trestle table. There are party nibbles still in their plastic compartments, tiny sailor's knot pretzels studded with salt, yellow crackers baked in the shape of playing-card suits, morsels of starch yielding texture but no taste. For the sweet of tooth the table offers two bumper tins of family assortment biscuits, iced rings and jammy dodgers and bourbon creams segregated in their indigo cellophane pens, a wee municipal treat. Danny pours two plastic tumblers of whisky, adding water to the first, then topping up the dilution with more whisky.

'I don't feel good about you seeing that.'

She is reminded again how illusory intimacy can be.

'If I hadn't, you might have killed him.'

He looks at her disbelievingly, but an exaggerated disbelief, a beginner in mime class.

She holds his gaze. 'If he'd gone over that balcony he'd have broken his neck.'

'What are you havering about?'

She grasps his sleeve, spilling his drink slightly.

'Danny.'

He laughs one of his platform laughs.

'Jeez, you must've led a sheltered life if you took that for a rammy. Look, Nan, I'll do you a deal: I promise I'll not try giving you tips on the perfect soufflé, so long as you don't kid on you can tell a butterknife from a chib. It's a hard city, my darling, the nasty boys play rough, but it's still playing. If it'd been anything else I would have made sure you weren't around.'

Man the protector, mighty, almighty, the one you talk to in the dark last thing at night, under the covers, the one you let inside your head, knowing that if you're a good girl, and you are a good girl, he'll keep you safe from harm. A nice bedtime story: sometimes she even wishes she believed in it herself.

There are moments when she feels bad about not telling him. After all, there is a possibility of damage to his career, if not a very real one; or at least, not real to Nan. Her imagination can't get beyond stepping into the dock, like a film, a monochrome weepie where even the barmaids speak RADA. After that the scene just dissolves. Fade to black.

'You don't have to be a man to understand the basics of violence.'

It takes him a second to catch her meaning.

'Christ on a bike, I forgot about the battered sisters. I didn't mention one-legged lesbians, laboratory beagles or the disappearing rainforest either. Thank God it's only you; your pal Imogen would have had me singing soprano by now.'

She was wondering when it was coming. Never a

meeting goes by without him mentioning 'your pal Imogen'. He takes it for granted that she is poisoning Nan against him whereas, in fact, since the day of the funeral she hasn't said a critical word. The student reminiscences have stopped dead, no more highlights from his career as sexual climber, hurter, and all-round shit, no arch references to the quarter-century age gap. Not that Nan has done anything to reassure him on these points. Secretly she enjoys his uneasiness, it goes a little way towards redressing the defining imbalance of their relationship, that perpetual disclaimer, the weight of a wedding ring.

Following his gaze, she turns to find a couple of Conservative Party helpers staring from the doorway. His face is a gargoyle of weariness.

'Anything I can do for you, ladies?'

Twitching embarrassed smiles, the women move on.

Danny picks up the whisky bottle. 'Let's find somewhere with a little privacy.'

It's a cleaner's cupboard: a coppice of brooms and mops, a jawbox sink and a grooved wooden shelf supporting kettle, mugs, caterer's drum of instant coffee powder and a greying bottle of milk. She hoists herself up alongside them, reflecting that she never used to spend so much time shut in confined spaces with members of the opposite sex. Only when she's seated is there room for him to step inside and close the door. She's reaching over to flick on the light when he checks her; while there's no one he'd rather be in a janitor's press with, he'd sooner the whole world didn't know about it. A cloudy light filters through the small frosted-glass window, just enough for her to reassemble his features from the concentrations of shadow. He gropes for the mugs and pours two slugs of whisky.

'Slainte.'

They clink pottery.

'Thought about you this week.'

Despite the darkness he catches her satirical smirk.

'I mean for a reason. On top of all the other times in the week I think about you.'

It seems there's a rumour in the Commons tearoom about the Post Office. They're talking about a new bill in the autumn, which means redundancies before the end of the year. Last in, first out. Just in time for Christmas probably. He seems disappointed by her silence.

She shrugs. 'I'm not banking on being around by then anyway.'

'Where do you think you're going?'

It's his incredulity that irks her, the absolute certainty that he has the measure of her life. Perhaps that's why she mentions the job offer.

He doesn't like it but is canny enough to focus his dissatisfaction on the reduced amount of time they'll have together if she's spending weekends and evenings waitressing.

'I didn't say it was waitressing.'

His eyes narrow, as if she laid that trap for him.

'What then?'

'Running a place.'

She wonders if Cal would be willing to trust her that far. 'One of Callum Macleod's brasseries.'

He becomes as distant as is possible in a cleaner's cupboard. She feels the old nervousness, the impulse to backtrack, to make it all right.

'I bumped into him at the health club he owns. Imogen took me for a sauna. He walked in by mistake.'

At the mention of Imogen's name the shadows tighten.

'Look before you buy?'

He pours himself another whisky without replenishing her mug.

'Christ Nan, you're that wet behind the ears they could sell you by the bottle. Doesn't it seem a wee bit unusual that a flyboy, an Olympic standard wide-o like Callum Macleod would walk into a steamroom, shake you by the hand, and offer you a job running a high-class washeteria for his drug funds without bothering to make sure you can boil an egg?'

'He's seen me cook.'

She knows immediately that she's said too much. All those pauses, those times conversation died on its feet and she pulled back from using Cal Macleod to revive it, all that restraint wasted. Now she has to explain, keeping the details hazy, skimming over the night at the tapas bar. Even with the bowdlerised version, Danny's not happy.

'Any other plans up your sleeve? Have you not thought of opening Stornoway's first nudist beach? There might be more of a future in it.'

'It's got to be more fulfilling than redirecting tax demands all day.'

This is lighting the touchpaper to a row, and they don't really know each other well enough to fight. She dampens the fuse with a downbeat murmur: it probably won't come to anything and, anyway – now a sly note of teasing – he's only annoyed because it turns out she knows someone he doesn't.

It's one of their private jokes, a reference to the wee men in bunnets who rise from behind their copies of the *Daily Record* to girn about roadworks or dog mess or all-seater football stands whenever he walks into a bar. If he doesn't smile, at least the set of his mouth relaxes a little, he runs a finger along her jaw like a housekeeper checking for dust.

'Steer clear of him, Nan, you wouldn't enjoy being a gangster's moll. Flushing your facepowder down the cludgie every time the polis turn up at the door: it's not what you want out of life.'

He starts to massage the back of her neck, one-handed, absentmindedly, fingertips straying into her hair. Electricity, or perhaps just the whisky, flutters in her gut.

'Danny, take it from me, he's not interested.' He raises a sceptical eyebrow. 'I don't think I've ever seen him without a chaperone: Imogen, his staff, Jack Ibster . . .'

For a moment, his hand hesitates.

'I thought you were just keeping your pal Imogen company at the funeral.'

'I was. I only met him the once. Didn't take to him, couldn't really tell you why.'

His fingers shift to her shoulder.

'You weren't the only one. Put him in a popularity contest with Pol Pot and the Boston Strangler and you couldn't guarantee he'd be placed. We were the Jekyll and Hyde of the City Chambers for a time. He'd kick their feet out from under them, I'd offer them a cigarette. Ran rings round the oppo. Didn't know if they were on this earth or Fuller's.'

He moves down, working the skin with practised fingers, closing in.

'Hardly saw him after I left the council. The odd ribbon-cutting, piss-ups for international cooperation and harmony, party conference once a year.'

Stealthily, as if she might not notice, he starts to unfasten her shirt.

'You know: five minutes' chat about Celtic's chances in the Cup, another five bellyaching about those clowns on the executive, then you change partners and do it all over again.'

She shivers. He pauses, enquiringly, then slips the final button.

'Jack's big problem was he couldn't be nice. Never get anywhere if you're not prepared to press the flesh a little.'

One hand drops to her waist, expertly negotiating the snares of skirt and underwear.

'Cultivated a reputation as the rudest bastard in politics and then wondered why he couldn't get a safe seat.'

She opens her mouth to ask something but her concentration is starting to slip.

'Tried it on with me in the early days. Soon packed that in. Once he knew what he was up against.' He grunts, shifting slightly. 'He was choosy about his enemies. Never upset anyone who could do him any real damage.'

'He obviously miscalculated once.'

As he unbuttons his flies she instinctively pulls his shirt out of the way.

'So you've decided to cooperate?'

She lets go of the fabric and lifts her hands in a gesture of renunciation.

'Who do you think killed him?'

He laughs, catching her wrists.

'A political assassination? Is that what you're getting at? The Militant, maybe? Dial M for murder? My money's on the Situationists. Had to be a message. I mean, arse about face in a dustbin: that's what I call making a point.'

She's not expecting the force of his entry. There are too many teeth in his kiss and her wrists are hurting with the pressure of his grip. He's hardly moving, yet the intensity of it surpasses anything she's yet experienced with him, every nerve-end receiving, sensations so unfamiliar she's not even sure they're sexual. His breathing is noisy but preoccupied, different from the histrionic gasps lovers use to communicate. She strains against him in an attempt to change position, but his hands hold her pinioned. In a dustbin. The implications of the remark

191

rise to the surface only to sink again, swamped by another priority, a greater claim on her attention, teasing, elusive, but unmistakable. She's resisting him now, muscles tensed, trying to fix her own coordinates, to pin it down, but he's working against her, moving faster, intent on his own rhythm. She holds out, an act of sheer will, tuning ever more precisely to the signal, hardly breathing in her fear of losing it. Then it takes over and she's talking, shouting, she doesn't know what but they're both past caring, the struggle suddenly cooperation, the world rushing towards her; anger, pleasure, suspicion, greed, all sucked into the roaring black hole of feeling.

He's almost himself again by the time her climax passes. She stares at him with unseeing eyes as his lips frame an odd smile.

'So tell me, Nan: who are you killing?'

'Where first?'

A silly question, but no sillier than the expedition itself. A shopping trip around the designer quarter undertaken without a fiver to her name. Imogen must know this, so to remind her of the fact would be a solecism, social one-downmanship, inverted boasting. Through the eye of the needle: no problem. Inside the portals of Versace is a different proposition.

That was the genesis of the outing. The existence of a store which keeps its door barred against the casual shopper. *Please ring for personal attention.* It's Maggie who buys there, Imogen tags along as chaperone, her scandalised intakes of breath adding savour to the widow's extravagance. More or less the function which Nan is now to perform. Nevertheless she's been looking forward to it. There's an implication of intimacy. Behind the exotic tourism of spaces normally closed to her is a more familiar prospect, the boredom of shopping, and behind boredom lurk the flattering assumptions of routine. Acquaintances may share a pizza or even a steambath, but only friends trudge round the mid-season sales. Especially with a toddler. Saul's childminder has selfishly chosen to keep a dental appointment and, beneath that formidable unflappability, Imogen is not pleased.

They start off in the Italian Centre, moving between hushed environments so underpopulated Nan finds herself mocking in whispers, tiptoeing over the carpet, awed by the humming breath of the airconditioning and the sacerdotal poise of the enamelled staff. Oblivious to intimidation, Imogen points out garments she finds particularly pleasing or particularly absurd, eye-rolling over the return of fashions consigned to the jumble twenty years ago. The names of these shops have entered the language, each now a shorthand for a particular socio-economic sub-group, but this is the first time Nan has seen the clothes en masse. Joking apart, she finds the best of them disconcertingly beautiful: unfussy, clean-lined, opulent with understatement. A simplicity only the rich can afford.

However rapidly their acquaintance is consolidating into friendship, for all their demonstrable pleasure in each other's company, Nan and Imogen are separated by what is euphemised as 'lifestyle': economic disparity presented as a consumer choice. Imogen belongs to the world of the three-hundred-pound cardigan, for Nan this sort of money is a biennial foreign holiday or two months' rent. Visiting Montpelier, opening the fridge in search of milk to pacify the bitter espresso or acrid Darjeeling (Imogen has a fondness for palate-stripping flavours), she has found vacuum-sealed chanterelle mushrooms long past their sell-by; a side of smoked salmon darkening at the margins; half-finished bottles of corkless champagne, flat as smalltalk. Nan has the unnerving tolerance of those who have lived under the volcano, but even she finds herself stiffening at such conspicuous waste. Theirs is an airport-lounge affinity, the improbable meeting of alien cultures, generating a subtly insistent awareness of difference which is, at least for Nan, close to the self-consciousness of courtship. These encounters with Imogen, two or three times a week now, are like seduction at one remove, charged with the strange parasexual excitement of female friendship, the heightened senses taking their cue from the music in the steaming coffee shop, the delicious pungency of the freshly painted storefront, the rush-hour glitter on frost-crisped leaves. Like seduction, it is the excitement of deferment, the promise of things to come, but what things? In Nan's grammar, potential is a masculine noun.

With the qualified exception of Althea, whose weekly pay packet clouded her status, it's been years since Nan had women friends. Her only template is the intensity of adolescent confidences, those two-hour telephone calls the morning after the fumbled date, screaming with laughter, blood surging with the endorphins of affirmation and relief. It was always an ambiguous intensity, those interchangeable spotty youths both mere pretext and the point, a rite of passage so traumatic that this elaborate feminine purification was needed to take away the madness before re-entering the world. Kilner broke the pattern. At first, flattered by his need for exclusivity, domestic *omertà* seemed a small sacrifice. What for her was entirely separate, as purely girlish a ritual as booking into the hairdresser's for copycat perms or singing along to the Sunday-night top forty, he saw as betrayal. And in so far as no experience was complete until dissected and reshaped, its current safely earthed, he had a point. Perhaps this explains the unreality of so much of her marriage. Later, of course, the injunction to silence was an irrelevance; by then, there were things that she could never confide.

Mid-afternoon they enter a shop where Imogen is a regular customer, or at least a weel-kent face. Snapping out of their anorectic disdain, the assistants are friendly and unexpectedly broadly-spoken. The celebrity shopper talks to them naturally enough, but with a telling economy, her thermostat on low heat, and they accept that this is as it should be, slipping away to return bearing coffee cups of vitreous china with Italian almond biscuits in their tissue-paper husks tucked into the saucers. Amaretti. Nan used to serve them at the restaurant but stopped on account of the yuppie contingent, the children who grew flushed on three glasses of wine but drove the Porsche home anyway, who developed a craze for setting the wrappers alight to see the flaming cylinder rising under the stately propulsion of its own thermals and then floating down, transmuted, like an autumn leaf.

'What do you think?'

Nan sets her lips and nods in an expression of approval some way short of enthusiasm. Imogen puts it back on the rail. 'Lovat green looks terrific on redheads.'

'*For me* you mean?'

Imogen flicks her gaze up to the ceiling. 'If I bought it they'd arrest me under the Trades Descriptions Act.'

Nan is flustered, unsure whether they're still pretending, window shopping in the warm, or whether the liberal conscience of the tabloid press really doesn't know how little the Royal Mail pays its Postmen Higher Grade. There remains a remote possibility that she is offering to buy her something, an impulsive gesture from the haves to the have-nots, a redistribution of the wealth she's saving on Michelle's visit to the dentist. But possibility is dwarfed by the embarrassment of presumption, the infinitely-expanding horror of being wrong. She reaches for a distraction.

'Now *this* would suit you.'

Imogen takes the hanger from her hand, fingers the fabric, then turns the coy cardboard label business side up.

'Nice bit of schmutter. Bit steep for art silk, but I like the cut and I need something for Venice. Might be a bit cold for the evenings, though. What d'you think?'

'Search me.'

Imogen dislikes these small snags in the conversational fabric.

'I thought you'd know. Didn't you say you had Italian family?'

That's right, she said it. But why? Why *Italian* of all things? (Not too many redhead signorinas around, either.) The identity supermarket has aisle upon aisle of options: spicy flavours of Russian or Pole, wholesome strains of Saxon and Scandinavian, cordon bleu leftovers from the Auld Alliance, and a full range of domestic produce, Celt, Pict, Viking, Glasgow Gael. Pick an ancestor from the genetic stew: an eighth, a thirty-second, a sixty-fourth, it makes no odds. Instant definition. Just look at Imogen. Nine times out of ten it's gender that comes up trumps but, challenged on her Englishness, she'll claim kinship with the lost tribe. Unless class happens to be the issue, in which case she suddenly rediscovers her workerist roots.

Nan shrugs.

'My grandfather, but I never knew him: he died before I was born. My mother reinvented herself.'

That much at least is true. A trait that seems to run in the family.

Kilner was a good Catholic boy from County Cork, via Liverpool. He used the withdrawal method the first time. She didn't know what he was playing at. Like finding yourself in an Edna O'Brien novel. Quaint really, a period detail to match the shark's fin Ford Zephyr he borrowed to take her on their second date. She had a cold. They sat in the snug drinking whisky macs while he explained the significance of the cladagh ring. She knew already but played dumb. It was a lazy way of flirting, slipping the scuffed band from finger to finger trying to achieve a fit, the nickel still warm from his calloused flesh; he'd been working on the lump, wielding the pickaxe until something better came along. He supported Celtic and knew the words to the rebel songs and refused to touch Guinness unless it was draught pulled in Dublin, and cursed – *Sweet Jesus* – with oaths that reeked faintly of incense, but he spoke Scouse like Ringo Starr. The bogus taint to his Irishness was one of those details she doggedly suppressed. Once recognised it became, like Rock Hudson's sexuality or the black-clad puppeteers skulking in the shadows on children's television, a persistent smear on the window of consciousness. For she was as much in love with the stick-on shamrock as he was, coveting his mythopoeic family history, his sepia stash of childhood images: schoolteachers still wearing the whittling corsetry and lisle stockings of a half-century before, strange urban saints who wound their soft bodies with chains then queued at the cheese counter behind Auntie Eileen, folk memories of famine, the derelict cow byre which once sheltered Captain Moonlight – or was it the Molly Maguires?

As often with this sort of bargain, what she acquired was not what she wanted but a persistent reminder of the lack of it. If his hold on the tricolour was tenuous, her grip was thrice removed. The alliance merely highlighted her isolation. Her lineage starts at birth; the family tree chopped for kindling; her father long gone; her social signals nonspecific, restaurant class. Beyond this, she's defined by those who get close enough to read the label, which at the moment means Imogen. In Nan's experience women run themselves down as a preemptive strike against envy, a socially acceptable way of eliciting compliments, an etiquette universally understood, but Imogen disdains such oriental indirection, crediting her own assets as objectively as she tallies her friends' and expecting others to be equally unblushing. At first, when praised, Nan would demur, to find her shrugging disclaimer received with a brief stare and a change of subject. These days she's learning to take her compliments straight and, as a result, finds her morning reflection looking out from the mirror more confidently.

'Nothing you fancy trying?'

Imogen has half a dozen hangers weighting her arm and seems to have reached the limits of strength, if not of acquisitiveness.

Nan shakes her head. 'I'll take a couple of things in for you if you like.'

But it seems changing-room rationing is strictly a chainstore habit. If she *really* wants to help, she can keep an eye on Saul. The child is going through a phase of intense concentration, newly awakened to the fascination of minor variation. His favourite toy is currently a model ambulance whose rear doors open to discharge a miniature stretcher and two moulded plastic paramedics. Thus equipped, he is hunkered down on the beechwood floor performing repetitive rituals of emergency.

Imogen's geometric fringe pokes through the curtain screening off the changing area.

'Nan, can you see if they've got the Nehru in a twelve?'

Eerily swift, the assistant is at Nan's side, handing her the jacket and casting a synthetically indulgent glance down at Saul's aubergine curls. Exempted from childcare, Nan penetrates the thick linen curtain. She is presented with a triptych of her friend in a russet shirt foregrounded by a rear view, naked from the waist down, a pearly layer of subcutaneous fat diffusing the dingy pigment like dappled cloud. Of course. They didn't just burn their bras, they threw their knickers away too. Time and gravity eventually rehabilitated the C-cup, but cotton briefs remain relatively inessential. Seeing Nan in the mirror, Imogen turns to receive the jacket, reproducing the buttocks in sextuplicate.

'Saul's not swinging on the bay tree yet?'

'Don't worry, he's being watched.'

As Imogen returns her attention to the clothes Nan experiences a rush of happiness so vivid it seems to rearrange the molecular structure of the air. As soon as she tries to fix the emotion it is gone but the memory remains, an atmospheric glint intensifying her unfocused sense of anticipation. Perhaps it's no more than the halogen spotlights, like the pallid gold of mist burned off by the morning sun, a technological gladness dazzling the surface of her mood. However steep the mark-up here compared with the high-street boutiques, they're all selling the same basic product. Transformation; the self, a life, made new. It is the promise Nan craves above all other, but what business has Imogen wanting it too? A woman who once performed an ideologically motivated striptease in the Garrick Club dining room is trying on capitalism's clothes, viewing herself in its doctored mirror, her high albedo borrowed from that halogen haze. Clumsily, as if still groping for the opening in that slubbed linen curtain, Nan grasps the absolute licence of a personality which embraces its inconsistency, not a conscripted identity in fear of the inspection parade. The reflections before her seem three different women: the left profile ill-assembled, a random trigonometry of nose, cheek, eye; the right presenting a near sinister contrast, purposeful, intent, the features like planets in alignment, exerting a powerful gravitational pull. And then, Cleopatra to these attendant presences, the full face, a droll forbearance confided to the glass. Regarding herself clear-eyed, assessing the effect without trying to alter it. No preening or tilting of the head, no comely positioning of the shoulders, deferring to no one, not even herself.

'What do you reckon?'

Nan nods. 'It's you.'

Clothes sense is a form of self-knowledge. Maybe that's

why she's never shopped in places with mirrors and fitting rooms. She didn't want anything to fit, she didn't want the Saturday girl to say how much it suited her. She didn't believe new clothes were worth the money, which was a way of saying she wasn't worth the clothes. Besides, dressing out of jumble sales and charity shops cut down on ambient attention from the opposite sex when she was out with Kilner, which saved her a lot of grief, although there was plenty to be going on with.

Imogen extracts a hanger from the bottom of her pile. 'Now you're here, try this on. Just to see.'

It's a green dress of light gabardine wool, the colour she believes is perfect for redheads. Nan finds the contrast a little obvious. Although she never wears it, she knows navy blue looks better.

Compliantly she peels off her jumper. No need to remove the jeans.

From behind, cool fingers lift the hair off her neck into an impressionistic bun. Imogen motions for Nan to hold the effect in place and her hands, now free, guide Nan's head until she, too, is confronting her reflection head-on.

'Get it cut, Nan.'

They've had the hair conversation only once before, but Imogen's low growl upgrades it to a regular wrangle. She has the skill of weaving off-the-cuff remarks into a sleeve of coded references, private jokes.

'I think you should see someone about this Delilah complex.'

Imogen sighs with luxurious exasperation. 'We're not talking about sapping your strength. I'm sure it's very effective, playing peek-a-boo through the split ends, but you don't have to come across like a teenage flirt to make the point that you're a woman.'

This hasn't been said before.

Imogen attributes the sudden chill in the cubicle to injured vanity.

'Oh God, I'm not impugning your choice of conditioner. I just mean you have an amazing face, Nan: why hide it? Peter was saying the other day, there's only two places you see faces that open to you, normally: in bed or on the couch.' She lifts her hand, curling the fingers to pluck this openness from the air. 'Absolutely present.'

'Are you suggesting I should sign on as one of his outpatients?'

Imogen's fingers relinquish their fruit.

'The other thing he said is that it's not suffocating. And that's right. It doesn't come across as neediness. Quite a trick, to be that up front and still keep something back.' The insinuating upper canine has acquired a smudge of damson lipstick. 'It's very powerful, passive aggression.'

She raises her eyebrows in acknowledgement of Nan's flick-knife glance, refusing the vitiating smile.

'You don't have to play those games, Nan. You don't need the people they work on.'

'Like you?'

Imogen shakes her head, her voice dropping to its lowest note.

'That's not what I value about you.'

Nan feels an uncoiling within her; the impossible promise, the benison of being known.

'How are you two getting on in here?'

The painted lady stands between the parted curtains, professional brightness transfixed by the abundant foliage of Imogen's pubic triangle.

'*Here?*'

Imogen's face radiates the deadpan satisfaction of a comedian who has found the perfect stooge.

'Why not?'

Nan's glance takes in the receptionist's afternoon monkey-suit, the velour ceiling, the track-lighting up the staircase, the imperial Axminster.

'Don't you have to be a member?'

Imogen's gratification intensifies.

'I am.'

Inside, the tiered chandeliers, despite a profusion of bulbs, shed an unsettlingly dim light. This is a matter of deliberate ambiance. No expense has been spared to create an impression of louche, faintly reprehensible decadence, an authentic Calvinist frisson. Nan's knowledge of casinos is based on James Bond movies televised on childhood bank holidays. Well past their original release date, full of actors conforming to outdated notions of glamour dressed in outmoded clothes. The afternoon gamblers bunkered in this windowless chamber are no one's idea of glamorous, but then no one is wearing a beaded chiffon cocktail frock or plum velvet tux. This must be counted an advantage.

Skirting the tables, Imogen heads for a corner furnished with high-sided, tasselled settees and mock-Ming table lamps with watered-silk shades.

'I like it here: free coffee and sandwiches and a rest from the same old faces. The West End bores me rigid: same names, same conversations. At least Jack,' too late to change her mind, 'kept them at arm's length.' She drops the carrier bags with unnecessary flamboyance, one more diversion now dragging her down. 'Nobody bothers you here. It's handy for the office. There's always something to watch. Of course it's tacky, but that's part of the fun.'

Fun? Those paunchy, lounge-suited 'businessmen' whose sources of income are nobody's business? The ebullient Chinese matriarchs yelling at each other in rapidfire Cantonese, bodies compact as children in their Orlon jumpers and Sta-prest slacks? She wonders if her reservations amount to more than a programmed Calvinist shudder. She is as prone to social stereotyping as any, pigeonholing the middle classes as petty bourgeois or shabby-genteel, believing the poor and deserving forever at odds with the reprehensibly flash, but these chancers defy her system of categorisation. Once, in Birmingham, idling without due care and attention through the Bull Ring, she was cornered by a clipboard-carrying market researcher, a manner like a brisk rubdown with an army blanket. In exchange for answering her questionnaire, Nan sought a decoding of the pollster's alphabet, those reductive building blocks of identity, and was amazed to learn that for the purposes of the survey a married woman's status was determined by her husband's rung on the socio-economic ladder. What she was was Kilner's to define. So where does that leave her now?

'Aren't you worried the sadness might be catching?'

Imogen flops into the straitjacketed softness of the settee, reaching up to take Saul from his perch on Nan's hip. 'You've got to learn to own your own feelings, Nan: stop you appropriating everyone else's.'

There is a theoretical offence to be taken at many of Imogen's personal remarks, but by now she understands the trade-off: the sharper the perception, the more persuasive the arguments against voicing it and, consequently, the deeper the emotional investment it represents. She has always been susceptible to the flattery of definition.

'Once you've had a go you'll see it totally differently.' Imogen speaks disjointedly, preoccupied with settling the child on the cushions. 'They don't want your pity. They just want to win. Think of it as an unofficial arm of the social services: instant self-esteem. No job, no prospects, the institutionalised racism of a culture that makes no effort to accommodate you . . . whatever your problem, if that ballbearing settles on the right number you know the Gods still love you. You must have done the Pools?'

'Never.'

Imogen laughs softly, as if she guessed this all along.

'Turning your back on good luck doesn't eliminate the bad, you know.'

Approaching the gaming area, Nan is gripped by awkwardness. Knowing that the punters are sealed behind the plate glass of concentration does little to loosen her up. She is handed a stack of plastic counters which turn out to be one-pound and five-pound chips. Imogen forestalls her protest.

'It's only twenty-five quid. We'll write it off as part of your education. If you come out ahead you can always pay me back.'

They circle the room, skirting the high tables where girls of little more than school age slip playing cards deftly from the shoe, their faces blank even when a departing player pushes a grimy chip towards them. Under their cherrybum jackets they wear leotards and black tights barked with horizontal pulls, some bearing the tell-tale stiffness of nail varnish. Their posture, that sullen stiffness disowning present circumstances, suggests the teenage offspring of stage-struck mothers. Maybe this is what happens if you don't make it into the chorus.

Imogen tires of the spectacle and drifts towards the roulette wheel and by the time Nan catches up her friend's stack of chips is growing. The shiny wood circling the spinning numbers, glowing orange against the grid-marked green baize, has a Wild West saloon-bar gaudiness. Frontier spirit. New money. The croupier heralds the spinning of the wheel with a curt, Glaswegian 'no more bets'. No fancy French lingo here. Time after time the wide-browed Chinese at the table takes these words as the cue to move his chips, as if bucking the system to this extent will tip his luck at the wheel. The third gambler is white, small, ferrety-faced, with lines like concentric sets of parentheses either side of his mouth. He projects the sort of insistent mateyness that can tap well-springs of unsuspected sadism in its targets. Nan studies the croupier's clip-on bow-tie, a red satin Easter-egg ribbon. She can feel the gambler's breath straining towards her neck, the dense reek of cigarette smoke transferring itself to her clothes. Imogen, her eyes following the clattering circuit of the silver ball, has yet to notice. She is winning, not every time but more often than not, and usually when her stake is highest. The stack of chips increases. Every so often she will remove her counters to the unmarked baize, watching the wheel with the same rapt expression as when she has something to gain, or lose. Then she'll re-enter the game, stacking the chips one by one, with a series of discreet clicks. Nan wants to ask the meaning of the ritual, find out how she knows when not to play, but she fears to utter the word that breaks the spell. Unobtrusively she adds her untouched store of casino chips to Imogen's stockpile at the table edge.

'You're not playing?'

Imogen's trance is less complete than it seems.

Nan shrugs. 'I don't trust my luck.'

Imogen watches as five chips are removed from her square.

'You mean you do, but you trust it to be bad.' She places new chips on the adjacent number. 'If you lose, it's confirmation that you're a loser. If you win, it's an anomaly.'

Nan's silence is a grudging acknowledgement.

'Nobody wins at roulette, Nan. It's a business with built-in profit margins for the operators. There's only one proven system. You pick a number and you bet on it all night and you lose, and every time you lose you double your previous stake, and eventually you'll win. And then you quit.'

The Chinese gambler sucks his teeth as a pile of twenty-five-pound chips are raked across the table.

Nan screws up her face, trying to master the maths. 'And you come out ahead?'

'You would, but they operate a stake limit so even if you've got the money to cover your losses, it doesn't work.'

'But in principle, if you start out with a lot more than everyone else, and you're willing to risk the lot, you can't lose?'

Imogen grins.

'That's the way it works.'

Nan retrieves her chips and places a five-pound counter on number six.

Imogen is right. It does seem different from this angle. Like most games, the enjoyment depends on the degree to which it is taken seriously. Normally this would rule Nan out, but Imogen's fascination is catching. Technically they are competitors at the table, rival suitors for the favour of lady luck (or the silver ballbearing), but the steepled tilt of their bodies as they watch the blurring of the segmented wheel suggests the secret tug of collaboration. Their interventions in the game have the instinctual rightness of golden anniversary couples quickstepping around a sprung floor, an affinity with overtones of art. Their eyes gleam with forbidden pleasures, or the light of these low-wattage chandeliers, two positivists indulging in a superstitious holiday treat, intoxicating as the abstainer's thimbleful of Christmas sherry. Watching the ball so nearly settle on the desired number before rattling over into the next compartment, their bodies slew with synchronised laughter, hilarity drawing the sting of loss. She never experienced such exhilaration on the north-facing playing field, the loamy earth dragging at her plimsolls; is this what others find in the collective uncon-scious of team sport, the symbiosis of player and player and ball? But for all her enjoyment, she recognises a point at which the game loses savour and she is chafing to walk away, before her stash of chips is exhausted, to claim her independence of capricious fate. With all pleasures there comes a moment when she wants to stop, before enjoy-ment is sated, fearing the fun will turn to ashes, one more reminder of ultimate hollowness. Whatever the rec-reation, the underlying game is brinkmanship, played against her own appetite. Imogen, by contrast, is a pusher of boundaries, a taker to the limit. Despite her hard-headed assessment of commercial realities, she will not quit until she is ahead. She is suspended in a net of probability, any one of whose holes could let her fall, but her whole life to date has been a demonstration of her superiority to the common laws of chance.

The wheel spins. Red. Black. Nan is fidgety with impending disaster yet her suspense implies the alternative possibility. Hope. The torturer's secret weapon. You know what's coming but it might just be delayed. Her eyes flicker over the room, seeking some relief from the almost-inevitability playing itself out in front of her, coming to rest in the sitting area where they left Saul. Where Saul is no longer to be seen.

Amid the chinoiserie, Nan revolves twice, as if such tawdry magic could make the child reappear. And it does. A heavily-made woman spared the indignity of the leotard, a knee-length skirt below her marching band jacket, approaches. Her face wears the circumspect dis-approval of the working mother.

'Lost anything?'

The child is fractious, tired of the meaningless progress from shop to shop and this final, interminable wait. Nan's presence produces a bout of luxurious crying, confident at last that comfort is at hand. She holds him until his breathing calms and grief's rictus gives way to a shaky, peg-toothed smile, but she knows his distress is only in temporary storage and won't be fully assuaged until Imogen gets her share.

Heads turn, distracted, as she crosses the carpet, the child in her arms. The blackjack dealers lose concentration, wondering whether to intervene. Saul isn't a tantrum thrower, not having inherited his mother's taste for dramatic effect, instead he shows distress by fretting, a high-pitched sound like kittens in the litter, an abstraction of pure unhappiness shorn of strategic purpose, as if he's long since acknowledged that attention-getting never pays off. By the time she reaches the roulette table Imogen's pile of chips is further depleted. At the sight of his mother the child draws breath in a tremulous arpeggio, like the dregs of fizzy liquid being hoovered up through a straw.

Crossing the carpet to the cashier's window half a step behind Imogen's piston stride, Nan suspects her rescue may be insufficiently appreciated. Providing she refuses to acknowledge it, the loser's sulk will probably pass. She chooses the words to sound flatly conversational, but they flutter in the delivery like a white flag.

'Ever play blackjack?'

The window is deserted. Imogen clicks her handful of chips on to the laminated counter.

'Of course. But I never had a hope in hell of winning at that.'

Belatedly, Nan makes the connection.

'You used to meet him here?'

Imogen cranes her neck, seeking the absent cashier.

'Now and again. He was more of a poker-player. He had the face for it. All-night sessions in some back room in the East End. Some of them were pretty heavy characters. I always wanted to sit in just once, to watch, but he said they wouldn't wear it in case I started signalling cards. Not that he needed any help. Must have been some winning streak to afford what he threw away here.'

Losing at roulette seems to have tapped into some darker humiliation. Her voice is viscous with rancour; these inconsequential words swimming in a slow thick tide of bitterness.

'So he took you in the beginning?'

Imogen's nostrils quiver with sour amusement.

'Oh, he took me every step of the way.' Her voice is pitched so low Nan can't be sure even she is meant to hear. 'He took me for a cunt.'

Nan glances down, startled, but Saul is oblivious, deep in the adenoidal purr of infant sleep.

'A shame newspapers are so prissy. I spend hours trying to think up other ways of getting the message across. *Dear Morag, he was taking you for a cunt*. Great phrase. Means exactly what it says.'

A shiny smile like a wipe with a damp cloth. All gone now.

'Here comes the man with the money. About time. OK if I grab the first cab? I'd better get Sleeping Beauty here home to his bed.'

'Hope the clothes are tighter these days.'

'I'm sorry?'

'I used to think pale and emaciated was best but with all those junkies and You Know What and starvation rations on the dole, thin is tantamount to a guilty plea these days. You might as well wear a bomber jacket into the dock.'

It's Tarquin. Calling for a chat; in other words, some not-so-gentle nagging. He's given up asking exactly when she's coming back, and now puts his energy into auxiliary questions which assume her return. Has she found a character witness yet? What about giving evidence herself?

'Juries are rum duckies. Have their own ideas about happy ever afters. They might be sympathetic; on the other hand they might not. No good trying to second guess them, they don't like that. You have two options: tell the truth. Or say nothing at all. The thing is, poppet, keeping mum might not be so dumb. I want you to try a dry run in front of a friendly audience. See how it goes down.'

It doesn't take much to fob him off. He's itching to get back to Gino or Nino or Dino or whoever's currently cooking his carbonara.

'OK, Tarquin, I'll stage-manage a rehearsal.'

But that doesn't mean she'll make the first night.

Once upon a time she would have found a seaside resort in a torrential downpour enjoyable, exotic even, its very drabness perversely evocative, like the silvery otherworld of black and white movies. But she's long since lost her fascination with the romance of provincial life, her nostalgia for the boredom of childhood, that time when everything was imbued with significance, nothing happened, but the world passed before her like a continuous IOU. The inexplicable thing is that when life started to make good its marker, when she was exposed to occurrences the world could catalogue as events, the experience should have proved so uninvolving, like an argument heard through the walls of another room. Perhaps Imogen is right, that's what depression is.

Looking around the tearoom at the dainty dancing academy chairs painted streaky gilt, the brown and orange abstract expressionist carpet, its hideousness rendered almost highbrow by the passage of time, the formation of empty tables serenaded by the muzak's grinding strings, she wonders why he chose this place. And why, having chosen, he was unable to offer her a lift. Outside, the rain should have washed the dirty shingle clean by now, but the town retains its smudged look, shops, houses, places of entertainment blurring into the dullest common denominator, an undifferentiated mean. Hardly his natural element. Poverty breathes through the place's pores. Not the very bottom of the heap, not desperation, but the qualified pleasures of the habitually careful. Families like the mother and toddlers at the next table, still wearing their bubblegum anoraks as if they can't trust their luck to stop a hole from opening in the roof above them.

Hard to believe that the mannerly seafront outside the window with its begrudging strip of green turf and sadistically pebbled beach ever amounted to paradise, but thirty years ago it served as a cue for release, a week or two of freedom away from the drudgery of earning a living. Now there's no work, and getting away from it means all the comforts of home under the Spanish sun. The town is reduced to daytrippers with disappointed expressions measuring their enjoyment in ice creams and one-arm bandits, invaders exterminated and fortunes told.

The waitress, a thick-waisted teenager with crimped yellow hair, brings her tea in a tiny stainless-steel teapot and a thimbleful of milk in a matching jug. She is dressed in black and white, a pastiche of the efficient frills of the Lyons' nippy calling to mind the skimpy-skirted nurses' uniforms and St Trinian's gymslips sold through small ads in semi-respectable magazines. Pouring the tea, Nan dribbles an archipelago of tannin across the table top. The cloth is far from pristine, speckled with sugar and grained with flecks of cigarette ash, but still the waitress turns away tight-lipped.

And now here he comes, bursting through the doors in his toothpaste-white trenchcoat, his fringe straggled with rain, the technicolour confidence dazzling enough to fade her fellow customers' dayglo rainwear. Passing their table he peers into the tarnished silver goblets, performing a sitcom double-take at the unappetising paste within.

'Not late am I?'

He opens the teapot, grimaces at its contents, and winks at the waitress. Irritatingly, she approaches to take his order. Worse, he flirts her into hanging his trenchcoat on the hatstand by the door. Catching sight of Nan's expression, he hams a spinster's disapproving simper.

She's not sure now what possessed her to ring him. If anything she was thinking of Danny, trying to put some distance between them, crowding him out with other complications. Not that she's reached the firm conclusion that Danny was responsible for Jack's death, but it's becoming increasingly difficult to dismiss the possibility. Cal's transgressions don't bother her the same way. She now takes it for granted that he is bankrolled by drugs and, after her initial surprise, the knowledge barely flutters her pulse. It makes little practical difference, just another reason not to trust when she wouldn't have trusted him anyway. Nothing personal. She's long since abandoned the habit of sorting people into types: all men are capable of all things. Deviance, antisocial behaviour, amorality, are part of the continuum of personality. That doesn't eliminate the need for discrimination, but it changes the relevant question. Ask not *what does he do?* but *will he do it to me?*

Cal's sundae arrives, parasolled and flagged, looking almost as disgusting as the toddlers' mush. He picks up the long spoon and excises the green glacé cherry from its aerosol alp of cream, offering it towards her then, shruggingly, depositing it on his plate.

'Imogen sends her regards, by the way.'

He lowers the spoon.

'I bet she doesn't.'

'Why do you say that?'

He flashes her his lighthouse smile.

'The lady hasn't told you?'

She raises a bluffer's eyebrow and the beam broadens.

'Well, well, well. Normally she's broadcasting on all frequencies. And I thought you two were bosom buddies, in the sauna cabin anyway. Or are you just a little treasure when it comes to minding the baby?'

This needling is not malicious, not even idle curiosity, just idleness; the devil making work. A random shot, but one unluckily on target. What Nan desires most of all is to be stitched into the fabric of life, but Imogen's life is full, the rectangles of time in her mock-croc filofax crammed with ciphers and initials, hours and half hours and fifty-minute appointments slotted end-to-end, friends and contacts allotted their precise span; she's a boon to the taxi trade. So much leisure is spoken for so far ahead that to be with her means swooping on the scraps, scavenging the offcuts of her day: amusing Saul at the radio station while his mother is quarantined by the red light above the studio door, hanging around afterwards on the promise of a canteen coffee and a pooled postmortem, trading a listener's perception for the tensions and glitches off-mike. She performs other services, too: picking up the cashmere jacket from the invisible mender's on her way home, posting the birthday present to the sister in Singapore, dropping by to make the pâté sucrée the morning of Peter's birthday dinner. The fact that involvement in Imogen's ménage is exactly what she wants does not banish the possibility of being used. Nothing so stark as exploitation, more an unflattering ambiguity of definition: friend, certainly, but also Imogen's little helper. As ever, there is the vexed question of parity. Having no life herself, no rich tapestry into which the successful journalist can be threaded, Nan cannot offer equivalent satisfactions, even assuming her friend were disposed to value them. Is Nan, then, the exploiter, the one who's taking a little more than her share, or providing a little less? This is the point at which she recognises the futility of the emotional balance of payments. Perverse to resent the acceptance of a gift freely offered; as pointless as toothcombing her own trespasses without a glimmer of complaint. So she rejects these anxieties, without quite dispelling them, knowing them for what they are, insurance, small premiums of mistrust set against the big pay-off. In the days since that afternoon at the casino, the nature of their connection has changed. No longer a connection at all, in fact: the careful bridge between self-contained subjectivities has been swept away, leaving a friendship that is elemental, boundless, variable, constant, manifest, like weather. No need to ask if Imogen feels the same. They are two notes in a chord, harmony and counterpoint, wisecrack and backchat, star turn and audience, a double act; if it weren't mutual it wouldn't work. To acknowledge the mystery, even, especially, to Imogen, would call its self-evidence into question; why desecrate the miracle of affinity beyond doubt?

She smiles. 'We have better things to do than talk about you, Cal. Endlessly fascinating as you are.'

His mouth closes on a spoonful of chopped banana, a bead of chocolate vermicelli lodges provokingly in the corner of his lips.

'You don't know the half of it, toots.'

It turns out that he's been visiting one of his old teachers, a housemaster currently packed away in one of the retirement homes lining the seafront on the outskirts of town. After a lifetime in a boys' public school he's ended up in a granny farm, his Y-fronts tangling with frilly bloomers in the wash, raising the toilet seat every time, gagging down his lunch through a filter of lily of the valley and parma violet, every battle between the Test Match and *Mrs Miniver* a foregone conclusion. A confirmed bachelor, straight no chaser, or at least so deep in the closet even he doesn't know he's there, and the first time in his life he gets close enough to sniff a woman, let alone a houseful, they're thinning on top with chin growth like a Kleeneze brush.

'Never even spent a tenner on a trick, stingy old sod. It's not as if he had anything else to do with the moolah. Must be minted by now.'

'So that's your angle.'

'I'm sorry?'

He withdraws his smile like a slap.

She's been caught out before by these unaccountable outbreaks of highmindedness, moments when the playful tone falls away and all at once he's offended that the bad boy posturing has been taken at face value. The first time, wrongfooted, she felt a mixture of shame and aggravation, she was playing his game and suddenly he changed the rules. Now, when it happens, she's interested, a pattern is emerging: once again she's been tripped up by the old school tie.

He's the product of an institution founded to turn out pillars of empire, arrogant enough to defend an indefensible system, docile enough to do its bidding. It's quite an art, the moulding of individuals both conformist and egotistical, although individuality is a strictly qualified concept here. Whatever the Latin motto above the headmaster's lectern, the gist is the same: surrender yourself and we give you the world. It's hardly surprising that social subversion becomes a point of principle. Flouting convention, defying consensus, mocking pieties, these are matters of high moral seriousness, the public school boy's sole purchase on identity. In a boarding school it's no more than healthy rebellion; in the world outside it makes for that most dangerous combination, the self-righteous psychopath.

The rain is taking a short break to gather its strength. They leave the café and cross the road to the promenade but he shuns the neat runner of turf and steps on to the shelving beach, the scree shifting under his feet. Reluctantly, she follows, trying not to identify the decomposing clumps of debris between the stones.

The trippers are out in force, if wisely keeping to the prom, their only neighbours at the shorefront a quartet of small boys skimming pebbles, and the occasional flap-landing gull. The sea is a sheet of gunmetal, the sky hanging close as a marquee, the air teases with chemicals she cannot identify. The unpleasantness in the café forgotten, he's chatty again.

'So what did you want to ask me, Nan Megratta?'

The job, responsibility, wages, hours . . .

'Who killed Jack?'

He flips a matchbox over with his toe and the sodden cardboard disintegrates. Captain Webb all washed up.

'Is that your question or Miss Reiss's?'

She feigns incomprehension, but she's convincing nobody.

'You know about them, then?'

He smiles at her capitulation.

'It wasn't the talk of the steamie, but someone had to be in on the secret. Where do you think they did it all those years? Car seats and al fresco kneetremblers lose their romance after a while.'

'Your house?'

'Please. I don't live in a knocking shop. I told you. I used to be in property. Buying. Selling. Sometimes letting, though it's a mug's game. Usually had a dozen or so flats on the go.'

'Were they furnished?'

It's such an unselfconscious bark of pleasure she barely minds it being at her expense.

'I know this will come as a shock to you, Mizz M., but the verb to bed need not be taken literally. The furniture isn't an integral part of the experience.'

Something moves an inch below the horizon. Squint-ing, she makes out the tip of a submarine slicing through the waves. Over by the jetty a skipper tosses a pail of unidentifiable scraps on to the water. The screaming gulls converge like a cloud of midges.

'I didn't realise Jack was such a good friend.'

She seems to have stumbled on a private joke.

'The lady really is operating on the need-to-know. Jackieboy wasn't a good friend of mine, not even a bad friend, though that would have been more likely. You tell Imogen if she's wanting a list of suspects there must be a couple of hundred frustrated home-improvement freaks with the motive. Apart from that it's anyone's guess.'

'What about the man he was blackmailing?'

Cal laughs the hair into his eyes, then flicks it away with a sideways toss of the head.

'How do you make that one out?'

'Why else would you kill him?'

She only says it because it seems so unlikely. The next moment, she's not so sure. He turns towards her, his face expressionless, but holds the pose a fraction too long. She knows he's fooling before he takes the first step towards her.

'Do I look like a killer?'

Retreating from him, she loses her footing and lurches sideways, he grabs for her and suddenly, although it's not clear who started it, they're running on the treacherous shingle. She expects him to give up, or at least settle into a gentle jog, but he's fast for a man of his bulk, and she has to sprint to stay out of reach, slithering on the shale, losing her balance, recovering it only to find the ground shifting under her next step, laughing, half-squealing in panic, or exhilaration, or perhaps both. She's charging up the slope, heading for the steps which lead to the prom-enade, desperate for solid ground, but he catches her before she makes it, hurling forward in a lumbering tackle, trapping her against the sea wall. The impact knocks the wind out of her. His weight holds her and she's inhaling the salt tang of the crumbling surface, stomach and breasts crushed against the algae-greened concrete, his breath hot on her scalp.

When he releases her, the sea air seems colder than before.

They're sitting on the jetty, their dangling feet just inches from the choppy, scum-flavoured water below. The afternoon has brightened into an early sunset, backlit clouds, oyster and green, swirling across a sky like a tarnished teaspoon. A stiff breeze musses his hair, exposing his roots and the beginnings of a receding hairline. Not only a bottle blond but a clever comb-over too. Before them is a cut-price marina with a dozen fibreglass dingies, middle-management toys, the wind plucking and slapping their rigging against the hollow aluminium masts, tapping out carnival rhythms. She turns her collar up and tries to pull the second-hand coat tighter but it's a Utility garment dating from the frugal days of pencilled-on stocking seams and make-do-and-mend; its primary purpose was always morale-boosting, rather than insulation. Unexpectedly he wraps an arm round her shoulder and huddles her against him. Warm flesh gives under the trenchcoat. Knowing that it's not a sexual overture doesn't make the gesture any less charged.

'So I've got myself a new manager?'

He wants her to run Nineteen Canteen, a budget bistro concealed down an unadopted lane in the west end of the city. The idea is to take it upmarket, attracting a more profligate clientele than the parties of students who hog the tables for hours, eking out a bottle of house red and a basket of garlic bread. He doesn't mind how she changes the menu, she can even redecorate, provided it doesn't cost the earth, but she must have it breaking even within six months. If she pulls it off and the food gets a reputation, he'll think about giving her a shot at one of the bigger restaurants. It's the sort of offer she used to fantasise about as things got more difficult in England: autonomy without the paralysing burden of ownership. Or marriage.

'I don't know yet. I'll need to take a look at the place, find out what I'm getting into.'

She frowns; her tenses seem to be running ahead of her.

His arm tightens slightly, signalling agreement, unless he's asserting control.

'OK, Greasy Nan.'

'And if you're going to call me that the deal's off.'

He smiles perfunctorily, as is often the case with other people's jokes.

'I have a couple of conditions too.'

There is a tenuous intimacy to sitting side by side, faces in parallel, sharing the same view. Once he turns towards her the impression is destroyed. No one should be looked at this close.

'I think it's time you came clean, confessed your sins to father Callum. What's a nice girl like Nan Megratta doing on the wrong side of the law?'

Instinctively she leans away from him but there's no give in the encircling arm. With his free hand he turns her face towards him, the pressure of his fingers too firm on her cheek. To the old couple walking their wind-drunk labrador along the prom they must look like lovers.

When he breaks the silence it's with a new voice, shorn of the usual trimmings, and unnaturally quiet, although there's no one to hear over the percussion of wind and sea.

'I don't care what you've done. A pound to a penny I've done worse, but that's why I have to know. I can't carry any unnecessary risks. If Tarbert Lane works out I'd like to cut you in, we'd work well together, but I can't afford any skeletons in the closet.'

All of a sudden she wants to tell him. All the bet-hedging and subject-changing, the months of carefully worded evasions wash back at her like sewage up a drain. Why not? she thinks, as she's thought from time to time with Danny and Imogen, even Rab, but with them there was always an answer. Because you'll lose them. Because even if they cloak their shock in sympathetic words and supportive embraces, you'll be someone else to them, someone to whom they've no obligations, and they'll drop you.

With Cal, there is no love to lose, no answer to the question why not? Not even the risk of jeopardising the job offer, discarding the golden apple that's landed in her lap. Maybe she will go back to Birmingham, ask Cal to take the stand. There's a twisted but appealing logic to the idea of producing an inner-city drugs baron as her character witness, someone who can vouch for her as a viable member of the free-market economy. Tarquin thinks her employer should testify, and for that, he has to be told.

Cal sits silent, waiting; she notices how long his eye-lashes are.

'I killed a man. He was my husband.'

He lowers those heavy lids with their extravagant lashes, then opens the blue eyes very wide.

'Divorce is slower but I've heard it works just as well.'

She's furious. This is her life and he's turning it into a pretext for smart remarks. He believes her all right, it's just not real to him, whereas to her it's the only reality, like living in a photographic negative. Her eyelids sting

222

with aborted tears, with sudden anger and thwarted exhibitionism and a deep-tamped emotion that might even be grief.

'Maybe I just couldn't wait.'

The fingers release her face.

'Extension three five one four.'

'Engaged at the moment. Do you want to hold?'

'Please.'

That is, not particularly, but she'll do it.

'Still engaged, caller, are you holding?'

She visualises the newsroom, ergonomically designed workstations in injection-moulded plastic, the mushroomy light cast by those computer-friendly uplighters, identikit women in pillarbox lipstick standing around in clusters, bending over photographic contact sheets, drinking coffee on the hoof, almost anything but sitting at their desks.

'Putting you through now.'

The phone purrs twice before the receiver is lifted.

'Features.'

So she was hanging on for the wrong extension.

'Is Imogen Reiss there?'

'Not sure, who's calling?'

'Nan Megratta.'

'Hang on a minute.'

The line goes dead. Once upon a time they just muffled the mouthpiece with a hand, now they've got mute buttons, a lead-lined coffin allowing no leakage. The mechanism is released, flooding her ear with sounds she failed to notice before: other telephones, the bleep of a fax completing transmission, a burst of shushing laughter, human hum, but still no voice in the mouthpiece.

'Hello?'

The secretary again.

'I'm sorry, Imogen must have popped out for five minutes, but I can take a message.'

'I'll call back.'

F or years she used to watch herself in shop windows; in art galleries, too, although she stopped visiting those after leaving college. Perhaps that's why: the shame of commandeering genius to offset her own reflection. Then she met Kilner and somewhere along the way the habit left her. Perversely she mourned its passing; it might have been vanity but it was also an affirmation of life, a reminder, however trivial, that she did exist. Just recently, however, she's caught herself slipping into old ways, her gaze drawing back from the chisel-hipped mannequins and artistic arrangements of embroidered towels to the panes of glass themselves. Today she's walking briskly, her second self an intermittent presence in the corner of her eye, ectoplasm dematerialising across dustbin alleys and bill-blinded shops. Outside a café she swerves to avoid a fearless pigeon, mouths an apology to the over-alled shopgirl whose progress she interrupts, and looks up to catch her reflection tapping a woman on the shoulder.

'I thought it was you.'

The misapprehension takes barely a second to sort out. It was the new hairstyle, she realises, that and the shape of the handbag: from such fragments we assemble identity. All the same it's an unnerving error. Not her reflection but Maggie's, suddenly so close behind her; the shoulder accosted not a stranger's but her own. She takes in Maggie's black hair, lustreless as spit mascara, her deoxygenated complexion, the knitting-needle elbows sawing through her lime-green tailored jacket, the laundered jeans and soft leather loafers with their dinky gold chains, the whole merry widow kit, expensive, gaudy, shiny-buttoned.

'Fancy a coffee?'

Still numbed by the mistake, Nan finds that her face wears an acquiescent smile.

Given that they have exchanged fewer than fifty words to date, Nan knows a great deal about Maggie. She's a constant reference in Imogen's conversation, namedropped to a point beyond affection. It's almost as if forgoing the comparison would upset her equilibrium, undermine her very identity. Her relentless capacity for survival and Maggie's status as professional victim are more than the coordinates of friendship, they provide the bearings for her whole life. Redundant to wonder what they have in common: their differences, of course.

While it's easy to see what Imogen gets out of it, Maggie's percentage is less obvious. Even professional victims must find the role claustrophobic at times, especially as it wasn't always thus. There's the curious business of their identity switch, Imogen's tales of a time when her friend cornered the market in glamour and she scuttled along in her shadow. Maybe this was the real betrayal, and adultery just a comprehensible cover.

The *pas de deux* into the teashop leaves Nan slackjawed with admiration. Maggie accepts the courtesy of the opened door and still manages to hang back, so that it's Nan who must find the table and Nan who's left with the narrow space behind the Kelvinside matron in her waxed-cotton riding mac, while the older woman simply slips into the corner seat and waits to be served.

Queuing between the open-sandwich trade, the career shoppers with their hard-won carrier bags inching towards the till, Nan stares uninhibitedly, knowing that Maggie is too myopic to be aware of her scrutiny. Her eyes look dim-sighted, not so much bloodshot as yellowed, rendered by Rembrandt in candlelight, and framed by the sort of stagey application of warpaint Nan associates with female impersonators. Her skin, too, is over made-up, clogged with a curiously old-fashioned shade of powder suggesting pretensions to porcelain beauty, although its chief effect is to collect in the fine down of the jawline and highlight the purplish tinge to her skin.

'Funny. I was just talking to Imma about you the other day.'

Nan squeezes an interested smile, wondering how she can be so certain that the hurt is not inadvertently caused, deciding the clue lies in that bleating grace note, forcing you to choose between a victim's complicity and the guilty freedom of the oppressor. Even when she's being unpleasant she manages to suggest you're doing her wrong.

'She was saying she hasn't seen much of you recently.'

Dipping into her bag, Maggie places cigarettes and lighter on the table and rests her right hand an inch and a half away from them. At the next table a pair of comfortably built women in uncomfortable clothes are drinking black coffee and enduring extremities of misery at the proximity of all those chocolate eclairs. Their glances flicker enviously over the surplus denim draping Maggie's fossil thighs and back to their calorie-empty plates. Maggie, meanwhile, is watching Nan eat, her fingers twitching beside the softpack of menthol cigarettes.

Nan wonders why she is doing this: bolting her soup so her companion can light up, wishing away her precious break, trying to calculate just when it would be socially acceptable to make her excuses. Genuine excuses. Lunch hour is a strict forty minutes, but somehow the urgency of her desire to leave makes the justification feel bogus. Gorr's wrath is as nothing to the misery of lunching with Maggie Ibster, who can't be enjoying it much either.

Surely she can't need company to drink, despite the charade of asking a waitress for a second glass. Or is it that she's so used to the noncommittal expressions of the sober that she can no longer tell friend from conscript?

Talking or listening, the widow has a habit of rubbing thumb and fingertips together, a disconcertingly arhythmic movement, like a pastrycook sifting floury fats, an industry of gesture at odds with the absent gaze, a hint that her mind is otherwise engaged. It may be simple irritation, or even a reluctant sympathy, but those restless fingers are almost unbearably distracting. How can Imogen stand it? Nan has to admit to a blind spot in this department; some of Maggie's mannerisms are winsome enough, that dipped gaze before she pulls the puckered grin, but she cannot warm to them. It's not that the woman is unappealing, just destructive, like poison ivy, or Virginia creeper, decorative but working her tentacles deep into the masonry.

Conversation labours along, a long way from lively but never quite dead. There's no point trying to second-guess her, to interpret the random sequence of pleasantries and stony looks. Shamefaced by a couple of early smiles, Nan makes the mistake of mustering some show of social enthusiasm only to be deflected with an uncomprehending stare. Brain dead or actively hostile? If it's the former, Nan has to admire the skill with which she maintains a semblance of normal conversation; only the relentless efficiency of carafe and glass indicates where her true attention lies.

She promises herself she'll go when Maggie finishes her drink but it is gradually becoming apparent that Maggie *never* finishes her drink. The level in the glass remains the same while the carafe steadily diminishes. At one point Nan makes the mistake of visiting the lavatory and on her return a second bottle has appeared. Her own glass remains full to the brim, much like Maggie's bowl of soup, marks of mutual obstinacy and silent reproach.

So Maggie's a drunk. The question is, what sort of drunk: capable or incapable? Exactly how near are they to the point at which she becomes either maudlin or belligerent? Such is the strength of Nan's distaste that she hopes it's the latter. Flailing and shouting wouldn't be enjoyable but are greatly to be preferred to greeting over squandered chances or, the ultimate horror, kissy protestations of lifelong friendship, those sapless arms round her neck, the flopping head lifeless as a ventriloquist's doll on her shoulder. She has to get away before the critical moment, the point at which she won't be able to leave. It's one of the great unwritten laws, part of the unbreachable etiquette of a city that swims on alcohol, obedient to its rhythms as a fishing village observes the tide: drunks have to be looked after. They're not answerable for their safety, let alone their actions; somebody in the vicinity has to pick them up, wipe them down, see them home. The trouble is, they never want to go home.

Nan remembers the relief of those Edwardian beer palaces of the English Midlands, masterpieces of ceramic and etched glass, where drunks were drunks, comical maybe, or mildly disgusting, or full of pack-hunting bravura, but not existential heroes on metaphysical quests. They might boast of quantities consumed once the hair of the dog had started to work its magic, but they knew it was just getting pissed. It's not a question of shame. Maggie has shame, that's why she requested that extra glass. But here shame is an accessory, it adds to the dignity of the drunk, becoming another component of the rite of passage, that mortification of flesh and spirit which pushes them through the portals into knowledge.

Nan checks her watch. They've only been together twenty minutes and, yes, the second hand is still turning.

She can't decently make a move for another quarter hour. Meanwhile, she really ought to make some reference to Jack, offer her condolences. She sorts and discards standard forms of words, unable to find the right cliché. Odd how quickly you forget the arcana of death, its endless footnotes of meaning; all that's left is the gratitude for how much you cannot know.

'How have you been. Since the funeral?'

Maggie exhales a cloud of smoke.

'OK.'

Nan drains her glass of water, an action which usefully precludes response.

'Imogen's the one I feel sorry for.'

The yellow eyes seem uncharacteristically sharp. Her companion seems to have entered a pocket of clarity, unless she's been there all along.

'You know she was fucking him for years?'

The moment feels dangerous. Nan doesn't have sufficient data to construct a reply. She is almost certain Maggie is bluffing, in which case one careless word will trigger incalculable devastation, but she can't sit here with a noncommittal look on her face indefinitely. Even this constitutes an admission of sorts.

'I find that hard to believe.'

Maggie laughs, a laugh that says she knows Nan is lying and doesn't really mind. This is itself a lie, part of the victim's pose of self-effacement. Nan used to do it herself, really believed she didn't matter, but underneath the organism was fighting for survival.

'It happens all the time: best friends and husbands. The oldest story in the book. You must have seen it yourself?'

There it is again, the invitation to join the united front, to acknowledge their mutual interest, the solidarity of the not-Imogen. And coming from anyone else it would be a temptation. Briefly she reviews the past ten days, the fruitless phone calls, the resolution not to try again, the slippages of will, oddly-timed compulsions, always at the moments she is guaranteed not to be there. The object of the exercise is not to make contact with Imogen, not directly, for that she could ring the house. What she wants is for Imogen to return her call, to lift a finger, make some sort of overture. So far it hasn't happened.

Once in a while the contaminating feeling of rejection gives way to a sudden conviction that there must be an explanation, to believe otherwise is mean-spirited, a failure of trust, and then, like the returning tide, comes the knowledge that she has been abandoned. Not just by Imogen, it's as if her withdrawal has tilted some balance, tipped the wink to the rest of the world. Too much has been invested in the friendship; through loving Imogen and the things Imogen loved, she was almost beginning to like herself again. Fragments which hadn't seen the light of day since Kilner emerged like prehistoric gold. And now as she traverses the familiar streets she finds her treasure-trove self scattered all over town, in the Polish deli among the chorizos and ricotta taschen, between the yachting blazers and linen-mix sweaters in the window of Imogen's favourite boutique, lying on doorsteps, jettisoned in lamppost litter bins, discarded, dumped.

Walking back from work the other night she found herself stepping over a child's chalked message on the pavement: *Kazza hates Stevo*. In a similar spirit she dissects their time together, putting barely-remembered slights and misunderstandings under the microscope, searching for flaws, unpicking the intricate fabric of their friendship. What else is there to do? She's exhausted herself with permutations, the possible explanations, the amnesiac colleagues and gremlin-ridden answerphones.

She's tried telling herself that she's a victim of unfamiliar etiquette, that it's quite acceptable, even routine, to leave a call unanswered for ten days in Imogen's world. She's spun guilty fantasies of disaster and sudden bereavement, tolerable priorities. She's even tried the luxury of despair, bouts of orgiastic self-loathing, pushing her reason to rejection-point, hoping to persuade herself that Imogen's disaffection is a piece of the same paranoia. None of it works. The truth is she doesn't know and never will unless Imogen decides to vouchsafe the information. The most she can realistically hope for is that one day she will no longer care.

Right now, she cares very much, which is why it's so difficult listening to Maggie, the favoured sister, bad-mouthing her friend.

'Or isn't that an issue?'

Nan's eyes take a furtive tour of the tablecloth. No clues there.

'Is there a man,' Maggie simpers to disclaim the phrase, 'in your life?'

'I'm a widow.'

She wonders idly where that bit of fustian came from. Whatever its provenance, it seems to have been a mistake. Maggie's interest has quickened.

'Imma said you were divorced.' She smiles slowly and not wholly pleasantly. 'So that's the bait. You had me wondering. She doesn't usually go for the top-button type. Likes her cases with a bit of melodrama. The more gothic the better. You strike me as more Barratt homes than Bluebeard's Castle, but I suppose a dead husband is worth a few points.'

Nan gathers that the threshold of belligerence has now been crossed.

'I'm surprised you've lasted so long. She usually wears them out within the month. There's always a nastier mess in the queue. It makes me laugh, our Mother Teresa of the tabloids, ministering to the sickos. They're so grateful to find someone willing to wallow in it with them, they never think to ask why. She likes the ones that give good pain. Kinkier than black leather any day, which is why you're such a turn-up: such a straight little postie. What's your problem, Nan? I'm dying to know. Which wounds do you let her lick in the privacy of your own home?'

Nan lifts her stare from the soup spoon.

'Is that the way she is with you?'

Maggie stubs out her cigarette inexpertly; it lies bent in the ashtray, trailing a wisp of acrid smoke.

'Oh, I'm the exception. That's why I'm permanent. She doesn't try to sort out my head, I know how the trick works.'

The second carafe is almost finished, Nan notes with relief.

'Maybe I'm an exception, too.'

'Is that what Jack told you?'

Nan is caught off-guard. She recalls the boozy sniping on their way to the funeral, old Mrs Ibster's gorgon glare.

'I shouldn't think he had an opinion on me one way or the other.'

'Which is why you were pen pals?'

Behind her, the Kelvinside matron has finished her open sandwich and is attempting to extricate herself from her seat. Nan is aware of the straining against her chair-back, but it feels a long way from the drama being played out at her own table.

'You posted that empty envelope?'

Maggie's lipstick is bleeding into the scores radiating from her upper lip. Her teeth, gappy and domino-square above, capacity-crowded below, show briefly in an approximation of pleasure.

'What did you expect to find inside?'

234

'I wasn't expecting anything. I thought you'd burned all his papers.'

'I'm not the one worried about incriminating evidence.'

Maggie is telling her something, but Nan isn't sure what, possibly no more than that she's suffering from a drunk's reality-slippage, that she's reached that point where disorientation mutates into higher insight and the universal conspiracy clicks into place. She wonders if that face was entirely sculpted by booze, or if the genes had sealed her fate long before the first sip. Worse than the vellum eyes is the way the skin around them is gradually coming away from the bone and muscle underneath, puffing like a vol-au-vent. The next instant the pouches are ruched by a snigger as Nan is pitched against the table by an ample Kelvinside rear. Its possessor is mortified, but also indignant after her extended efforts to sidle out with a minimum of fuss. Rising from her seat to give the woman free passage, it occurs to Nan that she won't get a better opportunity to make her escape. Grimacing at her watch, she turns towards the door, then, on impulse, swivels back again.

'Oh Maggie, I wasn't sleeping with your husband. Just in case there's any confusion.'

The woman in the riding mac stands frozen like a squirrel on a suburban lawn, hoping for invisibility, mouth ajar, a shred of parsley visible between two top teeth. Standards in Kelvinside are obviously slipping.

Maggie smiles for the audience, draining the last of the carafe into her glass.

'Of course you weren't. You're not his type.'

'How did Gorr take it?'

The significance of the surname does not escape her. Gorr enjoys a variety of aliases: Gorbals, Blimey, Poison Dwarf and, for reasons now lost, Captain Spam. Rab's refusal to use any of them amounts to an excommunication.

She shrugs in a passable impression of her old manner with him.

'Didn't listen to what I was saying, of course. Did a number about the great future I was throwing away. Then he just flipped, got quite nasty: it'll all end in tears and I needn't think the Post Office will bail me out. People like me are destroying this city, too many waiters, not enough welders, yuppies drinking cappuccino when there's weans can't get enough to eat. Seems to think I'm sleeping with Callum Macleod as well.'

'You mean you're no?'

She's not surprised by his attitude. Why should he be pleased for her? There's nothing in her opportunity to give him hope. By taking their griping to its logical conclusion, not realising that the escape committee was just a social club, something to pass the time until retirement, she has betrayed him. As far as he's concerned she's already over the wall. In the past fortnight they've hardly spoken. They still place their trays side by side when meal breaks coincide, swap observations on the previous night's television, but it's not the same.

He's perched on the edge of one of the battleship desks, chewing a hangnail and kicking his left foot rhythmically against the metal drawers. She has a feeling he's waiting for her to tell him to stop so that he'll be able to justify an eruption of grievance. Considerate as she is, she's not going to oblige him to that extent.

'Have to organise a swally to see you off.'

She sees the smoky pub, the gallons of Heavy and the whisky chasers, herself swilling gut-rotting orange juice after the third beer, some joker spiking it with vodka, her eyes burning a hole in the clock, condemned to be the last to leave.

'How many were hospitalised after the last mass piss-up?'

He stops kicking and looks at her.

'I meant you and me. No point putting a note up: naebdy else would come anyway.'

The old Bakelite phone rings suddenly, the sound of homburgs and black Wolseys and decent policemen. She seizes the handset with relief.

'Well, you're about as easy to come by as a rosary in Larkhall.'

Pressing the receiver to her ear, unthinkingly she half turns her back on Rab. He slides off the desktop and before she can remedy her rudeness the door slams shut behind him. A pile of letters levitate in the draught before drifting down to earth.

'Hello, Danny.'

She strains to detect hints of aggression or sulk but his friendliness sounds unalloyed.

'Where have you been hiding yourself?'

Cinemas mostly. Over the past week she's seen more of America than she has of Glasgow: LA lawns, the helter-skelter topography of San Francisco, autumnal New Hampshire and a downtown nightmare she thinks was New York. He's easy enough to avoid; he never leaves messages at Catriona's and, since they became lovers, the same caution has restrained him from ringing her at work. But now he wants to see her, says he's leaving the House early to make sure they have a decent stretch of time. There's no getting out of it, so she suggests they meet at Nineteen Canteen.

The bistro is tattier than she was expecting, the gingham oilcloths peppered with cigarette burns and biroed games of noughts and crosses. She suspects a lack of cleanliness rather than indelible ink. The walls are hung with Woolworth's imitation oils, garish sunsets in white wipe-clean frames, palominos cantering through the sea-spume, Mediterranean urchins with big eyes and petted lips. It's always struck her as the worst kind of tastelessness, that which passes itself off as knowing, joke kitsch. The tables offer ketchup in dispensers shaped like giant tomatoes.

Her official reconnaissance has been arranged for tomorrow night but she can't resist visiting the place anonymously first, indulging her secret sense of potential. For the next twenty-four hours anything is possible, nothing ruled out, like those afternoons painting her toenails before teenage parties, or boiling up bouillabaisse for summer evenings, or taking slow trains to romantic rendezvous. In her experience, anticipation invariably bettered the event.

Straight from the airport in his legislator's suit and tie, Danny is uncomfortable. Nan can't see what the fuss is about. Even she feels geriatric among this crowd; a forecourt hustler's leather jacket would hardly count as camouflage. The tables are crowded with gangs of adolescents displaying their tribal marks, a narrow strand of hair plaited and bound with embroidery thread, a circle of beads around the little finger, a leather thong tied tight on the left wrist. They smoke self-consciously, drawing with exaggerated sensuality on inexpertly-packed roll-ups, eyes watering in the self-generated fug.

Working on the principle that if they're going to have a scene it might as well be an early one, she explains about the restaurant. Surprisingly, he takes the news in his stride.

'So that's what's behind the Houdini act?'

All heads turn as a bottle, complete with lighted candle, explodes on contact with the floor. Horseplay at a neighbouring table. A couple of girls are trying to pick up the fragments, giggling between exhibitionism and embarrassment. Their male companions re-enact the moment as mime, adding battlefield sound effects, redoubling the group's amusement.

He looks away.

'I see the raggedy-arsed look is in this year. Any tattier and social services would have them on a register.'

At moments like this the years between them stretch very wide.

'They're kids: haven't got two beans to rub together.'

His look suggests this is unworthy of an answer, but he supplies one anyway.

'They're middle class, you can smell it a mile off. Students. A couple of years in a bedsit with dodgy wiring, enamelling the Baby Belling with packet soup, drinking Lambrusco out of the toothmug, dressing like they shop in Soweto. It's romantic. Something to reminisce about when they've got two cars in the drive and the managing director coming round to dinner. No permanent scarring.' He smiles thinly. 'Where I come from, eating in restaurants doesn't count as the breadline. It's dishonest, but then you're more comfortable with that than I am.'

So she should have worn body armour after all.

After the meal he follows the road hemming the north

bank of the river through a shantytown of caravan snack-bars with their illiterate bills of fare, lock-up garages dispensing dodgy MOTs, trailers sheltering watchmen employed to keep the roof-strippers and stone-throwers away from the empty factories. Not that there are many windows to break. The architecture is industrial monolithic, sheer faces of blind brick. Just beyond the wintering ground of shuttered fairground amusements he stops the car.

'Come on.'

She slips through the crevice between the buildings easily enough, but he has to stop, go back and remove his jacket. She wonders if the Alsatians on the Keep Out signs are to be taken seriously. After too long he reappears, tucking in his shirt, tugged loose by the scraping walls, remarking that he can't understand it, his size hasn't changed since he worked in the yards.

'But I bet your tailor has, and flattering the customer's all part of the service.'

About twenty feet from the quayside the brick corridor gives way to an uninterrupted view across the water to the shipyard. The tanker sits in dry dock, keel and propeller fully exposed. Perhaps because every inch has been painted a uniform oxydised red, it looks at once as huge as she knows it to be and as dinky as a child's bath toy. Half a dozen cranes are ranged around like consultants at a private patient's bedside, attentive but supernumerary. Only the welders silhouetted in their magnesium halos, tiny as cereal-packet toys, indicate the proper scale of things. Odd snatches of shout carry across the river, above the banging of hammer on metal, the low rumble of the generator, the gushing of compressed air feeding the oxy-acetylene torches. She stares, transfixed, at the unpredictable points of illumination, benign explosions, flashes of light that burst grey in the shipyard's sodium glow. The river is low tonight, exposing the layered tidemarks on the ridged wooden quay opposite, the cushioned buffer of weed above the subfusc stain of petroleum and, just above the waterline, a darker, more viscous stripe. Perhaps this accounts for the smell, pervasive, almost palpable, a thick brown odour that clings to the palate. In Birmingham, where there were no ships, the engineering quarter smelled just the same, this rank, generic secretion of heavy industry; close your eyes, and it could almost be the whiff of the farmyard.

She resents the astuteness of his bringing her here, an insight so sharp it carries the suspicion of exploitation. The thing she really likes about Danny, the quality that sets him apart from other bespoke-tailored neds on the pull, is his mythic resonance. On the rare occasions that he talks about the yards the simplest story, the most banal reminiscence, is smoky with the poetry of the unintelligible. The black squad. Welders and platers and caulkers and jogglers. The heater boy and the holder-on. He spans epochs now impossibly distant, times whose glamour is inextricably bound up with the fact of their being finished, over, boxed, one more picturesque episode in the heritage pageant. The face of Labour is now Malcolm Foy, not sinewy sons of toil. Men with limbs white as stripped branches under their baggy suits, complexions fresh as boys but hairlines thinning, as if ambition is scorching through their skulls.

The silence between them is in danger of becoming eloquent, she can sense significance massing like distant thunder and in that recognition she realises the remarkable lack of heavy weather in their dealings to date. Sexual static, yes, but no heaving emotions, no pain and, perhaps in consequence, no real exhilaration either. She shivers extravagantly, hugging her shoulders, but he doesn't take the hint; however spellbinding the view, she's had enough of this scarred landscape, not quite a waste-land, still worth protecting with bayonet fencing and dogs, but futureless, forsaken.

His face is indecipherable in the Lucozade light. The wind off the river seersuckers his shirt. Finally he turns and nods towards the activity on the opposite bank.

'See that? That's what I'm supposed to represent.'

Something tells her he's not talking about the con-stituency.

'You should try it sometime, being a walking advertise-ment for a dying way of life. Does wonders for the self-esteem. Half of them blame you for selling out the Wobblies, the other half for not moving with the times. You're either a scab or a dinosaur, or just a user.'

He draws breath sibilantly through his teeth.

'If Rangers have lost at home I can hit the treble.'

Only when she feels the relief does she register fully the anxiety it displaced.

'So that's what it's about.'

'What what's about?'

'The bear with a sore head act.'

He looks at her and the anxiety returns, which means she has to take the offensive.

'Somebody's nipped your head down at the House, and you're taking it out on me because for once I haven't spent the week sitting on top of the phone in case you ring. I'm sorry you couldn't get in touch. Now you know what it's like. Some of it anyway. You still don't have to intercept the knowing looks, watching them guess your bra size, or stand there like a dummy while they ask *you* what *I'm* having to drink. Not that I can blame them really.'

'Well, don't blame me, sweetheart. You get the same breaks as the rest of us, it's your problem if you don't take them.'

Suddenly they're in the middle of a row. Or he is. Nostrils dilated, moustache pulled taut, his voice guttural, almost a growl, starting just south of his Adam's apple. He wants confrontation, physically needs it, aggression pours off him like rut. She wonders if sex would serve as well and decides probably not: the whole evening has been leading up to this. A shame she can't oblige. She feels adrenalin's acid burning her chest, but she's done with all that, doesn't have arguments, isn't the type.

'There's no point pursuing this, Danny.'

'Who says? If I'm in the dock I'm entitled to know the charges.'

'No one said anything about being in the dock.'

Wear him down with his own strength, that's the strategy; like shadowboxing, eventually the lack of resistance will get to him. Providing she can sustain it. The heat in her thorax is spreading up her throat, contaminating, corrosive.

'No, you want to play Doctor Freud, let's play. The patient is suffering from an excess of testosterone. Well, let me tell you something: I'm sick of carrying the can for masculinity. You have problems, they're problems with me, not the XY chromosome, I'll take the rap. But you don't want that. It might mean taking a closer look at Nan Megratta instead of passing the buck to biological conspiracy, and we couldn't have that, could we?'

'Danny, you've done the masked lady rant before.'

'Don't flatter yourself, you haven't the tits for Margaret Lockwood. It's more like pass the parcel. Every week you unwrap another layer but I never get to the fucking prize.'

She feels the old fear. But of what: his rage or her need to retaliate? One last shot at appeasement. She forces her shoulders into a submissive droop, massages her eyelids with a penitent's weariness, but the sigh hisses like a punctured tyre. Her body is ready for nine rounds with Rocky Marciano.

'And what do I know about your life apart from a few punchlines, my weekly quota of after-dinner anecdotes? It's a two-way street. I don't expect you to tell me what your wife wears in bed, but you've not even been square with me about the blackmail.'

'What the fuck are youse daein'?'

So the 'keep out' signs weren't lying: a security guard and his dog, a pit bull, its albino body flexing like flayed muscle. No muzzle.

'Can youse no fuckin' read?'

He's a young man, too young to spend his drinking hours in a Portakabin in the dead zone. A Slavic economy to the eyelids, spots shining purple in the unearthly light. His flat-top haircut aspires to pick-ups and American beer.

Danny tends to the short-sighted, although too vain to admit it, and the watchman advances another ten feet before he registers the implications of the boyish figure inside the mansize uniform.

'OK, pal.'

But the youth isn't Danny's pal and doesn't seem too keen on being addressed as such.

'Freeze or I let the dug aff.'

Nan is tempted to put her hands up, but there's no guarantee that he'd get the satirical point, and even if he did it wouldn't necessarily amuse him.

Danny has yet to grasp that a pit bull in the hand cancels out the intimidatory advantages of manly middle age. He takes a step forward.

'Ah'm no fucking aboot.'

Danny aborts his second step, placing a reassuring hand on her forearm and murmuring into her ear.

'Don't worry about the dog.'

By now she's worked that one out for herself. It's the handler's movements that bother her, the subtle change in direction as he walks towards them, like a compass needle settling on north. His eyes, too, are fixed on her. He's barely ten feet away when she makes the connection: Danny jacketless, her unseasonal outfit chosen in antici- pation of an evening divided between steam-fugged bistro and the toasty interior of the BMW. Surely the girls haven't patrolled the waterfront since the sailors went away?

He stops twelve inches off, directly in front of her, and allows the dog to snuffle her ankle. She can tell from Danny's electricity that he's suffering on her behalf. Apart from the indignity of being robbed of his role as protec- tor, he *is* worried about the dog. She's fairly sure it won't attack without its master's voice, and right now its master has other things on his mind. She meets his stare and is surprised at the nature of the challenge. Not power, not coercion, but friendliness, complicity, a claim of right way beyond the familiarity of established intimacy. This is what it feels like to lose the last remaining power, the right to withhold. This is what it feels like to be so far down the pecking order that a plooky kid earning ninety quid a week to walk his dog along a derelict riverbank can assume she's his for the asking. This is what it feels like: treacherous organs stir as his eyes travel the length of her body, breaking the journey at breasts and crotch. She stands there while he inspects the merchandise, uncomfortable and faintly roused.

Danny still doesn't get it.

'Gonnae let us out the front gate, pal?'

She almost smirks at the outbreak of unparliamentary language. Reluctantly, the watchman turns his gaze.

'This is private property.'

'Aye, I know. I used to work over the river.'

His hand twitches in the direction of the tanker, but at the dog's growl he thinks better of the gesture. 'We just wanted a look at her.'

The slow leer returns to the boy's face, although this time his eyes resist the temptation to go walkabout.

'I wouldnae turn it down, masel'.'

She's been steeling herself against the point at which it dawns on Danny, the geysers of aggression can't have cooled so quickly; and now she senses him tensing beside her, knows that she's powerless to restrain him, that even a touch might upset the precarious equilibrium of the moment. Miraculously the eruption doesn't happen. Instead, he spans a hand around the base of her neck and grins in an uncannily close approximation of the younger man's smirk.

'We're out of here now, big man. Gonnae open up the gate for us?'

The security guard, while mollified by that 'big man', isn't about to relinquish the night's entertainment so easily. The graveyard shift must get pretty dull. It occurs to her that maybe he's holding out for a playmate. Judging from the proprietorial grip on her neck, Danny suspects the same. The youth has now relinquished his X-rated eye contact and is addressing his remarks to Danny. His body language is still locked on target, however.

'Any trouble, I've to get the polis.'

But it's a half-hearted threat, little more than a stalling tactic. She takes a step towards him, stopping just short of the sliminess of his synthetic cavalry twill. If she's going to be taken for a hooker then at least she'll pimp for herself.

'Be a honey and let us out. We'll get off and you can get back to your cabin.'

Beside her, Danny radiates wariness verging on con-fusion. This isn't like her. She plants a flirtatious hand on the guard's arm. 'No point in standing out here in the cold.'

His lips part in anticipation, exposing furred teeth. Unpredictability flickers in his eyes. For one terrible moment she thinks he might ram his hand between her legs.

'Gonnae come in and have a warm, then?'

She smiles regretfully, wrinkling her nose in the intimate whisper reserved for babies and children.

'Another time.' She glances in Danny's direction, not quite catching his eye. 'Prior engagement.'

They cross the yard, faces blank with the effort of self-control, not daring to exchange glances until they're out of the gate, across the cratered pavement and inside the car. The doors click, sealing them into the safety of leather upholstery and German engineering. They're still laughing when the barman hands them their drinks a mile and a half down the road.

It's too cold to sit outside but she agrees on condition that he doesn't want a replay of their debut in the beer garden. They settle at a picnic table under the intricate buzzing of the electricity substation, dwarfed by the looming black outlines of transformers and coils, insulators and isolators, the cat's cradle of high-voltage lines. The air is sweeter here but still dank. Nearby a foot ferry shuttles doggedly between the two banks, empty of passengers. She huddles deeper in his overcoat. Apparently the temperature doesn't affect him.

It's part of their ritual before the first touch, when they're still pretending that they might be acquaintances out for a casual drink, that he warms over the week's Westminster gossip, tidbits of embarrassment and hypocrisy, whispers the lobby correspondents' antennae don't pick up. She too has a role in this. Sometimes she teases

247

him for boasting about his access to the inner circle, feigning a boredom she doesn't really feel. Other times she's an eager audience, laughing before the punchline with a relish that's equally inauthentic. Now, as if to signal that proceedings have returned to normal, he embarks on a tale involving the racial and sado-masochistic predilections of a prominent Labour feminist.

'Basically she likes screwing the natives. Wonder what your pal Imogen would think about that?'

Nan could point out that Imogen's principles do not make her morally liable for the libido of every woman who calls herself a feminist. But she doesn't.

'If I ever see her again I'll ask her.'

It was a stupid thing to say. He seizes the news like a terrier, worrying at it for detail. She makes a reasonable job of keeping the self-pity out of her voice but he's not fooled.

'Pretty much the procedure you've been putting me through.'

She tuts in perfunctory rebuttal.

'It's been ten days now.'

'Nine.' She corrects him automatically.

'Ten. Unless you count seeing you last night.'

She turns her head too quickly, as if there were something he could have seen.

'I thought you were in London.'

'I was. You've got me dreaming about you now. Nearest I come to getting you into bed these days. Funny: I never dream, not really. Just action-replay stuff: select committee, Saturday surgery. If that's all the subconscious has to offer, give me *Take the High Road* any day.'

'Ta very much.'

He lifts his hand and with the ball of his thumb lightly smudges her nose, like a sculptor working with wet clay.

'I was in a house, big place, high ceilings and peeling

walls, no furniture downstairs, and upstairs just this kist with all these drawers. Tell you what it was like: staying at home in Fair Fortnight when I was a wean. That feeling that you're the last one left on the planet. I opened one of the drawers and it was lined with newspaper, nothing inside, just this sheet of paper with one corner torn out.'

She had forgotten the banality of other people's dreams.

'So I opened them all. Same story every time, the same sheet of paper with the same bit missing. Until the last one. All brown and foosty so you could hardly make it out, but the photie was you all right. I tried to get it out of the drawer for a better look, so I could read it.'

For a moment she almost believes in revelation. He shrugs apologetically.

'That's all I remember.'

Belatedly it occurs to her that he may be making this up, a middle-aged philanderer trying a few teenage tricks. With the cold eye of the caricaturist she notes his incipient turkey wattle, the promise of crêpe ruff contrasting cruelly with the theatrical vigour of Cossack eyebrows and charcoal moustache. She remembers such startling alterations of perspective from her other life, knows them to be symptoms of mood, not objective takes on reality. In the course of a minute she can swing from acceptance to pitiless judgement and then, just as suddenly, turn partisan, protective. Tomorrow he may be handsome again. But tomorrow he won't be there.

He taps her lightly on the forearm, a habit of his, as if attention were an infinite commodity and he could never have enough.

'I've been thinking: why don't we go away? A weekend somewhere: mountains, good food, find out if your snoring's any worse, wake up in the same bed. If we get any sleep.'

But his smile is a flimsy garment, behind it his face is stripped of both senatorial assurance and street-corner brio. She feels immense heaviness, an all-enveloping, dragging reluctance, along with a faint undertow of nausea.

'You could always buy a pair of earplugs.'

He sighs.

'Always the romantic, eh?'

But in her experience romance is largely a masculine indulgence, a luxury few women past adolescence can afford. All the mystic paraphernalia of saved cinema tickets and letters conned by heart, glimpses of the beloved from the tops of buses, occult readings of coincidence, the palimpsest revealed. The terrifying implications of transcendent love. Maybe this world isn't all there is, and he's still out there, waiting.

Before she can stop herself, she's shrinking from his touch.

'Christ Almighty, Nan, what is it with you? No Queensberry rules in the bedroom but if I lay hands on you without a hard-on you'd think the sanny man had slapped an order on me. If you're trying to tell me I haven't been reselected, I'll quit now. Spend more time with my family.'

She realises she has been thinking of him as a man at ease with his emotions, and he is, with the easy ones. Candour for the cameras, bonhomie at the bar, various modes of platform anger from whispery menace to pistol-crack indignation: all readily accessible. But faced with that unmarketable product, rejection, he's reduced to weak parliamentary puns.

Maybe he puts his drink down a little too smartly but it must be a flawed glass, for it shatters almost pleasingly into five neat sections, like paleolithic blades. Time fractures in sympathy, imploding with the apprehension of larger disasters, moments when the predictable universe lets us down. After the split-second hiatus of shock he starts to curse, over and over, the shards cupped loosely in his palm. Gently, she opens his hand and removes the glass to the end of the table, turning his fingers, checking for cuts, his flesh glinting wetly in the phosphorous light.

'You're lucky.'

He smiles grimly. 'Not from where I'm sitting.'

Now finally she registers his suffering and, in spite of herself, feels a flicker of adolescent triumph, as if all over her body flaccid cells are tautening, nerve-ends crackling with a sense of their own power. But separate from that, the recognition touches her more deeply than any amount of armchair affection, or their bouts of outhouse sex, getting rougher and readier of late to her inexplicable satisfaction. For the first time she considers the possibility of a future beyond their next assignation and identifies the nameless dread. It's not a question of four hands on the supermarket trolley or strange smells in the loo, domesticity isn't an option even if she keeps out of gaol, it's the other life sentence that threatens her: a world where everything matters.

She never understood those confected images of erotic felicity, hand-in-hand through the cornflowers, sunshine on freshly-washed hair. What about dislocation, hallucination, the charring of flesh, surrender to forces far from benign? And yet she too is conditioned by the clichés. Sitting here flanked by clearance sites and closed-down factories, in this buffer zone between industry and leisure, redundant past and the purposeless present, the dread is suddenly swamped by a tidal wave of hope. In that instant an entire future assembles, impossibilities click into place, a lifetime, shiny as advertising, is revealed in the pulse of a second. Has it been waiting, unguessed at, all this time?

She closes his fingers within her own.

'They say Skye is worth seeing this time of year.'

'Must be eighteen months ago now.'

He pats his jacket pockets in the desultory manner of an airport bodysearch, seeking the inevitable book of matches, latest souvenir of the constant round of bars and restaurants beside the Mother of Parliaments.

'I heard that fat clown at the Home Office was coming up to look round the Bar-L, clap the governor on the back before handing it over to TrustHouse Forte. Cup of tea with the screws in the afternoon, shuffle round the Special Unit, macramé and cake-icing demonstration by the drug dealers and multiple murderers, then into the penguin suit for a heart attack on a plate. Supposed to be a surprise visit; top security. Amazing what you pick up over a swally with a pal in CID.'

At last. He retrieves the matches from an inside pocket. *Hooray Henry's!* a gold scribble on matt black. That'd go down a storm with the constituency.

'I saw Kropotkin and his pals on the other side of Buchanan Street one Saturday morning and crossed over. Spur of the moment. God knows why. I suggested maybe they'd like to arrange a wee reception committee, demonstration of popular feeling, remind the overfed slug that getting the voters out in Tunbridge Wells doesn't mean he can stroll into Glasgow any time he fancies it. Seemed a good idea at the time. I didn't know what headcases they were then.'

The cigar end glows and fades. He looks up as if expecting her to supply the punchline.

'I was down at the House when it happened. One of the press boys said there'd been trouble. I checked the

Teletext: the polis always like to talk up their injuries so I wasn't that worried. They stub a toe and it makes the casualty list. I didn't know about the poor bastard until next morning when I turned on the radio.'

Evidently she isn't showing the appropriate reaction.

'You remember, for Christ's sake? The George Square riot. That polis that got cracked on the head and ended up with the cabbage patch dolls learning to tie his shoe-laces again.'

A year and a half ago she had her own problems.

'Wife at home knitting bootees: he'll still be singing nursery rhymes when the kid's bringing home a wage. I know I should have told you, Nan, I thought about it, but,' he shrugs, sifting the words, 'how many endorsements does it take before the ban? The past week it's looked like I was getting my jotters anyway. It was a fucking stupid thing to do, but ninety-nine times out of a hundred I'd've got away with it. They changed the itinerary at the last minute. He wasn't supposed to be anywhere near the City Chambers. It was me tipped them off.'

He shuts his eyes.

'We're talking incitement, maybe conspiracy.'

He seems to be looking for absolution, but all she can think about is where Jack Ibster might fit in to all this.

He screws up his face.

'Jack? No. The only people who know are you and the Wild Bunch out there. Anyone else finds out and that's me finished. Not too many vacancies for burners in the job centre these days. What's Jack got to do with anything?'

'Quite a lot if it was you he was trying to blackmail.'

Afterwards, replaying the conversation, asking herself just when she took the decision to believe him, she's not sure that it wasn't even before the subject was broached.

But his reaction to those twelve words clinches it. There's no faking that sort of surprise.

While he fetches a final round of drinks she too leaves the table, walking a few paces towards the river to the point where the relentless monotone of the substation drowns out the clashing treble of the pub's juke box. The water is black, with a manmade orange shimmer on its restless surface. The sky gives out the first tentative spits of rain, diffusing the oyster coronas of the street lamps into dandelion clocks, intensifying the thrill around the wharf's green landing lights, beads of primary colour in the city's umber wash. Below her the ferry completes its forty-yard crossing and grinds onto the cobbled slipway, allowing a sole passenger to disembark, and for a moment she pities the loneliness of the unknown traveller, as he finds his car, fumbles with the lock, and fires the engine into life. Reversing, his headlights catch the opposite bank of the river below the silhouettes of grain store and dockyard crane, casting huge circles on the slanting concrete, and she marvels that, even after identifying the source, they still strike her as mysterious. Maybe she was off school that day; or dreaming at the back of the class, leaving physics to the boys with greasy hair and quilted anoraks; maybe it's a perverse act of faith, superstition in the teeth of science. What does it matter? She's glad to find explanation superfluous. She's lived life by the text-book too long.

It's too late for anything but home so he hails her a cab, pressing a ten-pound note into her fingers through the open window just as the wheels start to roll. She's grateful for his timing: her purse isn't up to a principled refusal.

An invisible rain has polished the midnight pavements. The taxi passes a stationary police car, tails a cruising colleague until he stops for a fare, otherwise the roads are empty. Hitting the grid of streets in the city centre, their route stretches ahead, an unbroken vista of red lights, yet as they approach each intersection the signal flickers through amber to green, obliging their progress like the unravelling of a red carpet, or the parting of the Red Sea, allowing them to ride the length of the rollercoaster road without even changing down.

The driver crumbles the silence into a bronchial chuckle.

'Looks like somebody up there likes you, hen.'

As always, she selects the spot on the platform to give her the earliest glimpse of an oncoming train. It's easy to be fooled by the slicing hiss of current on steel, the sinister whispers of compressed air, the *trompe-l'oreille* of Victorian tunnels, but from here she can see the parallel skis of white light curving towards her through the darkness. She feels the fierce, cold blast of air, its pull stronger than usual, then a tepid backdraught. Two trains, clockwise and anticlockwise capsules of the subway, are drawing into the station simultaneously. The jumbled passengers on the central platform turn toward their destinations like country dancers, do-se-do. Nan enters her train and, settling in the tartan upholstery, looks up to see Maggie and Imogen in a compartment on the opposite side of the platform.

They're huddled on a padded bench marked out by double doors to one side and a vertical steel support to the other. Next to Maggie is a woman evidently planning on feeding the five thousand without the loaves and fishes trick, either that or the message bags at her feet contain a light snack for the man-mountain beside her. It is on his account that the two friends are occupying a space much smaller than their entitlement, a proximity only intimacy could sustain, thighs seamed together, torsos angled, one leaning forward, one sitting back, so that Imogen is in danger of inhaling the brittle wisps of frizz escaping from Maggie's careless contrivance of a hairstyle. Their expressions are blank, thoughts not wanted on voyage, but their closeness is more obvious than if she'd spied them sharing a joke, a bond stronger than liking or interest or fun, just a fact of life.

As the doors close Nan looks away, fearing discovery, but she's safe enough. Sealed behind two layers of reinforced glazing, she couldn't be further from their minds. The trains pull out in opposite directions.

C al is taking his fifth telephone call since her one o'clock appointment began. His Bart Simpson novelty clock indicates that it is now seven minutes past. She swings the imitation-zebra swivel chair through 360 degrees, taking in the stainless-steel vase of Aaron lilies, the buttermilk linen sofa, the lithograph by the up-and-coming Glasgow artist and the huge Victorian desk, leather-topped, brass-handled, glowing like a lovingly polished conker.

Finally he replaces the receiver.

'Touch that phone once more and you can find yourself a new manager.'

The telephone emits its single electronic peep. He catches her eye. The ringing continues. Neither one speaks. Finally she cracks, lifting the receiver and handing it over.

'Borgia Catering: Lucrezia speaking, how may I help you?'

It's his accountant calling to check some detail about the books. It seems the taxman is cutting up rough. Cal stands and hunts through the topmost drawer of the filing cabinet, retrieves the relevant sheet of paper and reads out a string of dates and figures. Still listening to the voice on the other end of the line, he shrugs off his jacket, first one sleeve then, switching the phone to his left hand, the other, grunting intermittently to indicate his continued attention to the conversation but keeping his eyes unwaveringly on Nan. Next he's loosening his tie and slipping his braces, unbuttoning his shirt, beckoning her over with a matter-of-fact flick of the head. Warily, she approaches his side of the desk. He indicates that she is to examine his back. Her face assumes a blend of resistance and disbelief.

'Hold on a minute, Bobby.' He gags the mouthpiece. 'Near the shoulderblade.'

The gaping shirt exposes chest hair, bark coloured, sparse and straight like the growth of pubescent boys, incongruous against that hothouse tan. Furiously she studies the shirt, its freed tails, French seams and mother-of-pearl buttons. Only now he's taking that off too, trapping the receiver between neck and shoulder, still making those small noises of assent into the mouthpiece. The manoeuvre proving impractical, he takes the phone in his hand again and, after a couple of ineffectual twitches of his left arm, offers it to Nan to remove the sleeve. Despite his preoccupation with the voice in his ear, the situation feels like a test. Power hangs in the balance. Like that custom-made shirt – half off? half on? – the moment is open to interpretation. Its logic demands one of them at a disadvantage, but the roles have yet to be assigned.

Moving behind him, she pushes the heavy cotton out of the way and, seeing the raised mole on the upper back, traces its contours with a slow, deliberate touch. His skin is soft as a girl's, the pores invisible, a broad blank canvas dotted here and there with caramel pigment. She can see why he's worried by the cindery pink nub on his shoulder, a freak outcrop on this blemishless plane, but it looks harmless enough, an apparently igneous crust with a yielding, almost moist texture. It quivers fleetingly under her fingers as a faint spasm passes through the generous flesh.

The door opens and Tinkerbell bounces in with a pile of mail.

It's the girl's lack of surprise that embarrasses her. As if it happens all the time, as perhaps it does. She places the letters on the desk. Nan withdraws her hand and Cal smiles, the moment being his again.

'I see the coven are in.'

She follows his sightline to a quartet of middle-aged women in the centre of the room. The table is strewn with the debris of langoustine shells, avocado skins, raspberry vinaigrette and abandoned bowls of cullen skink, a preliminary skirmish in what is evidently to be a lengthy engagement. They're drawing out softpacks of extra-long cigarettes, flicking laminated thumbnails on shiny gold lighters. Furls of smoke catch in the spotlights' pencil-beams. She notes the straining waistbands, the brittle candyfloss hair, a glittering of ring and watchstrap, a certain appliquéd glamour. Then one of them, the plumpest of the party, tilts her head back in a full-throated cackle that shakes the table, and judgement turns to envy, the pang of the new girl in the playground. The joker was once a small woman, her still-dainty fingers and feet now at odds with the compacted white jeans and swelling sweatshirt, its rhinestone-spotted leopard ready to spring. Her hair is a puffball of lacquer, her nose has the dropped septum of surgical correction, dusky cheekbones are blazoned on the bottle-browned face in defiance of nature or art. At this distance it has to be an illusion, but Nan can smell her perfume. Behind the teased fringe, her eyes flicker around the table, gauging her audience with a professional's timing. Suddenly, painfully, Nan remembers Imogen, but when she catches Cal's eye she realises she must be smiling.

'Who are they?'

'Lift-and-Separate's married to scrap metal, Miss Ibiza '69 used to be a dancer, married a footballer but didn't rate his goal average, the honey in red I don't know, and of course Jungle Jenny with the big game across her central reservation is the good lady of your very good friend the Labour MP.'

She should have guessed he'd marry a blonde.

'I know him, I wouldn't go any further than that.'

He cocks an eyebrow. 'From what I hear you've gone a lot further than that.'

He starts to laugh.

'Don't worry, I won't bring it up in the witness box.'

Once again she wonders why he seems so little disturbed by her situation. Beyond enquiring after her chances of acquittal, he's asked her nothing. Even the prospect of making the papers doesn't seem to worry him unduly. She's grateful for his broadmindedness, but not too grateful to be aware that her gratitude could be useful to him.

'Has Imogen said something to you?'

This redoubles his amusement. 'Let's just say that I like to keep abreast of what my friends are doing. Or who, in this case.'

The centre table breaks into a few bars of a pop song, surprisingly melodiously, until foiled by the inevitable raucous mirth. A look passes between Cal and the head waiter who is suddenly at the women's table, clearing away their plates.

'Why do you do it, Cal?'

His gaze returns, whoopee-cushion innocent.

'What?'

'These fireworks through the conversational letterbox, cryptic comments about Imogen and Danny. Stripping off in the office. You know what I mean.'

'Did it bother you?'

Hard to remember that outside it's still early afternoon. The restaurant, with its expensive gloom, seems to exist in a timewarp of the wee small hours. Late-night conversations, smouldering cigarettes, your place or mine?

'If you mean was I driven to a frenzy of lust by the sight of your warty back, the answer's no.'

'I was talking about Dannyboy. I'm surprised he hasn't mentioned he knows me. Still, he probably has his reasons.'

'How *do* you know each other?'

He selects a toothpick and channels underneath one immaculate nail. Briefly, under the table, his foot brushes hers. Maybe accidentally, maybe not.

'It's a small town, Miss Megratta.'

It took her some time to acknowledge that she was physically interested in Callum Macleod but the fact is now a given of her dealings with him and, sometimes she suspects, of his with her. Guilty fears. Reason reassures that there's nothing incriminating in the way her eyes feast on the fatted cheek or that sensual wad of flesh easing the gradient from jawline to throat, the voluptuary's sheen to his buttery skin. It's not as if she harbours illicit desires. Hers is a disinterested physical interest. The features she finds so absorbing, juxtapositions that can surprise her to tenderness, are not the man. At first she was misled by the charged quality of their encounters, the unrelenting attention, but it's to life he's paying observance: a form of narcissism, not personal homage. She knows it now, and has learned to ignore those rosebud pouts, camp as picture-house cupids, the unwavering gaze under that languid blink, all the promises of latent satyriasis. Unless she's altogether mistaken. There's always the possibility of misunderstanding, the old reluctance to shake off the hand on the buttock, to stonewall the stare, for fear of taking umbrage at shadows. *You wish* . . . And it may be no more than imagination. There's something almost innocent about his sexual exhi-

bitionism, tossing that fourth-form fringe to the gratification of maternal instincts everywhere, while offering
those too spotty and awkward and message-overloaded at
the time an opportunity to revisit the hairtrigger thrills
of adolescence.

The waiter arrives to take their order, monkfish for
him, smoked salmon scrambled eggs for her.

He raises his glass in salute.

'To the taste of things to come.'

She's given a lot of thought to the canteen, spent a
couple of Saturdays in the reference library with back
copies of the local papers, checking out the restaurant
reviews, following up with on-the-spot research. Of
course she can't afford to eat in any of them, and Danny
has never taken her anywhere fashionable, so she has to
make do with a peek round the door and scribbling
down details from the window. Now she presents him
with sample lunch and dinner menus, a torn-out hi-fi
advertisement from a glossy magazine, several swatches of
curtain fabric, and a paint chart with five colours circled
in biro.

'I thought we'd try for New York loft. I know it's
been done before, but not here, or not well. There's
more speakeasy booths than Prohibition Chicago in this
city, it's time we opened things up, with the atmosphere
and the food. I know what you're going to say: all those
places that made it into *Blueprint*, some Spanish trendy
does it over in mock-Mariscal, and the punters sit there
stiff as pokers, bolt their designer lager and never come
back. It doesn't have to be like that. What we've got to
do is create a place where people want to be seen.
Somewhere where you're going out just by stepping over
the threshold. A performance space where anything can
happen. So . . .'

Clearing condiments and cutlery to one side, she smooths out the plans on the table.

'We know Glaswegians smoke like chimneys, so what do we do about the punters who don't fancy inhaling Players Navy Rough Cut with their mangetout? We take the ceiling off. What's up there besides the staff washroom? A dralon armchair and someone's prize collection of mucky books. Who needs it? Then we've got some air circulating, and a really dramatic space. Next, we get some performers, stand-up, singers, bands, acoustic only probably, or at least a strict decibel limit, and the odd novelty act, magicians, ventriloquists, whatever. Kids just starting out. And we hire them as table staff. Casuals. We don't have set spots, no performance times, they walk on, they do their thing, start clearing tables again. No backstage, they have to be there, part of the whole experience. The punters talk to them, get involved. Nothing coercive, none of that audience participation fascism. There's a karaoke machine. If it takes off we have an hour a night, or one night a week. Obviously we have to have a core of non-performing staff, and obviously the performers will get paid extra. But we cut down on the numbers by having the customers collect their own food from the counter. They're called by name, maybe there's a bit of backchat over the mike, maybe they order under a pseudonym, maybe they want to be recognised: it's a party. And then we have the menu.'

Cal takes advantage of the arrival of the food to hold up his hand.

'Permission to interrupt?'

'Just hear me out. What's the problem with eating out in Glasgow just now? You've got pasta, bastardised Indian, bad French with wallpaper-paste sauces. Even here, look at the menu: apart from the fact that it's about as legible as a doctor's prescription, even when they do know what

264

it says they don't understand it. The days of intimidating the punter are gone. Look at it: far too long, it screams freezer and microwave at you, and you can go all the way to the bottom without finding anything you actually fancy eating. OK, it suits the sort of alcoholic poseur who just wants to be seen here, but don't kid yourself anyone's interested in the food. At Canteen the clientele is twenty years younger so we base the menu on vegetarian, lots of raw, interesting textures, bright colour combinations, but we do it with fish and meat too. Same with the puddings. It says healthy, but not puritanical, and the cooked dishes are really special. We've failed if they think they know what it's going to taste like, so we have to let them take a bit of everything. You know why people like Chinese and Indian, apart from the fact that it's cheap? Because they can mix and match. It's a social occasion not a pig-out. The chat's going round the table, so's the food. Tapas almost got it right, but if you have any more than two dishes you need a second mortgage, so we say try anything you fancy, everything if you like, and pay by the weight of your plate. They've been doing it in New York for years.'

His face suggests he's catching her excitement.

'You've never worked for Bettaware by any chance?'

'It's the right idea at the right time. It'll make your name.'

'But will it make me money?'

'Cal, by the end of six months they'll be queuing on the pavement Saturday nights. You'll feed more famous faces than the BBC canteen, and they'll get up and do a number if they're pissed enough. We'll never be out of Tom Shields' diary. Probably get written into a gag in *Rab C Nesbitt*. And then, after eighteen months, we completely change it. Start the buzz all over again. That's the big mistake of fashionable places, they forget the

Carnaby Street principle: what comes in, must go out. Punters get bored, so we anticipate, strike just before it happens. If we plan it properly we can do the conversion inside a week, not even missing a Saturday. What do you think?'

'I think your eggs are getting cold.'

His gaze flickers towards the waiter and instantly he's there. Proprietor's perk.

'Fetch us another scrambled eggs, and tell Kevin the lady's claiming the prize: she found the smoked salmon in the last one.'

She waits until the smirking boy is out of earshot.

'Thanks a million. All I need is for you to start causing trouble with Kevin.'

He refolds his napkin, fiddling to align the creases exactly.

'You've got to expect a little creative temperament in the kitchen, but I'm sure you'll work together very well.'

It's not the words themselves so much as the way he says them, something a little too studied in their casualness.

'But we won't be working together.'

He meets her eye.

'There's been a change of plan. The Canteen can carry on as is a little while longer. And we really need you here. I've interviewed the world and his budgie for the second chef and no one's up to it. Kevin's got enough days owning to take him up to retirement. He says I'm working him to death. Can't have that, the insurance premiums'll go stratospheric.'

Her first thought is that she mustn't cry. All that work, all her planning. Childish to believe that it might have happened, that she might have windfalls and lucky breaks like the rest of the world. Letters to Santa. She's glad she didn't finish her eggs, what little she did swallow is curdling in her stomach, threatening to defy gravity all over his graphite damask table linen.

'You'll learn a lot, Kevin's a genius, he's worked with all the names.'

Now suddenly she's angry. They had an agreement. He gets her to give notice on her job, not a job where she's happy but there are comforts in not being a contender, and then he unilaterally ditches the deal. Second chef. Scullery maid. Is it a change of plan? Or the one he always had in mind?

'Nan?' He clicks a finger in front of her face playfully. 'Still with us?'

'Don't. Just don't you fucking dare dump on me and try to tell me you're doing me a favour.'

He looks surprised. Perhaps it hasn't occurred to him that this is her life he's playing with.

'What do you think I am? Some skivvy you've bought in from an agency? A bimbo just out of catering college? I don't care whether Kevin's worked with Anton Mosimann or Albert Roux, he cooks like a cowhand. If they ever stop making catering vats of raspberry coulis he's in trouble. The only thing I could learn off him is how to turn perfectly good produce into pigswill. Only reason you haven't had a gastric epidemic yet is that nobody can get more than a couple of forkfuls of the shite down. If I were you I'd check that he's not on the take from Alka Seltzer . . .'

The fact that he's laughing makes it worse.

'You think you've bought me, lock, stock and barrel? I'm some domestic machine and all you have to do is select the setting: manager, second chef, dishwasher? Some kitchen slag? I don't have a lot going for me, no money, no home, no private life unless you count a timeshare in somebody else's husband. You can fuck me around all you like, nobody's going to give a damn, but

I can cook, and you're not going to fuck around with that.'

The centre table is watching, fascinated, their revels suspended. Why couldn't she manage this with Danny? This sudden, limitless rage? She can feel her pulse racing, the searing in her chest, the prickle of fear, or excitement. A Pavlovian response, pure conditioning. What happens next is he hits her.

But not this time. So many experts tell us how badly we communicate, how flawed and fallible the messages we send, but when it came to the point he understood. He'd heard it all before, threats and denunciations, the setpieces of domestic melodrama, wearily predictable as afternoon films, but he knew this time was different. She remembers the smell he gave off, sour, unfamiliar but unmistakable, an atavistic odour of crisis triggered by primitive genes.

'Who's Kilner?'

His voice is casual.

'Just now, you called me Kilner.'

'You must have misheard.'

But the thought police are already carrying out house-to-house enquiries. Sometimes when her brain is idling, screening the out-takes of the day, she finds herself saying his name. She tells herself it's meaningless mental static, her subconscious spring-cleaning, but it slipped out with Danny too.

Now her tantrum is spent his tone has hardened.

'I run a business. As part of that I have to allocate staff and resources to maximise profits. That means: when you work for me you do as I say. Got it?'

She takes a long pull of wine.

'I get it. I'm just not sure I agree to it.'

'Well, let me know when you've made up your mind.'

The encounter is over but, trapped by the etiquette of the table, neither moves.

'I've just remembered something.'

She delves in her bag and places the letter on the tablecloth.

'You were right, it was for you.'

He raises an inquiring eyebrow.

'Process of elimination. Jack had no reason to blackmail the others.'

'He had no reason to blackmail me either. Not that that's anything to do with anything.' He shakes his head at the approaching waitress and her dessert menus. 'Jack wasn't blackmailing anyone. He was being blackmailed himself.'

His delivery is crisp, efficient, reminiscent of that night at the tapas bar.

'He didn't tell Imogen.'

'Now there's a surprise.'

'Why should he tell you?'

'He thought I was the one doing it.'

Alarm bells are ringing in her head. For a moment she considers the possibility that Jack might not have sent those letters. The world rearranges itself, but her brain isn't agile enough to take in all the adjustments. Of course he's lying. He'd be crazy not to.

'Why?'

'Why was he being blackmailed or why did he think it was me?'

'Why was he being blackmailed?'

'I can't tell you.'

'Why did he suspect you, then?'

'If I told you that you'd know why he was being blackmailed.'

She shrugs. 'Suit yourself.'

Not taking her eyes off him, she reaches for the envelope. He leaves it until the last minute then brings his hand down soundlessly, trapping her fingers. She expects him to puncture the moment, release her, say something. Her knuckles are stinging in his grip.

'If I'm wrong about Jack I still need the letter. You can't have it both ways.'

'Can't I?' He's not letting go.

'If you're worried I'll go to the police, forget it. I'm not interested in bringing anyone to justice, I just need to know.'

Has it really taken him so long to make the connection? His anger is like a magnetic field, everyone in the room can feel it without knowing what it is, its silence more arresting than her recent leap in volume. Danny's wife is staring again. A table of business-lunchers stop drinking and turn their heads as one. Time passes. Within the dead weight of his hand she detects the first flutterings of muscle fatigue, he can't maintain this pressure indefinitely. Yet when, without warning, he gets up from the table, she registers the breaking of contact as a loss.

'It's the fifteenth today, you're due to start on Monday. You'd better think it over. If you really believe I killed Jack Ibster, you've taken the wrong job.'

Like many markets, the Barras retains something of the medieval, a gaudiness amid privation, the illusion of abundance in a climate of need. The fluorescent plastic tat proliferating over these weekend stalls conjures the same doomed, fleeting gaiety as the sweetmeats and gewgaws of six hundred years ago. The people, too, seem a throwback to earlier times, leathered traders, men held together by scars and spectacles, women boldly but inexactly painted, as if the wind has worn away their features leaving them free to improvise as they wish. The punters display a variety of boxers' noses, boss eyes, faces pulped and randomly rearranged in the healing, inherited quirks that cube the cranium and foreshorten the chin, suggesting intelligence similarly botched. Drunks with raspberry complexions and a strange, jittery watchfulness stand aside as women roll continents of flesh along the pavement. What better antidote to the lie of advertising than these teeming streets and covered warrens, this comforting reminder of common humanity, a state where regularity is freakish, imperfection the norm?

Just inside the wrought-iron archway she pauses, overwhelmed by the sudden apprehension of other people's lives, the philosophical impossibility of all those clashing normalities. Containable panic. A few minutes and her skin will harden into that shrugging acceptance of which Danny so disapproves, although she can see he enjoys the disapproval, the moral superiority it allows him to indulge. Doubtless it is shameful, callous even, but it's the same cold shoulder she turns on herself. Without it would she have survived Kilner? On the other hand, without it, maybe she wouldn't have stuck around to find out.

It's one of those days which acknowledges no season, overcast but oddly bright. As ever in the market the weather is bitter, swirling gusts of wastepaper and grit, the susurration of cellophane in the gutter driven by the nose-running wind. Her eyeballs ache with the relentless whiteness of the sky, the frost-blanched concrete pavements, the merciless acid yellows and lime greens of the signs offering quantities no one needs at prices nobody can ignore.

All around her there's a smell she associates with grime: hot fat floated far from source, carried congealing in the cold air, now and then diffused by the welcome tang of vinegar as a chip-eater huddles by. Here, by the entrance, the food-sellers congregate. Rotating signs, tormented by the wind, whirl their promises of hamburgers and chips and tinfoil trays of yellow curry sauce and suddenly, cutting through the grease, there's the blessed scent of popcorn, clean as the singe of fresh ironing. A stallholder with a microphone, a man who seems to have discovered the commercial possibilities of personal abuse, harangues the crowd from the back of a truck, tossing out shallow boxes, while a sidekick weaves among the punters reaping the harvest of ten-pound notes. He's selling some kitchen device, an unfamiliar configuration of scarlet plastic and stainless steel which will eliminate the need for a whole range of conventional utensils. Men and women thrust their money into the air like school children bursting to impress. How many of them are plants, she wonders, lemmings with a refund, leading the masses to destruction?

Just in front of her a trio of boys with the unnervingly knowing eyes of late-twentieth-century prepubescents are sniggering and elbowing each other in what she initially takes to be some esoteric game. But the pretext is a third party, a woman of unnaturally narrow frame in a vivid orange raincoat. Even from behind, Nan can tell she lacks the temperament for such a colour. There's a desperation about her exhibitionism, the way she seems to be courting the trader's jibes while he, with the performer's instinctive aversion to anything he cannot control, maintains his abrasive patter as if she didn't exist.

The woman half turns, as if to stake a rival claim on the audience, and although Nan slides her eyes away instantaneously it's too late. The moment of recognition passes between them. Neither really wants this meeting but now there's no escape: they are bound by the iron laws of acquaintanceship.

Forcing her glance to return, clamping the smile to her face, she finds that Maggie's attention has switched back to the trader and his improbably versatile gadgets.

'You know how much they cost in Debenhams? Eighteen ninety-nine.' His consonants crackle as if picking up dust in the amplifier. 'And this wan: twenty-two ninety-nine in Boots. Sold out now. This is the only place you'll get them for love or money. Sorry, hen, in your case it'll have to be cash. Now, what's eighteen ninety-nine and twenty-two ninety-nine?'

He pauses to allow the more complete humiliation of his target, a mousy woman in a purple ski-jacket that never yet saw snow.

'Come on. I'm not asking you to explain nuclear fission: eighteen ninety-nine and twenty-two ninety-nine? Jeez. I cannae wait all day. Forty-one ninety-eight. Right? Aw look, the light's come on. Now I'm no going to sell you one of these for fifteen quid, I'm no even asking a tenner each. I'm saying – and God knows why, because you dinnae deserve it – fifteen quid the pair.'

Maggie is watching, predatory, waiting her chance with a smile perfectly poised between malice and vulnerability. Among the carbohydrate-clouded faces of the women in the crowd, her features stand out like a cartoon. Eyes and lips too sharply defined, a garish stain of colour on those desiccated cheeks. Booze or bad blusher.

'You huvnae the sense to buy them because they're the best bargain in Glesga, but think about it: you'll be going on your holidays soon. Gran Canaria, Lanzarote . . . OK, a weekend at Butlins if you're lucky. And holidays mean bikini time, which means you lot are in dead trouble. Who wants to look like a couple o' pound of pork dripping on the beach –'

'Does it bother you?'

The crowd titter, less in amusement than disbelief at the hubris of challenging this tin-pot dictator. The trader turns, slowly, knowing he can no longer ignore her.

'I can see it disnae bother you.' He appeals to the punters. 'Two of her wouldnae make an anorexic. Now, what do they diets always say? Hunners of fresh fruit and vegetables down your gub. With this you can shred your cabbage, chop your onion, grate your carrot. Two minutes: all the coleslaw you can eat.'

'What's wrong with using a knife?'

How drunk can she be at eleven-thirty in the morning? A wee voddy with her cornflakes? Not that she sounds particularly inebriated, but why else would she be heckling a complete stranger in the street? Unless he isn't a complete stranger.

'Time, missus, something none of us have enough of. The clock's ticking. Faster for some than others.'

Nan studies him more closely: mid-fifties she'd guess, losing his hair but gaining in virility, something unignorably penile about that tough pink tonsure, a something echoed by the high-riding bulge of the gut. Hardly a snappy dresser in his burgundy-coloured V-neck gathering bobbles around the overdefined pecs, but with a wash and a warm-through and the flattering filter of the drink, not unthinkable. An ill-advised pick-up on a rainy night?

The forest of eager arms seems to have had second thoughts, or perhaps they don't want to detract from the spectacle. Maggie addresses a woman who, absent-mindedly, is still offering up her fifteen pounds.

'If you really want to save time you'll cut out the visit to the Trading Standards when it snaps in half.'

Embarrassed, the woman lowers her hand.

The outdoor cabaret senses that he's losing. Faces in the crowd show an assortment of grins. Nan watches his expression change and feels her stomach shrink. Some primal equation has been upset: man's absolute right to be unpleasant if he chooses challenged by woman, whose duty is to charm. There's indignation alongside the ugliness. Maggie has broken the unwritten law and he can't be responsible for the consequences. Nan is not the only one to recognise this. Around her, shrewd-eyed punters strike poses of lip-licking anticipation. But she's the only one who feels afraid.

'The mince counter's over there, darling.'

'Thanks but I've had all I can take over here.'

'Well, fuck aff and spoil somebody else's view then, ya miserable bitch.'

Even Nan wasn't expecting the sudden crumpling of that paper face. It only lasts a second. No tears come, she doesn't make a sound, but the moment leaves its after-image branded on her vision. She sees now that the backchat was a sort of flirting, unlikely enough given the volatile combination of audience and masculine ego, but intended as a tribute. The crowd, too, seems sickened by the kill. A couple of men drift away to another stall. No hands in the air now. The deadpan insults rained on complete strangers were a joke, a perverse proof of good nature, but this humiliation colours everything that went before and now, belatedly, they feel offended, slurred. Maggie is heading towards her, garden-party smile cutting a swathe through the shell suits. A pair of junkies with skin the lemony-mauve of ancient bruises turn and stare as if Nan too has become part of the show.

They make their way through the towels and teeshirts, past the tooth-tingling barrows of cheap sweets, in the direction of the fleamarket, displaying perhaps exaggerated interest in the wares to either side of them. Despite the defensive gait of the shoppers, the wind-insinuated silt crunching between their back teeth, the street seems an intimate space, domesticated by the frills and ruches of the curtain stalls, the dinky watersilk scatter cushions, those three-piece suites sitting proud in the gutter, their suburban surrealism pricking half-remembered dreams.

Nan wants to keep the encounter brief but they're moving as if toward an agreed destination. And with Maggie, it doesn't take three guesses. But no, she's stepping through a doorway into the vicious tang of shellfish, handing over coins for two polystyrene tubs, then, outside again, passing one over. Mussels. Smoothly uneven like half-chewed caramels forced from the mouth. Soft yet gritty to the tongue. Nan tries not to look too closely: however invulnerable the shell might seem, underneath we're all blubber and tissue. The knife went in not easily, but more easily than it should. She spears one into her mouth with the rudimentary plastic fork, breathless with the astringency of brine, the wind stinging the vinegar down her fingers. Maggie seems unaffected, but then maybe if you drink as much as she does the tastebuds need a kick start.

As they draw closer to the second-hand stalls the punters change. Physically they're no different, the same graveyard complexions, the random juxtapositions of angularity and stodge, but here they shun the rainbow profusion of synthetic jackets for recycled tweeds and raincoats in the no-colour fashion houses call 'stone'. Little berets worn at a jaunty angle, carelessly knotted tartan scarves. Nan too used to dress this way, as if the second-hand sweaters and shapeless skirts held a richness of nuance denied to new clothing. Putting on these colours that didn't suit her, in sizes which didn't fit, she felt as if she were wearing the century, great swathes of experience draped on her back. When she moved to Glasgow she left everything behind. She had a history herself by then, and found it a much overrated commodity. Yet passing a trestle table of bric-à-brac as they progress through the market, she automatically checks its contents. Two plaster ducks, incomplete hookah, barnacled soap dish, pile of chipped saucers . . . Once upon a time even here she might have found something worth salvaging, some fragment of another life to add ballast to her own.

'I wouldn't have thought that was your style.'

Maggie's assumption that she knows what is, and is not, Nan's style is starting to irritate. Her mortification in the marketplace buys a certain forbearance, but it's not inexhaustible.

'The dealers are too efficient nowadays: ship anything decent down south or over to Germany. Or maybe we've just run out of stuff. There can't be an infinite number of old ladies sitting on treasure troves of junk. You don't get the bargains any more, it's mostly trash.'

'Same thing's happened to the man supply.'

Nan tries to laugh but finds she doesn't like Maggie enough to be amused.

There's a bar on the next corner. Level with the

entrance, Nan slows down. Inside, a soprano is belting out a Seventies disco hit, slightly sharp.

Maggie looks incredulous. 'At this time in the morning?'

Now Nan smiles, taking the remark as self-mockery, an alcoholic jest, until she sees Maggie's face. The widow slips ahead into the disorientating blare of the saloon.

'If I had any say it'd be banned altogether.'

Evidently this is a minority opinion. Karaoke is good for business, the only free table is right beside the machine, where the singer ordering her lover out the door is revealed as a dumpy man in white jeans. Maggie peels off her coat. Underneath, she is wearing a siren-red zip-fronted jacket reminiscent of a frogman's wetsuit and black leggings which, while bagging decently from hip to ankle, outline with pornographic snugness the vulval cleft. Anxious to deprive the lunchtime trade of further anatomical exhibition, Nan is only too pleased to buy the drinks.

'Stick a microphone in their hand, they think they're playing Las Vegas.'

Nan, who has been tapping her foot underneath the table, hums a small note of dissent.

'I'm always amazed how tuneful they are.'

In the slight hiatus which follows she realises that once again they are talking at cross-purposes. Her mind throws up an image of Maggie jaywalking across the M8 with a drunk's invulnerability, herself darting and weaving through the traffic, trying to keep up. She could drag them both back to the kerb, conduct the conversation on her own terms, but that would imply a degree of investment she doesn't want to make; she has nothing to say to Maggie. And yet here they are, knee-to-knee under the chipboard table. The choice is between presence and absence, which means the choice is already made. Disengagement is simply self-deceit. This *is* happening. And they do have something in common. She can still feel the force of his anger, that luncheon-meat flush as he swore down the mike.

'Can you honestly say he's that different when you're on your own?'

As a conversational gambit it's a little on the personal side but nothing to warrant this glassy stare. Dilute sunlight forces an entry through the grimy window behind them, exposing the warp and weft of tobacco smoke. Maggie shows no sign of replying.

'I mean afterwards, looking back, how much is there that we don't see, or guess at, within the first meeting? We ignore it, or forget, or make excuses, but it's all there. Right from day one.'

'What are you talking about?'

Nan feels immense weariness. Is it really so difficult making herself understood?

'The kitchen devil back there.'

'So when am I supposed to have been on my own with him?'

'I thought you were friends.'

So much for laughter as a social lubricant. Maggie's brand of amusement only holds enough for one.

'What gave you that idea?'

If only she could surrender now. Give in and go home. All around them people are luxuriating in the annihilating glamour of overloud music. Eyes shining, conversations continuing without misunderstanding, because no one is really listening to what is said. Meanwhile she and Maggie are shut out of this Eden, labouring to communicate when all that connects them is dislike. That and the Imogen-shaped hole Nan carries around.

'Imma tells me you've got a new job.'

The mike passes to a lanky man with a rhinoceros

quiff who betrays his rock 'n' roll haircut with a Sex Pistols number.

'Never a dull moment with Callum, I'll bet you.'

Something about the familiarity of her tone tells Nan they've never met.

'You know him?'

Maggie opens her purse and extracts a five-pound note.

'Mostly by reputation. Bumped into him a couple of times when Imogen was going through her fag-hag phase.'

Smoothing the knees out of her leggings, she straightens up and points a finger at Nan's glass, still half full.

'Same again?'

Nan's stomach has just plummeted twenty-five storeys. Compared to this, the possibility that Callum Macleod killed Jack Ibster seems a mere detail. It isn't that she objects to the idea of him being homosexual – although for her own reasons she does – it's the unlikelihood of it all. *Turd burglars, shirtlifters, fudgepackers* . . . He's always been camp, of course, but the things he *said*. Is she the sole butt of this joke or does it have a wider constituency?

Kilner always said he loved her more than she loved him. It was one of their ground rules, the facts they took for granted. She spent a large amount of her life making up for this differential. The incompatibility of his loving her, and his hitting her, never arose. Just as hitting her did not alter the fact that he was the injured party. Love was like that. Looking back now, the metaphor that suggests itself is hypnosis: when you wake up everything will be perfectly normal, excepting the way you see black as white. Once the influence is broken the whole spectrum becomes suspect, nothing is normal ever again.

One day, perhaps soon, she will have to tell the story of her marriage, but which particular version should she

tell? The part-time punchbag? A personality systemati-
cally dismantled? The betrayed wife? Her best option is
probably self-defence in the heat of the moment, the
animal instinct for survival: him or me. It's a reliable line
in courtroom drama, an easily understood context for
the bewildering escalation of that night. It may even be
true. But in her heart events arrange themselves into a
more mythic pattern, tragic flaws, poetic justice, a little
Old Testament retribution. He deserved to die. It's not
that she cared about the other woman, but the implications of the lie were limitless. So much time and effort
spent on squaring this circle, eight years sacrificed to
solving the great conundrum, the mystic complexity of
unhappy love, when the answer was staring her in the
face. *He was taking you for a cunt.* He'd often told her he
couldn't live without her, so she took him at his word.
He owed her a life.

Maggie's back with the drinks, slopping gin – Nan's –
on the rickety table, deliberately crossing in front of the
doorstep stage. She bends to slip into the gap between
seat and table, close enough for Nan to catch her breath,
a raw toluene smell, like nail-polish remover, an oddly
synthetic odour to issue from the interior darkness. Seated
now, she lights another cigarette. The cloud of smoke
she manages to extract from a single puff would show up
on the meteorological satellite, remarkable even in this
miasma of carcinogens. Must be a peculiarity of the
brand.

'Didn't you know? About Callum? They're all like that,
public school boys. Straight window dressing. Wife and
two point four kids in the showhome – or a string of
Merchant City secretaries – but behind closed doors,
camp as a row of pink tents. Still, at least you won't have
to worry about sexual harassment.'

As always when caught off guard Nan's instinct is to

lie, not because the fiction gives her an edge, just for the comfort of concealment.

'It's the fact that he's pally with Imogen that really surprises me.'

'Not any more. They met at some party and hit it off. Let's face it, everyone does with our Imma. She liked him and she hadn't got one in her collection yet. Screaming queens, yes, the Kelvinside opera-lovers, but not a Hugo Boss suit with a squash racquet in the back of the Porsche who just happened to prefer doing it with boys. No night sweats, no rent boys trying to put the squeeze on, not even hiding it from his mum and dad. No fun at all. You know why she got friendly? To buy herself some time to find his problem. She couldn't bear the thought that he might be doing OK.'

It may simply be the effect of the atmosphere, the engaging fug of bum notes and boozy breath, but the pickled eyes seem brighter now, the puff-pastry skin flushed into something approximating life.

'He had her number. She was looking for a lamb to save from the slaughter: he supplied one. Asked her to find a job for a kid he knew: HIV positive from an unlucky brush with the cottage industry, lost his job when the floor manager found out, crazy for a start in newspapers. Real tale of woe: right up her street.'

She pauses, stringing it out.

'And?'

'She got him a job as a runner, a gofer with prospects. Smart laddie, popular around the newsroom. A couple of reporters were doing a bit of digging around Callum Macleod, investigative journalism, but for some reason nobody could work out he was always one step ahead of them. They had to jack it in, getting nowhere, and guess what? Little boy lost found himself a new job.'

'Was *he* gay?'

Maggie exhales another environmental disaster.

'You tell me. If he was it was the only thing he wasn't lying about. Imma wasn't very happy but what could she do? She wasn't going to start kicking up a fuss if no one else had made the connection.'

'If Cal set the whole thing up, he's quite capable of pretending to be gay to gain her confidence.'

Maggie's lips split in a piano-key smile.

'Got the hots for him, have you?'

'I'm more interested in working out exactly how devious he is.'

The split broadens, exposing a stripe of gum.

'Think of a number and double it.'

Lunchtime comes and goes without either of them having lunch. An unbroken string of drinkers render a selection of hits from the past thirty years. After a while she realises that the talent on display is not singing but a highly accomplished mimicry, a perfect reproduction of the original recording artist. That small, stringy woman, eyes magnified to joke-shop proportions by the bulging lenses of her spectacles, produces the whipped cream and chopped nuts contralto favoured by tulle-swathed crooners in the Fifties. Close your eyes and you'd swear her pallid, eczematous daughter, wailing her way through 'The Greatest Love of All', was an African-American in thigh boots and Hiawatha suede. Ask them for an unaccompanied verse of 'Happy Birthday' and who knows if they'd hit the notes? The punters seem to judge each singer before they've taken the stage. At times they listen with the solidarity of an audience, staring mesmerised at the prompting screen, unselfconsciously lipsynching the song. A new singer takes the stage and the crowd is suddenly fragmented, each table hosting a different debate. Yet even those relegated to the status of background music find an acceptance, a tactful ignoring of their shortcomings. Nan grieves a little at her exclusion from the party. Much as she'd like to scapegoat Maggie, she can't offload all the blame.

The talk between them is inconsequential but never quite moribund. It turns out that Maggie has the most tenuous of connections with the abusive market trader. She was given one of his previous gadgets by her daughter as a birthday present, only to have its plastic parts suffer meltdown in the dishwasher. Normally she'd have shrugged it off, but the kid tried to get her money back and came home in tears. Maggie knew he was a chancer but she didn't expect to find him *literally* flogging the stuff off the back of a lorry.

'Wasn't expecting him to turn rabid on me, either.'

Nan aligns the beermats with the edge of the table, the memory of Maggie's collapsing face still too vivid to look her in the eye. Some reply is evidently expected.

'I thought only lovers were that aggressive.'

A young man in a baseball jacket takes the mike and selects a Beatles number from before his mother was born.

Maggie drains her glass, laughs her individual-portion laugh.

'You really are a case, aren't you?'

Is she? Maggie's tone isn't sufficiently hostile to dismiss the possibility. What if it really is like the songs: all pairing, sharing, caring, hardly wearing at all? She's always assumed that happy-ever-afters were more the exception than the norm, but no one really knows if their experience is representative. Who can say for sure what the word means? The colourblind know the grass is green, but that doesn't mean they see the same shade.

Her turn to buy again. She really ought to slow down. She scans the yellow mixers lined up below the gantry without enthusiasm. What the hell.

'Two gin and tonics.'

After her fourth, she finds herself mentioning Cal's broken promises over Nineteen Canteen. After her fifth, she asks about Imogen.

'She's fine.'

This is not the information Nan was seeking.

After all this time, the pain is still palpable, lodged in her chest like a stone, almost comforting in its solidity, not to be dissolved by tears, impervious to the distractions of irony or melodrama or the discriminating voice of reason. Imogen saw the best in her; now it seems that the best is without value. The experience is closer to annihilation than rejection, but it's an all too living death. Even in absentia Imogen remains the arbiter, a madhouse twist on the piety of seeing the other's point of view. Not that she hasn't imagined revenge. As always with pain there's the temptation to turn it to use, to torture the other with guilt, but what would be the point? Where does guilt get its purchase if there's no acknowledgement that she exists? There is nothing to do but wait. For the nerve-endings to numb, the rawness to pass, for the partial death that signifies survival. Hard to believe that there was once a time when contact was so easy that she had dialled the telephone number without any inkling of what she was about to say. That a dull day at work could be transformed by the dragging ring of the internal line and Dod's voice informing her that 'Mrs Rees' was waiting at the front counter. That describing the engine's knocking to a black-fingered car mechanic, or patiently shuttling overpriced clothing between display rail and changing room in a Merchant City boutique, she could murmur an aside that left her friend foaming with laughter. Afterwards she would turn each encounter over and over like a lucky pebble in her pocket, wearing it smooth, so that now their friendship seems a fairytale, as much a

285

fantasy as the welling emotions it generated. It is the nature of love to assume reciprocation, even a kind of telepathy; the illusion shattered, how much can be taken for granted? Did she misread embarrassed kindness in the face of her own too-obvious need, or is Imogen under the impression that they were casual acquaintances, temporary friends whose season has passed? And if that is her impression, does that not make it true?

'I've been seeing a lot more of her lately.' Maggie laughs in a way that has more to do with the alcohol than any actual humour. 'Feeling guilty about Jack. She still thinks I don't know. *Poor Maggie*. She'd be surprised what poor Maggie has picked up. She wasn't the only one. That was the thing about Jack: as soon as he made any sort of commitment he just had to be unfaithful to them. He was a bastard, my husband,' she squirms her latest cigarette butt into the brimming ashtray, 'but I miss him.'

'Do you? Or do you just miss being married? Knowing your enemy?'

Funny that, now, they have no trouble communicating. It's more than the indiscriminate intimacy of drink. At some point over the past two and a half hours a truce seems to have been declared. Maggie has taken to touching her, lightly, on the upper arm when making points of particular emphasis. Nan even finds that her eyes are no longer straying, with horrified fascination, to that black lycra crotch.

The widow lights yet another cigarette. 'Is that what Imogen says?'

'I'd be the last person to know what Imogen's saying, she's dropped me like an infected needle. Haven't seen her since I last saw you.'

Some restlessness in Maggie's face is placated. She draws deeply on the tobacco.

'Tell me about *your* brush with the enemy.'

Still infiltrating each other's dreams, reading each other's minds, wrenching at the root when the other was hurt, lodged in the entrails of each other's lives. But not in love. He was the jealous type, obsessed with the idea that she had more fun with other people, which she did. But what was fun compared with the metaphysical awe of their connection? When you find the meaning of life, it hardly matters that it's not tied up with pink ribbon.

'I fell in love with him and it was wonderful, then one day it wasn't wonderful any more.'

'The end?'

'Well,' she fishes the semicircle of lemon out of her glass, a white pip nestling amid the bitterness, neatly sliced in half. 'One of the ends.'

There were others. Finding out that he'd been dipping into petty cash, the knowledge suddenly illuminating all the accusations she'd never understood: how she emasculated him, shut him out, was obsessed with the need to control. What Imogen calls projection; though she'd worked out the mechanics before she learned the label. Not that that's any cause for smugness: it did take her eight years. So many of their fights are a blur now but that one she does remember, the two of them half-dressed, screaming across the satin eiderdown. This time he didn't touch her. It was she who felt the impulse to get physical, one little push to jar his head against the door frame. The thought of it frightened her more than he ever had. And in the bathroom, sitting on the lavatory pan in the silence between the artillery bursts of kicking on the door, noticing that the toothpaste speckles on the mirror could do with a wipe, wondering how many disposable razors it'd take to open up her veins. Even then she knew she didn't want to kill herself, it was just the next step in the argument. Self-mutilation: the penultimate taboo. Next day they had to replace the pane in the door with a mismatch; you couldn't buy that sort of frosted glass any more.

'Oh no, not this.'

Maggie is complaining about the song, a pudgy East End Jagger barging through 'Satisfaction' in a hoarsely rhythmic shout.

'Always reminds me of Paris. Staying with my god-mother in the Sixteenth. Didn't do much for Imma's revolutionary credibility but she was glad of it when she got arrested. No festering in the cells if you've got friends in the right *arrondissement*.'

Nan feels that familiar pang of exclusion.

'That was where I met Jack. I'd spent the morning on my own. Doing some shopping, propping up the bour-geois capitalists. He picked me up in a pavement café, ordered me a *pastis*. I paid. He'd bummed lunch off a different bird every day since he'd arrived. Two days later Imma brought him back to the flat. *Hello again*. Should have seen her face.'

She takes a long slow swallow of gin, as if toasting the memory.

'She could have had him, I wasn't that desperate. All that summer everywhere you went you heard the Stones. Every time you switched on the radio. In the *tabacs*. He preferred me, anyway. Of course he would have dropped me for a better offer. He kept on bumming the lunches. I used to check his pockets after he'd fallen asleep and find the phone numbers scribbled on serviettes. It was like his signature tune.' She mimes along with the singer, ... *some useless information ... to fire my imagination ...* 'The walls were like paper. She had the room next door.'

She tightens her lips on a tonic-water burp before continuing.

'The police think it's a *crime passionnel*.'

Nan has drunk too much to be able to tell whether this is anything more than random thoughts strung together on a rope of schoolgirl French. Even by their idiosyncratic standards of friendship, trying to frame your best mate for murder is going a little far. Unless it's a question of self-preservation. Which would put Callum Macleod in the clear. Gay, but OK. Give or take the odd drug deal.

'What's yours? The song that brings it all back?'

Nan's gin-washed brain sees everything very clearly, as if she's just arrived from outer space. In a far corner two women in short-sleeved blouses are handjiving to the song's final chorus, forearms like heavy, mottled hams, the looser flesh above their elbows a fraction behind the beat.

'I don't know, anything by Van Morrison I suppose. Kilner liked the way he looked like a loser.'

Maggie is suddenly up on her feet beside the karaoke machine, pointing the remote control device with a wavering aim.

'You're on.'

Nan shakes her head then realises she isn't in any condition for violent exercise.

'No way.'

'Go on: everybody's looking.'

A woman in a black crocheted cardigan who has been staring aggressively at Maggie now turns her hostile gaze on Nan. There seems to be a queuing system which the widow has managed to circumvent. Nan raises one hand in a gesture intended to indicate that she will wait her turn, but Maggie shoves the microphone into it.

And so it happens that Nan Megratta, married name Kilner, steps a little unsteadily on to the toytown stage and sings a slow sweet ballad of requited love. The tele-prompt spills its white couplets onto a pale mauve screen, each syllable ripening to an insistent yellow as its moment arrives, then gone, swallowed by the blankness of the background. Panicked by that inexorable yellow, she quavers the first line and the tables fall silent. She gets a flash of childhood, posing in front of the mirror, dressing-gown wrapped back-to-front, hairbrush mike in her hand: you open your mouth and everything goes quiet. In the fantasy they were always entranced, here they're merely expectant, heads tilted towards her, drinks momentarily forgotten. She muffs the next phrase out of embarrassment but the wincing awfulness of missed notes is preferable to the shame of drying-up. She doesn't need the prompt. She must have heard it a hundred times over the years yet it was always his song, they were all his songs. Now, belatedly, she acknowledges it as hers too, part of her life, her history. Why should the devil have all the best tunes?

As she sings, releasing inchoate sounds on trajectories which so nearly converge with the actual notes, she remembers. Not specific incidents or occasions, just the smell of things, perverse stirrings of nostalgia for a time she would not willingly revisit. By the second verse nothing matters, not standing on a pocket-handkerchief stage in a crowded bar with her eyes tight shut, not the thwarted chanteuse in her crocheted cardi, or the dead hush at the tables, or the tears streaming down her cheeks, not even the sympathetic bubbling in her nostrils. Never mind that the feeling is a lie, a prop used in the ritual of tenderness and abasement that followed their fights. Never mind that she was the one who was lying, in the absolution of her embrace. *Forgive me, never again.* Too right, pal. Never again. And yet through all the contaminating layers of deception and delusion, some truth survives. The music rises above its own banality, shameless in its predictable harmonies, the inevitability of its rhymes, and as her lungs fill with the luxury of sound she knows that, given the right song, she can still carry a tune.

S he arrives back at Catriona's to find Max loitering in the closemouth.

'You took your time. I was beginning to think you were gone for the weekend. Julie Andrews wouldn't let me wait inside. Obviously I look the type to lose control and take her on the pink dralon.'

This is almost certainly what Catriona did think, but Nan is not about to offer confirmation. It's a long time since she's seen Max, more than long enough to have cancelled out their tenuous acquaintance. He's looking more normal these days, not so meticulously groomed; in fact, now she looks closer, downright disordered. The waxy complexion is flecked with a sparse stubble, that tow-coloured hair striated with grease, the dandy's silk shirt under his biker's jacket crumpled with more than a day's wear. Amid the stair ghosts of tobacco smoke and other people's gravy she detects the sweetish hint of male genitals too long without water.

'What are you doing here?'

'Funnily enough I'm waiting to see you. Indoors if it's all the same.'

She replaces the keys in her pocket. Reintroducing him to Catriona does not strike her as a good idea.

There's a café at the end of the road, a housewife's hobby full of the crafty offerings of the night-school classes: handthrown sugar bowls, rag rugs, semi-abstract seascapes, exorbitantly priced and about as aesthetically pleasing as the home-baked tea loaves sagging on top of the yellow pine counter.

He returns with two coffees and a small piece of currant-studded masonry.

'I asked for yours black. You look like you could do with it.'

There seems little point in disputing this.

'You don't look too crisp yourself.'

'Yeah, well, been overdoing it a bit recently. Sleeping badly, probably not eating right. And my house burned down last night.'

His expression says he isn't joking.

'Would have been a chip-pan fire only I don't eat chips, so it'll probably get written down to an electrical fault. I was round at a friend's for the night, otherwise I'd've been kippered as well.'

He attempts a bite of the cake but, finding it resistant, lets it drop back on to the plate with an impact that sets off sympathetic vibrations in the teaspoons. In Cal's hands this bit of stagecraft might have amused her, but then with Cal, it would have been performed to amuse.

She knows she should be preparing herself for the moment he mentions Danny's name, rehearsing the right blend of indifference and irritation. Whatever he wants to ask her, the answer is no. A brief conversation, then, if it rates as a conversation at all. The signs are none too promising. She is used to a certain level of attention from men, not in the tongue-lolling category certainly, but they usually meet her eye. Or avoid it. Max's body language barely registers her presence. He seems more interested in the coffee, lifting the cup to his lips two-handed, the way actors in television commercials demonstrate the life-restoring properties of packet soups. As he leans in for the first sip she catches a glimpse of tiny unclean teeth.

'I want you to call Macleod off.'

It's not the tone of a man asking a favour.

'I didn't tip Foy off and I've no intention of ending up under the Crossmyloof relief road to teach me a lesson I don't deserve. The guy's an environmentalist, he doesn't need me to tell him the site's an unexploded bomb.'

She has the suspicion that admitting how little of this she understands would destroy any possibility of illumination. Under the circumstances, silence seems the best tactic.

It isn't.

His chair scrapes alarmingly on the patchily varnished floor as he pulls back from the table.

'I haven't got time to piss about. Your friend just tried to get me killed. You tell him the last whore I'd get into bed with is the Labour Party. The new boy wants to grab a fast headline, it's got nothing to do with me.'

He sits there detached from the table, faintly ridiculous, cast adrift on his raft of floorboards. Watching him, her eyeballs have the pan-fried feel of sleepless nights, heightening the photosensitivity she has experienced all day, a premonition of hangover's iron mask. Oddly, considering the quantities of gin consumed, she doesn't feel incapable, but the world reaches her complicated by the extra dimension of drink, a pinpoint clarity of vision that shoulders surrounding objects into soft focus. If Danny had wanted him dead, dead is what he would be. On the other hand, if he only wanted to frighten, it seems he's achieved the objective. No. Even this is unthinkable. Childish melodramatic suspicions, a combination of her own freakish history and too much bad TV. Since that lunchtime at the Greasy Spoon she's regained some sense of proportion. However untrustworthy Cal may be as an employer, in this matter she believes him: Jack wasn't sending poison pen letters, neither Danny nor Cal had any reason to wish him ill. Now Max is jemmying up the floorboards, uncovering another body, albeit a corpse that didn't die. He could be lying but somehow she doubts it. She has finally identified the odour hovering about him: a whisper of smoke, the cloying residue of unwholesome combustibles, synthetic upholstery, moulded plastic, man-made fibre. Could Danny be so stupid? She remembers the tendons in his neck like steel hawser as he staggered towards the balcony rail, Sean clinging to his back, and her blood thrills with the certainty of bad news.

'You should have left him alone.'

'Writing letters is now a capital offence?'

'Depends what you put in them.' She stops, registering what he's just said. 'It was you?'

Finally he grants eye contact. Those pencil-lead pupils behind their shields of glass.

She wants there to be no mistake.

'Guilt is like love –'

He lifts his head, enlightened.

'So that was the one that went astray.'

'How many others, for God's sake?'

He shrugs.

'Just the two.'

Her brain pleads fatigue the way it used to on those Sunday evenings when her once-a-fortnight father would try to fulfil his duties, the complete paternal service, by explaining the principles of calculus. Desperate to please him, nodding with wary agreement as he completed each line of hieroglyphics, knowing there was an answer, tense with the strain of pretending to understand.

'You're telling me Danny MacLeod set fire to your house because you're blackmailing him?'

His incredulity has a nasty edge. He pulls the chair in again, leaning forward over the table, his voice a hard murmur.

'Try again. Shouldn't be too difficult. Your boyfriend

wouldn't have the bottle, Ibster's dead, who does that leave?'

About 4,999,999 people. She plays a hunch.

'Callum Macleod.'

Doll's teeth peek out of his lipless smile.

'Bingo.'

Whatever connects Cal to the other two, it's unlikely to be an anti-government riot in George Square.

'So you give him the message like a good girl.'

She's always had an aversion to blond men: overfine eyebrows, those indefinite lashes, a suggestion of something epicene, or is it just resistance to her charms? Doll's fingers too, those miniature ovals pressed into the flesh. The coffee cup is drained. Another ten seconds and he'll be gone.

'Tell you what, Max: you deliver your own messages. They don't make any sense to me.'

The chair grinds across the floor again. Abruptly he's on his feet.

'All right, let's see if we can enlighten you.'

She remains seated, unsure of what's involved in this challenge until he hooks a hand under her armpit and hauls her upwards. The move is so unexpected, she's yielding to the pull before she's identified its source. Her chair, propelled backwards, falls deafeningly to the floor. Faces swivel towards them. No one intervenes.

Outside umbrellas are being furled, collars tentatively turned down. The flat sky has curdled into lumpen cloud towards the horizon but up above there's a jagged tear of blue and through it the late-afternoon sun is putting in an appearance just in time to set, bringing to stone and street the enhanced colours and heart-tugging glow of family snapshots, summers created in the darkroom, Ma and the weans on the prom. His motorbike, dated but shiny, its petrol tank the brittle red of Christmas tree baubles, is parked fifty yards up the road. He zips his jacket, knitting a diagonal stripe across the black leather, the neatened outline that of a tin-chested adolescent.

She doesn't have to get on, she can think of worse fates than unsatisfied curiosity, but since the worst has already happened she has very little to lose.

There's only one helmet and he's wearing it.

'What about me?'

'You're going to have to live dangerously for a while.'

As the machine starts to move beneath her she clutches at his waist. The leather tenses under her touch.

'There's a hand-grip behind you.'

She's never sat on a motorbike before, never wanted to either. To her relief he takes it slowly through the homecoming traffic and after the first heart-stabbing corner, where she attempts to correct the angle of the machine by leaning the opposite way, she finds instinct informs her posture. It's the hybrid nature of the experience she enjoys, to be as exposed as the pedestrians yet always leaving them behind, among but not of them. Feeling the chill on her face, watching the blacktop blur under her feet, smelling the river's cabbage reek and the chewy diesel smog and yet blessed with a kind of invisibility. With Max, too, there's an ambiguity, indeterminate status. Even with her hands on the back-rail, it's an intimate way to travel. For a while she holds herself stiff, keeping a modest strip of black vinyl on the seat between them, but it interferes with cornering and amid the vibrations of road and engine she's not even sure that he registers the contact. Odd that he should manhandle her back there in the café. Maybe it's a trick he learned in prison: a bit of strategic furniture-tossing when all else fails.

Looking down, she notices that between the end of his jeans and the contrasting cuff of that high-laced lumberjack boot the band of cotton sock is precisely the same sage green as the soiled silk shirt. Such fastidiousness of dress calls to mind art teachers and local government planners, self-consciously exotic subversives among the ranks of check viyella and fawn corduroy, flaunting shirts in egregious shades of mulberry and apricot but never quite daring to forgo the toning knitted tie. Max has had his shot at rebellion, so why bother with the dressing-up box? The sartorial fussiness nags at her, for all her openmindedness towards female plumbers and men who frequent the tiered counters along the cosmetics aisle. She least of all can afford the taint of sex stereotyping, being gifted with that most traditional of aptitudes, for table and stove, but something in her fails to recognise Max's masculinity, finds it unconvincing in a way that, whatever his bedroom preferences, Cal's could never be. It's more than a matter of chemistry, pheromones failing to spark. Watching Danny has taught her that politicians are born of personal slights and the need to sublimate them into matters of principle. What subliminal affinity with electoral impotence made Max a terrorist?

Heading into town, they pass shops, tenements, huge brick-built relics of industrial glory and stand-alone bars saved from the bulldozer, boxes of community spirit so redolent of loss it might be kinder to the community if they'd gone. Like the other amenities, the bingo hall and pizza takeaway, they occupy patches of eloquently redundant space seeded with municipal grass or showing the Hiroshima shadows of vapourised buildings. Regardless of whether she believes him about Cal, she's relieved that he's not accusing Danny. Safely distanced now, she toys with the fantasy that he *had* tried to kill Max, confronting him with her discovery, but the exchanges are formulaic, clogged with the stale rhetoric of Radio 4 plays, and she abandons the reverie feeling obscurely shamed. These days she sees Danny from a new perspective, yet one that seems to have been there all along, as if the condensation has cleared from a window to reveal a forgotten landscape. The way he cups his hand to the back of her head, drawing her face in to the stiff-tailored niche of neck and shoulder when they say goodbye on the street; the fusewire growth poking out from his ears once in a while (and the next time they meet, savagely cut back); the simple fact of him being a father of daughters. It's not the first time she's known such random access of sentiment, even when she had little enough cause; with Danny there are at least defensible grounds, moments when conversation turns off the bantering highway to bed and his honesty is like looking into a mirror. Rab used to confide in her, even Gorr, occasionally, happened upon in that mood when just about any mother surrogate will do; but while sympathetic, a corner of her remained apart, sorting through the confession, separating out the strands that did her and her kind harm. It's a question of biological opposition, necessary to the propagation of the species, a little grit in the oyster, a tension so fundamental to her she only recognises it when it disappears. When Danny opens up to her. At such times they have no need of the obsessive eye contact of adulterous couples, she feels his presence contiguous, complementary, like a sheet of metal from which her template has been cut. The apprehension is so precious it's almost a relief when the fit slips and they're back to their habitual abrading flirtation.

Slowing down now as the sliproad approaches, her mouth dries. Max is taking them onto the motorway. She tries to tap him on the arm, to attract his attention, but it's not compatible with the act of holding on. He must be aware of her agitation, but his only acknowledgement is to accelerate. She registers the needle's climb

299

somewhere around the collarbone, that flat certainty that she has used up all her choices and used them badly. The only thing that can help her now is fate, which has hardly proved a friend in the past. How quickly the body forgets the temptations of fear. It isn't so long since she lived like this day and night, fighting the seduction of surrender, the impulse to give up, let go. If you don't care whether you live or die, maybe it doesn't matter any more. Is he trying to scare her? The scuffed curve of helmet affords no clues. His body is blocking the speedometer but it seems to her they're moving very fast, more than keeping up with the traffic. On the inside lane, close enough for her to reach out and touch, a red Audi is travelling at exactly the same speed but erratically, threatening to stray on to their section of road. She fixes her eyes on a silver BMW two cars ahead. Seeing the danger, Max pulls into the outer lane a fraction too sharply for his speed, the wheels executing a skittish little jump. Saliva bitters in her gorge. Terrified into recklessness, she relinquishes the rear grip, left hand, right hand, and grabs him round the waist, curving her body into his back. As if in reaction he opens up the throttle, leaving the BMW far behind.

He pulls into a lay-by beside a shuttered snack van, kicks down one of the stabiliser legs and dismounts, offering no explanation.

The slope they're climbing is slum country, an inter-mediate zone straddled by electricity pylons, a strip of ersatz pastoral at the city limits. Although not steep the uneven ground is hard going and his stride too efficient to encourage conversation, it's as much as she can manage to stay a couple of paces behind. A captious wind is sweeping over the tussocky grass, brushing lustreless green to a dull silver. The drabness of the landscape defeats even the technicolour sun, though she feels its heat and the unaccustomed exercise drawing the blood into her face. Finally she gathers that they've arrived. The ridge of a small escarpment, hardly a beauty spot. Beneath them stretches a series of large windowless sheds, single storey, splay-sided, with shallow pitched roofs and connecting corridors made of corrugated metal; an arrangement with the neatness of a toy, something to be picked up and packed away at the end of the day, leaving no evidence. To one side is an enormous carpark, empty but for a single hatchback. Its frosted bodywork collects a grainy image of the sun, sending it back as diffused dazzle. The air is fresh enough, not second-hand as in the city, but without the fragrance of growth, as if nature were boycotting this corner of the country and the scrub under their feet just a clever imitation, a technological breakthrough by the whitecoats in the factory down below.

Max half unzips his jacket and fumbles the top button of his shirt. His waxy cheeks are stained a dirty pink. That pace wasn't achieved without effort. She too feels the need to loosen clothing, despite the whipping hilltop wind. The hiatus intensifies into silence.

'So?'

He gives no sign of having heard, but continues to train his eyes on the buildings down below.

'Thousands of acres of derelict industrial land in Scotland but the Japanese have to put their factories in a field. It's *cultural*.' He gives the word the inverted commas of contempt. 'And nobody says anything in case it looks like they don't like the Nips. Which they don't. Who's going to stand up to them? They can always take their factory somewhere else, and bang go seven hundred jobs. So they bend the rules a little, chairman of planning gets an early Christmas present. Who's it hurting? Local MP gets his face across the papers and a couple of thousand votes in the bag come the next election. The council chalks up some brownie points for a change. Developer gets his planning permission. Fifty acres of agricultural wasteland are suddenly worth seven and a half million quid.'

He cranes his neck slightly to look at her.

'Ringing any bells?'

'Not for me.'

His gaze returns to the factory.

'Usually works out fine. Council corruption is a grand old Scottish tradition. But now and then something goes wrong. Planning officers just up from England. How are they supposed to know the place was an illegal tip? Could be anything under there. Chemicals, toxic waste, asbestos. The locals know it was a midden, but nobody thinks to ask them, and why should they bother to say? Their MP knows fine, and their councillor, and they're both shaking hands with the suits and ties at the Lord Provost's reception, so it must be all right.'

The sun finally drops below the cloudline.

'The developer knows, that's why he's so generous with the gratuities, as I'm sure you're discovering, now you're on the staff. And it looks like the new boy for Clyde East has worked it out. Only his snout isn't in the trough. You know, I know, Uncle Tom Cobbley and all. But nobody knows if, or when, the place is going to go up like the Fourth of July.'

So that's where Cal got his money.

'I didn't know.'

He turns his head slowly, as if giving her a chance to vanish by the count of five.

'You've been running errands no questions asked? I thought you were brighter than that. Everyone has their price, I just assumed yours would include information.'

He has a point. Her eagerness to swallow Danny's

explanation amounts to collusion. Anyone else would have had their suspicions. But she isn't anyone else. Life for Nan Megratta is an uncertain dribble of unearned favours, not a quota of rights. Besides, information is a reciprocal deal. Give-get . . . But this is hardly the moment to rehearse the case for the defence. Unless that's why she's here, in the middle of nowhere with an ex-terrorist she knows just well enough to dislike. Because she needs to be weighed in the balance, away from the mitigating pleas of hormone or sentiment, to receive the definitive word of judgement. Or condemnation.

'What was Jack's cut?'

His nostrils pinch with distaste, triggered as much by her use of the Christian name as by any detail of the bribe.

'Whatever the going rate for a socialist conscience was six years ago. I wouldn't give you fifty pence for it. I understand your boyfriend came a little more expensive.'

'And you thought you'd get yourself a piece of the pie.'

The contempt in his reply seems genuine. 'Don't judge me by your own standards.'

'How you pay is up to you?'

He smiles, gratified at this reminder of his handiwork.

'A gentle hint about the jeopardy of his eternal soul.'

'With a bank-account number?'

'Theirs not mine. Just so they knew I wasn't bluffing. Two Bank of Scotland slush funds in the names of John Maclean and William Gallacher. Callum Macleod's idea of a joke. Dannyboy had the pin number and card for one, Jack got the other. DIY graft: a quick trip to the hole in the wall every time they're feeling short. No unexplained deposits showing up on the bank statement, no hanging about in motorway service stations waiting for the brown-paper parcel . . .'

Out of the corner of her eye she registers movement. A black cat with a butler's white shirt front and cuffs is trotting through the billowing grass, its head weighted by a long-bodied dead rat. Surprised, it freezes, jaws tightening on its prey, watching with a wariness in which the submission of the domestic animal is countered by the aggression of the feral. Then, freed by some signal that she does not see, it slinks off again, to be swallowed by the shifting topography.

'Danny told me you were leaning on him over the George Square riot.'

Max's lips twist in a sucked lemon smile.

'What a cretinous caper that was . . .' Remembering he's not among friends, his tone turns facetious. 'But the boys have to make their own mistakes or they'll never learn. And if you're going to balls it up without comeback, Dan's your man. Cal Macleod's a different kettle of piranha.'

Despite the offhand tone, the subject is agitating him. He stows his hands in his trouser pockets. Too late. She has already noticed those tiny pink nails, not bitten but peeled, down to the quick.

'Still, what else can you expect? It's the representatives of the people really stick in my craw, the red in your bed who put seven hundred people at risk to swing a few more votes. Our chairman of planning taking his mistresses to knocking shops where one night in a kingsize bed costs a month's benefit. Peeling the notes off his wad at the poker table. Whoever took him out of the game did us all a favour.'

'Whoever . . .'

She's not sure she's ever heard him laugh before, the sibilant rush of a carving knife whetted against steel.

'Ten years ago I posted a few indoor fireworks. Most got intercepted, one or two were opened: not a blister. If you're talking about hurting people, take a look at your boss. Think about how many junkies they find dead in public toilets with a needle in the groin. Kids injecting their eyeballs because they've run out of veins. What about the casualties if the economic miracle down there goes boom? How will you feel about having Desperate Dan's hand in your knickers then?'

She grabs at the crudeness, grateful for a pretext to feel aggrieved.

'You don't like women much, do you, Max?'

He allows her another moment of eye contact before replying.

'Not women. It's you I don't like. Walking through the sewer and thinking none of the shit sticks.'

They were up to their elbows in calves' liver that afternoon. Nan knew the punters wouldn't go for it but Kilner had instituted an economy drive. Althea had a way of circling a conversation, like a sparrowhawk stalking its prey. God knows what the decoy was this time, all Nan remembers is that her friend put the knife down on the board with undue care and remarked lightly,

'But he doesn't *like* you.'

So?

She'd known that all along.

The day is fading quickly now. Tilting her head back, the sky seems light enough, but the ground is already losing definition. Dusk is drawing out the factory's molecules, attacking its geometric lines with a pointillist busyness. It's time to leave. Out here, once night falls, there'll be no sulphurous glow to guide them down the hill. She tries to remember if there's a moon but unless it's blood-red or aspirin-full, matters lunar tend not to register on her urban consciousness. Even her menses follow an erratic cycle; perhaps she's attuned to Saturn's rings. The wind is at them relentlessly, battering them on all sides, tugging at the roots of her hair like a wire brush. Max's cheeks are blanched of colour again, tallow pale, yet still he hangs back. He didn't bring her all the way out here to tell her she disgusts him.

But Max and his motives are a dwindling priority, displaced by shreds of memory sharper than cinema, vivid as litter, a backlit insistence giving way to sudden darkness; the abruptness with which life plunges into loss.

It was late when she got in from Althea's, the storm still blowing, jostling the dustbins in the side passage, clanking the wrought-iron gate at the corner. As soon as she turned the key in the lock the wind forced an entry, smashing the front door against the coat hooks in the hall. She fought the gale to shut it, by which time there was little point in tiptoeing around in her stockinged feet. He'd be waiting up anyway. The radio was on, the DJ reading out an apocalyptic list of traffic warnings, trees toppled, bridges closed, lorries that had shed their loads. At first she didn't know where to find him. The lights were off downstairs. Bed and bathroom empty upstairs. She padded back down again to the kitchen and found, when she touched the switch, that the fluorescent tube had gone, it strained and flickered at either end, forcing lurid mushroom light towards the centre, producing spasms of energy that revealed the familiar room piecemeal, in flashes, like fragments of time. She saw the breadbin, the broken milk jug she was planning to glue, the soup plate of waterlogged mungbeans just beginning to sprout and, peculiarly, for he was tidy in the kitchen, the ten-inch Sabatier lying on the empty worksurface. She turned to put the light out of its misery and found Kilner right behind her, his hand covering the switch.

'And how did the do-it-yourself terrorism achieve a cleaner world?'

For the first time Max's face shows something like pleasure. 'Let me guess: you don't approve of violence. No, sorry, you don't *believe* in it. Tell me, what will you call it if the poor bastards down there are blown to kingdom come? I suppose it's not violence when the loan sharks go round the schemes confiscating the Monday books and getting in some baseball practice with a few heads? How about the girls around Anderston agreeing to do it without a condom because the broo doesn't give them enough to feed the kids? Democracy's really looking after them. You know why your fancy man and his pals take backhanders? Because they can. So how do we stop them? Shop them to the polis? How hard do you think the fiscal's going to pursue that one? But just for the sake of argument, let's get really hypothetical, let's say it gets to court *and* there's a result *and* they get a custodial. We could put them in an open prison for a few weeks, until they go down with reversible Alzheimer's and get compassionate release. Shame they've shut the Special Unit: we could have introduced them to the improving influences of art. But they don't come from a room and kitchen in Wine Alley, they've heard of Mozart, they can afford psychoanalysis if that's what they need . . .'

Without warning, the wind drops, leaving a ringing stillness like the accumulated silence of a long-shuttered room. Suddenly they're standing too close for the expanse of hilltop, their half-shouts are redundant, intimacy has intruded. Lowering his voice, he creates an inadvertent complicity.

'They do it because they can: it's that simple. So we show them they can't do it any more. "You know all that bad stuff you were elected to put a stop to, but doesn't seem such a priority now? Well, some of it's coming your way." It's uncivilised, I know, but that's what happens at the bottom of the pile, they don't provide soap and towels to keep your hands clean.'

She shouldn't have jumped, it reminded him that she had reason to be scared.

'Where the hell have you been?'

'I've been to London to look at the Queen.'

She used to think their rows were like lists of prime numbers, a weird, apparently random escalation, no deducible pattern, words whose literal meaning wouldn't take the weight.

He didn't know what she saw in that fat slag. It was bad enough they had to have her in the kitchen. The kid could be anybody's: they ought to raffle the paternity suit down at the Trafalgar. It'd be dealing crack by the time it was eleven. Had it crossed her mind that he was waiting for her? They had things to talk about. She might think all he did was sit on his arse and pick fights with the bread man, who'd fuck anything in a skirt so it was pitiful to see her creaming herself over him, but he was all that was keeping them from the bankruptcy courts. She was bleeding them both dry for the sake of a rave review in *Table Talk*. She should grow up, face a few facts. TrustHouse Forte would always see she didn't starve but she was never going to be discovered by Raymond Blanc. If she was really such a hot ticket didn't she think she'd have had a better offer by now?

Other people had arguments like this, she knew. There weren't that many variations on the theme. She'd overheard them all over the years, in supermarket queues and airport check-ins, but Kilner was the maestro. Kilner lent the notes an expression all his own.

When did she start to stop loving him? Was his

aggression a reaction to the changed emotional temperature or was it the violence that caused the thermometer to drop? When they first met all those years ago she'd had the impression that he admired her, saw in her qualities he lacked. Later she couldn't say whether this was true or simply a reciprocal illusion, infatuation's flattering mirror, but her instincts told her she was right, and possession had effected a critical change. The characteristics he had sought to annex, through her, became enemy forces, a Trojan horse he had invited inside the city walls. Her individuality was a threat, an invasion. Loving him amounted to a declaration of war.

'If that was the rationale behind crossing Callum Macleod it looks like it backfired on you, he was always going to use a bigger stick.'

In the dusk Max's eyes retreat further behind his glasses.

Sensing an advantage, she pursues it. 'What did you think you were going to achieve?'

He laughs softly.

'Oh no, you're not putting me in that little box. I don't believe in the revolution any more, or Santa Claus, I just felt like throwing a spanner into the well-greased democratic works. If we can't clean up the pigsty, at least we can make sure the pigs don't have it all their own way.'

'You certainly got Jack rattled. He even sent a letter warning *me* off.'

'Did he now?'

For a moment the air between them seems warmer.

'So you want me to tell Cal it's all been a misunderstanding?'

The moment is over. He fastens his jacket with those peeled, blind fingers.

'You tell him that if he doesn't get off my back I'll go

public, and if the papers won't touch it I'll flypost every wall in the West End. He'll be the new Poulson. And you can tell your boyfriend they'll be fumigating the Labour Party as well.'

Once he made the mistake of marking her face. In retrospect she can see that, for one so out of control, he was remarkably careful as a rule. Trousers and poloneck sweaters covered a multitude of sins, but this time only a rapist's balaclava would have obscured the evidence. Her swelling cheekbone pulsed radioactive at the marrow, the eyesocket was a pulpy tenderness which made her nauseous with apprehension. The might-have-been expressed itself in strip-cartoon terms, the popping eyeball squirting its jelly, but there was a comfort in these grotesque imaginings, infinitely preferable to the clinical reflection that, a fraction to the left, and the blow could have cost her her sight.

It was very bright in the police station, studio-lit, the artificial shrubs stripped of their artifice, the nylon weave of the leaves clearly visible, a light so relentless it conjured the whiff of disinfectant, although when she looked, the place wasn't particularly clean. The counter was unattended. She pressed the buzzer for attention and a sergeant emerged, his white hair cropped to a reassuring even bristle, like teddybear fur. In the first unfocused glance, his face took on the fatherly-flirtatious concern she habitually elicited from teddybears of late middle age. Then as she turned towards him he registered the slow-blooming cheek, the squinting eye, and knew without question what crime she was there to report. In that moment his face closed like a conjuror's cabinet.

The grey linoleum floor in the interview room was speckled with flattened dowts, matching the dirty ochre walls and the membrane that formed over her half-drunk cup of tea. She was asked questions carefully framed to elicit preordained answers. After her replies they repeated the gist of her words in subtly and not so subtly different language and, on her shrugging assent, laboriously copied their own phrases on to the statement sheet, sometimes improvising a further variation in the transcription. Patiently she watched them misspelling words that were not of her vocabulary.

After the painstaking detail of the night's events came the broader enquiries. Had it happened before? Were there witnesses? Why had she not previously made a complaint? Was she pressing charges? Seeking a divorce? What *did* she want? A reasonable question. She wanted to believe that he could be removed from her life, that it was a philosophical possibility, an ambition so limited it was difficult to explain. She was handed over to a pair of constables, one chunkily overweight, the other long-necked, chinless and extraordinarily tall, so that together they seemed an apparition from the hall of mirrors. They took her home in a squad car, escorted her inside and waited while she ascertained that the house was empty, turning noncommittal eyes on the kitchen cupboard ripped from the wall, the debris of plate rack and cutlery drawer, the gash in the plaster where the radio-cassette had landed, the table lamp that had shorted so spectacularly as it went down. Next morning there'd be averted glances when she met the neighbours in the passageway.

He didn't come back for three days, by which time it seemed a little late to dial 999. She'd just got the units back up and replastered the dado. You'd hardly have known the difference.

If she gives herself up she will have to produce contrition. Her chances of acquittal, or a nominal sentence, depend on the quality of her remorse. It's always been an emotion she finds difficult. As a child, when bickering boiled over into fisticuffs, she could never do it. *Say sorry.* She regrets meeting him, she regrets marrying him, she does not regret killing him.

Or is that a lie?

Most things in life are irrevocable in their small ways, few feel as if they are. How often in her history had she been aware that a deed once done, a single heedless act, could never be undone, and that henceforth all the tributaries of her life would flow from that? The certainty of having flunked her final exams, her unlicensed hands on the wheel when a child ran into the road, the tadpole swimming within her adolescent belly, all disasters which failed to materialise. This time there was no reprieve. She had found the one irreversible fact, defying amendment or adaptation. Not until that moment did she realise that time cannot be spooled back. The dented ice-cream van where, the week before, she'd bought two nougat slices, one with extra raspberry sauce, still parked on the corner. The boxer shorts mouldered in the dirty-washing basket. The mungbeans sprouted in their soup plate of tapwater, requiring so little to thrive. She threw them away, appalled that life, even vegetable life, should continue so heedlessly. So you could say she was guilty of a double death.

That night she dreamed of opening the grimy rear doors of a windowless van and finding him sitting on a slatted wooden bench among the toolbags and tabloid newspapers. Without the exigencies of domesticity there was nothing to say. He was separate from her, a stranger. Only then did she recognise that that's what he'd been all along.

Max stops the bike and indicates that she is to dismount. She was under the impression that he lived within walking distance of Byres Road, in the natural habitat of the West End ponytail. She wasn't prepared for a stone-built cottage in the green belt, a townies' fantasy of rural bliss with moss-napped slates above gingerbread eaves and doll-size mullioned windows framed in grey and ochre stone. The paintwork is too perfect for rental. Unless there's some starter grant for reformed terrorists, housesitting seems the most likely explanation. He doesn't strike her as the green-fingered type either, and even in the baldness of a Scottish spring, all rain and earth and the stark lines of the lithograph branches, it's obvious the garden is well-tended. Squinting in the dusk, she surveys the roof: it seems he was exaggerating the extent of the blaze. Just short of the iron-studded door he veers off the path and across the grass to disappear around the corner of the building. She follows to find him standing in the mudded furrow between house and lawn, sliding a camping knife under the catch of a small casement window. Now that strung-out adolescent's body comes into its own, clambering through frictionlessly. His face emerges out of the shadowy interior, a blue moon gathering what little light remains to the day.

'Go round the front and I'll let you in.'

With Max she has the feeling that responsibility is an all-or-nothing affair: a straight choice between taking over and being stripped of any independent will. In some ways it's a curious relief.

'Do you mind telling me whose house we're burgling?'

They're standing in the narrow hall. Max has found a torch in the course of his journey to the front door. He flicks the concentrated beam over a wall covered with paintings, etchings, charcoal drawings, all in black and white. An art-lover, or someone with a lot of money to spend on colour-coordinated interior design.

At the end of the hall is a large map chest. He opens

the shallow drawers, sweeping the torch over their contents.

'Let's see if we can find any clues, shall we? We're looking . . .'

Breaking off, he holds up his palm like an old-fashioned traffic cop, switches off the torch, listens. Nothing. The rummaging resumes.

'We're looking for a Beretta self-loading pistol. Six inches long, weighs about twenty-two ounces. Mafia gun. Designed not to spoil the line of an Italian suit, so you can leave any 357 Magnums where you find them.'

She knows whose house they're in.

'You're off your head, Max.'

She's back at the door, her fingers already turning the Yale.

'You don't want to do that.'

In the moment before she turns she has the distinct impression that he's drawn a weapon on her. Facing him, she finds herself blinking off the dazzle of torchlight.

'We find the gun, we go home, we all sleep safer in our beds, all right?'

Technically this may be classed as an appeal.

'The idea of you with a firearm doesn't make me feel particularly safe.'

The voice behind the biting light is impatient.

'It's a lot safer in my hands than it is in Callum Macleod's arsenal, believe you me.'

'Why?'

The beam drops from her eyes leaving a violet afterburn.

'It's the gun that killed Jack Ibster.'

She's always assumed that if she were ever confronted by a rapist or a murderer – or a terrorist – she would be able to talk them round.

But he doesn't like you.

'So who pulled the trigger: you or Cal?'

'Neither of us, as it happens.' Carefully he closes the final drawer. 'But my fingerprints are all over it. And Sean's.'

A three-quarters moon has emerged from the cloud, making the torch redundant. He moves into the adjoining room and resumes the search.

He's standing before a large roll-top bureau. Finding the cover locked, he inserts the penknife and yanks upwards. It gives with unpredictable enthusiasm, clattering like a Bren gun. The incident seems to loosen his inhibitions. He treats succeeding drawers more roughly, careless of leaving traces.

'Who was it?' Her voice rises into the register of disbelief. 'Not Brendan?'

He grunts, forcing open the door of a corner cabinet to reveal a Victorian teaset, the teacups' gold rims worn thin by genteel lips. 'I haven't got time for twenty questions.'

Belatedly it occurs to her that the balance of power may not be as disadvantageous as it feels. For all his expressions of hostility, he's the one who wants her there. Maybe it's time to claim this advantage.

'You haven't got time for twenty questions, I haven't got time to be arrested as an accessory to murder. See you around, Max.'

'All right.' The timbre of his voice, close to alarm, seems to take him by surprise. Seeing that he's succeeded in stopping her, he lowers the volume. 'It's my gun. I've had it for years. It was borrowed without permission. Nothing to do with us. But we did a little ex post facto clearing up, moved the body to Callum Macleod's. Sean got jumpy, hid the gun in a half-finished toilet, covered the top of the toilet bowl with manufacturer's tape: it looked fairly convincing, convincing enough for the plods anyway. Thought he'd get a chance to retrieve it before it was found. Maybe it's already at the bottom of the Clyde, but Callum Macleod doesn't strike me as the type to look a gift heater in the mouth.'

'And that's your definition of having nothing to do with it?'

He makes a pneumatic noise of disgust and her neck prickles with the old dread, the certainty that whatever the offence, she is guilty as charged.

'Listen, I'm not interested in what you think. You're a friend of Imogen Reiss, you don't want Sean to get into bother. Nor do I. So get looking, we'll be out of here a lot quicker.'

'If our host doesn't get here first.'

He clicks the torch on and uses the beam to indicate a portable writing desk on the other side of the room: her assignment.

'Let's hope for both our sakes he doesn't.'

Half-heartedly she fumbles with the inlaid box. Opened, it presents a perfect slope of leather which has kept the cushioned feel of living skin, the brass inkwell snug in its hole. She releases the catch and raises one half of the writing surface to explore the trays and compartments beneath. There it is: smaller than billed, almost snub-nosed, cold to the touch in its nest of temperate rosewood. She slips it into her coat pocket and continues the search.

The bangs and curses overhead are becoming more frequent. Max is not the patient type. He knows he's getting to the end of the nooks and crannies; she can feel the tension through the joists and plaster. The moon doesn't reach this side of the house so she's working in the dark, dutifully opening drawers and cupboards, fingering fish scaler and oyster knife, tracing the science fiction curves of the worktop appliances, the ingenious plumbing of the espresso machine and the chunky industrial chrome of the Dualit toaster, reading Cal's life by braille. Whoever stocked this kitchen knew what they were about, even the saucepans betray the touch of an expert, perhaps even loving, hand. There are no clues as to whether it was male or female but increasingly she doubts the former option. It's not hard to imagine Cal's 'coming out'. All it would take is a throwaway remark at first meeting, some inadvertent ambiguity or misfiring joke, and then the possibility of pressing the misapprehension into service.

What is she doing, haggling with herself over Cal's sexuality while upstairs Max is subjecting his bedroom to more rigorous enquiry? What is she doing here at all? However aggrieved she feels about being cheated out of the manager's job, she shouldn't be a party to this. If Cal's got blood on his hands one way or another, who is she to cast the first stone? She should leave, phone him from the nearest call box: after all, they're more than acquaintances, if less than friends. What holds her back is curiosity and that tempered streak in her, the detachment that doubles as courage or cruelty or just indifference to her fate. It's a hard world.

Up above something very heavy hits the floor. The impact resonates in the foundations, hitting her diaphragm with the panic of childhood accidents that can never be put right. Dense objects being forcibly overturned, tremors on a larger than human scale are shaking the building, as if he were driving a tank at the walls. She climbs the stairs. After the apocalyptic noises, the chaos is banal. Being simply but expensively furnished in the butch minimalist style, the bedroom offers limited scope for vandalism, and what there is reaches her softened by shadow, aesthetically redeemed by the furred

outlines of a pastels sketch. The chest of drawers eviscer-
ated, the linen on the kingsize bed deposed, the adjoining
bathroom ransacked, shower curtain ripped down, handbasin filled with broken glass, the air stinging of aftershave, a scent half-familiar but lacking the alchemy of the
wearer's native musk. Over the years she grew hardened
to the debris, but never to the electric charge, the draining of strength in the crescent of tissue from oxter to
breast, the buzzing in her sinuses. Fear, fight or flight.
An incomplete list, but then, death doesn't rhyme.

Max is on the other side of the bed, straining against
the clean lines of a monolithic wardrobe. The leverage is
poor but its resistance only feeds his rage. She must be
visible to him, even when cloudcover withdraws the
rectangle of muslin light across the carpet, but he gives
no sign of knowing she's there. Touching him she can
feel the frustration jump like lightning as she becomes
the shortest route to earth. Before she hits the wall she
has time to think that he must be stronger than he
looks, then she feels the impact rearrange her organs, the
rippling displacement of liver and lights, the shock to her
skull clearing the head like smelling salts. So time doubles
back on itself after all. The old symptoms claim her:
thinning of the blood, the vacuum in her lungs, a dizzy-
ing tang in her nostrils, disgust at herself for harbouring
the delusion that she could ever get away. This is the state
psychologists term 'arousal', picking up signals, processing
data, mouth dry, cunt wet. They say the hanged man
dies with an erection. She never liked it, whatever the
pornographers choose to believe, and now it's the cue
that brings her most alive.

He drew on an escalating repertory of violence, starting
with shaking, a humiliating gesture, yet comfortingly
controlled, offering a better-than-even chance that things

would go no further. Next the open-handed slap, *outré* now but possessing a respectable pedigree. Classically inflicted, with a take-off of no more than twelve inches, it carried an elegant echo of the golden age of Hollywood. The macho variant, a wide arc gathering momentum before the spectacular soundburst of contact, was painful but on the whole preferable. Demanding arm's-length delivery, it opened up possibilities of avoidance. His coordination was not all it should be, which was probably the reason he never attempted the backhand. After that it got serious: close range, fists or feet, teeth or improvised weaponry. Once this phase started, all bets were off. The foetal position was best, she found. Once, one of the good times, sitting on the runway at Birmingham Airport, six days in Amsterdam ahead of them, laughing about the call girls and the hash cafés, she dutifully extracted the safety card from the stitched pocket of the seat in front. Scanning the efficient diagrams, the quaint instructions to remove stiletto heels, the exhortations to selfless mothers to secure their own oxygen masks before their children's, she recognised the 'brace' position, for use in emergency landings. And she thought she'd invented it. Yet even then the idea of their fights as systematic, behaviour patterns familiar to the rawest social-work recruit, never occurred to her. It had nothing to do with statistics and labels, other people's categories. He just hit her. Because she didn't love him enough.

'Am I interrupting something?'

Cal is standing in the doorway. With a snap of ancient wiring he switches on the overhead light, momentarily blinding all three of them. The trenchcoat gives him the air of a Chandler detective, agent of restored order. In spite of everything she's pleased to see him, but the pleasure is short-lived. Anger shows as a thin, white shine on his basted tan. Max seems paralysed, but she has a feeling that, like her, he's assessing height, weight, the squash-to-sunbed ratio of Cal's health club visits, and the unknown quantity that renders all the rest redundant. It is a moment of pure, unweighted potential. When it ends it is by an imperceptible signal, a contraction of the pupils, perhaps, or a tightening at the corners of the lips, a quiver in the room's magnetic field, but at whose instigation she couldn't say.

Cal grabs Max by his straggling seaman's ponytail and swings his head against the wardrobe, following through with a kick to the groin. Make it quick and make it count, that's what they used to say at her women's self-defence class. Cal has obviously been given the same advice. Watching from the wedge of safety between wardrobe and wall, she can tell he's not at home with violence, his movements have the arhythmic disconnection of a dancer who's only just learned the steps, but he has a bulky, rugby player's force and something extra that may also come from the playing field, the winner's instinct.

Doubled up by the blow, Max lunges at knee-level, trying to take him off balance. For a split-second they're poised in a scene of supplication, a burlesque of land-owner and serf. Cal looks down uncomprehendingly, then buckles, falling heavily onto one of the discarded drawers. Max tries to get to his feet, to capitalise on the moment, but Cal is quicker, despite the extra ballast, and by luck or judgement targets Max's supporting arm. She is used to the soundtrack of violence, Kilner's stream-of-consciousness fury or those broad-accented war cries of skirmishing outside pubs, not this speechless absorption in the exchange of fist and foot and shoulder, action and reaction, advantage seized and retaken. Background noises she never noticed as participant or pavement spectator are grotesquely amplified: the guttural straining before a sudden move, the protesting of floor and furniture, the muffled percussion of impact, flesh and bone.

Cal catches the yielding spot below the ribcage and, realising he's struck home, redoubles his efforts. Her stomach balls in sympathy as the victim twists away, and then suddenly he is the aggressor, up and kicking, a mechanical momentum packing each swift retreat before the follow-through. Max is the more skilled, with a streetfighter's efficiency, a butcher's cunning in the selection of prime cuts, but both are handicapped by lack of leeway. In the arena circumscribed by bed, wardrobe and dresser, boobytrapped by the drawers underfoot, the fight has a panicky limiting of possibility. The energy that would be expended in evasion and pursuit is here channelled into the business of hurting. Without either of them choosing, the stakes are higher. The outcome is predetermined, the only question is which one of them it will be?

The first blow caught her on the temple, rattled the brain in its suspension of brine. The second cracked her head backwards against the freezer's precision edge. As long as she was upright it was containable; like a boxer, you must never go down. Then that scramble around the kitchen table, like Whitehall farce without the frilly knickers. She'd almost made it when he caught her wrist in the door: the attenuated bones in sharp relief like chicken wings, so easy to snap. Strangely, she didn't feel the pain. Where does it hurt? In the kitchen mostly. In fairness the blow was accidental, intended but unaimed: it was never sexual. That was one thing she could say about him; saner than her, perhaps, as things have turned out. But she was in no state for fairness, and she saw the knife, as far as she could see anything because there was blood in her eye from a wound she couldn't remember and she was on the floor, although you must never go down, and she knew it would be a long time before she saw the hospital.

Max has Cal on the carpet, but in getting him there he's used up his chief advantage, the bigger man's uncertain centre of gravity and consequent fear of falling. Now they're a two-man scrum, that wiry adolescent's body trapped by the pure beef of his opponent. Even at this range fists miss their mark, scudding off-target into the anticlimax of space or the bathos of mattress springs. The level of engagement fluctuates erratically, now dwindling to a frustrated scuffling, almost a marking of time like boxers between rounds, now, unpredictably, sharpening into the promise of serious injury, as Max's cheek is forced onto the dovetail joint of the dressing-table drawer. She registers the fight in the solar plexus, belly contracting blow by blow, lips framing wordless circles of anticipation or pain, at once combatant and witness, and yet neither, insulated from harm and denied the instinctive partiality of the spectator. Cal's lower lip is split like an overripe tomato, the buttons of his shirt are gone, the golden swell of stomach blotched carmine as if scorched from too long in front of the fire. Somehow he's managed to shed the trenchcoat while Max is still wearing his motorcycle leathers, armour and straitjacket combined. His ponytail has all but slipped its rubber band, creating a windsock effect, a lank balloon at the back of his skull. These details present themselves distinctly, almost clinically, to her eye while her nervous system has tripped the old circuit. Fear, fight, flight, equal and opposite forces. There came a point where damage was in the air, there was no getting it back in the bottle. He wanted to hurt her. She was reluctant to fight back, but reluctance didn't diffuse the rage. There are no choices, only compulsion. The will to destroy or self-destruction.

All at once it seems obvious. She draws the gun from her pocket.

'Enough.'

Cal turns his head in the direction of the word. His face is unfamiliar, dark with exertion, the eyes closed to applause. Reading Max's intention, she shifts the angle of the barrel downwards by six inches. Cal's chest starts to heave with the deferred breathlessness of the fight.

'Get up.'

He is already complying when his body acknowledges the armistice and personality clicks back into place. His mouth puckers into a minimal smile.

'Yes, ma'am.'

Max seems recovered, almost calm, or perhaps just in shock. His glasses are long gone. She gestures him over to the door. Glancing between her face and Cal's, he steps onto the small landing. Cal looks set to follow; again she trains the gun on him. He cancels the move, spreading his hands in a pose that proclaims the innocence of the Easter lamb.

'I take it this means you won't be joining the payroll, Miz Megratta?'

M ax stops the bike outside Catriona's tenement. She has to lean in close to make herself heard above the engine.

'Where are you going to sleep? Your girlfriend's?'

The face in its frame of helmet is neutral, acknowledging that power has shifted but uncertain where the balance now lies.

'It's not a regular fixture.'

The temptation to see him vanish into the night, a blip removed from her personal radar, is a powerful one.

'You can stay here. Tonight.'

'What about Julie Andrews?'

'She'll be furious, but she's too polite to object in front of you.'

The problem is deferred. Catriona is out. Nan is only half-relieved: for all her assurances there remained a possibility that her landlady would have thrown him out. Now she's stuck with him. He's eyeing the decor, the clover-sprig curtains and mob-cap lampshades, that tapestry-by-numbers home sewing kit on the sofa arm. The scimitar grooves where his nostrils meet the planes of his cheek deepen.

Beyond warming a plate of baked beans in the microwave she has never cooked in Catriona's kitchen. She opens the fridge, scanning the rows of low-fat yoghurt and cottage cheese, arranged according to sell-by date: not just bringing home an unexpected guest but cupboard-raiding too. As she heats the oil and takes a knife to the onion she wonders why she forgoes this daily pleasure, why it takes a stranger to push her into exercising her principal skill. He watches her, salivation blunting his sceptical edge, eyes following her between fridge and cooker with an almost childlike fascination. Not for the first time dislike is overcome by the involuntary affection of the feeding hour. Maybe that's why Kilner never really liked her cooking for other men. All that belly love coming her way. Not that she usually received it direct, but why else did they flirt with the waitresses?

'How is it?'

Bent over the plate, his face has the furtive look of an animal interrupted at its meat. Twin ropes of spaghetti trail from his mouth, but instead of spooling them in with a final splatter of tomato sauce, those sharp little teeth nip together and the falling pasta snags on his fork.

'Could have done with you in Barlinnie. The food was indescribable. If you didn't smoke or do drugs or fancy brain damage from the tattie poteen, there weren't too many of life's little pleasures left. You even shat in company.'

He pauses; evidently objecting to communal defecation is too personal an admission. 'Still, I paid my debt to society.'

She wonders which of life's little pleasures she will miss. Sausage sandwiches in the Post Office canteen? Gassy beer in the sort of phoney howff where Danny knows he won't bump into either the bon viveurs or the spit and sawdust diehards of the Labour Party? Their subsequent couplings, those bouts of wild abandon when he never removes his watch? She's hardly the last of the great hedonists. All they can take from her is freedom itself, her ill-gotten gain. The price is high enough already, without having to lose the thing so dearly bought.

'Did it change you?'

He laughs without observable amusement.

'You mean am I a reformed character? Back on the straight and narrow? I tell you what prison did for me: I went there with no thought of taking a life. I didn't have it in me. I'd had the odd run-in with the fascists. Lewisham, Toxteth. Administered the odd kicking. But nothing you couldn't cure with an aspirin and an early night. After eight years inside, I knew that with the right provocation I could finish someone, and I knew exactly how far they'd have to push to get me to do it.'

'Like marriage, then.'

He treats the vacant air to a brief, blank stare before returning his attention to the spaghetti. The temporary truce seems to be over. Once again she's the sewer-walker, the Tammany Hall moll, Salome under the gaze of John the Baptist. But they're more alike than he would allow. She too knows the seductions of pariah status, the freedom from responsibility outwith the city walls. Perhaps that's why she grants him the right to judge her.

Watching him doggedly working through the mound of food, she's aware of a tension along the leylines of rib and pelvis, her sinews pulling like purse strings, stomach barricaded, posture hunched. Without thinking about it, she knows the discomfort is connected with Danny. Why bother throwing her a confession as damaging in its way as the facts he wished to hide? That night by the river she bought the whole Valentine's card, padded satin petals, copperplate verse, the works. She can hardly believe it now. Falling in love is always a triumph of hope over experience, in her case amounting to a lapse in sanity.

Max has the antisocial habit of biting his cutlery, puncturing the silence with the irregular click of tooth enamel on fork. It is to drown this soundtrack as much as anything that she speaks.

'So you had the option of cooking for yourselves? Inside.'

He looks at her with sly interest.

'I wouldn't pin your hopes on it, everyone wants to work the kitchens.'

She suspected he knew, but the hairline crack between suspicion and knowledge runs deep. He guesses the unspoken question.

'Sean told me.'

Even as her worse fears are realised, she feels the indignation of a broken bargain. This isn't supposed to happen. The fear is meant to head off the ambush. Pre-experience the worst and it may never happen: a standard bluff when playing poker with a thrawn God.

'Who told him?'

'His mother, I think.'

'She didn't know.'

Max is looking bored again.

'Well, she knows now.'

He severs a clump of spaghetti with the edge of his fork. 'How long do they reckon you'll go down for?'

Going down. Doing time. Porridge. Bird. The argot of a million cop shows, the gamey flavour of Cockney rhyming slang, sawn-off shotguns, spindle-wheeled Jags. The defiant patina on the daily round of waking up, wearing down, slopping out.

'Depends how dim a view they take of me granting myself bail. Unfortunately he didn't maim me, so I can't count on the sympathy factor. They may even decide it was provocation. He was screwing someone else. I'd known about it a couple of weeks. To bring it up then, and tell him I was hiring a bookkeeper to take over his side of the business . . . they might think I was setting him up, knowing he'd take a swing at me, to give me an excuse to have a go back. They might even think I decided to kill him.'

He stops chewing.

'And did you?'

Very slowly she turns her head towards the door. Cuckoo clock, chest freezer with magnetic ladybirds clamping good intentions to the white enamel, two-tier spice rack, the Impressionist Masterpieces wall calendar. April: Seurat's *Bathers*. Is it Catriona's taste she abhors or simply domesticity, the sitcom props used to carry a surrealistic plot, the promise that normality exists? Now the return journey: cooker, calendar, spices, the upright ice coffin, Korean alpine clock, aluminium-frame window with its macramé plant-pot holder and candy-stripe blind.

'I don't know.'

How to distinguish what happened from what was meant to happen? The idea of being free of him was so impossible, she can hardly believe she was capable of framing it before it became accomplished fact. And yet he was worse than she could remember seeing him: angrier, and perhaps a little afraid. Why else but because he knew she meant business, even if she didn't know it herself?

Things had been so bad for so long in the unrelieved terrain that was her marriage that it was difficult to accept the concept of a critical mass. Her principal objective was to avoid the overview, the aerial shot that would reveal the pitiful outlines of her insect life. She had learned to break it up, taking time in bite-sized pleasures. The breakfast coffee drunk French-style from the handle-less bowl, the political sketch in the newspaper, her daily flirtation with the young ned who delivered the milk, her tongue itching to probe the alabaster hollow at the back of his skull before the ginger stubble grew back:

neurotically exact satisfactions, apt to be spoiled if the bowl broke or the sketchwriter went on holiday or the boy found a new barber. Planning was for menus. How could she premeditate a murder when she couldn't see beyond the next half hour?

The meal is finished, the last twists of spaghetti abandoned, cleaned of their sauce, like sandworm casts at low tide.

Why not? How else are they going to fill the hours before bedtime? And she did promise Tarquin she'd attempt a dry run.

'My friend Althea had a baby . . .'

No one could call him a good listener. He possesses a series of distracting mannerisms, running a questing tongue over his teeth behind the curtain of his upper lip, inserting his little finger tentatively into one ear, raising his eyebrows in a commentary resolutely out of sync with the rhythm of her account. But in a way it's easier without his sympathy. She doesn't have to mime remorse she doesn't feel, or watch guiltily as he goes through a vicarious distress more real than her own. He isn't fretting over the sensitive response, twitching with indecision about the arm round the shoulders, wondering if it would be seen as a pass, or might offer the potential for one. Free of such secondary considerations, she can focus on the truth. Whatever that may be.

'He'd left the Sabatier on the worksurface. He'd use anything for buttering bread – filleting knives, grapefruit knives – maybe he did it to annoy me, although I don't know how he could tell. We had a strict division of labour: he was the one who got annoyed; I was the provocation. I still don't understand why he left it out. He always put everything away. He was tidier in the kitchen than I was, it was a way of saying I couldn't do

329

my job. He'd stacked the rest of the washing-up by the sink, it wasn't as if he left the bread out, or a dirty plate, it didn't look like he'd been interrupted. Sometimes I think maybe he did love me after all. Maybe he left it there deliberately.'

She pauses. 'Does that sound mad? Yeah, well, it's not a theory I'd try on the police.'

'What did you tell them?'

She wonders if his jumping ahead in the narrative betrays impatience or simply a clumsy expression of interest.

'It was a couple of hours before I called them. I knew he was dead, so there was no point getting an ambulance, and I knew I wouldn't have a lot of time to think once it became official. I should have called them straight-away, it would have looked better, more like things had gone horribly wrong. I knew that at the time. I should have dialled 999 too, not the local cop shop. You're supposed to lose control, that's what gets you off, pre-meditation equals murder, it has to be the heat of the moment. But who says the moment can't last a fortnight? What if it lasts a lifetime?

'The woman on the other end couldn't believe it. I probably sounded too calm. She thought it was a wind-up, I could tell. There was a noise, like she was doing something and trying to keep it quiet, and then a gap, dead air, and she started asking me everything all over again. I was still talking to her when the doorbell went. I knew the two at the door, they'd brought me home once before when I made a complaint against him. The fat one went straight over and knelt down to take his pulse, and I saw him flinch. He must have been stone cold by that time. And I suppose there was the blood. There was. There was the blood.

'Policemen look so big indoors, much bigger than on

the street. Have you noticed that? I told them I killed him, pointed out the knife, in case they missed it, went to get my coat. I thought they'd take me to the station. It was all a bit quick for them, they looked a bit shocked, I think the tall one must have felt sick, I could tell he was trying not to look so he kept moving his eyes very quickly up the wallpaper. And his partner said we ought to go to the hospital first and I thought he was being funny, and then I thought *no, he's still alive, I didn't kill him.*'

Her mouth is a clown's rictus, the stretched skin tracked with tears and snot.

'But he was talking about me. He took me up to the bathroom. I thought when it was all washed away I was going to be fine underneath, it was just blood. But when I wiped it with the flannel, it kept coming back. Just above my eye, an old wound; he'd opened it up again. They wet a towel and wound it round my head. I looked a real sight. And then they had a row over which one was going to stay with the body and which one was going to sit with me in the other room; they wouldn't let me back in the kitchen. I wasn't sure which counted as the short straw. They were looking after me, talking about getting me medical attention, but they weren't sympathetic. I suppose they knew I was going to be charged. Which is fair enough. I knew that. But I couldn't believe they could see me and not. Just not respond to me as a human being. The tall one had these huge hands with club nails, you know? curving over the ends of his fingers. We had seventeen bookings for dinner the next night, Terry was getting me some swordfish, I'd said I'd pick it up from the market first thing. I mean, I knew it wasn't going to happen, but I was still worrying about it, wondering if I should trust the oven with a pavlova or just do the clafoutis. My head was bursting, pushing out all these thoughts, on the one hand this, on the other hand that, I had to sort it out or I'd go mad, but there were just more and more things to think about. I wanted to ask for a priest, not because I believe in God, I just needed someone skilled in morality, someone who could draw the line between right and wrong, and then I thought if he was a Catholic I was going to hell anyway, and if he was Anglican he'd just deliver a spot of amateur psychotherapy, try to make me feel better, and the last thing I needed was to feel better; I wanted the day of judgement, not a cup of cocoa.

'Then the house was full of people. This doctor came out of the kitchen and told us he was dead. In case we didn't already know. There was a detective inspector, a real wide boy, top button undone, tie half-way down, wrinkled seams in his cheap-tack suit: he asked me all the questions the other two had already asked. The doctor told him he'd have to get me up to Selly Oak, to the hospital, but I couldn't face all the Saturday-night drunks with their exploded noses, teenage toughs getting their chib-marks sewn up. So I said no. There was a storm blowing, more like a hurricane really. They radioed for a policewoman but she never turned up. The doctor wasn't happy but in the end he said OK, so they took me in. The tall one drove because the fat one didn't mind staying with . . . The tall one drove. The inspector in the front, me and the doctor in the back. He signed the form and they took me into a room with no windows and asked me if I wanted a solicitor and I said OK.'

Tarquin has risked a lot for her, one way or another. She doesn't know why. Dislike of the DI, covert revenge for barely covert homophobia. The drama queen in him responding to the tragedy queen in her, perhaps. Some people will do anything for a bit of excitement.

'I was in there for hours. They found a policewoman

in the end: she had hair like a doll's, like nylon. As soon as I saw her I thought: you want to make me cry and if I don't you're really going to go for me. She kept calling me "love" but every time she did it she'd look over at the boss, trying to get a rise out of him. There was her and the solicitor and this inspector in his Prince of Wales check, four of us in this tiny room with no windows and this smell, really rank and intimate, almost not there, so you couldn't help straining for it, trying to pick it up, wondering who it came from, worrying if it was you. Me. I don't know if he was showing off for her but it was like he didn't believe me, there had to be something else. He was asking me where I bought the knife and what I bought it for and Christ it was only a bloody Sabatier, and he wanted to know exactly the sequence of the fight: where he hit me first, which hand, when did my eye start bleeding, and I didn't fucking know, it's like sex, it happened, you can't remember afterwards who put which hand where. And that was *really* the wrong thing to say. He was leaning so far over the table I could see the bulge through his trousers and I thought: I just want to go to sleep. Even with three people in the room all watching me, and the tape recorder going and this gorilla with the body odour and the monster erection in my face, I felt my eyes closing. And then Tarquin started kicking up a fuss, said there was something wrong with my pupils. They were all looking at me like I was doing it on purpose. He said I had concussion, and if they made me spend the night in the cells without medical attention they could have a death in custody on their hands.'

The look on their faces, more primitive than any law-enforcer's reluctance to breach procedure: it was fear, the acknowledgement that he might be right. And she felt fine, fine, just very very tired. Strange to see three people crackling with adrenalin and to feel the creeping blanket of sleep. As if it had nothing to do with her.

Why did she buy the knife? Why not? She was a cook. So why when she picked it up would she hold it horizontally, blade flattened, gauging its weight in her palm for an untranslatable moment before reangling her fist to address the parsley to be chopped, the chicken to be quartered? Who's to say it wasn't an unconscious rehearsal, the tendons working of their own accord?

'The policewoman went to the hospital with me. It was about four in the morning. I thought they'd be over the Saturday-night rush, but the place was packed out. There were a lot of storm injuries, broken glass; some kid who'd swallowed a sewing-machine needle; a goth who'd been trying to pierce his nostril for a nose ring and made a real mess of it; and this woman with a massive gash on her face – awful – and when she saw me *she* looked away. It was an Asian doctor, he kept making little jokes, *knock-knock: who's there?* I suppose it was nerves because I was with a cop. She didn't like him, I couldn't tell whether it was because he was black or because he was an arsehole, which he was a bit. They took me down to the ward and gave me a gown like an ironing-board cover, all these tapes to hold it together down the back. There was a little glass office over by the door where the night sister sat and Sindy went to talk to her. I think they knew each other already. She was telling this really long story, it must have involved sex because she kept dropping her voice. I couldn't hear anyway, just lay in bed listening to the noises.'

Snoring, sleeptalking, a snuffle that might be suppressed crying, the squeaky wheel on a trolley in the corridor, and the silence, the eerie, heightened silence of bright lights and high ceilings.

'I needed to pee. The nurse showed us the way and

waited outside in the corridor with the policewoman. I thought hospital toilets would be cleaner. No bogroll either. I sat there looking up at the window. That glass that looks like frogspawn. They'd fixed the frame so it didn't open all the way. It was a bit of a squeeze.'

Five o'clock in the morning in a surgical gown, barefoot through the Birmingham suburbs, past the rhododendron bushes and the monkey puzzle trees, picking a path through the debris of the storm. The wind had dropped and it was almost warm for November. She'd kept a spare set of clothes at the restaurant ever since Kilner pulled that stunt with the guacamole. She always had some petty cash inside the fish kettle in case Althea needed a loan, so she didn't have to ask him. He would have said no anyway. She caught the first bus to the station, full of nursing auxiliaries on early shift at the hospital. It took her right past the gates. She saw them outside, a couple of photographers, the BRMB land cruiser with the aerial on its roof. Half a dozen car coats drinking coffee, laughing, cold air snatching the steam out of their polystyrene cups. A real picnic. One sleazeball even had a set of aluminium stepladders with him. He was the one who fetched up at Jack's funeral.

'I don't know why I picked Glasgow. I was happy here as a kid, I suppose. Sunday afternoon outings. And there was no chance of being recognised, nothing to connect me with the place. Not that I was in any state to make that sort of calculation, I just put one foot in front of the other. It didn't feel like absconding from police custody. I saw the card in the job centre window and I thought: just a bit of time to sort myself out . . . It's amazingly easy. You get an address, a library ticket, a job, stall them on your national insurance number. Suddenly you exist, this person you've decided to be. A new identity. More real than the old one in some ways.'

The end of the narrative takes her by surprise: nothing more to say.

Max is slumped in his chair, legs stretched out, torso indigestively compacted. For some time now his face has worn the absent look of those who know nothing is required of them, an expression that could be read as boredom but for the glint of satisfaction, a personal stake in the fallibility of authority. *She put one over on them.* One of those pared fingernails nicks a dot of dried sauce from the tablecloth.

'Did you mean to kill him?'

She studies the spillage of salt on the table, the unused sideplates and stainless-steel serving spoon, the crossbones of abandoned cutlery. Such a simple question. But she can't answer it.

Max sits up suddenly. 'Which hand *did* he hit you with?'

He's toying with the bone-handled knife, a relic of the 1930s, shaped for buttering the white end of the loaf before the shaving of the slice. He drums out a rhythm, the sprung blade bouncing lightly off the cloth. Deftly he flicks it off the table edge, sending it spinning through a brief, crazed orbit before catching it in his other hand.

'Right or left?'

What is he doing?

Slowly he brings his right hand towards her cheek.

'This one – Or this?'

She catches at his wrist blocking the mock-blow, and he leans in close, reaching with his free hand to take the gun from the pocket of the jacket hanging over the back of her chair. Panicked by the sudden move, she swings backwards, the seat tipping with her, but before she can fall he's grabbing

He was on top of her yet she was still upright. His face raging and screaming, flushed dark with exertion, yet inexplicably still, telling her she was a bitch, a *fucking bitch*, but not moving, not hitting her. She was fighting for breath, for balance, for the pain to stop, but this time he wasn't hitting

She drove the blade home and the pressure on her windpipe eased, his grip fell away. One clean cut, between the ribs, straight to the heart. Luck not judgement. The shock of blood, and so little of it. He was still on his feet, waiting for something. And then, as if through trick photography, the inches between them stretching to infinity, he fell, his body pulling away at immense speed, sucked down the long tunnel of diminishing perspective, leaving only the look on his face. Not surprise. Recognition.

Now he knew.

They arrange to meet at the corner of Kelvin Way and Sauchiehall Street, where the grand vistas of Victorian planning hit the happenstance of inner-city blight. Spring has arrived, as it will at this latitude, five weeks behind the forecast and apparently overnight. Yesterday's diesel-stained vegetation, those winter lawns outshone by the jaded green of municipal railings, are suddenly vivid with new life. Pink-edged daisies crown the bowling green, beech branches fur with a penicillin-coloured growth. In this corner of the city the works of nature and man have a drab homogeneity, a landscape of leeching greys and browns, the palette of decay. The plastic traffic cones and corroding supermarket trolleys under Partick Bridge are perfectly at home in the swirling scum of the Kelvin. Down a blind alley, the castellated flour mill squats in its purdah of dust. But this morning, under a postcard sky, the virgin leaves are still pure of the taint of traffic. At a distance, you could almost take the beery froth riding the current for white water, an innocent distillation of speed and light.

Imogen is dressed for work, navy-blue box jacket and long pleated skirt, an ensemble that stakes its claim to elegant middle age with a teasing suggestion of schoolgirl gymslip. These things don't happen by accident. Nan is trousered, free of Gorr's sartorial preferences, indeed of the need to please any employer. It is the day she was to start working for Callum Macleod.

Arriving at the corner, she stops short of the rendezvous, the yards of pavement between them still too wide for speech. Imogen closes the gap with three swift strides and a shoulder-clutching hug almost mannish in its force. In spite of herself, behind the defensive breastbone, Nan feels a liquid trickle of peace. From this angle it's not possible to see whether Imogen's eyes are closed.

'It's good to see you.'

The words come out choked, or perhaps clenched, a product of the continuing embrace. Nan recognises the apology implicit in such emotional extortion but you don't cancel two months' cold-shouldering with a wrestler's grip. Finally Imogen takes a step backward, releasing the armlock but holding her eyes.

'How've you been?'

'Fine.'

Always the good girl, no trouble to anyone. Tell them what they want to hear. Unless they fancy themselves the Mother Teresa of the tabloids, in which case discretion is the ultimate snub.

'Lucky you.'

A little tug to bring her to heel.

Nan shrugs.

'I'm lying.'

'At least you're honest enough to admit it.'

The coffee shop across the road isn't open so they head towards the playpark, an asphalt dustbowl containing the obligatory swings, chute and roundabout and a couple of unfamiliar amusements, climbing frames, she supposes, although the intersecting iron bars showing dark through the scabbed paint suggest medieval tortures, ingenious pain. The children are in school, the truants shoplifting on Argyle Street. Only a bin-trawling skipper, anorak-hooded in defiance of the season, disturbs the solitude. They perch on the bars of the smaller frame. Sunlight bleaches their eyelids but the metal is cold.

Only now can Nan appreciate the full weight of those

weeks of absence, the loss not just of a friend but of the self that flourished in her company. Imogen's faith in her, implicit in all their dealings, amounted to self-fulfilling prophecy. Even chatting over coffee at the kitchen table their meetings held a sense of occasion, a glamour and speed. The earth turned more quickly. Self-consciousness was part of the pleasure but there was also an obverse satisfaction, the gift of spontaneity, a knack for the sharp and funny that she dimly remembers from those early days with Kilner, before the teeming sense of how much she had to say became the desert where there was nothing to be said. Discovering that the world's stock of conversation was after all limitless meant more to her than an evening's good company or the affection of a few weeks. Those with a religious cast of mind might call it redemption, but that's never been her style.

And now here they are again, Imogen delivering highlights from her morning exactly as she used to, the same drily comical set to her jaw, that snaggle tooth denting the cushioned lower lip, a few disobedient threads of dye-resistant silver in that disciplined curtain of hair. The faint familiar citrus of the soap she uses, overlaid, when her lipstick is fresh, with a marzipan sweetness. Each detail brings a rush of gratitude at the unexpected restoration, a retrospective connection through the anchorless weeks of absence. But connection implies obligation, and unfulfilled obligation resentment; love and punishment share the same breath.

For a long time she banished all memory of those evenings in Montpelier. Sieving the week's letters with wicked laughter, singling out the foot fetishists and the regulars in Readers' Wives, speculating on the euphemised perversions, deconstructing the appeal of dysfunctional attachments, sorting and labelling, playing God. Now, retrieved from limbo, images surface with the store-bought clarity of second-sight. An impromptu sing-song over the sink when an old Ronettes hit came on the radio. The sweet breath of freesias in a jar. Cheap red wine decanted until it tasted like claret. Saul's cheeks rosy from the bath as she read him his bedtime story while Imogen sorted out some suppliant on the phone. Now and again, pleased by an evening swarm of starlings or the pavement cats sprawled like discarded slippers rearing up to anticipate the stroking hand, it has occurred to her that these moments, too, have their small perfection. But it isn't the same without Imogen. Nor, necessarily, with her. It takes the alchemy of trust.

'So why now, after all this time?'

Imogen looks up, surprised, as if this were a subject they'd agreed not to broach.

'I know I should have been in touch, Nan.'

On second thoughts, maybe she doesn't need her humiliation spelled out.

'No problem. When you wanted to see me, you saw me. When you didn't, you didn't.'

Imogen draws breath to argue but, abruptly, changes focus.

'You knew Max McWilliam, didn't you?'

An odd thing to say on several counts.

'Not well enough to know his surname was McWilliam.'

Imogen pauses as though giving this serious consideration.

'The police have been round looking for Sean. They found Max's motorbike on the canal bank up by Partick Thistle. Don't seem to think it was stolen. Apparently he hasn't been seen for weeks.'

'One week.'

A noise in the night, a jump cut in her dreams, the click of the latch, a draught of cold air as the outer door swung and closed. If she'd taken him to her bed would he have crept away before dawn?

'He stayed over at Catriona's the Saturday before last. On the sofa.'

It's as well to clarify these details.

'Came round to ask me to get Cal off his case. That's what he said anyway. He must have known there was nothing I could do. Really I think he just wanted to talk to somebody who wasn't afraid, put his paranoia into perspective. Looks like he wasn't paranoid enough.'

Imogen is listening intently, but with a concentration running just ahead of the conversation.

'Callum Macleod? Come off it, he may not be Andrew Carnegie but I can't see him setting the muscle on to small fry like Max. Reading between the lines of what Sean's said over the years, suicide's more likely. There's nothing more depressive than a revolutionary who wakes up to find the world doesn't want saving after all.'

She wonders if Imogen was always so casually dismissive of her point of view. Maybe she just didn't notice.

'Last time I saw Cal he was knocking eight bells out of him. And getting as good as he gave.'

Imogen's eyes widen in deliberate drollery. Theoretically she disapproves of violence, but the image tickles her.

'Well, that strikes him off the suspect list. Callum Macleod's not going to take any chances on you telling tales in the witness box. Or do you think he might try bumping you out of the way too?'

'You seemed to think it was within his capabilities at one time.'

But Imogen's inconsistency is a subject best avoided. Once upon a time a lot of things were different.

'Did the police get to speak to Sean? I mean, there's no possibility he's gone AWOL as well?'

Imogen is amused. A *what are we going to do with you* smirk, not one Nan remembers from her repertoire.

'He called me a week past Friday, an unexpected honour. Reverse charges of course. Harangued me for ten minutes about testing shampoos on rabbits. Not an issue that moves me one way or the other but I know he likes to think of Mum as the wicked witch of the west and I do my best to oblige. He was asking for you: were you still on the South Side or had Callum Macleod got you living in? At least now I know why he rang, little bastard. Running errands for the Byres Road Guevara. What were they after? Trying to recruit you to the gang?'

Nan takes the question as facetious but Imogen seems to expect some response.

'I don't think Max saw me as a comrade-in-arms.'

The implications of the past tense depress her. In the end, for no real reason, she almost liked him.

'So what else did he have to say that night?'

Nan feels the need to thwart the returning easiness between them, to force some further acknowledgement of her weeks in the wilderness.

'This and that.'

That your dead lover and my live one were lining their pockets with Callum Macleod's money. Or is that old news?

Imogen dangles one shoe from the end of her foot, exposing a small nylon run on the underside of her heel.

'If you were the last to see him, I suppose you should go to the police?'

'I have my own problems in that department, as you know.'

The frontier is crossed. Anticipating this moment, Nan used to taste the warm syrup of her friend's concern, unsure if the bubble in her gorge were craving or disgust.

In the event, Imogen looks neither shocked nor sympathetic, just careful. The sun is hotter now. Nan feels the shininess on her forehead, her armpits damp. Imogen is unbuttoning her jacket, revealing a white lawn blouse – a souvenir from their trip to the designer quarter – sticking, here and there, to the skin. She wears no wedding ring today, her fingers bare as if surgically scrubbed or ready for making pastry.

'It doesn't seem that much of a problem.'

Nan shrugs, a gesture of contradiction often misread for compliance.

'I've been pushing my luck staying so long.'

'You're moving on?'

Hearing the urgency Nan lifts her head, bright-eyed, but she's mistaken. Whatever triggered that staccato enquiry it wasn't dismay. She recalls that Friday afternoon of shopping and gambling and feels the shooting pain of remembered happiness, a phantom twinge from a severed limb.

'Something like that.'

Imogen's gaze wavers, distracted by a dog, an ageing red setter whose patchily-dulling coat draws the eye like talcum-powder combed through the hair of a juvenile lead.

'I once met a civil servant, a friend of a friend in London, and afterwards found out she was the woman who leaked a cabinet memo about nuclear power to the *Guardian*. You remember all that fuss about the cost of decommissioning? Questions in the House, rumours that some minor minister might have to fall on his sword. No one did, needless to say. She was the perfect mole. Walking wallpaper. I could tell you what we had for lunch that day but all I can tell you about her is that she wore glasses. She was born to get away with it.'

Nan frowns, not quite seeing the point. 'Are you suggesting I belong in the Vymura catalogue too?'

'Well, they say Napoleon was killed by his wallpaper.'

'How do they make that one out?'

'Cyanide in the green dye.'

Her smile evaporates.

'I'm sorry, Nan, I wasn't thinking.'

'It's OK.' And it is. Her only regret is that the moment of playfulness is over. She doesn't even mind Imogen playing dumb over Kilner all that time, although she would like to know how she found out.

'Sean told me.'

Nan nods.

'Max said it was you who told Sean.'

'No, Sean got it from Callum Macleod. That time he disappeared, it turns out he was labouring at the wine bar on the river, cash in hand, last-minute panic before opening night. Once the place was finished Cal asked him to keep in touch, on the promise of more work. Took him out for a drink one night. I suspect his interest wasn't entirely . . .' She censors the rest of the sentence. 'But don't ask me who told Cal.'

She doesn't have to. The only surprise is that she's surprised. With gossip that good he'd have to tell, no matter how insignificant she was. Walking wallpaper. But ego will out, however complete the camouflage. Government moles blow their cover on the North London lunch-party circuit, Nan did it on the seafront, reckless with repressed lust for an ambidextrous drug dealer. What is anonymity but a form of arrogance, the belief that you can control what others perceive? Arrogance, or arrested development. When infants close their eyes, they think they can't be seen.

But there's a more pressing claim on her attention. She remembers the weight in her palm, the pleasing neatness

345

of the squared-off barrel. Cigarette lighters, boys' toys crammed into saloon-gal garters and Christmas stockings. So many imitations, it's the genuine article that seems unreal. As improbable as her Sabatier in its vacuum-seal polythene. *Exhibit A.*

'Did the police say anything about a gun?'

For a second Imogen's face is blank, perhaps thrown by the change of subject.

'What gun?'

'Max had a gun. Sean's fingerprints were all over it.' Nan's too, now. 'He told me it was the gun that killed Jack Ibster.'

Like a word she never uses, a fragment of non-menu French or the name of a flowering shrub in someone else's garden, it comes to her, a detail she didn't know she knew. 'You remember the gun: it's the reason you rang me this morning, the reason we're standing here now.'

Imogen laughs once, an involuntary spasm like a cough, a hairball of nervous surprise.

Nan speaks quickly to forestall any more lying.

'Max had it last. Said he was going to take it for a swim in the Clyde; maybe he chose the canal instead.'

She remembers the underground train, their bodies' instinctive accommodations, Maggie in front, Imogen behind. A love beyond reason, self-interest, the safety of her child.

'They'll nail her in the end, you know, and then Sean's incriminated himself for nothing. You must see that.'

Imogen tilts her head back in a sun-worshipper's pose, puckering throat stretched smooth, the uncharitable light picking out a tidemark of foundation.

'It's not her, Nan. It's me.'

The one possibility she never even considered.

'But you loved him.'

As soon as she says it she wonders why. She more than anyone should appreciate the distance between reality's leavings, the compost of expedience and denial, and that plastic phrase, gaudy, unbiodegradable. She musters a shrugging retraction.

'I suppose everybody's relationships look good to me. My speciality is men I have nothing in common with at all.'

Imogen's face is unnervingly still, mouth slightly ajar, her lipstick too shiny, as if melting on her skin. It's almost startling when she breaks silence.

'Maybe that's what you want. Some people need recognition, some need left alone. What Jack did for me was so much like nothing it was a fucking miracle. No one else has ever managed it. No contract, no demands, and he put me in touch with things I thought were gone for good. Like when I was a kid: running over the moors, the others miles behind, just me and all that sky. Those adjectives that get lost around puberty: brave, strong. He made me self-sufficient again. Hell, we all need a catalyst. I've known women who managed it with a diesel-dyke haircut and a pair of dungarees; with me it took Jack. It wasn't because he was hers: he was made for me. And I'm under no illusions that it was a reciprocal deal.' She sighs, a short, sour, amused breath. 'Why shouldn't I love him? He made it possible for me to love me.'

Nan is only half-listening, her attention still snagged on her own contract with Imogen, her big mistake. She should have cared less.

'You know how many letters I get about infidelity? One in five are complaining that he can't get it up. The other four are because he's got it up somebody else. And you know what they always say?' Her voice cracks, a dry fissure. '*How could I have been so blind?* I was out every night: workshops, rallies, group sessions. Spreading the good news. All that consciousness-raising, but I felt so bad about Maggie I couldn't see beyond what a bitch I was. Men, you didn't expect anything of them anyway. It was what women did that mattered.'

'You told me you didn't feel guilty.'

Imogen's eyes spark briefly, the instinct to retaliate striking on self-reproach.

'Given the choice between believing you have control over your life and the possibility that you have none, most of us will take the guilt. Until there's no option. I was prepared to beat myself up about being the bit on the side, I wasn't going to take responsibility for the whole fucking reserve team. We were in bed when I told him I knew about the others. Didn't even put him off his stroke. He said if I didn't like it I could walk. No negotiating position: classic mistake of industrial relations. You want to hit back, but you don't want to do without him, so you're shafted. It would have hurt him, to leave, but it would have hurt me more.'

She pauses to slide a sweetening tongue around the corners of her mouth.

'I've used up a lot of trees over the years warning women how they'll feel after splitting up if he gets custody of the self-esteem. I never realised it makes you dangerous. Amazing what comes into your head: finding somebody else, fucking them across the street from his window. Teenage fantasies. But you have to do *something*. I thought PMT was bad; this is Vietnam. You want to destroy; you have to. If you don't, you're destroying yourself.'

Nan knew. She must have known. Otherwise it would have occurred to her. How could she not recognise something so close to her own boiling?

'You understand now why we couldn't afford to go around as a matching set, Nan? Apart from the fact that

I didn't know when you were going to get lifted. I'd already said more than I should.'

'It's that welcome mat I've got for a face.'

'But watch out for the wallpaper.'

Their laughter strikes a holiday note, chiming with the sunshine; Nan has a sudden irrelevant hankering for an ice cream.

Imogen's smile dissolves.

'Without the gun it would never have happened. I'm not the Lizzie Borden type. I found it behind the water tank when Sean moved out. I knew about it before then of course, they looked after it on a rota basis when Max went to prison: I wasn't crazy over the idea but I knew none of them would ever use it, just liked to keep it around as a virility symbol. I took it with me for pretty much the same reason. I was getting boxed into a corner, making hysterical threats we both knew I didn't mean. He was calling the shots,' another ironic breath, 'I thought I'd take a little extra reality along, tip the balance in my favour.'

How many times has she rehearsed this to herself? Often enough to believe it? But until you filter it through an audience you can never be sure how it will play in Peoria. Nan is flattered to be chosen, but she has no illusions about the paradoxical status of the confessor, that pact of power and dispensability. Strictly a once-in-a-lifetime opportunity.

'You're right about Sean, I wish to God I'd kept him out of it, but he was already involved because he knew about the gun. And I needed him to move the . . . If I'd left him where it happened they'd have picked me up within the hour. We used to meet down below the Botanic Gardens when it was fine, not to screw – my Lawrentian days are long gone – sometimes we did the crossword. There was a woman we'd see pretty regularly walking her Labrador. I knew if that dog found him I was finished. Sean was staying with Max, I'd bumped into Brendan's girlfriend that morning and she let it slip. He'd been working at Cal Macleod's, knew his way around. Didn't remember it was the bloody opening night though, and once they realised, there wasn't time for second thoughts. Ditching the gun in the toilet was a bit of a balls-up, but they *were* under a certain amount of pressure . . .'

Nan becomes aware of the chugging of a road-gang generator without knowing how long her pulse has been following its rhythm.

'. . . Looks like we got away with it, anyway. The police are winding things down. They can't admit it in public, but they've handed all his stuff back. Filofax, desk diaries. I haven't seen a *Contract Killer Riddle* headline for weeks. It's over. Even Maggie's moving on.'

She looks at Nan, gauging how welcome the mat really is.

'I did her a favour, you know. We might even wean her off the skoosh now, get her back to something like the way she was.'

The agony aunt and the agony, Imogen and the drunk, bound by ties Nan can only imagine: schoolgirl confidences and half a lifetime of deceit. Time lends a tragic dimension to human relations. What can she offer to compete? Laughter, conversation, a paddle in the shallows of gratification. Fun you can have with anyone; how often are you tugged by the primaeval tides of passion and taboo?

'For all the propaganda he was a controller. Ran people like laboratory rats. Jack in his white coat applying measured doses of stimuli. Just enough to make us squeak. You'd think we'd've noticed the rows of cages, but we all like to think we're unique.'

'Maggie didn't.'

There's still time for Nan to take the tactful way out, the issue could be fudged, but she doesn't feel like being tactful any more.

'She's known about you and Jack for years.'

Shocking to see a face drain of pigment, a complexion suddenly grey as dishtowels flapping on the line, as the letters from the troubled with their illiterate rounded scrawl. As other people's lives. The make-up remains, its discreet shadows and skilful bloom garish and arbitrary. Nan feels queasy stirrings of excitement, a window-smasher's rush.

'She told me.'

Imogen slides off the bar, heels jarring on contact with the earth.

'What the fuck were you doing discussing it?'

Nan has never heard her raise her voice before, but then she never invested enough to be angry.

'I got stuck with her one Saturday lunchtime. Conversation was running low. Your name came up. I tried to look surprised and embarrassed, which wasn't hard; changed the subject as soon as I could. How was I supposed to know what she was going to say?'

But the moment for self-justification has passed. Imogen is riffling through the card-index of memory, absentmindedly fingering an invisible drip from the tip of her nose: the deceiver's tic, a sign that mind and mouth are at odds. Not that she's speaking. Perhaps she's lying to herself.

'No, I don't believe it. She would have used it, sometime. She hasn't the restraint not to.'

There's something to be said for this line of reasoning but Nan can think of other explanations. The possibility that Maggie's inadequacy is a selective phenomenon. Abandon, too, can be an instrument of control.

Nan watches the realisation dawn in Imogen's face before echoing it.

'There's a good chance she knows you killed him, too.'

A woman walks past pushing a double buggy, dark skins showing through pink crochet. The sheeny synthetic of her salwar burns orange in the midday sun. Nan smiles with reflex maternalism, a cost-free courtesy. The pushchair wheels generate an irregular ticking, leaving a voluminous silence in their wake.

Imogen rebuttons her jacket. Her face is already fastened.

'I have to go. Good luck, Nan. I hope it all works out for you.'

So this is how friendships end. Posted into the world with all good wishes. Have a nice life. Another fantasy she's not prepared to sustain.

'I'm going back to Birmingham.'

'*What?*'

A smell of bitumen carries over the trees from that calmly chugging generator.

'After all, I can't hide forever.'

Imogen doesn't recall the reference. 'I don't see why not.'

But wherever she was going she would get there sometime, and then there would be here, the strangers known, the new life as familiar as the old. That's not really the problem. She likes her life, even wants to take full possession. It's Nan Megratta she's ready to escape.

'I always said I'd turn myself in.' Not that she always meant it. 'You're the one born to get away with it. I'm going back to haggle with reality.'

A shadow of hesitation crosses Imogen's face, like a

child waiting the perfect moment to jump the skipping rope.

'But you'll keep the other business to yourself? We can count on you?'

We. Mother and son? Or has Maggie already been accommodated as an accessory? Either way the Megratta-Reiss axis is over. It's in everyone's best interests, Nan's own most of all.

But having said her farewell, Imogen now seems loath to let her go.

'It's masochism, Nan. Don't tell me you're expecting justice because neither of us are that gullible. They'll lock you up and throw away the key.'

In another fortnight this tangy spring will have ripened to the funereal lushness of high summer, dark with the promise of rot. The scent of urban hedgerows, the peppery pollen of Motherdie and Queen Anne's lace. What will the remand cells at Holloway smell of? Carbolic and shit probably.

'It's not as if I have anything else to do. Signing on and a weekly roll in the sack with Danny McLeod? Not my definition of life, liberty and the pursuit of happiness. I want it cleared up. OK, it's a lottery: I might get life, I might get probation, but it won't make any difference to what I know happened. It doesn't matter how they judge me . . .'

She pauses, surprised. Over the past week her outlook has changed beyond recognition. Not once and for all but moment by moment, each new horizon yielding to the next. Among the bewildering burgeoning of possibilities she hardly noticed the loss. So guilt has a half-life, like radiation.

Imogen curves an arm around her shoulder, drawing her in to the disconcerting softness of adipose tissue. A gesture that doesn't quite fit the occasion, off the peg maternalism, but still affecting, charged with the indiscriminate power of archetype.

'Well, love, it's your life.'

'What are you doing four o'clock Saturday?'
     Suffering every expanded moment of bemused silence on the other end of the line, she realises she doesn't have the constitution for this sort of stunt. Eventually, almost instantly, he identifies her voice.

'Poppet, how are you?'

She's timed the call carefully between the possibilities of a late dinner and an early night, nevertheless he sounds preoccupied, otherwise engaged. Let's hope she's not in competition with anything too tactile.

'I'm planing a trip to Birmingham.'

He has picked up the call on a cordless phone. Faint electronic gurglings, interplanetary wow and flutter eddy up the line.

'Thought I'd call and see my old friend Cid.'

She has the impression that he has just taken a gulping breath of air, but it may be a trick of the telephone interference.

'Tarquin, say *something*. Four months ago this was the only tune I could get out of you.'

'Sweetpea, I'm delighted.'

His voice moves away from the receiver which, perversely, permits the words to carry more clearly, refined by Victorian acoustics and a lull in the galactic storm.

'No, *carissimo*, it's a client.' The mouthpiece is restored. 'I'm sure Cid will be thrilled as well. Get him to give me a ring the minute you arrive. Four might be a bit tight, though. Gino's bribed me into taking him to watch Aston Villa and there's no knowing what the traffic will be like. I'm quite excited, haven't had Bovril since Marlborough. Can you make it four-thirty?'

'No problem.' She wouldn't want to interfere with his enjoyment of the skin show at Villa Park. 'And thanks.'

'My pleasure. Um . . . Cid does enjoy a sing-song. Have you rehearsed anything?'

The joke is wearing thin. Is he worried about being overheard, afraid of Gino shopping him after a lover's tiff?

'I thought I might tell them what actually happened.'

'Yes, of course, I'm sure that'll go down very well, but I was thinking about something a little more up-to-date. You remember what we discussed . . . ?'

Proof that she's been leading a model life as a productive member of the community. Something to show for the past six months. *Well, m'lud, I've been having an adulterous affair with an MP who was being blackmailed over a dodgy planning deal by an ideological nemesis who was also leaning on the local councillor before he was killed in a crime of passion by his mistress who happened to be my best friend. Then I was offered a position by the restaurateur who was paying off the bent politicians, but the job fell through after he caught me searching his house for the murder weapon.*

'My character witness turned out to be a local drugs baron, so I thought I'd just tell them I've been working for the Post Office and leave it at that.'

Tarquin does enjoy a joke.

'Well, you know best. See you Saturday – don't forget your sponge bag and some clean undies, by the way. He'll insist on you staying over. You know how hospitable Cid is.'

'I shouldn't be here.'

It's an arguable point. What isn't debatable is that, being here, it's better not to be seen talking to herself. A nervous reflex. There must be ten thousand people standing on the quayside. The workforce and their families, kids in Rangers' strips and pushchairs, have been herded into the further enclosure and fobbed off with plastic union flags. It's not so easy getting the measure of the more privileged cattle pen. Tribes she would normally consider mutually exclusive are here rubbing shoulders. The county set, tired of playing shepherdesses, slumming it in the shipyard; the gold-plated tap brigade of testimonial diners and directors' box seat-holders; and a cross-section of the committee-serving classes, if not exactly the great and the good, at least the prominent and well-meaning. Royalty is expected, a spanner in the sociological works throwing everything out of kilter. The women's outfits have the afashionable look of best dresses, styles which may just have made it home in the carrier bag, or been preserved in dry cleaner's polythene for years. Egregious shades of lime and turquoise and tangerine, dinky little clutch bags on brassy chains, scene-stealing picture hats, heather sprigs tied with tartan ribbon and pinned to the patriotic breast. Some of these women must be councillors, the people's representatives, one or two of them even working class, the rest are serial shoppers, leisurely lunchers, professional wives, but God knows how you tell which are which. Tastelessness is a great leveller. Even she's at it, skin creeping with the synthetic caress of one of Catriona's floral numbers, anticyclonic air currents catching in her voluminous skirts. The men are generally less conspicuous in their finery, but self-conscious all the same. A number of faces she recognises from the newspapers as solid figures in the trade union movement, some a little too solid, buttons straining in their double-vented suits, dandruff speckling shoulders shiny with the suspicion of man-made fibres. The Labour Party powerbrokers look more comfortable in their best chalkstripes, relaxed among the burghers and merchants of this crowd. And why not? They are the establishment now; their status confirmed on the point of extinction. There's nothing so monolithically powerful as yesterday's men.

It's a jolt to see Imogen here, although now she thinks about it, the widow's tragic status, compounded by the guilt that they never much liked her husband, is more than enough to have secured an invitation *plus one*. Nan recognises Maggie's hat from the funeral, stripped of its veil, teamed with a silk suit in extravagant black and white polka dot, the skirt short with a flirtatious little ruffle at the hem. She wears white stockings with an opalescent sheen at the curve of calf and squared-off kneecap, as of sunburned flesh showing through, an illusion instantly belied by her complexion, its fine dusting of wisteria pollen. For the first time in Nan's experience Imogen is inappropriately clad. A wine-coloured coat dress, its regimental buttons too shiny, the neckline exposing too much toneless flesh; she looks like a spinster schoolmarm attending her first party a quarter century too late. Back in the kitchen at Montpelier she will judge this company, etching its absurdities with a scalpel wit, but for the moment her presence tacitly acknowledges its values and in this garden-party atmosphere of sanctioned vulgarity, she is ill at ease. Nan tries a halfhearted wave, but she isn't receiving. Her face registers nothing but a sincere wish to vanish into the crowd.

It crossed Nan's mind not to come today but she dismissed the impulse out of hand. As the prospect of prison becomes firmer she's aware that it might be useful to receive the odd envelope embossed with the thrupenny-bit portcullis, although how this is to be managed without the draining business of explanation, not to mention confrontation and recrimination, she couldn't say. Of course, there is always the possibility that *he* has stood *her* up. But no, she spots him below the launching platform, in a circle of Labour Party apparatchiks, among them the member for Clyde East, who is taking his new responsibilities seriously enough to be dressing like an insurance salesman these days. Danny, in a go-getter's, plane catcher's suit whose grey wool is verging on lilac, looks oddly American, carotene coloured from his recent all-expenses-paid tour of the Pacific Rim. He phoned from the airport, waiting to pick his suitcase off the carousel, a silk kimono folded carefully on top of his dirty washing, something concealable tucked into his pocket for her. *Don't let it be underwear.* As she approaches, the group subtly rearranges to admit her: they've been briefed in advance. She volunteers a handshake and he pulls her in for a kiss. On the cheek. A flurry of confusion as she remembers to avert her lips. For Danny, this is part of the kick. A couple of the dandruff-shedders exchange glances, but the innuendo is merely speculative, the smirk forever latent when women are around.

'What do you reckon to an MP's life then, Nan?'

Lank hair ploughed backwards from his vistavision forehead, a teddy boy who never stopped buying the Brylcreem. She smiles warily, stalling. Is she meant to be a Commons researcher or a student working on some unspecified project? It doesn't matter as long as she does the right thing. *Keep smiling*.

'Better than working.'

Danny laughs.

'I work a lot harder than these idle bastards, that's for sure.'

The bodies politic realign, as if phototropically. That's her quota of attention. Now she's included, they can carry on as if she weren't there.

Man talk. The rules are so simple it took her a while to grasp that there's nothing more to it. The ground is well trodden, a ritual arena. Should an amusing remark be made, and the definition is a loose one, any inherent humour is then beaten out of it as it is passed from mouth to mouth, although all heard it the first time, circling the company until it comes to rest with the original wag who usually has the restraint not to repeat it over again. It's an authentic Glasgow tradition, an expression of the spirit of the tenements. They say a whole close could wring soup out of a single bone. In her teens, fired by the rhetoric of Imogen Reiss and her sisters, she despised the sex-segregated social lives of her elders, those couples' nights out, women roosting at the tables, men on their feet at the bar. Now it seems eminently practical. Far worse to see women on the sidelines of conversation, acknowledging male preeminence while bored out of their minds. Alone with Danny, he's grateful enough to speak her language, unpacking his emotions to lay them at her feet, but she's careful not to read too much into this. Just a little psychic plumbing, a blockage to be discharged so he can get on with the serious business of repeating other people's jokes. Women don't feature, she's noticed, although she'll never know if that's the norm. Maybe they're not ignoring her at all, on the contrary, every word not spoken screams awareness of her presence. She cannae want them to *talk* to her as well?

The quay she last saw from across the river, littered with off-cut pipes and rusted oil drums, scrap metal and swarf, has been swept and hosed and staked out with bunting and balloons. A helicopter circles in an unpredictable sky crossed by clouds of grey wadding so that the sunshine sears and fades. The light is sharp as a bromide print, the superreal intensity she associates with highland games and miners' galas, events that even as they happen belong to the past. Now and then the breeze forces female hands to their heads to secure the lifting brims with the ragged synchronisation of a light operatic chorus. A pipe band is playing, which means it will almost certainly rain. She scans the crowd, edging away from the circle, straying definitively out of range, at which point she feels a finger tracing the length of her spine.

'Love the frock, darling – but where's your hat?'

Cal, billowing in cream linen, fresh from some summer fête on the village green, an outfit so ostentatiously traditional he looks foreign, like men in kilts on Sauchiehall Street. She didn't think to see him again, already he's been consigned to memory's attic, an item of exotica that once, inexplicably, passed for an everyday object in her life. Out of the corner of her eye, some twenty yards away, Danny changes colour.

A clash of fabrics trips past on perilous heels. Cal raises his eyebrows. A suggestion of semaphore in his gestures shows he's aware of Danny's discomfiture and doing what he can to heighten it

'Come to wave the flag on behalf of Her Majesty's Mail?'

'I don't work there any more. Packed it in for a better offer, remember?'

Apparently not.

'So you're here as a geisha, with the pride of the Clyde?'

'That's right, we'll be sneaking off for a session behind the pipe sheds once the speeches start.'

The image is inadvertently graphic. For a moment he looks almost prim. Beneath her own embarrassment she's quite pleased with herself.

'Have you heard about your friend?'

'I have more than one, Cal.'

'And which of us can say that hand on heart?' His eyelids droop into the slow blink that telegraphs a punchline. 'Maxwell McSemtex: vamoosed, I hear.'

She shuts down her smile. 'Missing, presumed dead.'

'Really?'

He knows this, but he wants to hear it anyway.

'According to Imogen.'

'And you? Do you think he's pan breid?'

'What do I know?'

'I was under the impression you two were close.'

She remembers his face as she left the bedroom, the hostility she assumed was residual from the fight, not new-minted for her. The satisfaction of knowing she'd just escaped the narrow lines of his definition. Leaving with Max was to press home the point; it never occurred to her he might be ignorant of his preferential claim.

'Cal, that night at your house.'

'Ye-es.'

'I didn't know it was your place.'

'Whose home did you think you were trashing?'

His bulk blots out the sun, a mainsail of cream linen. His breath tastes faintly of buttered toast.

'Max turned up at my flat that afternoon acting pretty strangely . . .'

'I noticed.'

362

'. . . dropping hints about Danny and Jack. I wanted to find out more so I tagged along.'

'And what did you find out? About Danny and Jack.'

Moisture prickles her armpits.

'I don't want any more to do with this, Cal.'

'No? What do you want then?'

To live her own life. Not much of an ambition, but grander than it sounds.

'Just tell me you didn't do it.'

'Do what?'

She remembers how unreasonably he reacted the last time she accused him of murder.

'Forget it.'

Over by the launching platform a tall woman in yellow greets Danny with a sharp cry of delight, airbrushing his cheeks with puckered mouth. Left, right, left again.

'How's your own little local difficulty going?'

She shrugs. 'I'm heading south tomorrow. Turning myself in.'

'Still want me to give evidence?'

She's not sure whether he's making a genuine offer or scoring a point.

'I'm not for sale, Cal.'

A smirk infiltrates his lips.

'Just as well, since I'm not buying.'

She could just touch him. Defy his definition of her still further, and not only his idea of her, her own too. Nothing so crude as reinventing herself, more like Imogen's ideal of recovered girlhood, a reconnection with the tomboy treeclimber who always went out on a limb. Running out of time must be restoring her reckless streak, unless recklessness is a redundant concept, having nothing left to lose. The condemned woman ate a hearty breakfast. He leans a little closer. Buttered toast and sweet tea.

'So you're going to make a clean breast of it, are you?'

She lets the provocation pass.

'I don't want to wake up as one of those people who know they're lying but can't remember what the truth is any more. Sooner or later it destroys you.'

His eyes, over her head, are trained on the crowd.

'I wouldn't know.'

The moment, whatever it was, has slipped away. Levering herself up with a hand on his shoulder, looming into a lunarscape of pore and eyeball, she kisses him lightly on the mouth. The smooth cheek grainy with late-afternoon stubble but the skin quite soft. A lick of butter. His lips remain closed.

'What was that for?'

Maggie was right: he didn't like it.

Knowing Cal, the worst she would have predicted is mockery, milking her embarrassment, extracting his pound of flesh, but they've gone beyond playfulness. And beyond playfulness, she doesn't know him at all. A kiss isn't just a kiss, it's the staking of claim, the taking of power. Who knows, he might even have interpreted her pulling a gun on him that way, although Max told her later she'd left the safety catch on, which takes some of the heat out of the situation. She smiles through a face like cardboard, already backing off.

'I might not get another chance,' she twists a look over her shoulder, Danny is still chatting with the comrades, 'to say goodbye.'

The pipe band is playing *Flower of Scotland*. Danny appears not to have noticed that she's come back. Unless he's pretending not to have noticed her absence in the first place. Either way, he probably saw the kiss. On the platform, under a bunched canopy of red, white and blue balloons, men with tense, official faces are consulting their watches. The dignitaries make their way up the steps. Sun glints off the Provost's chain as he follows a small figure wearing hat, coat, shoes, all of the same cobalt blue. Only royals and air hostesses go in for outfits so obsessively matched. The pipers switch to the National Anthem, sending the loudspeakers berserk with feedback. Conversations are suspended, peeled apart with uncertain smiles. Nan skirts around the circle to address Danny from behind.

'We'll see better from over there.'

It's such an obvious gambit that snubbing her would only make it worse. He smiles his excuses and detaches himself from the group.

'You've decided to speak to me, then?'

She leans towards him, riding the wave of recent bravado.

'Come on, Danny, you know you wouldn't have talked to me with the politburo around.'

She can sense him rising to the sexual challenge, but warily, suspicious of its provenance. Brushing against his flank as they clear a path through the polyester, she steers him forward.

'Where can we go?'

He nods to indicate a clearing to their right.

She presses closer.

'No. Where can we *go*?'

'Christ, if I'd known royalty was such a turn-on I'd have booked us in for a week at Balmoral.'

'We have to talk, Danny.'

'Talk is it?'

Physically he has this directness, a trick of arranging body and limbs to create an intimacy almost philosophi-cal, a claim of common humanity. With women, it pro-duces an inevitability long before the question is asked. Politically, too, it's his trump card. Few manage to hate him face-to-face. After three weeks' absence, it may be that she's forgotten the exact flavour of their meetings, but it seems to her his trademark ease has an extra, proprietorial confidence today. Troubles at home shifting the balance in her favour? A lifting of worries? Max's disappearance? She pushes the thought aside. People are packed more densely on this part of the quay and now that the first of the speeches is scratching through the loudspeakers there's less tolerance about letting them pass and sacrificing a vantage point that may not be regained. Tuts and sighs chart their progress. Threading a way through, they move from clearing to crush and without warning the gathering loses its gentility and becomes that rude animal a crowd, lit by a crowd's avidity, obedient to its unfathomable rhythms. The helicopter is circling closer now, one minute threatening to land, the next climbing, only to descend again, a clattering parabola drowning the chairman's words. Up ahead there's some obstruction. Heads are craning away from the tiny figure on the platform towards the bobbing advance of two peaked caps. Policemen, travelling with an urgency that promises an impending arrest. Nan feels her impetus drain as the crowd's resistance becomes an equal and opposite force bulging against her, a thwarted stampede of colour-coor-dinated stilettos displaced by the need to clear a pathway for the police. There's a freak alignment of the undersized and for a moment she glimpses the machine pistols, held two-handed against bulletproof bodywarmers, matt black metal cushioned by navy-blue nylon. Her breath seems lodged in a bale, polythene sheeted, at the base of her throat. Quick enough to be an optical illusion, a juggling of the rods and cones, something else catches her eye. Buried in a terrine of bodies, a trawl of faces split with Halloween grins: her own unreasoning panic in another face.

At the sight of Imogen, Danny's body expands, hackles rising in an aggression which carries a shiver of sexual display. Maggie is scratching a shoulder of polka-dot silk with a hand like a purpling chicken claw, scaly-backed but shiny at the knuckles, oblivious to the drama at her side. Looking up, her face is suddenly taut with recognition, its sags and puckers hoisted like a marquee, but this isn't the moment to renew old acquaintance. The crowd is pressing on them like a wall, closing the brief sightline, sucking the oxygen from their air-pocket. Nan strains towards the fresh wind overhead, but as her lungs expand in readiness the breath is thwarted. Danny grips her upper arm and she's dragged as in a dream, unsure if her feet are touching the ground. New faces multiply before her eyes. The armed police pass on and her fear passes with them, like the crowd's temporary madness, a false alarm, a faintly embarrassing joke. Overheated men are wrestling with buttons; manicured hands patting at millinery. This is the ugliness of the January sales, not the bloodlust of the mob. With the steadying of her pulse Nan experiences a welling sadness. So the Mother Teresa of the tabloids finally found a problem that wouldn't talk itself out.

Danny is up on his toes, squinting myopically towards the sheds.

'There's another load of goons with semi-automatic truncheons over there.'

'I thought they were after me for a second.'

He snorts perfunctory amusement, still scanning the distance, only half listening.

'Being wanted for murder.'

'What?'

She holds the moment, half-hoping he heard, half-praying that he didn't. Fate hangs on his good ear and the direction of the wind. Over by the ship a bell rings

367

and one of the cranes, a blue giraffe whose body sits too high on spindly legs, creeps a few metres along the quay.

She shrugs, the decision taken.

'Nothing.'

'No, tell me what you said.'

He still has the old agitator's sixth sense.

'Nan?'

A patter of applause gathers momentum as acknowledgement of the chairman's closing witticism shades into a welcome for the dumpy woman in blue. She steps forward to the microphone but her first word is severed by the jagged notes of a speaker system turned full volume. Distortion rakes Nan's fillings, bass notes dissolving her sternum. She recognises the song but for an instant wonders if the resemblance is accidental, a random snatch of melody thrown out by rank industrial noise. Around her heads are swivelling like searchlights, trying to locate a source, but the sound is coming at them from all sides, bouncing off the corrugated metal walls of the fabricating sheds. Danny laughs, a single involuntary bark left over from another life. Across the river, in front of a derelict factory, an old-fashioned open-backed lorry has appeared. A green tarpaulin thrown back exposes a bank of speakers like washing machines in a black-painted launderette.

God save the Queen
Ya fascist regime.

She's too far away to identify the shadows in the driver's cab, but she has a fair idea who they are. No one could call it a sophisticated political statement, but they deserve full marks for organisation. The helicopter swoops, an intimidatory gesture posing no actual threat; the anthem continues. After the first shocking soundblast the music assumes the inevitability of any pop classic. Nan finds her mind singing along, waiting for the grinding chord change, the switch from bellow to rasping sneer. The focus of this tribute stands straight-backed, gaze fixed on the middle distance, a pose familiar from airforce flypasts and calendar shots of Trooping the Colour. The crowd too is frozen, imprisoned in its cage of noise, docile with certainty that there is nothing anyone can do. The thrashing guitars are ploughing into the final verse before Johnny Rotten's vocals acquire the descant of sirens. A sudden wash of sunlight renews the tarpaulin, blessing the scuffed paint on the speaker cases, neutering the winking light on the first of the police cars now closing on the truck. Three black-clad figures jump from the cab and start to run. One head swarthy, stubble-cheeked; one hairless and white, extruded from the neck of his clothing like a bead of dried glue on the end of the tube; the third a dirty-blond ponytail. The sideshow is over. Danny's face wears a slack, abstracted smile. He lets out a whistling breath of what could almost be grudging admiration.

'Those bams were lucky not to be taken for the IRA.'

She tugs at his sleeve.

'Can we move? I'm feeling claustrophobic.'

This isn't strictly true but it's a declaration of need he's comfortable with, much simpler to express than self-referential anxiety at the prospect of watching a triple arrest. He acts promptly, as she knew he would, pushing her towards the boundary where the metal crush-barriers meet the margin of deserted concrete lining the quay.

This close, the sheer bulk of the ship is awesome, its shadow a sanctuary of cool, clear light. Unthinkable that anything so massive could be other than a permanent fixture on the landscape. A looming iron wall, behind which, on the opposite bank, the Sex Pistols succumb to a premature silence. The sirens, too, cut out. Immediately, the vacuum is filled by cocktail party babble, a hum of speculation, and then as the woman in blue steps forward to resume her place in front of the mike, ecstatic applause. Laughing, Danny grasps Nan's hands and manoeuvres them into a single ill-coordinated clap.

The public address system relays a high, quavery elocution, conjuring brandy butter and cracker novelties, the fifteen-minute lifespan of a fortune-telling fish.

His good humour gives way to rancour.

'Here we go: she'll be giving it dokey about this island nation and its seafaring tradition. No mention that the buyer's permanent fixture in the torturer's top ten, and the profits are going straight to Oslo. Still, I suppose it's not the bloody Japanese.'

'I thought you were very pally with the bloody Japanese.'

It's a delayed reaction, a straying of the glance in a minimalist double take; he isn't sure until she withdraws her wrists from his grip.

'Who told you?'

'What does it matter?'

'It matters to me.'

She has to remind herself that she's the one in possession of the moral high ground.

'It wasn't Cal, if that's what you mean.' That overfamiliar monosyllable slips into the space between them. 'The point is, Danny, you *didn't* tell me.'

The crowd is sparser here, they stand within a charmed circle of pebbled concrete, no one within earshot, every face in focus intent on the tiny figure up on the dignitaries' platform. He lowers his voice anyway. 'What have you heard?'

'That you and Jack got a nice little nest egg, tax free.'

He shakes his head so forcefully that for a second she really thinks she's got it wrong.

'I never wanted the money, just the jobs; it was Jackie and your gangster pal insisted on me taking a cut. Golden handcuffs in case I came down with a dose of conscience later on. Made them feel more secure: all for one and every man for himself. Oh, I spent it right enough. Blew it on sweeties: just wanted it away.'

His left hand strays towards the spot over his inside breast pocket and plucks at it as if the memory were burning a hole. He removes the rogue hair from his lapel. One of hers.

'Christ, we were in the middle of a global recession, factories shutting up left, right and centre. Half the city lying derelict and that was the only site they'd accept. Cardiff and Liverpool were breathing down our necks, Brussels had promised them the dosh. We were only in the running because they'd been to Gleneagles and fancied the golf. Seven hundred jobs, seven hundred men with something to get up for in the mornings; aye, and women too. Weans with new shoes in the winter. Christmas presents that hadnae been shoplifted to order. Couple of hundred people off the moneylenders' books.'

Up on the platform, the matching coat and hat is saying something about tradition and a seafaring nation.

'So Callum Macleod made three or four million. Or five or six. There's always some bandit creaming it off the top. What were we supposed to do? Tell him to go fuck himself and watch the factory go to the taffs? Get Scottish Enterprise to send in a couple of consultants, see how many we could take off the broo making speciality jams and tartan ovengloves? These are real jobs: decent money and a bit of pride.'

Now he can never leave me. The thought takes her by surprise: an irrational assumption, but revealing in its way.

'And if there's an accident?'

'Gie us peace, Nan. I've had enough of the millenarian keech from the balloon Foy. Until the whips had a few words with him about backbench promotion prospects.

371

The site's been stable for years. Okay, there's a risk. The Victorians were worried sick about piano legs, Orson Welles had them shitting themselves over the War of the Worlds, AIDS was going to wipe us all out until some pocket Einstein worked out that by their calculations half the country should have been pine-boxed by now. One week coffee's going to kill you, then it's the stuff they use to decaffeinate it. Fertilisers in the water table, holes in the ozone layer. Ten years ago they were telling us schoolkids couldn't get off to sleep for worrying about the bomb; now they've got no social skills because of computer games. It's mass hysteria. You know what the fatality figures were like in the yards? I'm not talking worst case scenario, they *knew* that come Hogmanay another twenty-odd were going to be first-footing at Peter's gate. No one said, Let's stop building ships. Then. Life's a gamble, risk against profit. You take your chances. Driving a car, crossing the road . . .'

Another access of caution. He brings his lips to her ear. She can feel the baritone vibration in the gradient of her hip, a bluebottle against the bone.

'How did you know what you were getting with me? The first time it got . . . boisterous. How sure were you I'd know where to stop?'

It's the great unmentionable, the source that they never tap even when the conversational shallows run dry. He jokes about the games, or more precisely, puns about them, arch references to her liking a bit of rough or wanting to tie him down, but neither of them have ever acknowledged the dark shape at the end of the bed.

She pulls back to bring his features into focus. Above the knowing twist in his lips, the faint draught of breath through their imperfect seal, his eyes are uncertain with appeal. He's asking her to trust him, but her body made that leap of faith some time ago. She trusts him enough, which is to say she's comprehensively mapped the contours of her mistrust. All that remains is for her to trust herself.

Their seclusion is breached by two shipyard employees in factory-fresh protective headgear and newly-laundered boiler suits, one cornflower blue, one white, who stop the other side of the crush barrier, on the fenced-off margin of quayside, conferring anxiously, glancing towards the tiny figure at the mike. One of them murmurs urgently into a mobile phone.

Danny's mouth dips in derisive amusement. 'If she doesn't wind it up quick she'll be wasting her breath. They're going to miss the spring tide.'

But you don't sit on a throne for forty years without being able to stick to a schedule.

There's a splatter of foam as the champagne bottle makes contact, and an instantaneous dunt, an echo-blunted impact of solid metal. Almost imperceptibly, the hull starts to move. At first infinitesimally slowly and then, as gravity takes over, picking up speed, like a building slipping down the street in a cartoon landslide, alarmingly fast for its bulk. Nan feels her face exercised by unfamiliar emotions, hilarity too powerful for laughter, astonishment at what was always foreseen, elation that the world can still pull such stunts. The hull hits the river, stern then prow, sending up an almighty backwash of water, the waiting tugs blaring their foghorn welcome. There's a moment's hiatus and now a hellish sound. Disorientated, her body tenses, then she sees the ponderous drag chains jerking past the yellow taffee grease on the wooden runners, paying out along the slipway, churning clouds of rust and singed metal and vapourised paint, and with a bathos of cheering and flag waving and a soaring of helium balloons, the ship is launched.

Danny releases the breath he's been holding in a gust

like the sigh he gives just after climax, and starts to chafe
at the four-bar bracelet of pressure welts around her wrist.

'Well now, Nan Megratta, what did you think of that?'

She lifts his fingers from her arm, laying his hand on
hers like a palmreader, or a plaster saint, or a lover.

'I think it's time you started using my real name.'